I0525792

Readers love All the Beautiful Lies Book One

Erotic Romance With a Heroine You'll Love

"As a former editor of this genre, I can't tell you how many promising stories are ruined by a heroine who couldn't tie her shoes without the hero's help. Not the case with All the Beautiful Lies, though. Aleah, the protagonist, is a strong, self-sufficient and, most importantly, imperfect woman. It makes the drama gritty and the romance explosive. The fact that Sarah Atlas is also an amazingly strong writer is icing on the cake. I'd even recommend this book to those who claim not to enjoy erotic romance. It's that good. Can't wait for the rest of the series!"

—H. Claire Taylor

Finally, an erotic read with integrity

"I received an advance review copy of All The Beautiful Lies, billed as mainstream erotica with a real story. I was a bit dubious, as usually anything with an erotic label quickly descends into smut with no plot. I'm glad to say in this case I was pleasantly surprised to find a strong, intelligent, witty and above all honest narrative that drew me in before hitting me upside the head with sex scenes. Since the book deals with love and adultery, the sex scenes aren't just integral to the plot, they are the mainstay of it. Thankfully, they're neither glossed over nor overblown, just a natural part of the action. I'm looking forward to reading the rest of the series to see how Atlas handles the situation she has so deftly created in Part 1."

—S. Gail Seymour

Hot, Breathtakingly Hot

"Meet Aleah Clayton, a young woman filled with warmth and lustrous beauty. She is just your average girl, not a big deal at all, that is until she awakens her "other" side, and some sexual encounters she least expected sent her down a path exploring her own deep, dark desires sleeping in the most unexplored realms in her mind.

Texan beauty Sarah Atlas brings this short erotic novella to life. Fasten your seatbelt and be prepared to experience some heart-pounding thrills, some sensual strokes and rhythms, so breathtaking you will be roused to mental climax. Intimacy has never tasted so good on pages and though new to the publishing world, I have a feeling the world can expect great things from this author.

This book was fast-paced, well-written, characters truly defined and grabs a hold of your attention until the very end. Sarah, well done."

—Al-Khemet Book Club

Hot!

"This is the kind of writing that you don't see often enough in erotica. Aleah's story is relatable and interesting. The attraction builds quickly but in a believable fashion. The sex scenes were HOT. Really looking forward to book 2. Well written and engaging. This book deserves five stars. Looking forward to more from this author."

—JR Leinen

I want more!!!!!

"I read it in a heartbeat! Now it's 5am where I live...

This story has great characters and a contemporary and real plot. You can identify yourself in Aleah, she's a everyday girl with her insecurities and her struggle but also with her strength...she rule her life, she can speak out the things that make her feel sad and unfulfilled, she understand that her life and marriage lack something but when occur something that make her feel alive again...when Blake occur...she doesn't take it lightly, she has doubt and feel guilty like every other person...but then I think that when you are sad in your life and something good happen to you...you have to take it...and so she does, with fear of course, but without regret or agenda, she simply live the moment thinking only about herself for one time!!!

I loved this character and this book and I can't wait to read what will happen next!!!
I think that Sarah Atlas is a great writer, who can dug deep into the characters and create plot that will take you glued to your e-reader!!!"

—Blue London

Leaves You Hungry For More

"Not all erotica is created equal. There are authors who fail to create a compelling storyline around a great sex scene, and then there are writers who have a decent storyline but include unrealistic passion with characters who don't seem to mesh. Sarah Atlas's novella has the perfect blend of creative storytelling and a sexual intensity that leaves the reader hungry for more. The protagonist, Aleah, is a strong, realistic character who is moving through a loveless marriage, when a deep stirring from within compels her to explore her desire for a friend. The novella ends at the height of their passion-- leaving the reader craving for more.

The best part about this book, aside from the sex, is how real the characters are to me. It's rare for a short story to include characters that readers develop a connection with, but I feel as though I know them and their situation. It's not predictable, per se, but it's familiar in a realistic sense. That, in my opinion, makes for some great storytelling."

—Melissa Strickland

I can't wait to read the second book!

"I was hooked from the first paragraph and didn't put the book down until I had finished the story. But the story is really just beginning and now I can't wait to see what happens between Aleah and Blake and Aleah and Glenn in the second book. The passion sizzles and Aleah is so real real and so vulnerable.

Sarah Atlas has a captivating writing style and quickly engages her reader. She writes descriptively about longing, frustration, lust, passion and loyalty. What I don't know yet is which emotion will rule Aleah. Time for book number two!"

—Barb

`We don't always recognize the moments that alter our path in life and send us ricocheting through the universe out of control.'

"Texas author Sarah Atlas writes erotic novellas. ALL THE BEATIFUL LIES seems to be in four volumes to date, this being Book 1 (she has also published a book PRECIOUS CARGO which is classified as an erotic short story. Sarah has talent - reading just one of her short erotic novellas assure the reader of that fact...

This rather short novella deals with a needy woman Aleah, married to Glen who refuses to be checked for fertility, and on New Year's Eve she strays out of the house away from her ill Glen to attend a poker party (a section rather overwritten for non-card playing readers) and there she encounters the lusty Blake. `Blake and I had been friends forever. I'd known him almost as long as I'd known my husband. They'd been roommates when Glen and I were dating. He's funny and sexy and I was always happy to see him.' That out-of-the-house situation become an in-house sex party and the manner in which Sarah develops this ménage a trios works quite well - given the drives and propulsion of the story.

Sarah Atlas works words well - and that is a refreshing finding among debut authors. She likely will make it strong -especially for those who enjoy the flavors of erotic."

—Grady Harp

Five Stars

"Well-written, sexy, and it keeps you hooked. I will definitely keep reading!"

—C. Hornsby

Interesting Storyline

"This book was a quick, but highly enjoyable book. I read it in about an hour and it left me wanting the next book! I really like where this story is going and I'm interested to see what the future holds for the main character, Aleah.

Aleah Clayton's life is not what she expected it would be like. A husband who shows no passion for her, or their relationship anymore, and boring days filled with unfilled wants and needs.

When a forbidden kiss comes from someone she least expects, all those wants and desires unfold. But she knows her actions will cost her eventually. Question is, is it worth the risk of losing everything?

I really enjoyed the plot of this story. It was interesting and fun to read! I liked how the story was about forbidden romance. It added to the suspense to the story and made the book that much more enjoyable. I can't wait to see what happens next!

My favorite quote: 'We don't always recognize the moment that alters our path in life and sends us ricocheting through the universe, out of control.'"
—Jocelyn S.

The romance scenes in All the Beautiful Lies left me wanting more from this author
"Ouch! These pages are hot!!! The romance scenes in All the Beautiful Lies left me wanting more from this author. This book is a fun read and a nicely set modern romance. Aleah and the other characters are authentic and believable which makes me able to place myself in her shoes.

I look forward to finding out what happens next and just how long and far this affair can go. Will it end in doom and gloom or love and butterflies? Or somewhere in between? More please..."
—M. Zvezda

Compelling Story
"The prologue is wicked, totally captured me from the get go... I felt the loneliness and heartbreak that was living in Aleah's heart. The words are descriptive and captivating and your heart and mind will be drawn in, you will want to know more. Be prepared it's an awesome book and I cannot wait for book 2."
—Gale Albright

All the Beautiful Lies

PASSION ALWAYS COMES WITH A PRICE

Sarah Atlas

First Edition
February 2015

Parnassus Cloud Publishing, LLC
Austin, Texas

www.parnassuscloud.com

for Ryan,

who encouraged me

every step of the way

Book One

Prologue

I can't recount how often I've been implored to write this book, to tell this story, and each time I have resisted. Fear has held me back. Fear of exposure, and of revenge. Even now I am haunted.

But clutching this to my chest, holding it in, knowing that if I don't share this with you of all people—this haunts me more. You deserve this story and this compels me to write.

Regrets collect like old friends... I can still feel the whispering caress of his hand on my cheek, his words to me: "People need to know, Aleah. People need to know how good it can be." *And how bad*, I think.

And so, I tell you my tale. While I fear you may not like me in the end, I'm not going to make it pretty. I'm not going to gloss over the strangeness of it all. I will be honest, though, and so even if you hate me, which I expect you will, you will understand me. You will know your own power. More than anything, that is what I hope for.

Chapter One

We don't always recognize the moments that alter our path in life and send us ricocheting through the universe, out of control. Sometimes the action in those moments is so slight, so seemingly inconsequential… It's not until much later that we comprehend their significance. But when we cast our glance back, we notice the light breeze that grew until it changed the tides of the ocean. For me, the breeze stirred on New Year's Eve. I've always hated that holiday. Crowded streets, ever-flowing alcohol, and icy roads never seemed like a good combination. This year we were supposed to play poker with the boys. At least that took place in the neighborhood.

Glen was sick. I wasn't feeling great either—my throat hurt a little—but given the choice between a neighborhood poker tourney or staying home with my miserable husband, I decided I wasn't nearly ill enough to miss out on Hold 'em. I grabbed some Sucrets, tucked Glen in, left a humidifier running, and drove to the game without him.

Frost crackled in the gravel as I walked the path to our friend Erik's man cave. You could maybe even call it a man lair. The thing was an enormous suite with a bathroom, full wet bar, band room, and the card room. I crossed the threshold into warmth. "Hey guys," I said, shaking off my jacket.

"Hey Aleah," a few called back. We had fourteen players. It was a two-table night. I paid my entrance fee, found my seat, and settled in to count my chips. I loved the rich black suede, the way the cards slid across it, the thick oaken beams Erik had used when he'd meticulously made the tables by hand. I was the only woman at the table. I'm sure they would have welcomed more; it's just that none of their girls were interested. I loved the game.

However, this night I was mostly card dead. Sometimes lady luck is just like that, smiling on other people. I made the final table, but two poor decisions put me out of chips early, around eleven. Normally I'd just go home. It was New Years, though. The other guys who'd busted out already were hanging in the band room. I felt like I should stay up but I was too tired to move, so I watched the boys play for a bit. The cards rolled out and hit the table, rolled out and hit the table. The world grew hazy through my tired eyes. I could barely tell what was on the board. Hand after hand, it got so all I was seeing was red and black. Maybe I was sicker than I thought. My eyes drifted shut.

The world grew quiet and I caught myself on the verge of sleep. I blinked and jounced myself back awake in time to hear Blake Porter announce, "I'm all in." His large hands swallowed his chips as he shoveled them onto the playing field.

"Good luck, all in," I said out of sheer force of habit. He threw me his best puppy-dog grin and winked at me.

"You back with us, sleeping beauty?"

"I wasn't snoring, was I?"

He shook his head, no, he was just teasing.

I looked at the board. King of spades, queen of clubs, king of hearts. I looked at Blake's chips. He was unusually short-stacked. I figured him for a king in his hand. Or else he was bluffing. I never could catch Blake in a lie, but he played just a few too many hands not to be bluffing at least some of the time. Nobody was that lucky.

Erik folded to Blake.

Johnny folded to Blake.

Jack, on the other hand, the chip leader, stared intently at Blake, pushed his chips in, and said, "I call."

Erik was dealing. "On their backs, please, gentlemen."

Blake flipped his cards up. King and four of clubs. There was that king.

Jack flipped his ace and eight of hearts. Dead man's hand.

"Trip kings," Johnny said, his long curls bouncing as he smiled. "Dominated." I wondered why Jack had called. He had shit. Maybe he felt like I did. The blinds were up to a decent amount. He probably thought Blake was trying to buy the pot and his ace high would beat Blake's crap. The turn came, three of hearts. No good for anyone.

Erik picked up the final card. "No hearts, no hearts," Blake chanted. It's a testament to how tired I was that I hadn't seen the flush draw before then.

Erik dealt the river. Seven of hearts.

Holy shit. Flush on the river. Jack had taken Blake out. He extended his hand across the table. "Nice game, man."

"For you, maybe." Blake laughed. "I'll get ya' next time." He cleaned up his empties, then stuffed his smokes, the few beers he had left, and his lucky rabbit's foot into his pack.

I decided it was as good a time as any to go, before I got too tired to drive. At least we weren't in the city. I wouldn't have to avoid a slew of drunks on the road. I gathered my things. We said our goodbyes and our Happy New Years and Blake walked me down the path to the car. I shivered, pulling my arms in tight to my chest.

"Need a jacket?" He laughed.

"I have one." I zipped it up a little higher. My teeth chattered. "And my car's not twenty feet away." I shook my head, smiling at him, and kept walking.

Blake and I had been friends forever. I'd known him almost as long as I'd known my husband. They'd been roommates when Glen and I were dating. He's funny and sexy and I was always happy to see him. He resembled a young Dave Matthews, a fair bit. Short curly dark hair, greenish gray eyes. Except built.

"Is that little thing even gonna get you home, missie?" he teased, lightly kicking one of the tires of my yellow VW bug. He was always giving me shit about my car.

"Yup. And she won't hurt the planet like your gas guzzler," I said, jerking my head toward his monstrosity of a truck, laden with racks, ladders, toolboxes and equipment. "Damn, it's cold. I'm just gonna warm her up," I said, hopping in to start the diesel motor. The little bug purred to life.

"Your flower's dead," Blake said. I glanced at the dash. The flower in the vase wasn't only dead, it was brown. I liked to keep fresh flowers in there. Sometimes I just didn't do a very good job of it.

"Thanks." I turned on the heater. Icy cold air blasted me from the vents. I yelped and hopped out of the car, shutting the door. "Very helpful observation, that."

"Anytime."

"Brrr." I rubbed my arms.

"C'mere." He pulled me in close for a hug. I pressed against him and reveled in his warmth as I hugged him back, a long New Year's hug. I finally turned away, my hand trailing. "Happy New Year," I said.

"Okay, one more hug." He pulled me back into him. I pressed my cold face into his neck, felt his breath warming my ice-cold hair.

What happened next I never expected. Not in a hundred years. I pulled away and he leaned in and kissed me so softly. On the lips. I was sick and I must have tasted of Sucrets and cigarettes and it didn't matter because he kissed me again, another sweet, soft kiss, and his kisses tasted so good.

"I shouldn't be doing this," I said. *Ohmygod Blake Porter just kissed me.*

And he said, "Okay, buh-bye," and walked away, but I wanted to call him back to me. Blake fucking Porter. I sat in the car, fully awake. The blue digital readout on the dash said 12:03. *January first*, I thought. *It's going to be an interesting year.* I drove home and my thoughts were of nothing else for a good long while.

The softness of his lips, the way my body jolted to life at his touch, all of this haunted me for days. I mean, I had several *What does it all mean?* kind of moments. But eventually I came to realize it was just a New Year's kiss. It meant nothing. I had more important things to pay attention to. Like my marriage.

Glen and I were on thin ice. Had been for a few months. Well, much longer than that, but I'd only just a few months ago cornered him in the glorious kitchen of our newly-constructed home and demanded that we discuss the state of our eight-year-old marriage. I told him everything that had been building up; I ripped at the foundations of our relationship all at once. "I don't think I can do this much longer, Glen. I think our marriage is headed for disaster if we don't figure things out."

I stood across from our stainless steel dishwasher and leaned back on the solidity of the two-inch-thick engineered stone counter tops.

He looked genuinely surprised. I at least expected that. He'd always been a little clueless. I mean, usually in a sweet way, but generally a little late to the table.

"Like what? What's wrong?"

"Okay. First off, you know I want a baby. I thought *we* wanted a baby." I stopped, realizing I need him to confirm that. "Do we still want a baby? Both of us?"

"Yes," he said. No hesitation.

"But you still haven't gone through testing." All these years Glen and I had never used birth control.

His face clouded over and he stormed away upstairs to our bedroom.

I followed him. I was used to his style of argument, but this time I wasn't taking his resistance for an answer. "You remember four-and-a-half years ago, at Black Butte, don't you?" Aiden, our nephew, had been six months old. "While I held Aiden in my arms and danced in the restaurant I can't tell you how many people came up to me and asked when we were going to start our family. You saw it was breaking my heart. You leaned in close and promised you'd get tested as soon as we got home. Do you remember?"

Sullenly, he nodded. I was crying at the memory.

"I don't think I ever loved you more than I did in that moment. But then you didn't get tested. Months went by. And when I reminded you of it, you'd promise and not do it and promise and not do it... And then years went by."

He was staring at the floor, clearly ashamed.

"I'm sick of your empty promises, Glen. I don't trust you to keep your word to me anymore."

"You always give me mixed messages," he said.

"What? When?" As long as he'd known me, he'd known I wanted children.

"You did," he said. "You said you were scared."

"Of course I'm scared. I'm scared of doctors. You know I hate them. I'm scared of giving birth. That doesn't mean I don't want a baby. I'm scared it's going to cost a fortune. I'm scared I'm completely infertile and I'm scared there's nothing they'll be able to tell us and nothing we can do. I'm scared it's going to hurt like nothing else. I still want a baby. Being scared doesn't make you stop doing something you want more than anything."

"Oh. Well, I'll get tested, then," he said, like it was done already. I'd heard it before. I'd wait and see. "What else? That can't be everything."

It could have been, but it wasn't. "I need to feel more connected to you. I don't feel that way at all now. I need you to talk to me more. You're always so quiet. 'How are you?' I say, 'Fine,' you say. 'How was work today?' I say. 'Okay,' you say. I mean, seriously, you know I work from home, right? You know you're my main source of adult conversation? Glen, I fell in love with you because of how easy it was to talk to you. Now we can barely string two sentences together without getting pissed at each other. Take me on a date. Take me on lots of dates. Reconnect with me."

"Okay. I get that. What else." He crossed his arms across his chest. I could see he was closing down.

I was sick of telling him I needed him to keep his word. I had to find a new way to get through to him. "Every time you agree to do something for me I am disappointed by your lack of effort. I need you to be a man." I knew it was a mistake as soon as the words were out, but then it was too late.

"What the fuck, Aleah? I am a man." He glared at me.

"I need you to be more of one," I said. "I need you to do what you say you will. It's time to grow out of your twenties, Glen. You're thirty-two years old. I want you to cut the apron strings. Treat me like I come first. Every time there's a choice, start picking me, not your mom and dad, or your sister..."

"I don't know what you're talking about."

"I don't feel like going over every time it's happened. You can figure it out."

"Fine. Whatever." He walked past me, through the door and started to head back downstairs.

There was one thing, though. The most recent offense. Glen and I were DINKs. I worked from home part time as an insurance underwriter and did the housework and watched our dog. He was a programmer for a local software firm. We'd only just moved into this house in the Hills a few months before. Three bedrooms, two and half baths, new construction. We went with a slightly smaller house, but pulled out all the stops on our building choices. Gas fireplaces in the living room and the master suite, the most beautiful kitchen we could afford, with engineered stone countertops that went on forever. We had hardwood floors and gigantic front-loading washing machines on pedestals. We had a natural gas feed on the back patio for the grill we hadn't yet purchased. I mean, it was a pristine, gorgeous house. Until Bianca moved in. Or rather, out.

I followed him back downstairs. "You want an example of when you chose your family over me? Maybe start with when you bitched me out for expecting your sister to clean the bathroom before she moved out. You would rather do things for her than teach her to be responsible."

Bianca had found her boyfriend spending their rent on Internet porn and she and her son had moved in with us in our brand new house for six weeks or so while they figured everything out. I'd told her when she moved in that the only thing I needed her to do in exchange for staying with us was to keep the bathroom clean. They'd moved out a month ago. Bianca left a five-inch ring of crusty yellow pee on the floor surrounding my brand-new toilet.

"She's a single mother, Aleah. Aiden was potty training. Cut her some slack. Is that all?" He spat the last words out with exasperation, like I was flying off the handle for no reason at all. There was that, too. I always felt an undercurrent of disapproval from him. Had he forgotten it was my idea to let them come live with us? He was always finding ways to think less of me.

"No. That's the crux of it," I said. "Baby and connection and keeping your word." There were other issues, but I decided to let them go. Those were the big three. I was lonely as all get out in an empty marriage with dreams unfulfilled, a walking cliché.

"I need to think about this." He was crying; small tears escaped the corner of his eyes, but he had nothing to say. He walked away from me again, this time opening the French doors to my office, my sanctum, and strode in like he owned it. *What the hell was he doing?* We had three bedrooms in addition to my office, one of which we'd converted into an entire office of his own upstairs next to the guest bedroom. There was no reason for him to intrude on my space. He sat down at my desk.

I followed him. "What are you doing?"

"Go away. I told you I need to think." *Yeah, this is problem solving.* I squinted at him.

"Seriously, Glen? Couldn't do your thinking *anywhere* else?" I shook my head and walked away. I threw on a jacket and left the house. My best friend, Jennifer, lived just down the road. Her husband was always working late with clients. He was a psychiatrist. Psychologist? Whichever one sees patients but doesn't write prescriptions. I could never remember.

Jennifer cracked open a bottle of wine and I told her about the fight. She knew it'd been building up. She knew everything, from the shitty sex I'd always have to initiate to how badly I wanted a baby (she and David were trying, too), to my utter loneliness.

"I'm glad you finally told him," she said. "It's been eating you up." She had the most compassionate hazel eyes.

"I know. Well, something had to change."

"How will you know when it has?"

I chewed on the end of my hair while I thought. "Fertility testing. If he does that, I think there's hope for us."

"How long will you give him?"

"I don't know. A month, maybe?"

When David got home, the three of us played some board games and drank more wine until we were all yawning. I arrived home late, around two in the morning. Glen was still in my office, sitting cross-legged on the floor. I moved past him without saying a word and walked on up the stairs to bed.

The next morning, after not coming to bed, he finally talked to me. He had the decency to wait until I'd made coffee. "I've decided I'm not ready to walk away from our marriage just yet. I want to give it one more try."

"Who said anything about abandoning our marriage?"

"You did. You asked me for a divorce last night."

"What?" Is that what he'd heard? "I did not." I took a deep breath. "Glen, I told you we had issues I needed us to work on. I wasn't suggesting divorce when I started the conversation. Divorce never even occurred to me," I said honestly.

"I thought that's what you were threatening."

"I was worried about us heading in that direction. I wasn't giving up on us, Glen. I feel like we've barely tried to fix things. I feel like we just started talking last night for the first time in a long time." We had slipped into being roommates who occasionally fucked because we were trying to get pregnant. It was pretty sad. I thought maybe he would be different, as a dad. I thought it would bring out a side of him he'd been unwilling to show before, a more playful and affectionate side. I could see all of that in him. I remembered his sweetness, from our early days.

"Well, I promise I'm going to work harder on things. I love you."

I looked at him and took in his misty gray eyes, soft with tears, the way his hair was a little more ragged than my mother would have approved of, because he had more important things to think about than scheduling barber appointments. I did love him. He was a smart, good man. "I love you, too."

He told me then, "When I grow up I want to be just like my dad."

"Wow," I said. I couldn't stop myself. "When exactly is that going to be,

Glen?"

He gave me the *how dare you* look I'd seen from his mom before.

I squeezed my eyes briefly closed. I knew I'd hurt him. "I'm just saying you hold yourself back. You are your own greatest enemy. You are so talented and intelligent. You perceive yourself to be so much less than you are."

"Save your breath," he said, lips pursed. "I don't need any lessons in self-improvement right now, thank you very much." He took a big breath. "But I want you to know that I heard what you said last night and I'm going to make some serious changes. I'm going to do everything in my power to make you happy."

That night, he started his metamorphosis by going to sitting meditation at the local Buddhist temple. *Okay.*

The Thursday before Thanksgiving, I started to plan the big meal: the first one in our new home. I sat at the kitchen counter, thumbing through the new *Cook's Illustrated* and a *Better Homes & Garden* special Thanksgiving edition to find a few new recipes to try out. I'd been looking forward to this holiday for ages, since before our new house was even built. I had invited Glen's parents, as well as Bianca and Aiden, months in advance and they'd all said yes. I loved cooking and I especially loved entertaining and putting great food on the table. I was looking forward to a candlelit evening with fantastic food, music, and laughter, a time to remember.

Glen's mom called in the evening. I half listened to his bantering with her while I made some soup for dinner. I set the table and pulled hot, crusty bread out of the oven while he wrapped up his call. "Yeah, sure. Four o'clock sounds good. We'll see you then. Love you too, Mom."

"What was that about?" I asked as Glen sat down to dinner.

"Oh, mom was just calling about Thanksgiving."

"Oh? So, they're all coming over at four?"

"No," he said, giving me a funny look. "We're going over there."

"What?"

"Mom called and invited us to Thanksgiving dinner and I agreed and we're going over there at four next week," he said slowly and patiently, as though I had some kind of impairment.

"Okay, but I don't understand."

"It's not hard to understand, Aleah. Thanksgiving dinner—" he began even more slowly.

"I know, I know," I said. I hated it when he talked to me like I was stupid. "It's just that I invited your family to our house for Thanksgiving two months ago. Your mom, your sister. I started planning the meal today..." I gestured to the magazines in front of me.

"Oh. I didn't know that."

"You were there when I invited them, Glen." I decided to hold my tongue about the several times I'd told him how much I was looking forward to it. I'd gotten used to not being heard.

"I'm sure we can host it here next year, Aleah."

I couldn't keep the disappointment from creeping into my voice. "It won't be the same," I said. "It's our first year in our new house together. I wanted to start a tradition of our own. Besides, everyone already said they were coming. Did she just forget?"

"I don't know," he said, his voice flat. I could tell he was tired of the conversation and didn't want to talk about it anymore.

After dinner I called his mom. "Hey Christie," I said. "Glen told me about your Thanksgiving invitation and I'm so flattered but also a little surprised. I know it's been a few months since I invited you, but I thought you were all coming over here for Turkey Day," I said. "So I wanted to call before you went to too much trouble; will you still be able to join us?"

"Oh," she said. She hemmed and hawed a bit. "Aleah, I completely forgot," she said. "I'm so sorry."

"Well, it's no big deal," I said. "You can still come over. Glen and I were looking forward to hosting Thanksgiving the first year in our new house."

"Oh, well..."

"What is it?"

"The thing is, I've already invited other people here. My mom and step-dad are flying up from Nevada and Richard invited several people from his office. We're kind of expecting a houseful. Can you handle that kind of crowd?"

Our sweet little house could not and she knew it. "Oh, that's a problem," I said. "Have they all accepted?"

"Well, several of them have."

"Okay," I said, defeated. We couldn't comfortably host more than eight for a formal dinner. "We'll do it at your place."

I got off the phone before my tears made me sound like a fool. I bit my lip, tears sliding down my cheek.

"What's the matter?" Glen asked.

"Oh, I was just really looking forward to hosting Thanksgiving," I said, shaking my head.

He raised his eyebrow at me. "You're crying over that?"

I knew it was a silly dream. It just hadn't seemed silly to me. "Apparently," I said.

"There's always next year." To his credit, he was trying to be comforting.

I endured Thanksgiving with Glen's family. Really, it's one for the story books. Their ovens went out halfway through the preparation. Everything tasted raw and I was afraid I'd get food poisoning. We didn't even have turkey; it was too undercooked to eat. Glen's mom acted like it was somehow my fault. I said nothing. I didn't even feel smug, just disappointed. It felt a little like getting my period every month, like one more possibly happy future slipping away from me.

Regarding our troubled fertility, since all Glen seemed inspired to do was more Zen meditation, I made the first move and got a well woman checkup. It wasn't a fertility workup, just a precursor. But I felt like I was conquering Mt. Everest. My childhood had scarred me against doctors. I went by myself. I didn't ask anyone to hold my hand.

"All my blood work came back normal," I told Glen when I got the results.

"Yeah? That's great!" He sounded genuinely excited and somehow relieved.

"So now we can move on to the fertility specialist," I prompted.

"Right," he said. "I'm on that too. I've been trying to get a reference for a reputable clinic."

I was genuinely surprised. "Glen, that's great. Thank you." It was more than he'd done before. Maybe we were getting somewhere.

Soon after that Thanksgiving, we were bearing down on the three month anniversary of having moved in to our brand new house. It was early December and we needed to get a punch list to our builder of anything that needed fixing before the 15th. Blake was a contractor specializing in residential construction. Glen called in a favor so that we wouldn't have to pay $400 to an inspector.

Blake came over after he got off work one day, before Glen came home, to assess the state of the house for us. "Hey," he said. Blake's smile lit up his eyes. Just that one word and I was at ease.

"Hey," I said. "Come on in. How's it going?"

He took his work boots off and came in. "Hope my socks don't smell too bad," he said.

I laughed. "You're fine," I said. "Want a drink?"

"Yes, please. Iced tea if you have it."

"Sure thing," I said. I had to make the tea first, and zapped the water in the microwave as he took a first level pass around the house. I let the black tea steep for a few minutes, sweetened it with honey and stirred until I was sure the amber sugar had dissolved, then poured it over ice.

Blake took it from me and gulped it like soda pop from a fast food joint. "That was really good," he said, putting the glass in the sink. "Thanks."

"C'mon." He jerked his head to me. "Let me show you what I've found." He started a list of issues on his clipboard. I was impressed with his knowledge of caulking and soffits. As we walked, he made recommendations to me on how I should keep up the maintenance. I grabbed some paper and scribbled notes. I hoped I could decipher them later. Blake was a veritable font of information. We got up to the final rooms in the house, the master suite.

We walked in and he took his survey of the three rooms: the master bedroom, the master bath, and the master closet, which itself was so large that Glen and I had been able to set up a queen-sized air mattress in there—we'd needed to the first night we'd moved in, because we hadn't yet put up any curtains and the streetlights shone in through our bedroom windows too brightly for me to sleep.

Blake made his observations about the closet on his little log. "They didn't finish the patching." He pointed with his pencil to a few places on the ceiling. "Here." He pulled a few short pieces of blue painter's tape and jumped up and slapped them on the ceiling where the blemishes were.

We walked back through the bathroom to the master bedroom. "Damn, that's a nice bed," Blake said, sitting down on it.

"I know," I said. "I bought it."

I bent over to pick some clothes up off the floor.

"And that is a nice view." He whistled and patted the coverlet next to him. I laughed. "Come check out this amazing bed," he said. I glanced over at where his hand swept across the purple satin comforter.

"I know what it's like, Blake, I sleep on it every night," I said and then it dawned on me. Blake Porter was flirting with me. Him, with a wife and two kids at home. I rolled my eyes.

Blake patted the bed next to him again, his eyes sparkling. “Right here, Aleah. You know you want to.” He winked at me.

No, he was just teasing me. “Don’t you flirt with me, Blake Porter,” I said. He laughed and got up and the moment melted away.

I didn’t take it seriously, I barely even noticed, actually. My heart is monogamous. In fact, I thought nothing of it until three weeks later, until New Years and those first few kisses he’d placed on my lips.

Chapter Two

Glen and I arrived at our next poker game earlier than usual and I was glad to have some time there before Blake arrived. I'll admit I was a bit nervous. Flirty nervous, like my skin was somehow going to detach itself from my body and be lifted away by fairies. Except that it didn't detach. And so I just felt sparkly. A wired and tense kind of sparkly.

Blake arrived and completely ignored me.

"Hey Blake," I said. Nothing. I couldn't even solicit a "hello" from him. It pissed me off a little. We sat across the table from one another and began to play.

After a few hands I noticed he was getting out of every hand I was in and would only play if he had position on me. He'd fold or make a ridiculous bet early and I'd fold. *Why? So he doesn't have to talk to me at all?* I didn't get it. *Did that one stupid kiss ruin our friendship?*

I played a few more hands, and then decided to take a break. It looked like several players were interested in the hand—the action might last a while—and I glanced down at crap, crap off suit. "Just fold me if I miss my turn," I said as I stepped away and out into the cold February air for a cigarette. I stood under the second-story porch as I smoked, leaning against a thick support beam. The white stars sparkled in the chill of the night through the fringe of the Douglas Firs all around me. The air was thick and cold in my lungs, I could feel the tip of my nose start to freeze.

I heard the squeal of the door opening and saw Blake enter the shadows.

He came to me directly, took my face in his hands, and kissed me like he owned me, his lips supple and demanding at once. He kissed me again, like it was the last time he expected to ever kiss me, deeply. "I've wanted this from the first moment I saw you," he said and kissed me again and again and I melted. I was shaking. I hadn't tasted bad. He had wanted *me*. "I remember," he continued. "You were wearing skin-tight pants that went all the way down your long, long legs, and an oversized gray sweatshirt that night. I remember." His voice was husky, his kisses divine. "Those legs," he said. "You looked like Uma Thurman in the shadows, your hair, your straight nose, your lean, sexy body. I whistled to myself. I thought, 'That's my Uma.' And then Glen said to me, 'That's Aleah. That's the girl I like.' And my world crashed to an end."

He remembered what I was wearing eleven years before. How do you react to that? How do you react when a man you've thought was so fine for so long comes and claims you? He kissed me again, holding me under the porch light. "Let me kiss you," he begged.

I did. I surrendered to those kisses. It was like having a dream I didn't even know I'd harbored come true.

His huge hands stroked me gently through my slick jogging pants, they rode up to my breasts, back to my pussy. Oh, it was so good. But I was terribly nervous. Glen was just inside. I could only take it for so long. I slipped away from him and started to walk to the door.

"Don't go," he begged, grabbing my hand, pulling me back to him.

"We can't do this," I said. "We can't get caught." Even at the time, I realized they were two very different things to say. He let me go.

When we got back inside, the pull between us was so strong, like a rope of crystal shot through with light, I thought it should be visible to everyone in the room. Even though he sat across the table from me, I had to move my chair further away from him and still it was there. I was certain everyone would notice. How could they not?

I like to keep track of players and my wins and places when I play poker. I like to know how much money I make or lose, and why. I especially like to keep track of people's tells. Jack blinks a lot when the flop sucks for him.

And he sticks his tongue out—just a little—when he actually has good cards. And so I keep a little poker notebook that the boys are used to seeing me scribble in from time to time. That night, I wrote feverishly, in between hands.

Blake kept getting up when I was writing. Once he skirted around behind me, peering over my shoulder. I shifted so that he couldn't see my notebook. He slipped back and then inched forward slowly, thinking I wouldn't notice.

"Hey!" I chastised him. "This is for my eyes only. Private information." I loved teasing him.

"I'd like to see some of that private information," he said, somehow managing to keep his tone light.

"I bet you would." I laughed. He moved back to his seat.

Each time he or I stepped out for a cigarette the other one shortly followed and we'd fall together. I couldn't get enough of his kisses. Part of me thought it would be so obvious, but I knew no one would be suspicious because they wouldn't be looking for it. I certainly hadn't been.

"I wanted to call you, after New Year's," he said. "But I didn't know what to say. I figured you'd call, but you didn't. So I let it go. It was what it was, you know..." He took a deep drag on his cigarette and blew a stream of white smoke into the moonlight. I watched it swirl in the porch light. "At least, that's what I told myself. But then I saw you again tonight and it was back, full on. I can't stay away from you. I can't hold back what I feel for you any longer."

Do I have to tell you how entrancing those words were?

He kissed me again, his lips full and insistent and so good. But… It was a fantasy, a fairy tale with an unhappy ending. I couldn't walk that path.

"I can't. I can't do this, Blake," I said.

"You can," he whispered.

"No. It doesn't matter how much I want to. I'm taken. Off the market. For that matter, so are you." I found the resolve to go once more back inside to the rest of the boys, to my husband. But despite my best intentions, I kept finding ways to go outside, to pass him on the way to the bathroom. He brushed soft kisses along my neck, lifted my braid to breathe along the edge of my ear.

"You know you want this, too," he told me. "You always unleash something dangerous in me, the way you softly whimper and moan when you hug me."

"I didn't think it was just me," I said. "The way you always press my whole body to you. The way your hand lingers as I pull away."

Glen actually won that night, so we were there until the end of the game. Blake came in third. I loved every stolen, passion-injected second Blake gave me. I wanted more, more, more. But I knew I couldn't have it.

When the night was over we went home and I fucked my husband hard out of frustration. He seemed excited, probably still high from the win, and jack-hammered into me, whimpering like it was the best sex ever. His gray eyes shone with excitement and he grinned as he came. He fell asleep quickly and when I finally slept, I dreamed of Blake the rest of the night, of being locked in his hot, sweaty embrace. How his kisses made me feel like an English heroine on a moor, like every princess I'd ever wanted to be. I woke up wet.

Why now, Blake? After all this time? I had always been attracted to him, but I'd buried it because I never dreamed my feelings were reciprocated. And now there was so much at stake. I couldn't imagine letting things go on with him and I couldn't keep my thoughts from him. Every spare moment, every idle thought turned there. *What's going to happen? What the fuck am I doing?*

Chapter Three

I swallowed hard against my nerves and chewed on my lip a little as we walked up past the line of cars parked in the Porter's circular drive. I'd felt tingly all day and now I'd have to face Blake again, this time quite publicly, at his birthday party. The front door was open, Blake was welcoming another couple to the party. I saw him, saw his happy smile, and breathed a sigh of relief. It was like it had always been. Friendly, comfortable. He was a gracious host. "Glen! Aleah," he said, seeming to savor my name in his mouth. "It's good to see you."

"Yes, Blake, it's been forever," I laughed. It had been all of eighteen hours. He pulled me in for a hug.

"You have no idea," he said huskily in my ear. With his words the world closed in around me and suddenly I felt like the only person in the room. My body tingled anew.

He shook Glen's hand. "There's beer on the back porch. Wine on the counter and," he cast a glance over his shoulder, "in the fridge if you want the white crap Cami drinks. Make yourself at home." He smiled at me and shed the good host veneer for a moment. He really smiled. There were so many people there, the house was packed and more people were spilling out onto the back deck. "I'm glad you came."

"Wouldn't have missed it, birthday boy." I gave him a playful swat on the ass as I walked past him. I hung my coat on their rack and headed for the spread. Once I had a decent plate full of chips, salsa, and fruit, I headed to the kitchen to get a glass of red. I mingled a little. I sought out people I knew should be there and found a few of them. Erik and I exchanged hellos and then Donna winked and indicated I should follow her out to the garage. She got me stoned and I zoned out with her for a good, long time.

"How ya' doin', honey?" she asked after I'd passed the pipe back to her the third or fourth time.

"Great," I said enthusiastically. It was as close as I could come to telling her that I was spending every spare moment dreaming about her brother. "Glen and I are hopefully actually going to see a fertility doctor soon," I confided in her. She was one of the few who knew how badly I wanted a baby, all the books I'd read, all the things I'd tried. I mean, we'd had discussions about cervical mucus. We'd been friends a long time.

"Well, it's about time."

"I know. You know I get scared." It was an understatement. I don't do doctors. Not well. Not on my own. Not since my father died.

"Yes, honey. I know" She did, too. "How's the depression treating you these days?" It had been Donna several years back who had originally marched me to the doctor's to get anti-depression meds in the first place. Honestly, I'd most likely have killed myself by now without her intervention.

Depression is the most subtle poison. It creeps up on you day by day, robbing you of any kind of enjoyment until all you can think about is how you mean nothing and everyone would be better off without you around, everything would just be easier. Life becomes the perpetual gray of a nine-month-long Seattle winter. I knew if I went off the meds for too long, I'd start slipping. I'd hard-wired one red flag in my brain. When that flag triggered, I knew I had to get back on the meds. I'm not sure why I ever stopped taking them, actually, except that they're expensive and there's something about depression—even though I knew it was just a chemical imbalance—because it's centered in the mind I somehow thought I should just be able to overcome it. Mind over matter. I mean, I'm smart. I'm an above-average bear. But somehow I can't handle it forever. Eventually, I have to go back on the meds.

"Your brother seems happy."

"'Course he does, it's his birthday." Donna is big on birthdays. She shrugged. "He's happy as he's gonna be."

"What does that mean?" I laughed.

"Oh you know, that shrew." Donna was not exactly fond of Blake's wife. "I really need to slip her some pot brownies one of these days."

I laughed. It was true. Cami was a force to be reckoned with. "You really should," I said. "She could do with a good dose of chill."

"You know it. That bitch has control issues rammed so far up her ass she's trying to make diamonds out of shit." Donna's blue eyes twinkled.

"Speaking of, we should get out of here before her majesty finds us smoking pot in her garage." Cami was on one of her abstinence kicks. And if Cami didn't partake, you'd better not dare partake around her. She'd been on this kick for a few months now. "You know, she actually chewed me out at Carole's baby shower because she thought I was stoned."

"She did not." Donna's face reflected her mock astonishment. She'd been on the other end of that lash, too.

"She did. In front of other people. People I didn't know. She stood up and pointed her finger at me and said, loudly might I add, 'Are you stoned Aleah Clayton? You look stoned.' Donna, seriously, she sounded like a priest in a pulpit screeching about damnation. 'Who comes to a baby shower stoned? Can't get through the day without it? What are you, an addict?'"

"She did not!"

"She did."

"What did you do?"

"I just looked at her. I was like, 'Cami, I'm not stoned.' I mean, seriously. I wasn't."

Later, I sat on a bench in the middle of their huge, grassy backyard. I had no idea where Glen was. I didn't really care. I just wanted some time to stare at the stars. I could feel the initial claws of PMS rip into my abdomen. Another baby I wouldn't have. Clumps of people stood all around me. I overheard parents talking to each other about how hard it was to find a good babysitter these days and how expensive they were. *Jesus Christ! Somebody, please, give me the hassle of having to find a good, expensive babysitter.*

A cigarette later, Blake stepped out onto their expansive back porch. Surprised at how happy I was to see him, I found myself involuntarily smiling. There were forty people in the yard, easy. He looked over, directly at me, like he knew exactly where I was sitting already. He smiled back at me and lit me on fire. I looked around. *No one saw us, right?* I was being silly, I told myself. A stupid kind of paranoid. *What would they see? Smiley happy people? People at a party?* Blake's attention made me feel naked, was all. I felt my cheeks grow hot. I was actually blushing.

Slowly, he snaked his way through the crowd, stopping to say a few words here and there, making sure everyone was taken care of, people had what they needed, they liked the music, and, of course, to accept their birthday wishes. I knew this because I had been to about eight of Blake's birthday parties and countless other parties he and Cami had thrown. Blake charmed everyone he met. Person by person, he made his way to where I sat, alone on a bench in the middle of their crowded yard, surrounded by his friends, her friends, our friends.

"Well, if it isn't Miss Aleah," he said, putting one booted foot on the bench next to me. He leaned forward and rested his forearms on his knee so his face was closer to mine. I found myself breathing slightly faster, shallower. I felt like every part of my being wanted to draw nearer to him. I was magnetized.

"Happy Birthday, Mr. Porter," I managed and swallowed. "Enjoying yourself so far?"

His whole tone of voice shifted. "I am. I was. And then I saw you sitting here all alone and so pretty and I wish all these silly people were gone and I had you all to myself."

A bolt of panic ran through me. "Blake. Hush." Someone could overhear.

"What? I'm just saying someone as gorgeous as yourself shouldn't be sitting alone on a bench. Where is your husband, anyway?"

"Good question," I said. "Could be anywhere. Probably with Johnny." Johnny was Donna's husband and Glen's best friend, as well as one of our poker buddies. We had a tight circle. I gestured vaguely at the house.

"Well, I suppose you'll have to endure my company on your own, then." He reached for my hand. "Take a walk with me, pretty lady?" I could tell he'd knocked back more than a few already. His Texas drawl was coming on thicker with every sentence. It was adorable.

His fingers softly brushed the palm of my hand. His touch set my whole body vibrating like a harp string, imperceptible to the eye but resonant. I let him help me up, but then withdrew my hand from his. I didn't trust myself, not with all these people. Cami was here somewhere too, though I'd managed to mostly avoid her other than a brief greeting.

"Don't be stupid, Blake," I said, quietly, walking ahead. "I don't know what you think you're doing, but I can't play this game with you."

"I'm not doing anything," he said, catching up to me. "Just going to refill—"

I stumbled in the dark and he dropped his beer to catch me before I pitched completely forward. His arms kept me from falling and he lifted me back upright like I weighed no more than a dress.

"Careful now," he said. "You have to watch out for those mole holes." He briefly caressed my lower back as he set me down. His arm fell away and I shuddered from the absence of his touch.

"Thanks." I swallowed to clear the huskiness from my throat.

"You all right? Everything all right?" Blake asked. I nodded. "I'm sorry 'bout that. Thought I'd filled all those suckers in," he said.

He retrieved the rest of his foaming beer, took a look at it, and set the bottle aside on a table. "As I was saying, I'm just looking for some company while I get me a new beer." We continued our way through the thick crowd. We got to the coolers and Blake grabbed a longneck for himself. I shook my head no when he asked with a raised eyebrow and a nod at the cooler if I wanted one. I did wonder where I'd left my wine.

"Reminds me of a story, actually." Blake said. "My daddy, when we were living out on some big property division in the Hill Country. That's Texas, of course. We were all kids, mind you, when this happened." A crowd started to gather around Blake. He did that, naturally, collected people to him. He'd had them at "story." I'd seen it happen hundreds of times. "Anyhow, my daddy had an armadillo problem." He said it *arm-a-diller.*

"I mean, he had a problem. They were tearing up holes left and right, digging all over his front yard garden. And if you know my daddy, you know he is mighty proud of his garden." I happened to know Rex Porter, and it was true. He was mighty proud of his garden.

"So, what did he do?" I prompted.

"'Bout the 'dillos? He did what every godfearin' Texan would do. He prayed on it. Then he went to bed. He set his alarm first, of course, and woke up when it went off—at 2:30 in the morning. Right when he had set it for. He had a plan for those critters. He crept out onto the front porch and threw on the floodlights." Blake's arms shot out from his body to illustrate the point. He almost lost his beer again. It sloshed at the rim, but he steadied it.

"Them 'dillos were everywhere." He smiled at me.

I felt my body turn magnetic again, everything under my skin trying to pulling me toward him. I leaned in closer.

"Way my daddy tells it, there were so many 'dillos that all you could see was 'dillos. There were 'dillos popping up out of holes, coming in from the neighbors' yards, and all these 'dillos were giving birth to baby 'dillos right there as he watched. So, you know. There were a whole lot of them. I think ten. Ten is a safe assumption." We laughed and so did the others listening. I found myself looking at him as he continued, wishing I were eleven years younger and this was an entirely different night.

"So, as he's seeing bazillions of these damn things in the yard, he does the sensible thing," he continued, "and he grabs up his shotgun and starts firing at those suckers as fast as he can keep his gun loaded."

I realized I'd always seen Blake socially, at a party, at a game. I'd almost never spoken to him alone. In fact, I couldn't think of a single time we'd been alone together for longer than the time it took to smoke a cigarette.

"Now, keep in mind, my daddy is living in a neighborhood sub-division. His across-the-street neighbor, I kid you not, his name was Earl, comes out and says, 'Rex? What the hell are you doing?' My daddy says, 'I'm shootin' 'dillos, Earl. Get yer shotgun.' Now—and here's the difference between Washington and Texas—" Blake spread his hands in front of him and waited, drawing out the suspense before going on. "That's exactly what happened. Earl didn't get on the phone and call animal control or the police. He got his shotgun and he and my daddy spent the wee hours of that morning shootin' 'dillos and ratchet jawin'." Blake drew one hand back to an imaginary trigger and squinted down the eye of his imaginary barrel and started taking shots at the gathered crowd, his imagined 'dillos. "Kablam!" he said. "Kablam! Kablam! Kablam!" His intended victims in the audience clutched at their chest and mock fell or stumbled back as he pointed at them. "But that's it," he continued. "None of this overzealous gun control. No excessive animal control. I mean, that's the difference right there. Texans do for themselves."

I looked at him with new eyes. *Uh-huh*, I thought. *They sure do.*

Chapter Four

Glen eventually came and found me at the party and we hung out with other people together. That is, we didn't really talk to each other. I didn't think his jokes were funny. I didn't want to have to laugh just because I was supposed to, just because he was.

To think there might actually be a life after this marriage—that it might actually *not* work out—was a revelation for me. Blake had me thinking about what that might be like and, for the first time, wondering if it might not be the end of the world.

"After all, if Glen's not perfect for you, you're holding him back from finding the perfect girl, too," Jennifer had said more than once. I had always resisted before, wondering if what I had was as good as it got.

Though we stayed late, the party finally waned. Glen took me home and for some reason we stayed up even later. Knowing he'd been drinking, I poured us both glasses of water and pulled the ibuprofen out of the medicine cabinet before plopping down on the poop-colored couch next to him.

Glen asked, "Is it making any difference?"

"Is what?"

"Everything I'm doing to try and save our marriage. I mean, I've been working really hard, Aleah."

"Try *to*," the grammar Nazi in me said softly before I could stop her.

"What?"

"Never mind."

I wasn't sure what he had been doing, but he seemed very stressed by all the changes he was having to make for me. I'll admit it, I was pissy and maybe a little uninhibited from the wine and the pot. The claws of PMS were tearing into my abdomen and I might have picked a fight. "Oh, you mean all the dates we've been on, how much more time we're spending together connecting as a couple?" I said innocently, knowing he would recognize the sarcasm in my routinely dry humor.

"Aleah." He said it softly, but I knew it was a warning. I ignored it.

"Or maybe like what you've done in terms of getting fertility testing done?" It wasn't nice of me to say. I knew he hadn't done anything yet; or at least I suspected. I was tired, my cramps were growing stronger, and he had asked. For once I was beyond caring if I were nice or not.

"No," he said. "Not just that. I'm talking about the meditation. I'm doing it so that I can release my need for things to be different. I'm doing it for us. So that we can connect better." He shifted on the couch and reached out for my hands, his gray eyes earnestly seeking mine.

I shook my head slightly. This wasn't the time to try to be holding my hands and he knew it. "Seriously? You're doing that for me? For us?" I said. "I thought you were going religious on me. I mean, I don't have a problem with it if you are... It's just..." I thought for a minute. Glen had been going to sitting meditation three times a week. He woke up in the morning and sat on his meditation pillow for a few hours before work. He came home and on the nights he didn't go to sitting meditation, he'd sit for a few hours before bed. "Glen, you spend so much time meditating... It's not like we're spending any more time connecting. I mean, do *you* feel differently?"

"I don't know. I guess not differently enough if you haven't even noticed a difference in me."

I half grimaced, half grinned. "I've noticed that you meditate a lot more," I offered.

"It's more than that," he said. I heard the familiar sense of desperation creeping into his voice; his defenses were going up. "I've been doing so much."

"Like what?" I said and winced. My cramps were coming on heavy. "Did you ever figure out which fertility clinic you want to go to?" My lips pursed.

I couldn't help it.

"Are you seriously pressuring me about that again?"

I stared at him. "Pressuring you? Glen, I told you this was a major issue—" I stopped to count on my fingers—"more than four months ago. Get real." I had let him blow way past my one month deadline. Of course, I hadn't exactly told him about it, so it's not like he knew he'd missed it. I guess it was more of an internal milestone. I'd have been really impressed if he'd addressed it that quickly.

"I am real. I am real... Busy."

"Right, with all that sitting around doing nothing it's amazing you have time for anything at all," I snapped.

"That's not fair, Aleah." He sounded resigned. I hated how he could be so completely devoid of emotion. I didn't understand him at all sometimes.

"Isn't it, though? I mean, it's obviously not important to you. I don't even know why I try." I turned away from him.

Glen stood up and brushed his way past my knees. "It's obviously way too important to you right now. Jesus, Aleah. It's four in the morning. Can't we just get some sleep and talk about it tomorrow?"

"Sure," I said, watching him head for the stairs, leaving me as he always did. Unsatisfied. I hugged my knees and my head dropped as the tears came. Why didn't he care? Why didn't he want to be a dad?

I didn't want to be in the same bed as him. Feeling pissy, I left the house, slammed the door behind me, and went for a drive. I took my Sadie dog with me, opened the window so she could let her tongue hang out. I drove the thirty-five minutes to Seattle and all the way back to our little woodcutter's town. I let myself get lost on back country roads. I eventually found my way back to Main Street and pulled up in front of the train car graveyard—a park littered with all the old logging rail cars from pioneer days rusting to their death in the damp of the mountains. I stayed to watch the sun rise and I just cried and cried for my non-existent babies. I cried for my shell of a marriage. I cried for my bleak future. A cop pulled over next to me and knocked on the window. In this town, the force was composed of truly good people. Salt of the earth Christians. I wiped at my face before rolling the window down.

"You all right, ma'am?"

"Thanks, I'm fine," I said, but I wanted to scream. "Just here to watch the sun rise."

I took myself out to breakfast at Twede's Café in North Bend. They had shitty coffee, but they brought it by often and it was hot. Sometimes, those were the most important requirements for coffee. They had good pie. I had pie for breakfast. I was in a tailspin. I couldn't see more than a moment or two in front of me. For the first time in the longest time, I didn't have any idea what my future looked like.

I'd recently told Jennifer my train had derailed somewhere and I didn't even know where. But after Friday and all Blake's kisses, our easy camaraderie at his party, I knew there was so much passion missing from my married life and it made me beyond sad. Every thought during every moment of every waking hour was filled with Blake. I was scared, confused, throbbing with want. I lived breath to breath, distracted, my head filled with dreams. I couldn't let any of it show. And I certainly couldn't act on it. Girls in my family didn't have affairs.

I managed to drive myself home sometime around eight in the morning. Glen wasn't out of bed yet. When he did wake up, he didn't even ask where I'd been. I supposed that was trust.

I made it through Sunday by sleeping since I hadn't gotten any rest the night before. We had Jennifer and David over for games that night. I was angry at Glen just for being there. I mean, I knew it was wrong to feel that way. It was his house. Our house. My whole marriage felt wrong but I wasn't ready to concede. Girls in my family didn't get divorces. I told myself I had to keep trying.

Monday morning my husband left for work and I was alone with my blissful, blissful thoughts of another man. I ached with desire for Blake. Every moment. I couldn't get him out of my head. I couldn't get him out of my body. At 3:00 in the afternoon I was still trembling, wondering what the hell I was—we were—going to do.

I called him.

"Blake Porter," he answered.

I plunged in. "I just called to tell you: I can't stop thinking about you."

He laughed. "I get that a lot," he said. I could actually hear him smiling. Then, "The feeling is completely mutual, my friend," and I knew there was someone standing next to him. My entire body tingled with the affection from his voice. He told me, "Sometimes I get off work early. I might come and visit someday."

"Oh really?" I said. I wasn't sure I was ready for this. "When?"

"Oh, it'll be a surprise. I'll just show up some afternoon."

"Call me first," I said. "I'm not always home."

He said he had to go. We got off the phone. Too late, I wondered what the fuck I was doing.

Later, Jennifer and I went out on one of our regular walks. Somehow, she knew something was different. She kept asking, "Aleah, what's on your mind? Earth to Aleah..." I was able to blame it on project stress and work.

I'd meant to take my phone, but realized after a short while I'd left it behind. When I got home an hour later I saw I'd missed two calls from Blake. I had also received an email from him. All it said was: *this is MY email address.*

I hit reply and wrote: *Good to know. Sorry I missed your call earlier—was out for a walk with a friend and the dog.*

I know you wanted to see it. So, this is what I wrote at poker the other night:

Since the first time I met you—me too.

Disbelief is tied to delight.

Awakening.

Longing to touch you, the table between us.

What might our lives have been, if only we'd tried something different?

I hit send and instantly regretted it. This was crazy. *What was I doing?*

When Glen came home that night, he made an announcement. "I made that appointment. At the fertility clinic. They're kind of busy. It's not for three weeks."

"Okay," I said. I was stunned. "Thank you for doing that." Inside, guilt gnawed at my belly. I was foolish for flirting with Blake. I'd make it stop.

"I'll email you the details of where the office is at so you can meet me there."

I walked over and gave him a huge hug and a sweet little kiss on the lips. "Thank you, love." I made myself take a hard look at him. His skinny face and belly had bloated a little in the years we'd been together, but he was still svelte overall. His eyes were full of kindness. He was a good man. He worked hard. He came home to me every night. He was smart. He trusted me. He was worth being loyal to. He was worth cherishing.

Glen was trying so hard. I shouldn't throw our marriage away, all the time we had between us. I should let everything I'd been feeling for Blake go. I promised myself I'd focus on Glen. Valentine's Day was coming. I could celebrate him, and us.

Over the next weeks, I did my best to do exactly that. Sure, the memory of Blake's possessive kisses rocked me to my core for a moment or three, here and there, but for the most part... I let him go. Blake called once or twice, but I didn't pick up and I didn't call back. I texted him once: *I don't think it's a good idea.* I was married. My husband came home every night for dinner. Divorce was not an option and I needed to stop playing with fire.

Chapter Five

Blake called me on Valentine's Day.

I was out with Jennifer, shopping for the evening's festivities. She was taking me from one boutique to another and all that was for sale was extremely expensive crap. I had absolutely no idea what to buy for Glen. I was getting ready to settle for some of that expensive crap when my eye settled on a nautical compass in a heavily stylized bronze casing. He was redoing his office steampunk style. It was perfect. He would love it. I sighed a breath of relief that I'd found something.

The price tag said $179. Fuck. Way more than I'd had in mind. That's what we got for shopping in Kirkland. I decided to get it anyway. It wasn't out of reach for us, financially, and I was tired of looking. More importantly, Glen would love it. I liked to give good gift.

Valentine's Day has always been a favorite of mine. I'm a sucker for it, judge me how you may. I didn't need a lot of love and affection the rest of the year, not in terms of flowers and chocolate, but—and Glen knew this from our first Valentine's, when he'd fucked up and got me the Whitman's sampler from Walgreens—that one day, I require it.

At least I was direct with him. "I expect a pound of really good, really dark chocolate with almonds. Don't skimp and get a half pound. Spend the thirty dollars. Get me flowers. Nice ones that won't wilt in two days. I'm not picky. But flowers, don't forget them. Take me out to dinner. A card with some nice words. I'm easy, that's all it takes. I don't need surprises. I don't need you to outdo yourself from the year before. But don't forget."

"Okay," he'd said. And from then on, he'd done right by me.

My cell kept ringing and for some reason I answered it. I couldn't imagine why Blake would be calling me on Valentine's Day. I guessed something must be wrong or maybe it was a desperate last-minute ploy to get a sitter. "Hey, lady," he said. My body shimmered at the edges upon hearing his voice. We exchanged a few pleasantries and then he said, "I was thinking today was a good day to come over and see you."

Instantly my whole body was on edge. I panicked. I told him, "I'm going to have to call you back," and hung up. Jennifer, noticing something, arched an eyebrow at me. "Work stuff," I assured her. "I don't want to deal with it right now." I couldn't talk to Blake in front of her. I didn't want anyone to know of my transgressions. We finished our shopping at a lingerie shop where I also picked out a little lacy thing I planned to wear for Glen at our own private after party.

I dropped Jennifer off and called Blake back. "Not on Valentine's Day," I said without preamble. "Not ever, actually. We shouldn't do this at all."

"I can't stop thinking about you," he said.

"I get that a lot," I said, teasing. I was suddenly shaking and my body cried out to be taken, to shudder. I still wanted him so badly. I was stunned at his effect on me. But I belonged to Glen.

"Seriously," he said.

"Seriously, Blake," I said. "It's Valentine's Day. Go and spend it with your wife. I am not playing around anymore. Put your attention where it belongs."

"I think I am."

His words hung in the air between us. I couldn't even begin to believe him. "Goodbye, Blake," I said and hung up.

That evening, I sat at our kitchen bar, clacking my heels against the side of the barstool, trying not to watch the clock. We had made reservations at Café Flora seven weeks earlier. I wanted a cigarette, but I didn't want to be all the way out back in case Glen came in from the front—which is where he should park, given that it would shave a few minutes off the drive if he didn't have to maneuver the back alleyways in the dark to get to the garage. I'd draped my black-sequined clutch and faux-fur-lined jacket on the chair next to me. I wore a short black, sequined cocktail dress and my shoulder-length, five-dollar-milkshake haircut was slicked to perfection. Glossy plum-colored lipstick and an extra coat of mascara were the whipped cream on my pudding.

I glanced at the time on my cell phone again. Our reservation time clicked closer and closer. It was forty minutes until we were to be seated. The restaurant was forty-five minutes away and Glen was not even home yet. Café Flora was not the kind of restaurant that would forgive you for not making your reservation time. Not on Valentine's Day. Further, this was not the night to lose your reservation in Seattle. Every restaurant worth eating at would be booked solid. If we didn't make it, we'd be screwed out of dinner and I for one did not feel like cooking.

I looked out at the dark skies and thought about how slick the roads must be. For the first time, I worried a little. Was he late because of an accident? Was he okay?

Then I heard the key in the door and Glen dashed in. He didn't even take a moment to stop and kiss me or say hello. My dad would have done those things. My dad had always taken the extra moment to celebrate my mother, her beauty, her intelligence. Of course, my dad wouldn't have ever been this late. Glen looked at me expectantly. He was dressed in jeans with a quarter inch hole in the thigh and a schlumpy white tee-shirt with his company logo on it. "Let's go," he said. "Are you ready?"

"Yes, but you aren't."

"I can throw on a jacket."

"Glen, you can't. It's Café Flora. It's Valentine's. Please. Go get dressed for dinner."

He sighed in exasperation and half-sprinted up the stairs. It didn't take him too long. He came down in a decent suit, like he was dressed for an interview. It would do.

We got in the car and I saw the glowing orange tank highlighted on the dash. "Are we out of gas?" I said.

He looked down like he hadn't noticed before. "Oh, shit."

"Glen, we're already late," I said. I couldn't help it.

"I know. I'll just stop and get a few gallons."

I called the restaurant while he pumped, pleaded with them to give us ten extra minutes. They said they would see what they could do. Glen and I spoke very little the rest of the way to Seattle. I drove myself crazy watching every minute slip by on the clock.

"How was work today?" I asked finally, as we pulled off of I-5 and onto the neighborhood streets, trying to break the ice. More than anything I wanted to have a nice night.

"Okay," he said.

"Yeah? What are you working on now?"

He shook his head. "Just work."

I thought of asking him about meditation, but since the whole point of that was to *not* think, it seemed rather toothless as a conversation starter. I gave up.

After a slight wait once we reached the restaurant lobby, we were seated in the atrium with a graceful lack of drama on the part of the restaurant staff. I loved the atrium. It was like eating in a huge, lush, tropical greenhouse, like summer trapped in the middle of Seattle's mausoleum of a sky. I placed my card and present for Glen on the white-linen-smocked table and sat down as the waiter tucked me in.

We ordered drinks. A martini for starters, wine to go with the main course. I put my hand palm up on the table, an invitation for him to take it, which he did. He held it for a moment, sort of loosely in his hand, then squeezed and let go. He shifted in his chair and swallowed a few times as he looked at the gift and envelope I'd set on the table.

"I'm really sorry," he said. "I didn't get you anything."

"Oh, okay." I meant it. Glen looked visibly relieved, his shoulders dropped. He loosened his tie and collar.

I didn't even have the energy to be angry. Not then. Instead, I completely checked out. All of my anger just drifted away on a cloud. It was the most amazing feeling of release. I didn't care anymore. I felt freedom. The air was humid with jasmine tea and I felt as though I floated above it all. I felt enlightened.

The waiter brought the first course, coconut soup with mung beans and cilantro.

Glen started talking on and on about the physics of gravity, his latest reading obsession. It was all well over my head and honestly, I couldn't give a rat's ass about the physics of gravity. I felt the ghost of Blake behind me, his lips playing upon the nape of my neck, little light kiss after little light kiss, nipping at my ears and I could barely focus on Glen's words. In truth, my consciousness drifted in and out of the conversation, but for all he knew I was fully there. I prided myself on being a good actress. Nothing was different between us. I felt Blake's hands on my skin, stroking my forearms so lightly the hair actually stood on end. I felt him hard behind me and my hips rocked imperceptibly on the chair. It was Blake's body I felt beneath me, not the woven wicker cane. I became lost to his lips, the way his ghostly hands knew me. I felt drunk with lust.

Glen started in on a new story about his meditation teacher, about her dharma lesson, about walking meditation, about being present and honoring the thoughts that come into your head and letting them go. I wondered at his newfound devotion. At some level, I knew he was trying to connect with me. He wanted me to care about the things he cared about. I just didn't. Buddhism was no doubt a respectable practice, but it seemed so devoid of passion. Honestly, it just seemed so boring. My hands stroked my thighs under the table and I wondered how I could be so fully in two places at once. I smiled at him and he told me how beautiful I was. I answered him with some words—I have no idea what I said—and I thought, *this is the strangest Valentine's Day ever.*

"I'll be back," I told him, went to the ladies' room, and locked myself in a stall. The light in the room was yellow and I felt half drunk and hazy from the lemon drop martini I'd swallowed too quickly. I sat down and felt Blake's imagined hands under my black lace panties; I reached under my skirt and traced where I could feel him, I spread my fingers into my trimmed but still curly hair, my index finger sliding into the place along my clit; I moaned. I touched myself, my fingers caressing the scratchy lace, my nether lips throbbing, trapped behind the sudden restriction of cotton panties. It felt so much as if Blake were there, behind me, breathing down my neck, rocking into me gently, fully, like the rolling of an ocean tide. I forced myself to relax into his languid, full rhythm. I imagined his hand on my breast and I mirrored his touch with my hand, teasing my nipple until it was tight and I could feel the echo of every sensation in my cunt. I remembered the flash of his smile and I shuddered, my body pulsing with a sweet little climax. I rode out the sensation. My head fell back and I moaned a little, and yearned for more, not caring what the woman in the next stall thought.

I pulled up my panties and left the stall, put cold water on my hands and face, but I couldn't exorcise the ghost of his presence. I shook my head, trying unsuccessfully to clear the dreamy haze from my vision. And then I walked back through the restaurant to Valentine's Day dinner with my husband.

We finished dinner and Glen paid the tab, seeming none the wiser that I was only a shade of myself. We were almost out of gas again and so he stopped to fill up the car, all the way this time. While he was outside, his phone rang. He answered it and talked for a while as the pump labored. I noticed he was laughing a lot. I wondered who he was talking to. He finished pumping the gas and slid into the driver's seat. Then I realized he was still on the phone. I squinted my eyes at him and mouthed, "Who is it?"

"My mom," he mouthed back.

"Tell her you're on a date and you'll call her back," I urged him in a harsh whisper. He kept on talking.

Ten minutes later I said again, "Tell her you're on a date and you'll call her back." I said it loudly. I didn't care if she heard.

"Mom, let me call you back in fifteen or twenty. Yes. Yes. We're almost home. I love you too. Okay. Bye."

"Fifteen or twenty?" I glared at him. "I meant you'd call her back tomorrow."

"She likes talking to me on Valentine's Day. She's my mom."

"You know what? I like talking to you on Valentine's Day, too. I'm your wife. I'm your fucking wife! Remember?!"

He clenched his jaw, his face grew red. He said nothing more to me in the car. I stared at the trees lining the highway the whole way home and tried not to think of this as just one more instance where his family interfered with our relationship. When we arrived home, he picked up his phone and called his mom. I closed my eyes and took a few deep breaths and tried to let my shoulders drop before sinking into the couch. I turned on the TV.

He talked with her for another forty-five minutes. I flipped channels and idly wondered how Blake's Valentine's night was going, if it was anywhere near as sexy as mine.

Glen got off the phone, finally, and came over to where I was watching TV. "You know I love you, Aleah," he said. "You're beautiful, intelligent, creative... I'm lucky to have married you." His grey eyes were hazy with passion. Was he actually trying to come on to me?

I shook my head. "Don't even. I'm angry." I ignored his compliments, rage suddenly blazing inside me. "Is this how you connect better with me? I mean, you want to know if I'm noticing a difference? If I am, it's not for the better, Glen."

"I'm sorry." He laughed, covering his mouth with a fist as if he could keep the bubbles of it from escaping.

"You're laughing?"

He was almost hysterical. It took a few moments for him to catch his breath enough to speak. “I don’t know what else to do. I’ve tried everything. I’ve tried so hard. I’m done crying.”

“It’s too late, Glen,” I said. His confession was not enough. I didn’t want to get the new lingerie out of the box.

“Too late for what?” he asked, suddenly concerned.

“Too late for tonight.” I sighed, and went up to our bed alone.

Chapter Six

I waited a full hour after Glen left for work the next morning. I didn't really have any clear idea of what I wanted to happen. I didn't have any idea what to say. All I knew was: I wanted to see him. I called him.

"Blake Porter," he answered, all professional.

I suddenly knew what to say.

"Blake Porter, Aleah Clayton," I said, all business. "I've been meaning to ask if you wouldn't mind checking out the siding on the house—I'm not sure if it's warping or if it's something structural. It would be great to get your opinion so I can go back to the builder if I need to."

"Sure thing," he said, not missing a beat. "I can come and take a look at your siding... What's your schedule like?

"Pretty open. What about yours?"

"It's looking good. I can come over today."

I laughed. I was nervous and relieved at once. "All right then."

"Yeah. I'll come over and check out what you asked me to and then—"

"We'll talk."

"Yeah, we'll talk... about..."

"About what the hell we're doing," I said.

"Right. So, we're talking now. Right?"

"I guess so."

"So since we're talking we might was well talk. Have you ever done anything like this before?"

"Like this? Like have an affair?" It felt both dangerous and somehow honest to give this dalliance its real name. "No." Of course I hadn't. I was a good girl. Affairs were not an option for people in my family. Divorce was not in our vocabulary. "Have you?"

"Do blowjobs count?" I could hear the grin in his voice. I didn't care if he'd had a blowjob or two.

"I don't think so."

"Then, no. No, I have not."

Part of me couldn't believe I was having this conversation. Part of me knew exactly what I was getting into. I'd made the decision before I picked up the phone. "Why are you doing this, Blake? Why are you risking your family?"

"Because I want you," he said. "It's that simple. I'm selfish and I want you."

"Your family, though. You're risking your kids."

"Aleah. It's my risk. And I don't mean to downplay it, but I don't intend for anyone to get caught."

"What happens if we do?"

"Well. Cami will freak out for a while and eventually I'll talk her down and everything will be fine."

I took his word for it. I guess I wanted to. I knew what I was risking. My marriage. My house. I blinked slowly, letting my eyes stay closed a minute as I truly realized I could live with that. I'd survive if it came to that, if I lost Glen. And the house... I loved it, but it was a house.

"All right. So, I'll see you this afternoon?"

"I can't wait," he said, and his voice was the sexiest thing I'd ever heard.

The hours crawled by. I was nervous and crazy with the want of him. I didn't know what the hell I was doing, I just knew I felt happy, attractive. And after years of being ignored in my marriage, it was so nice to have someone pay attention to me, to want me. I cleaned the house—I changed the sheets, I cleaned the bathroom, and I made a playlist. I listed to *Ceremonials* over and over.

At this point Blake and I had had a few stolen kisses, but I knew that's not where we were going to stop. Every song, everything I cast my eyes on that morning seemed to be about taking chances, about living desperately.

At noon I took a shower, shaved carefully. I put papaya honey lotion all over my arms and legs, my belly. I got out the packages of lingerie I'd purchased to wear for Glen: Black thigh high stockings with big rhinestones spaced down the back hooked into a new blue satin corset. I had never really worn a corset before. It was sort of complicated to get into. I hitched up the thigh-high stockings and fumbled with each of the garter straps. It seemed like I'd get two fastened and when I got the third one done, one of the first two would pop off. Finally, I got them all attached. Then I realized I had forgotten to put the matching blue satin thong on first. I took a deep breath, unhooked the four garters, slipped on the thong, and started again. That managed to eat up a good twenty minutes.

I finally figured out I could yank on the strings lacing up the back of the corset to tighten it. That helped a lot with my cleavage issue. I didn't have much to start with. Turns out, compression was my friend.

Over my lingerie, I wore what I hoped was an unassuming pair of blue jeans and a plain blue shirt chamois shirt. The minutes were agonizingly slow to pass. It was 1:15. I didn't know when he'd come over, but from the last time he helped us out I had the impression he didn't get off until three or four. I sat down at the computer to make myself get some work done. He called me at 1:45.

"You ready for me? 'Cause I'll be there in forty-five minutes."

"Good," I said.

I checked the bedroom again to make sure everything was tidy, turned on the radio, and lit a jasmine-scented candle. He rang the doorbell after thirty minutes, just as I took the toothbrush out of my mouth. I quickly spat and rinsed and raced downstairs to stop Sadie from barking.

I let him in and we danced away from each other. I could feel him so strongly. I was crazy with want and yet I managed to keep my hands off him. Our resistance was its own strange kind of foreplay. "C'mon, it's this way," I said. We went out back and I showed him what I was concerned about, how the siding was buckling just under the window.

"You really do have something wrong with your siding." He laughed. His green eyes lit up.

"Yeah," I said.

"I'll be god-damned. See, I thought you were just being smart and giving me a reason to come over." I loved the drawl in his voice. He peered at the siding for a moment. "Yeah," he said. "They should fix that. Now c'mon, girl. Inside with you." His eyes crinkled at the edges when he smiled.

"Cigarette first?" I asked, suddenly feeling shy.

"Sure." We grabbed smokes and headed back to the garage. It was too cold to be outside. We smoked and talked. He laughed. "I'm nervous," he admitted. "I don't know what this is. Some kind of wild crazy pheromones," he said. "Oh, and I knew exactly what you wrote at poker because I felt it too."

"Yeah?"

"Yeah. What you and I have." He pointed back and forth between us. "I haven't felt anything that affected me like this since, well... Ever."

"I know, it's crazy, right? I thought everyone would be able to see it."

"I know. I thought they would, too. It's like there's some kind of weird connection between us, like spider webs that stretch between us and bind us together."

My heart leapt. He felt it too. I wasn't alone in this crazy infatuation.

Blake leaned in and kissed me in the safety of the garage. He kissed my lips, my cheek, my neck, the hollow of my throat, and worked his way back to my eager mouth. His kisses were stakes, claiming me. Soft, pliant, and firm at the same time, urgently asking a little more of me with each gentle suck. They were exactly the kind of kisses I'd been missing. Sensual, authoritative, eager, unhesitant. They demanded my full attention. I wanted him. I wanted more.

He stopped and drew back a little, put his finger on my chin and lifted it a little. "I just have one thing to say," he said, his voice growing serious. "No matter what, I'm with Cami. No matter what happens between us. I'm with her 'til the end. I don't love you and I'm not going to marry you. Even if everything fell apart, I don't love you and I wouldn't marry you."

"I understand." He had children. It would be enough, just to feel his body. It would have to be enough.

"Okay," he said. "I mean it."

"I know. The last thing I want is for your family to get hurt." I believed my own words. I mean, I wished things were different, but I was a pragmatist. I yearned for his touch.

He kissed me again, lightly. "I'm really happy to be here, Aleah."

"Me too. Let's go inside."

He slipped his hands into my back jean pockets as we went upstairs. The barest touch from him set my body tingling. We made it down the hall to the bedroom. The jasmine scent from the candle filled the room. The radio spat out commercials.

I didn't know what to do. I was so nervous. I looked at Blake. For once he seemed like he wasn't sure about his next move either.

"You wanna hit?" I asked.

"Yes please." He smiled. "That might ease the tension a little." I got out my little glass pipe and packed it. I found myself relaxing with the familiar ritual and I passed him the pipe. He took a toke and passed it back. My fingers brushed against his as the pipe exchanged hands. Electric. I licked my lips. We sat on the floor of the bathroom and I started shaking. "What's the matter?" he said.

I didn't know. Maybe I'd realized what I was actually doing. "Just nervous I guess."

He put the pipe out of the way on the counter and pulled me against his chest. "Don't worry baby," he said, holding my trembling body in his strong arms. "You're safe with me. I want to take everything slow. We have time." He held me for a while. He stroked my hair, kissed my temple softly. He was so tender. I felt the shakes dissolve. I wanted this.

"You sure you want this?" he asked, like he was reading my thoughts.

I nodded, squeezed his arm. "I'm sure." He got up, helped me up, then turned and hoisted himself so he was sitting on the counter.

"Well, good," he said. "'Cause I've got something for you." He took another hit and spread his legs for me to see the press of his hard cock against his jeans. I smiled at his lewdness. I could feel such a buildup of electricity under my skin. *What the fuck*, I thought. *Let's do this.* I pulled the chamois shirt off over my head to show off the corset in a single motion.

"Ohmygod, let me see you." He stepped back from the counter and helped ease me out of my jeans. "Oh, hell yeah," he said when my ensemble was revealed. I turned around for him, my white butt cheeks bared in the thong. "Garter belts are the absolute sexiest."

"I'm glad you like it," I said. "It's all for you." The words sounded corny as they came out of my mouth, but he didn't laugh. He knelt and buried his face in my crotch, kissed my trembling thighs, stood and gathered my small breasts in his hands and caressed them with kisses.

"They're smaller than you're used to." Cami had a nice rack.

"What are you talking about? They're perfect. I like 'em small." Tenderly, his fingers brushed the fullness of my breasts; he pressed his face in to nuzzle them sweetly and eased a nipple out of its restraint. I gasped. He licked my nipple so softly it felt like I was being massaged with silk and then suddenly he suckled me urgently. My clit pulsed in response. My breath came deep and fast as he dropped a hand to fondle me there.

Is this real? Is this happening to me?

His hands traced my body as he knelt on the ground next to me. He looked up at me, "Seriously, Aleah. A lot of girls would kill for your legs." I did have really long legs. I was Tyra Banks tall. He breathed against the back of my knee and I moaned.

"Next time, put the panties on the outside."

Next time.

"I appreciate you playing hard to get and all, but I'm tempted to just rip those pretty little things right off of you. He worked the clasps on my garters with nimble fingers. "A stripper taught me how to work these," he confided.

"That sounds like a story I don't want to hear right now."

He laughed. "Yeah. I guess I can understand that. There, let's get you out of that." He slipped me out of the thong. "That's better. The tights are going back on, though." Deftly, he did up the garters and stood.

"Are you sure you haven't done this before?" I whispered.

He looked me up and down and met my eyes earnestly, an eyebrow raised. "Are you?" He smiled and I smiled and we laughed and we kissed and I reveled in the closeness of Blake Porter.

I helped him out of his shirt, surprised by his curly, graying chest hair, the firmness of his pecs, a few light scars I hadn't seen before. I tugged him out of his jeans, and pressed my face into his underwear to smell him. So yummy. I felt him under my fingers, slid his underwear off. "Oh my gosh," I said in a rush, like a little school girl. He was so much bigger than I was used to.

"It's all for you," he said, echoing my words. I licked his cock and teased him in my mouth a little, but I was afraid of getting him too excited. I don't think I needed to be, in hindsight, because any time he heard any sound he'd startle, pull back from me, and look around. "You're sure Glen isn't coming home early?"

"He never does. He'd call. He's very predictable. He's going to sitting meditation practice tonight. We have hours."

I fingered the rim of his sock to take it off, but he stopped me. "No, leave those on."

"Why? Are you cold? I can turn the heat up."

"No. It's just, socks. They're the easiest thing to lose and they take the longest to put on if you're in a hurry. Say if Glen came home. I wouldn't want to leave a sock behind. I wouldn't want to have to spend time looking for them and then putting them back on."

"All right then." I giggled. He'd actually thought this through. "But you don't have to worry. For Glen, getting home early is six-thirty."

He took his time with me then, kissing me deeply, slowing his breathing down until it matched mine, teasing me with guerrilla caresses along my inner thigh, my ass, my tits. He took a little step back every once in a while until he'd worked us up against the bed. He wound his fingers in my hair and slipped away from my hungry mouth, leaving a trail of kisses down my neck, over my collar bone, over the mound of breasts that the corset presented so perfectly. He stroked my wet and naked pussy with his authoritative hands. He knew just how to touch me. My whole body started to shake. When I thought I couldn't wait another moment he picked me up and tossed me onto the bed. My silk corset made me slide all over the satin coverlet. "Come here," I begged.

"It feels so good to be wanted," he said.

"I know. To want and to be wanted."

"Let me see you," he said, spreading my legs. "Oh my god, you're so pretty." He fingered my pussy. I glanced down. He looked like he was trying to memorize every nuance. "I forgot you're a blonde," he said, running his fingers through my trimmed hair below. I had been dying my hair auburn for a few years. "So pretty, the prettiest I've ever seen." He buried his face in my cunt. "So sweet," he murmured, "you taste so good."

All I could do was moan, his deep tongue kisses were so fine, flat against my clit, like nothing I'd ever felt before. I couldn't remember the last time Glen had gone down on me. *Had Glen ever gone down on me?*

I heard an unfamiliar sound of paper ripping and watched Blake slide a condom on. He shrugged. I nodded, swallowing. I realized it had been almost a decade since I'd used any kind of birth control, and that in my heart I knew it was me, that Glen's tests would come back normal, that the condom was extraneous. I said nothing and pushed the thoughts aside.

Blake surged up along my body and said, "I can't wait any longer." That was all the warning I got. I gasped as in a single stroke he fit himself into me like a hawk diving for prey. He was huge. He filled me so perfectly, I could just barely accept every last bit of him. All of my nerves sang out with pleasure. My mouth hung open, the feeling was an epiphany.

"Oh my god." He looked at me, eyes wide in surprise. "Oh my god, you feel amazing."

I was beyond wet for him and he lost control, riding me hard, long strokes continually filling me, each one somehow taking me closer and closer to the edge, my whole body pulsed from toe to ear as we slowly, rhythmically slammed into one another, hungry to go even deeper.

He fucked me like a master until I came—crying out at the ocean of orgasm that left me feeling engorged and satiated—and then he came, groaning against me, his teeth grinding as if trying to withhold the eruption. He held me for a while, after. "Unbelievable," he whispered, stroking my hair. "You're incredible."

"You're pretty incredible yourself," I said, still softly panting, deliriously happy. "I've wanted you for so long," I said. "You have no idea." But I think maybe he did. He was so adept, every move. "You're so good at this; I love the way you touch me."

"Your body is extremely responsive. Very sexy." His eyes seemed to intensify as he caught my gaze.

"You make me feel so pretty."

"I wouldn't think you'd need anyone to make you feel that way," he said. "You're one of the prettiest girls I know. It's not any one thing, either. Your amber eyes, those pouty lips, your cute nose... You're just pretty."

I sighed, leaning back against the headboard. It had been easily the best sex of my life. Granted, my experience was limited to just a handful of men outside of Glen. But I hadn't known it could be that good. I knew it certainly wasn't supposed to be that good the first time you had sex together.

It was impossible not to think of Glen. But I didn't know what I felt; I didn't know what I thought. I knew I should feel guilty. But I didn't, not really. I just didn't want him to find out and get hurt. I'd make sure he didn't.

"Thank you," Blake said earnestly, later, as he put his pants back on. "For all the pains you took today, the candle, the music, the corset, the way things smelled. It was really nice, Aleah." I was glad he noticed.

"I'm glad you liked it."

"I did, baby. I did." He kissed me, softly, his fingers lifting my chin to his perfect lips. "I have to go," he whispered.

"Oh, hey, before you do, I made you a mix." Knowing that Blake still limited himself to the anachronism of an analog phone—he claimed it was far too easy to drop and break any of the touch screen phones—I'd burned him a CD. I got it out and handed it to him.

He pressed his lips together and looked at me funny. "You shouldn't have," he said and I wasn't sure what he meant by it.

"But I did. So listen to it. You can throw it away if you hate it."

"All right." He drew in close for another soft, aching kiss. "I'll probably call ya' some time," he said softly and winked at me.

I shook my head, "Whatever." I smiled. Even if all we ever had was that day, it was beautiful.

I sent Blake off to his wife, pulled the coverlet off the bed, and threw it in the washer.

I'd like to say I was reflective and regretful and ashamed, but the truth is I was none of those things. More than anything, I was in the moment, putting the room to rights, acting the good wife, going to bed early. It was easier than I'd like to admit to disassociate the one thing I'd just shared with Blake from the other, my husband.

I took a shower, but I couldn't shed Blake's musky scent. I put on much more sensible clothing. Clothing Glen would expect me to wear. Jeans and a sweater sans the corset, garter, and stockings. I put the thong back on. I liked the pressure on my swollen pussy. I felt claimed. I couldn't take the smile off my face and I didn't want to.

Book Two

Chapter One

If I thought I'd have to wait long for Blake to call me after our first encounter, I was wrong. I was still in bed the next morning when my phone rang. I'd feigned sleep until Glen had left for work, having gone to bed before he'd returned home from meditation the previous evening. I needed time before I faced him. I wanted to dream a little bit longer. I think after the Valentine's Day fiasco, he was just as happy not to talk to me. The phone jangled insistently, vibrating its way across the nightstand.

I picked it up and saw that it was Blake calling. Happiness flooded me and I felt a smile growing across my face. I answered it on the third ring.

"Good morning, Blake."

"Good morning, sunshine. How are you?"

"Good. Very, very good."

"Yes you are."

I laughed. "Hey, just so you know, you got lucky this morning. Three minutes ago I would have had to explain to my husband who was calling me so early," I chastised him lightly.

"Oh, shit. I've already been at work for two hours."

"And he's just going in. It's why he doesn't get home till seven most nights. Or later, depending."

"Gotcha. So, can I come over? Or better yet, can you come over here? I'm alone on site today and the owners are on vacation."

"Seriously?"

"Seriously. I didn't get nearly enough of you yesterday. I need more."

Electricity zinged through my body.

"Where are you at?"

"I'm at a jobsite. On the lake. Please, Aleah? I mean... If you want to." He sounded strangely shy. "We'll have more time together if you come to me."

"I'd like to," I said. I'd like to do anything, as long as it involved more of him.

I had already picked out the next outfit I wanted to show him. I got dressed and wrapped myself in Glen's trench coat.

I found the neighborhood off the lake, pulled into the driveway where I saw his truck, walked in through the open garage door, heels clacking on concrete. "Blake?"

"I'm here," he said, hurriedly taking the steps down into the garage from the house above. He wore his characteristic jeans and a tight white T-shirt. He was wiping his hands on a rag. He smiled and everything got brighter.

"When do they get back from vacation?" I peered up at the giant windows facing the lake.

"Not 'til Friday next." I walked back through the remarkably empty garage to him. There were some kayaks on the wall. That was about it.

"Where do you want me?"

"Everywhere," he said, staring. "I can't believe you're actually here. Oh." He cracked a grin. "You mean right now. Come in here." He tugged me toward a door set at the back of the garage. I saw a bathroom. "This is what I've built out," he said. I surveyed his work. I didn't know what I was looking for. It looked like a really nice bathroom. "It's nice," I said. "A little cold." We were adjacent to the open garage and it was still February.

"I can fix that," he said. He set up a portable heating fan and shut the door.

"Whatcha wearin'?" he said, clearly intrigued by the long khaki coat.

"Not much." Slowly, I undid the buttons, then shrugged the coat to the floor. I watched his eyes. He took me all in at once and then let his gaze glide over me from top to toe: hair teased up a little, glossy red lips, a black satin ribbon tied in a bow around my neck, my black mesh bra, black thong, matching garters, black fishnet stockings, and knee high black boots.

He whistled, long and low. I found that I liked being whistled at by a construction worker. I giggled.

"You have no idea how fucking sexy you are. Fishnet stockings and boots." Shaking his head, he swooped in and pressed me up against the bathroom door, I felt every inch of his torso, his hard cock pressed into me, already large and rigid. His lips crushed against mine and he smeared red lipstick outside the lines. He nipped at me, he growled a little. I groaned. He kissed me deeper. We devoured each other. I can't tell you how sexy he was, how good it felt to rest my hands on muscle instead of flab, how his kisses were godlike. *I've wanted to be kissed like this my whole life and here I am with Blake fucking Porter.*

"Come over here, I want to see you," he said and pulled me toward the sink. He flipped on the lights. Only then did I see how pretty the bathroom really was. Granite countertops, beige flecked with a dark sable brown and silver. Brushed silver faucets filling translucent glass bowls—the faintest shade of green—set above the glistening stone expanse of granite. The lights were pendants, gossamer and glimmering above me.

"It's really pretty, Blake."

"I'll tell you what's pretty." He pushed me forward and I heard him unzip his pants. "God your ass is lovely," he said. "Just two perfect little moons. I wiggled it for him a little as I bent down towards the sink, resting my chin on my hands, my elbows spread out on the counter.

I couldn't tell you what came over me, but from the moment I'd left the house that morning, I'd been playing a role. I felt like the most accomplished actress on the planet, that somehow I was in a movie and my husband would understand this came with the territory. I crafted any scenario I could to rid my conscious mind of guilt. I wasn't Aleah Clayton. I was Marilyn Monroe. It was Marilyn wiggling her ass under Blake's possessive caresses.

"You're gorgeous, you know." Blake yanked my thong down my legs and out of his way.

"You're pretty fine yourself, cowboy." I caught his eye in the mirror.

I gasped as he slid into me. "Wet as I thought," he said. I stared at us in the mirror as he drove into me, my dark hair floating around my face... I gasped and fought to get enough oxygen as he pounded into me, filling me so completely with his giant, beautiful cock. I couldn't get over how he felt, better than I'd ever imagined a man could feel. He fit me that perfectly. My legs splayed out, wanting to collapse beneath me. I watched our faces in the mirror, then felt his whole body convulse. He let out a shuddering moan as he came, spilling his seed into me and half pulling out, spilling more on my leg. It dripped down quickly, toward my knee. I scanned the room, but there were no towels. Quickly, I scooped up what I can with my fingers and caught his gaze as I licked his cum. He groaned. "That is so sexy." He pulled me close. "You must be cold. You are so sexy." He wrapped me tighter in his arms. I was still cold, but no longer cared. "We fuck well together," he stated matter-of-factly.

"Uh huh," I agreed. He helped me get dressed after he'd pulled up his own pants.

"Oh fuck, the condom." Blake reached back and pulled it out of his pocket.

I hesitated before saying it, but I didn't want him to be anxious about it. "You know, not that it isn't ideal, but... I'm clean. And no one else has ever been able to get me pregnant." I sucked on my finger and met his eyes. I didn't think he needed to know that I was still several days away from ovulating. Too much information is still too much information.

"I'm sorry. I know you want that, right?"

I nodded. "Well, still. It was stupid of me to forget." He pulled me to him, wrapping me in his warm, strong arms. I fell against him. I felt safe.

"I hate to say this," he said, pulling back from me and petting stray strands of my hair into place. "But you should go. I'm paranoid my boss is going to show up any minute to check up on me."

"All right," I said. I supposed I'd be nervous too, were it my workplace. "Well, I'll see you around sometime." It was my turn to wink and tease.

"I'll see you Friday," he said, a smug grin on his face.

"What? Tomorrow Friday?"

"It's game night, isn't it?"

Oh lordy, it is. "All right," I laughed. *Fuck. I'll have to face Cami now.* "I'll see you tomorrow." He pulled me back to him and I kissed him again, a tender goodbye.

At least once a month we'd head over and help Blake and Cami get the kids to bed, then we'd drink and play board games until they kicked us out.

I imagined those evenings were about to become wildly more interesting.

A random storm started the power flickering on and off early Friday morning and woke me up. I started thinking about going for cigarettes, which is pretty much what I had gone to bed thinking about. I took my temperature and charted my cervical mucus, as I did every morning as part of my attempt to understand my own fertility. My cycles were wildly erratic and it was hard to tell when or if I ovulated without spending a fortune on those bloody test kits. I also charted when Glen and I had sex with green triangles. On a whim, I started to put a new symbol on the chart—a blue square. I put one on Wednesday and another on Thursday, but left the explanation in the key blank.

I went to a salon that afternoon. I'd been thinking about making a big change and I bit the bullet. I got a minor cut and a radical color—platinum blonde instead of auburn. It took three hours. My hair was still shoulder length, but with some blunt layers and a new, softer frame around my face. I loved it. I hadn't been a blonde in forever. Not since high school. I felt ten years younger.

I knew Blake was generally not in favor of things like tattoos, piercings, and hair color. I didn't think he would like it. But that didn't matter. I was doing it for myself. I got home just in time to get ready for game night. I put on a black T-shirt and my sexiest jeans. I slicked on my red lipstick and pulled all that blonde up into a severe pony tail. At the last moment I dug out a black leather jacket that I hadn't worn in forever—one with crisscross zippers and a leather belt at the bottom that screamed rocker chick. I caught a sideways glimpse of myself in the mirror and thought, *Damn, I look HOT*. Then I thought, *Fuck, I look like Gwen Stefani.*

I heard Glen come in from work. He shouted up the stairs, "Hey, Aleah, you ready to go?" I came down. "Whoa," he said when he saw me, and he smiled. "Blonde. I like it."

"Aw, thanks," I said.

We got to Blake and Cami's. Blake opened the screen door as we walked up and did a double take. Total shock took over his face. *I don't care if he doesn't like it—I didn't think he would,* I told myself rapidly. He opened the screen door. Just seeing him, it was on for me again. My whole body pulsed with want.

Cami came around the corner right then, "Hello blondie!" she exclaimed, pulling me into a hug. "Wow! That looks fantastic. I want to go blonde." She was as vivacious as ever.

"No," Blake said. He couldn't take his eyes off me. He was right, though, blonde would not go well with Cami's dark Italian looks.

"Come in; come in. Let's play! The kids are down already," Cami urged. Glen and I had introduced them to Settlers of Catan a few months back and it was currently the game of choice. Blake had already set up the board for us on their dining room table.

Cami sat across from me at the round table, Glen on my left, Blake on my right. He spent the night trying to surreptitiously play footsie with me; I had to keep scooting my foot away from his exploring toes. Anytime I put my hand under the table, he would reach for it, stroke my palm or the back of it so tenderly. Anytime Cami had her head turned, his hand was on my thigh. I could feel his strong pull, the bright energy linking us, and couldn't figure out why Glen and Cami were oblivious, not feeling it. I expected to be called out at any moment, it seemed so obvious to me. Still, I was beyond anxious. I kept pushing him away. I was furious with him for being so stupid, and equally furious that I wasn't alone with him.

Needless to say, my game was off and Glen was the decided winner of the first game. I declared a smoke break and Blake and I went outside.

"Do you have a lighter?" I asked.

"Yup. This way." He made me follow him behind the car, out of sight of the kitchen window, to get my cigarette lit. He grabbed me, caressed my ass, made it clear he wanted more. I pulled away. I wasn't stupid. I didn't need to be caught kissing him in his driveway by his wife.

"Light my fucking cigarette," I said. He did and walked away, his footsteps crunching on the gravel drive. I followed him and we talked for a while in front of the windows.

"You need to knock it off in there," I said.

"C'mon, it's fun." He scuffed his shoe in the gravel as he spoke.

"You're scaring me, Blake. You're playing with fire," I said. "Have you met your wife?"

"Yeah, I know."

"Do you?" Cami and I used to work at the same company. She'd gotten me the job, actually. I'd learned very quickly that she was a savage corporate power tripper.

She'd very often come back from a consulting gig and tell me about how her underlings were doing shitty work and they weren't doing it fast enough. "So I tell them the truth and they can't handle the truth," she'd claim, seeming proud of the cliché. Shaking her head, she'd continue, "Three of them broke down crying today." This happened on almost every job. She had a gift for routinely reducing grown adults to tears.

I think she thought sharing these stories made her seem like a tough, get-the-job done kind of project manager. She was still fighting the battle of being a female in a man's position in a man's world and thinking she had to overcompensate for her breasts. I also think she liked being a badass. Regardless, Cami was not someone I ever wanted pissed at me.

Blake turned and looked at his wife through the kitchen window. "She's given me two gorgeous kids. She's an incredible woman. She takes care of me." He said it softly and slowly, and I knew he was reminding himself more than telling me. Still, I felt a twinge of jealousy. I'd never be her. He turned back to me. "You know, I was going to ask you to color your hair blonde, after I remembered what your natural color was."

"I've been thinking about changing it for a while," I lied. "You like?"

"I like. You blow my mind, Aleah." I felt a little more glowy inside.

We were staring at the stars and Blake said, "Did I ever tell you about Orion?"

"I know Orion. But you've never told me about it, no."

"It's my favorite. I was in school, sixth grade, and my teachers couldn't get me to do anything other than write creative shit."

"Well, you are a natural born storyteller."

"Thanks." He took a drag from his cigarette. "Yeah. So one time my teacher assigned everyone a constellation for a science project, to research. I got Orion, the hunter. He just spoke to me. It got me into studying astronomy, and then I got into astrology. He's so big, up there, and naked. He's got a shield and just a loin cloth." He was quiet when he spoke and I knew it was important, that he wanted to share himself with me. "I mean, could you take on the world that way, so vulnerable?" Blake was in construction. He judged himself by his works. I treasured these little forays into his hidden soul. "I thought, if he could do it... Well, it gives me something to strive for." He stayed quiet for a while and while I sensed there was more he wasn't saying, it became clear he wasn't going to. Not tonight.

"Thanks for telling me."

"I like telling you things," he said. "You're a good listener."

I found myself as always staring back at the stars. I never got tired of the night sky, especially out on the dark country back roads. "It's such a beautiful night."

"Sure is," he said. I could feel him staring at me and I looked at him. His eyes were riveted on my face. He said, "Beautiful *what*?"

"Sky," I said. Only then did I realize what he was saying. I felt as pretty as the stars. I sparkled.

We were both quiet for a time.

"So. Whatcha doin' next Friday?"

"Mmmm," I said, daring to imagine him in my bed again. "Friday."

"Yeah, Friday."

"You tell me, Blake Porter."

"Okay."

I looked at him expectantly.

"Later. But you might start coming up with reasons why you need to spend the night at your girlfriend's."

"Oh. Wow." I was free falling and I didn't know what was coming next. I didn't want to miss a moment.

He walked toward the door as he finished his cigarette. He stopped on the porch, just out of sight of both the kitchen window and the windows on either side of their front door. I followed him.

"Don't do it," he said, and again as I drew nearer. "Don't do it." I knew he thought I was going to lean in for a kiss. I knew he wanted me to.

Instead, I leaned back on the porch railing, pushed my hips forward just enough to be suggestive and parted my legs a little. "I'm not doing anything," I said, and looked at him with my *come fuck me* eyes. It was extremely fun to torture him, to watch him swoon, his eyes morphing to green from their standard gray.

"Buh bye," he said and scooted into the house.

I took a moment before I followed him in. Glen was just finishing setting up the board for game number two.

"Aleah, I haven't told you yet—I'm super psyched," Cami said after we were settled.

"Yeah? What's going on?"

"I have a date with Justin Timberlake." Her eyes were huge with excitement.

Blake groaned and rolled his eyes. "You don't have a date—"

"I do too," she whirled and snapped at him. She turned back to me, eager to explain, her face bright with excitement. Happy Cami was fun Cami. The woman was nothing but extremes. "I'm going to the concert with Camille and Sandy." I knew them as friends of hers from New Jersey. They'd all moved out west together. "We're going to make a night of it and stay downtown at the same hotel he is staying at. I get to fuck him, right Blake?" she said, turning back to him.

"Sure," he said. "You can have a free fuck-my-celebrity-boyfriend pass for Justin Timberlake... As long as I get a free pass to fuck my celebrity girlfriend."

"And that would be?" she said.

"Gwen Stefani," he said, leveling his gaze at me. Somehow I kept from gasping and kicking him under the table.

"Good luck with that," I snorted. It was all I could do to hold back from slapping him.

Chapter Two

Blake called me Tuesday on his lunch hour.

"Hey," he said.

"Hey," I said back.

"This my celebrity girlfriend?"

"You know it, baby." I shook my head and laughed. "You really don't think Cami noticed anything?"

"Nah. She's not looking for it. You know she goes on witch hunts. She's all up my ass about smoking weed right now. She searched through the cab of my truck last night after I got home, looking for evidence."

"Did she find any?"

"Not for want of trying," he said. "I don't keep it in my vehicle."

"Note to self, don't leave any lace panties in the truck." I had spent quite a bit of time the day before shopping online for new lingerie. I'd considered a new vibrator. I was pretty happy with the one currently occupying my nightstand drawer, but those rabbit ears looked pretty enticing.

He groaned with want. "When can I see you?"

"I don't know," I said. "When can you?"

"Just for that I'm going to make you wait."

"Suit yourself," I said.

"You are coming over Friday, though?" He voice cracked and he sounded like he would be more than disappointed if the answer was no.

"When Cami's out with her celebrity boyfriend? I'll see what I can do." Of course I was. The idea of an entire night together was too tantalizing. I just had to figure out how.

I found Glen in his office that evening. It was a rare non-meditation night. I lounged in the doorframe. “Hey, I’m going drinking with a couple of girls from my book club Friday. We’re going to be downtown. We’re going to be walking or sharing a cab. Long story short, I am planning to have a very good time, stumble to Lizzy’s condo, puke my guts out, and crash until I am sober.” It wasn’t very much like me, but Glen knew that I occasionally liked to have reason to remember how much I hated getting drunk. He knew how much of a lightweight I was. If I were going to be doing any drinking at all, I shouldn’t be driving.

“Sounds fun,” he said, not looking away from the computer.

The days passed so slowly. I felt on strung out the entire week, like something big was missing from my life. I felt thin around the edges. I refused to be the first to succumb to the challenge and call Blake, especially after he’d said he was going to make me wait. True to his word, he didn’t call until Friday morning.

“Hey beautiful,” he said. My stomach tightened hearing his voice. I felt instantly slick with desire.

“Why hello, Blake,” I said.

“How are you?”

“Oh, all over the place,” I said. “But good. You?”

“I can’t wait to see you,” he said. “When can you come over today?”

“Oh, was that today?” I teased and left him hanging for a moment or three. “When do you want me?”

“Now,” he said, not missing a beat.

“No, really.”

“Cami’s not coming home after work,” he said. “I get home at 3:30.”

“I don’t think I can get there that early. Probably not until 7:30.” I’d been planning to make dinner for Glen before going out for ‘drinks with the girls.’

“Try,” he urged. “We won’t have this forever, Aleah. Make the most of it while it lasts.”

I knew he was right. Sooner or later we were going to have to stop and move on with our lives. Goddamn it. I didn’t allow myself to wonder just how short the time left to us was. I knew I should have ended it already. Maybe this would be our last hurrah. “Well, since Cami is going out, do you need a babysitter this afternoon for some reason? Something that might get me out of the house around three?”

“I do, actually. I’m sure I do. I’m just not sure what it is yet.”

“Why don’t you text me when you figure it out.”

The text came twenty minutes later.

“Hey, Aleah. I have a favor to ask. One of my clients wants to meet me this afternoon to go over blueprints and hopefully sign a contract, but Cami’s going to that concert... is there any way I could talk you into watching the kids for a few hours?”

“Sure thing,” I texted back.

Blake thought of everything. I loved that he texted in such a way that I could show it to Glen if I needed to. I texted Glen that I’d be doing the Porters a favor that afternoon and heading to Seattle directly after.

“Okay,” he texted back.

The lingerie I’d ordered arrived that afternoon. I’d ended up with four new ensembles to share with Blake. I decided on a neon green crotchless boy short with a halter top, both made out of neon mesh. I felt like a complete ‘80s throwback; like I should be wearing a black garbage bag, be a Robert Palmer girl. It was way over the top for me. I covered up with a black sweater and jeans.

I spent the entire drive to their house completely on edge. For the first time I understood, viscerally, why Blake had been so easy to startle when he’d come over to my house that first morning. Even so, Glen walking in on us was one thing. I mean, he was pretty much a Buddhist. Cami walking in on us was another animal entirely. She was a tough-as-nails Jersey girl. I was shaking when I got there, a little after four. He was waiting for me on the porch. I watched him standing there as my tires crunched gravel down their long drive. It took forever. I kept staring as I got out of the car. My sweater snagged on the door and I tugged at it fiercely. “You’re nervous,” he said, pulling me into a gentle hug.

“Yeah. That and scared.”

"Don't worry. I gotcha. I won't let anything bad happen to you." He held me until the shaking stopped, just held me. When I'd calmed, he took my hand and we went inside. "Stay here a moment." He put his fingers to his lips, then left me in the entryway and went into the living room. Blake closed the gate to the kid zone and turned on the television. He came back to me and pulled me past the opening to the living room, then turned right at the first door, their office that doubled as a spare bedroom. He sat on the daybed and pulled me onto his lap.

"We have twenty-three minutes," he said. "Or twenty-two and a half."

"Until?"

"Until *Yo Gabba Gabba* is over," he said.

I laughed. "Let's make them count, then." I couldn't stop smiling.

Then it was magic time. "Take it slow with me, okay?" he said. "Let's really enjoy this."

"I've enjoyed everything so far," I said, but I knew what he meant. "We can go slow." We had all night long. He cupped my face in his hands and kissed me, his soft lips barely touching mine, teasing at my mouth, and then backing away the moment I sought him out. I felt a little weird with the kids in the next room, but at least we could hear them. They were little, but not so little that they'd die without constant supervision. Two and three, I thought. Blake's lips were soft, insistent that I join him in that moment.

Slowly he worked up to letting his mouth linger a little, letting my tongue play with his, at his lips. I felt the buildup of desire within me, the hunger for him growing moment by frustrated moment. Such a sweet tease. Finally, he opened his mouth to me. After long, long minutes of those fluttery, soft whispers it was like surrendering. I fell into his kisses, forgot where we were going, forgot we had to go anywhere at all. The only thing that ever existed for me was him, those lips, his tongue, those amazingly fine kisses. For all of *Yo Gabba Gabba*, that's all there was. And then Desiree and Davis started hollering, "Daddy! Want more gabba gabba, Daddy!"

"I'll be right back," he said, smiling. One last kiss and he left quickly to attend to his kids. I wondered, *What the fuck am I doing in the middle of this family?* I went across the hall to the bathroom to pee and freshen up. I walked out just as the front door was opening and Cami stepped in.

Raw stress raced through my veins. I panicked a little, then remembered to breathe. *What the fuck is she doing here?* I kept walking, pretending nothing was out of the ordinary.

"Hey, Cami," I said, acting like she would be expecting to see me there. "What's up?"

"Hey, Aleah," she said, a slightly puzzled look on her face. "What are you doing here?"

"Oh, Blake called this afternoon. He said he had some work thing he had to do. Asked if I could watch the kids for a bit so here I am. What about you? I thought you had that concert to go to?" I was glad I had gone over the lie in my head so often for Glen. I knew it pat.

"I do! I forgot the fucking tickets. That's nice of you, though, to help out. Thanks for coming over."

"Anytime." I did feel bad that she was thanking me.

Blake came around the corner. "Oh, hey," he said to Cami. I watched him cover up his double take—only the merest glimmer of it showed on his face—and move on without skipping a beat. "What happened, your celebrity boyfriend cancel on you?"

"No, I need the fucking tickets! I can't believe I left them." Cami dashed down the hall and turned into the spare bedroom, the one *we'd just been in.* I caught Blake's gaze, my eyes wide with panic. He subtly shook his head. A minute or two in either direction and she would have walked in on a completely different situation. I was grateful Blake had wanted to take it slowly, that I still had my clothes on. He winked at me. "You're safe with me," he whispered.

"Got 'em!" Cami said as she emerged from the office, an envelope clutched high in her hand. "Time to go to the hotel and get ready for my date." She turned to Blake. "You have some work thing?"

"Yeah, Peter wants me to go schmooze a customer with him. You know that Sammamish job I did last fall? They're thinking about an add on. Apparently they like me." He shrugged as he walked up to her, a charming smile splitting his face. "After all, what's not to like?"

Cami groaned.

"Anyway, it's just dinner." He pulled her in for a quick kiss, a hug. "Don't have too much fun with your celebrity boyfriend," he said.

She smiled widely at him. "Oh, I plan on it," she said. "Okay, I'm out of here. Good luck tonight!" She dashed out the front door, waving as she went. I stood there, listening to the sputter and roar as her SUV started up. I waited for the sound of her tires crunching the gravel to fade completely. I stood there and listened to silence for several moments, just trying to breathe. So close, I thought.

"So, that was stressful," I said. Understatement.

"You did well," he said. "Perfect." He took my hand and with one backwards glance at the kids—who were once again mesmerized by the giant TV screen—led me through the kitchen towards the garage. "C'mon," he said. "I'll get you stoned."

"Yes, please." That would help.

His garage was a hoarder's dream. He had piles of leftover construction materials everywhere. Wood and blocks and tile and partially rusted Folgers and Maxwell House cans full of nails and screws. It was a cavernous room, but the piles of material everywhere made lots of nooks and crannies; it felt cozy. Blake flipped a five gallon paint bucket over for me to sit on and produced a little pipe and spice jar with a few nuggets in it. He loaded the pipe and passed it to me, brushing the back of my hand with his. Electricity ran up my arm and shot down and zapped my core. I blinked and took a hit and held it for a while.

"Shotgun," he said and leaned in to kiss me. I exhaled into his waiting mouth but then couldn't resist kissing him, ruining his hit. He leaned into me and I let the passion devour my fear. I forgot everything but the man holding me, kissing me. He pulled me closer. I wrapped my arms around him, clutched at the soft curls at the nape of his neck.

"C'mon," he said after a while, his voice gravelly, "let's get those kids down to bed."

I looked at my watch. "Blake, it's only 5:20," I said and sighed. "We should probably get them dinner and a bath first."

"Right," he said. "Damn it."

We played house together for the next few hours, making supper, putting the kids in the bath. I helped wash their hair and dried them off. I got Davis into his jammies. Blake let me read *Goodnight Moon* to them. We did the dishes. He stood next to me at the sink, loading as I rinsed, drying as I washed the bigger pots by hand. Glen never did that. Blake dried the last dish. "I'll just go check on the kids," he said. I couldn't help but dream a little, of what a life with Blake might be like.

Book Two

Chapter Three

"Come on," Blake said, walking into the kitchen and taking my hand. "They're both out. It's almost like I drugged them." He winked at me.

"You did not."

"I did not." He confirmed, laughing and tugging on my fingers. He pulled me past the kids' rooms and on down the hall into his master suite. It was a bit smaller than mine; the king-sized bed took up most of the room. I'd been able to put a damper on it for the past few hours, but the desire I felt for him took me over again, radiating from my center, making my belly feel so hollow. I could feel it pulsing, the energy of desire dancing out through every part of me. "Come here," he said, pulling me to him.

His soft lips found mine and he teased me again, darting in and pulling away, denying me the satisfaction of a full kiss. The energy coursing through me grew more insistent. I wrapped my fingers in his hair and pulled him close. My mouth demanded more from those teasing kisses, but he wouldn't give in.

"Not yet," he said, pulling away. "Not so fast." He backed away, letting his hand slip from my back down my arm and took my hand again. "This way." He tugged me into the bathroom. "I want to taste you," he said. His fingers deftly opened the button on my fly, unzipped my jeans, and slipped me out of them.

"Oh my god, what are you wearing?" His eyes widened for a moment as he took in the neon green boy shorts.

"What, these little old things?" I shrugged, smiling a little.

"Let me see the rest," he said, already grabbing at the bottom of my sweater. Obediently, I raised my arms into the air and he pulled the black cashmere over my head, exposing the matching mesh neon green top. "Oh my god," he said again, his voice brimming with appreciation. "You are unbelievably sexy, Aleah. I never knew this side of you."

"How could you have?"

"You're right." He laughed, "But I wanted to."

"I'm right here."

"I know it." He brushed my throat with his lips and he left a trail of soft kisses along the edge of the green mesh halter top as it plunged into my cleavage. His open mouth passed over my breast and I could feel his hot breath on my aching skin. My back arched toward him and he captured me in his arms to keep me from falling. His kisses traversed my skin to the bottom of the halter top and he slowly sank to the floor as he licked me, following the curve of my ribcage, down the hollow of my abdomen until he reached the rim of my panties. It was a little cold in the bathroom and the feel of the air on my wet skin sent shivers down my back. His hands cupped my ass and his fingertips brushed the opening in the shorts. I started a little at the rush of cool air where I wasn't expecting it.

His eyes opened wide and he looked up at me. "They're crotchless?" He couldn't keep the excitement from his voice. I nodded. "Oh my god, so sexy," he breathed. "Here." He put his hands on my hips and guided me so that I was standing in front of the toilet instead of the counter. He patted the lid. "Put your foot there." I did as he directed, exposing myself as he kneeled before me. I was slick with wet for him. He moved in close, pushed the edges of the panties out of the way, and thrust fingers in me—Two? Three? He inhaled deeply; I could feel the press of his face against my swollen skin, his tongue slipping between my nether lips so that he could gently tease and suckle my clit. *Oh my fucking god.*

My breathing grew slow and heavy, my eyes fluttered closed as I rode the sensations. He built up an insistent rhythm, sucking so sweetly, and I trembled. My legs started shaking and I put a hand on the counter for support.

"Too much," I whispered.

"Shh," he said.

"No, no, come here," I urged, tugging at his arms. I hated coming too early. My whole body would shut down afterward and I wanted this night to last.

He rose and I slipped my hands under his T-shirt, ran my fingers up his ripped abs and over his amazing chest, then lifted his shirt off and tossed it aside. I leaned into him, still a little shaky in the legs, and he held me firm. "Don't worry," he whispered. "I won't let you fall." I let go and his strength supported me like I was no heavier than a butterfly. I melted against him, melted into his kisses.

"God, you make me feel like such a man," he said.

I let my hand drift down felt his hardness through his blue jeans. "You feel like such a man to me, too," I teased, but I knew what he meant. I didn't have to be the driver in this. It wasn't Glen I was with. I could unleash my femininity. I could just let go. How often had I watched Cami, in her constant drive for more power, emasculate the incredible man in my arms?

"Your turn," he said.

Yes. I was hungry for him. I sank down to my knees, grateful for the thick rug on the cold tile floor. My fingers undid the button, then slowly unzipped his pants. I tugged down on the denim and nuzzled him through his boxer briefs. His engorged cock stuck out from the top of the elastic. At first I licked at the tip of it, teasing him as he had done all night to me, until he groaned in frustration. Only then did I take just the tip of his gorgeous cock into my mouth. I swirled my tongue around and flicked it lightly to arouse every nerve.

"Please, Aleah," he whispered. I cast my gaze up at him and as slowly as I could possibly manage, slid him in as deep as I could take him. His hardness was silky in my mouth. I took my time sliding back, my tongue lapping and sucking, stretching the moments out. Stroke by stroke I increased the pace until I found a comfortable rhythm. I got really into it, letting myself forget all the rest of the world. My eyes fell shut as I lost myself to his beautiful, rigid cock. I liked the feel of it, the smooth warmth of it, its firmness, and the way it throbbed in my mouth, against my throat.

The thing is, I'd never been all that good or interested or anything with blow jobs before. They weren't part of the normal repertoire I had with Glen. I didn't have all that much practice. But it felt natural to be in the moment, sucking on Blake Porter's gorgeous cock. It was about the most Zen thing I'd ever done.

After I don't know how long, he groaned, said, "Ohhh, you do that exceptionally well," and brought me out of my reverie. I became self-conscious. I looked up at him while my mouth was still wrapped around him. He reached down, caressed my cheek.

The lust in his eyes pulled me to my feet. I kissed him and told him, "I want you inside me."

"You got it, baby," he said as I leaned forward against the bathroom countertop, lifting my hips so that he could take me from behind. I stared at him in the mirror as he slammed in me, sliding, teasing. His hands softly stroked down my back, up my sides, and he clutched my hair as he rode me, harder and harder. I trembled at the way he felt inside, so big, so hard, and so slippery. He let go as he groaned and my head fell forward. I bit my own arm out of frustration; I was so close to coming.

I caught his eyes in the mirror, and watched his face tighten and contort as his spasm filled me inside. A guttural moan escaped his clenched teeth. The energy between us was unreal. It swirled up into a maelstrom, spinning under my skin. I was so close. He reached around, touched my sex and I lit on fire. My legs convulsed, sweet, sweet mother of goodness. I couldn't stop the shaking.

"I got you," he said, pulling me in close, wrapping his arms around me as I rode it out. I met his gaze in the mirror, his green eyes glowing with sated lust. "I got you," he whispered into my hair again as he teased me into a sweet ocean of orgasm with his fingers. I turned into him as my body quietly spasmed. I let him hold me. I let myself feel everything.

I wanted to stay there forever. I looked at the fading twilight through the window's frosted glass panes. I had the rest of the night.

He pulled me to the bed to relax.

"We should check on the kids," I said after spending a while in his arms.

"They're fine." He urged, "Stay with me."

"You're the one who should check on them; you're their daddy."

"You're the babysitter."

I rolled my eyes. "Fine," I said, grabbing his robe to wrap myself in.

"All right, all right, I'm coming." He groaned. I glanced back in time to see him hopping back into his jeans.

"I should hope so," I said, turning and flashing a wicked grin at him.

The kids were fine. After checking on Davis we stood in the doorway of Desiree's room, watching the little angel sleep. Night crept in through the window, shadows covering her face.

"Satisfied now?" Blake whispered, but he didn't sound snarky.

"I am," I whispered, and followed his tug back down the hall to his bedroom.

"You need anything?" he asked when we got there.

I shook my head. *Just you*, I wanted to whisper, but I didn't want to be that cheesy or desperate.

Something happened when the moon rose. If I had to choose the moment everything got more complicated for me, it might have been just then, when the white moonlight streaked in through his bedroom window and outlined his face, the way he looked at me with reverence etched in his eyes.

Blake lit a few candles on the nightstand and dresser. He placed scarves over the too-bright light of the bedside lamps, put music on, fiddling with the volume. He stood up and walked to the center of the open space in the room. "Come here," he said, taking me into his arms. "I want to dance with you."

This was a side of Blake I'd never seen. I put my arms up around his shoulders and swayed with him to the music. Dancing was never my strong suit. All the rhythm genes in my family had gone to my sister. But his lead was incredibly easy to follow. He made me feel like I knew what I was doing, singing along softly in my ear as the music played. His breath made my skin feel like it was coming alive after a drug-induced sleep. I turned my lips to his and let him sing into me.

"This one's perfect too," he said when the next song came on. "Even if it is wimpy Dave Matthews." I couldn't keep a small smile from my lips. I felt it in my eyes. The smile was much bigger inside me. I felt myself buoyed by the golden glow inside.

He brushed his lips against mine and used his breath like a weapon to draw in my soul. His lips danced just out of reach every time I sought them with mine. I stopped trying to force a kiss from him. I let go and found a magic in the sensuality, breathing his breath, feeling his energy. It was the most sensual sex of my life and all we were doing was twirling around his room, breathing each other's breath.

The night grew darker still; my eyes adjusted to the yellow light of the candles as one by one Blake turned off the bedside lamps. He found his way back to me.

"I'm so glad you're here," he drawled in my ear, then threw me on the bed like I was a bouquet of flowers. His legs straddled me and he leaned in to nuzzle my neck, his hips moved slowly down my body. As he nuzzled my neck, I could feel how hard he was for me. I knew I was dripping wet. "These are cute, but I think I'm done with them," he said, tugging at my green mesh shorts.

"Take them off."

"This too," he said of my halter top.

I looked at him. "Go ahead," I said, sitting up. I raised my hands high over my head. Blake smiled, his face bathed in candlelight, and lifted the shirt off. He pushed me back down on the bed and renewed his careful exploration of my body. I trembled beneath him. He kissed his way down my abdomen, stopped to inhale my scent and groaned. "So sweet," he said and flicked his tongue in my wetness. I felt his presence through me, every touch was beyond electric. "Oh my god, you're so sweet," he said. I clenched my legs and he moved on. He kissed a pathway along the inside of my leg.

"Please," I said. "Please kiss me." Part of me still couldn't believe this was real. A fairy tale, maybe. This couldn't be real. It was too good, too wonderful. Too much of everything.

He looked up at me with a predator's hungry eyes and crawled back up along my body. "Yes, ma'am." Blake was a masterful kisser. If kisses were music, his were a concerto: a brave introductory piece followed by the sweeter second movement, and finally the sweeping finale.

After almost enough time, he pulled away and without warning plunged deeply inside me. It didn't matter. I was so ready for him. He was sweaty, atop me. I kept staring at his gorgeous green eyes as he rode me, the length of him rhythmically fucking me, making more of his incredible music. He controlled every nuance.

I let one arm drop to the bed. He grabbed my wrist and held it down, his other hand was near my head.

I'm not sure what came over me. It seemed as natural as breathing, the thing I did next. I trapped his gaze as I took his hand and placed it on my throat.

"Oh my god," he breathed heavily. His hand was huge yet gentle on my trachea. My breath grew shallow, but I could breathe. It felt insanely sexy. He pressed a little harder and I found I couldn't breathe. I stared at him with perfect trust. Everything in me yearned for him and finally I let myself come, shuddering uncontrollably around him and he continued to fuck me, his rhythm a frenzy; he thrust into me relentlessly. I felt starry at the edges of my vision, the yellow candlelight got all blurry. I tried to breathe then, and couldn't. I felt my eyes flutter a little and the first pricks of panic flared. I clawed at his wrist. He glanced at me, instantly releasing his hold on my breath. I gasped a lungful of sweet, cold air and surged up into him, grabbing him to me, demanding his full kisses, my every nerve on fire as he came, my every sense tingling with him.

"Sometimes I think I should have been a porn star," he laughed once we were outside, sitting under the stars, smoking our cigarettes and weed. I sat alongside him on the floor of the porch, touching him, my head nestled against the crook in his shoulder.

"I imagine you'd make pretty good money," I said. "You have more stamina than anyone I've ever known."

I pulled away from him to light my cigarette. He shook his head as he stared at me in the moonlight. "When you put my hand on your throat..." He let it drift off for a moment. "I've always wanted to do that," he said. "But you... You amaze me, Aleah." He looked at me like I would just float away in a bubble, like Glinda the Good Witch, like he wasn't sure I existed at all.

Just being there with him was absolutely the most insane thing I'd ever done. I knew this story. Everyone knows this story. But I couldn't help playing my part.

It was late. 3:00 a.m. "Sleep with me a little," Blake said. "We have time yet. She won't be home until noon at the earliest."

And so I did. I fell asleep in his arms in his bed. It felt like being home.

I woke to the alarm on my phone before the kids got up. I left Blake to sleep. I walked down the hall to leave and all I saw was picture after happy picture of their family: of Blake and Cami, Davis, and Desiree. The kids separate, the kids together. Cami and Blake together. All of them together.

What the fuck was I doing? This had to end before anyone got hurt.

Except, on the way home, the love songs on the radio started to make sense to me. I knew I was in a little bit of trouble. Just the slightest bit. It was time to walk away, while I still could.

When I got home, I put four little blue boxes on my fertility chart. My resolve melted a little as I colored each one in.

Chapter Four

On Sunday, we went to Blake & Cami's to watch the Oscars. They were always asking us over to do something. More so lately than usual, it seemed. I thought I might know why. My determination to stay away from Blake was eroding before we even got there. My body tingled with excitement to see him. I liked being with him. It felt good, being so happy for the first time in so long. It felt really good. "How are you?" I asked when Blake hugged me hello.

"Happy you're here," he whispered, caressing my thighs only somewhat surreptitiously in front of everyone, seeming sure they wouldn't see because they weren't looking for it. Such a complex web we wove. I had to stop myself from moaning.

It was chaos at their house. Toys everywhere in the living room. The kids were shouting, crying, and hitting each other. Fun stuff. I volunteered to give Cami a break by changing their diapers for her and Blake followed to help. So dangerous. He whispered soft kisses at the back of my hair, held me close for a breath, fluttered his hands along my breasts as he passed near me.

Desiree was being a spaz and then Davis was crying, inconsolable. Cami was visibly frazzled, though it seemed to me like Blake and I had done the heavy lifting so far. I volunteered to help with bath time. Cami was so grateful for the break. In the bathroom, Blake kissed me in front of the little ones as they soaked.

Cami and Blake took the kids back for a story before bed. Glen and I cleaned the toys off the living room floor. Cami finally emerged and looked at me with complete exasperation. "See what you got yourself into? *You* wanted to see the kids—you're the one that had to be here when the show started. You could have come later when they were already in bed."

I wasn't sure where she was getting any of that. She was the one who'd invited us. She'd set the time. I just looked at her and said, "It's not a big deal, Cam." She had no idea just no idea how badly I wanted children, how I wanted them in my life every day, how jealous I was of her bedtime routine and having to bathe them and talk to them and teach them. She had no idea how lucky she was. It made me sad to see how heavy Blake could get around her and I wondered at how tired they must be.

"Right," she said.

"Really," I said. "I'd do just about anything to have those problems." I took the plunge and told her, "Glen and I are trying, well, we have been for a while now. We've got an appointment with a fertility specialist coming up."

"Oh," she said, looking at me appraisingly. "I'm sorry, Aleah. I'm hung over from the concert still, and cranky. I didn't mean to take it out on you."

"It's all right," I said, walking toward their couch. "Just relax now. They're down, right?"

She sighed. "Right."

We got back to watching the Oscars.

During the commercials, I told stories to Cami and Glen that I'd already told Blake so he didn't have as many secrets to hide, lies to tell. I'd never had a secret from Glen before and in the space of less than a month I had so many. Or one big one, depending on how you called it. I found myself to be the queen of manipulation.

I snuggled up to Glen on their couch and thought, *Take that*, at Blake. He hooked his arm around his wife's legs, rested his hand alongside her pussy, stroking her leg softly, like he was saying, *Oh yeah?* She actually squirmed away, uncomfortable. I took some refuge in that. He was somehow, inconceivably, repulsive to her. I wasn't taking anything from her that she actually wanted.

I had trouble concentrating on the television. My gaze was riveted by

Blake's strong arms, his callused hands. All I could think of was how I wanted him. We skirted the edge that night. Everything felt so dangerous.

I thought, *He's probably going to fuck her tonight.* I didn't want to know about it. And so we sent each other these strange mixed signals. Somehow Glen and I made it home with no one the wiser. My eyes kept closing on the drive home, but I couldn't fall asleep. I cast my own net to the stars, trying to change one belief only, that assertion that Blake didn't love me. I wanted him to love me. I knew it to be my biggest flaw and knew it would be my downfall in all of this. I didn't yet know how it would turn out, but at that moment I was not scared. Paranoid sometimes. But mostly just grateful to feel so alive again.

Blake called again Monday morning. Glen was in the shower.

"Hey lady, I'm in the neighborhood," he said. "Can I come over?"

"Can you give me twenty or thirty minutes? Glen hasn't left for work yet."

"Oh, shit. I'll call you later." I heard the jolt of panic in his voice. He hung up.

He did call me later, and came over to visit for a few delicious hours.

When he called me hours later on the drive home from the jobsite he said, "Almost got in hot water at work today. I told my buddy I was going to Home Depot. When I was gone for that long... The boss started hollerin'. My buddy had to cover for me. It was way too long to play hooky, Aleah. I can't keep doing that."

"No one's asking you to," I said.

"Well, maybe I'm having a hard time keeping myself from you," he said.

Oh.

In spite of how I'm sure it seems, I did work on my marriage. Somehow the freedom I felt with Blake translated into an honesty I hadn't exercised with Glen in some time. I opened the floodgates of communication. We fought and we cried and we ached. But mostly I was letting go of stored pain. I'd been hurting for so long. I cried as I told him how tired I was of being taken for granted. I told him I would try to make it work, and I would, for him, because he didn't want to lose me. But I worried it was already too late and that he'd lost me some time ago when neither of us had really noticed. I worried that when I said *I love you* I didn't mean it the same way he did. I told him that, too.

"Aleah, you could break my heart a hundred times a year and I'd still come crawling to try to get you back," he told me. I didn't know what to do with that. I wondered if I would throw my own self so ceaselessly at someone who didn't return the favor. I flashed on the previous Christmas, when Glen had presented me with a ring in front of tons of family and asked me if I would marry him again. I mean, you can hardly say "no" in that situation, but it's what I wanted to say. I played the good wife and said, "Yes," in front of everyone, but had he had the balls to ask me privately, I wouldn't have.

It's strange to me that I could exist in both places at once, that I could be such a harlot and wear the mask of the good wife, the wife who was trying, the righteous one. I believed our baby would help everything, if only we could conceive. Then we would have our own life, and our own family to cling to. Glen would have to be the man I knew he could be with a baby in the picture. He would realize he was a man in his own right, not always in his father's shadow. I would have every reason to truly be a good wife.

Our first meeting with the fertility specialist had me terrified. I was shaking so badly that Glen stayed home from work that morning to drive us both to town. I'd never felt so much a part of a strange science fiction experiment as I did entering the brick building with Glen. Inside everything was all light green glass and brushed chrome. I felt like the fluorescent lights were scrutinizing me. The receptionist was even dressed in a white lab coat.

Dr. Skanska called for us twenty agonizing minutes after our set appointment time. She was a small thing, silvery hair cut in a severe bob at her chin. She sat ensconced behind a giant oak desk and I think her chair must have been taller than mine because in spite of her obvious petiteness, she seemed to be peering down her nose at me. Her gray eyes stared at our chart behind her clear-framed glasses. She seemed like some kind of magician, someone who could wave a wand and make the baby we'd never been able to have. She had technology, after all. I had temperature charts, egg yolks, and progesterone cream. I felt like an herb witch next to her.

"So you are here today because..." She looked at us expectantly.

Part of me wanted to wait for Glen to say something but then the silence grew awkward so I filled in the obvious blank. "We want a baby. We've been trying forever…" I don't know what I expected. Maybe some kind of warmth or compassion? Glen said he'd checked this place out. The doctor continued to stare at our clip-boarded informational sheet.

"And this is the first time you've been in to see a specialist?" Was that condemnation in her voice?

Again I looked to Glen, but he seemed determined to leave me on my own. "Well, I've charted my fertility symptoms. I brought the last several months with me," I said, starting to fish through my oversized leather bag.

The doctor waved her hand at me. "You've been having intercourse regularly, though?"

I looked at Glen. We sort of had. "Yes," he said, his first word of the morning.

"I've been using progesterone cream—"

The doctor waved her hand at me again. "Don't tell me," she said. "You'll just make me angry. Self-medicating does more harm than good. Just stop it." She shook her head, then said forcefully, "We'll start with a fresh battery of diagnostics," and marked a series of boxes on a lab form. "You'll initial by the ones you agree with," she said. She talked through them quickly. Sperm motility, count, etcetera. Hormonal surveys.

Glen and I looked over the doctor's recommendations. Each had a price associated with it. The most expensive was one she explained took a certain kind of dye and shot it up into my ovaries, then used a special detector to confirm the passageway from my ovaries to the lining of the uterus was clear. That was one paycheck by itself. The other five or six assessments added up to two more paychecks. At my urging, Glen agreed to the basic sperm assessment for him to start with, while I submitted to hormonal assessments and blood work. The lab results would take a week to generate. We set up a second $300 appointment and I prepared myself to wait again.

At poker that week Glen went out of the game early. He looked tired and was pointedly yawning at me a lot. I, however, was the chip leader for once.

"You look tired," I heard Blake say to him. "I don't mind dropping Aleah home after the game if you want to leave."

"You don't mind?" Glen looked to me.

I looked at my chip stack. It was a completely plausible solution. "Not at all," I said. "With any luck I'll be here for a while. You should get some rest."

Other than knowing that Blake took fourth and I took second, I couldn't tell you anything about the rest of that game. I trembled as I climbed up into the cab of his huge truck. On the way home, Blake took a detour to the river. He pulled me out of the cab and we walked awhile along the rocky shore guided by moonlight. It was chilly. It was still early March, after all. By chilly, I mean it was fucking cold. I leaned against him as we walked, milking his body for warmth. "This way," Blake said to me after we'd left the road behind, and tugged me over to a little grassy knoll on the riverbank. He sank down and pulled me to my knees alongside him. I felt the pebbles through my jeans.

"I want you so badly." His words came out in a gush. "It has been torture tonight. Being in the same room with you but not being able to touch you." He kissed me, gently at first, then more urgently. He slid his cold hands under my shirt, up to my naked breasts. I shivered at his touch, my nipples instantly hard. He buried his face in my neck, and kissed me and kissed me. The cold air was its own aphrodisiac. I wasn't sure if it was raucous crashing of the nearby river heading for the falls or the blood pounding in my brain that filled my ears.

"I have to have you," Blake said.

"Here?" We were relatively secluded by tall bushes and grasses, but it was still a public park.

"Yes, here." He undid the fly on my jeans, pulled them halfway down past my knees. "No one's going to see us this late at night. Lie down here," he said, tamping down the grass behind me. He eased me backwards until my head rested on the cold earth. The smell of bruised grass filled my nostrils.

The moonlight was bright silver, almost too bright. It glistened on the river and heightened the shadows on Blake's face. He whipped his own jeans off and brought his body alongside mine. He fingered my wetness briefly before sliding into me completely. Because his body was so resilient at recovering from work injuries, I'd heard him joke that he was part werewolf. Maybe he was, because something wild took over and he rode me like a dog of the wild hunt. We hungered for each other, each pulling together closer, my arms holding him close for warmth.

"God, you're so good, you're so good," he panted, groaning in the throes of coming. He rocked against me, pulling out so that his seed spread all over my stomach, the ground, my thighs. There was so much of it. He fell against me, warm and slippery, and I reveled in his closeness until the cold overcame us both.

"Let's get you warm," he said and helped me up. I pulled my clothes back into a semblance of order and prayed Glen would already be asleep when I got home. I was dripping with Blake's cum and was sure I had seeds in my hair from the grasses. I swiped my dirty hands on my jeans.

"C'mon, girl. Let me get you home before I have to take you again."

We didn't quite make it home. He pulled over at the main drag, behind the train graveyard, and sucked my little clit until I was dancing with oblivion, then fucked me in the passenger seat of his new cab. I lay across the bench and his lips skated all over me, his hands deftly bringing every nerve alive. Every minute was so hot. Him sucking my tits, my pussy. Me going down on him, the urgency, the frightful wonder of it—how could it always be so fucking good? I came for him, windows steamed up—who knew if the cops were cruising by? Fuck that. Who cared? He brought me to the edge of orgasm again, his hands on my crotch as he drove me home. I stared at the stars through the window in delirium.

I caught a glimpse of myself in the side mirror, wild eyed, flushed with life. Who was that girl? That girl wasn't me. That girl was free.

"You know this is the kind of sex people write books about," Blake said when he pulled up to the house.

I said, "Oh, do they?" but I knew what he was really saying was that he wanted me to write it.

Glen *was* asleep when I got home, thank God. I took a shower and it wasn't enough to get the thought of Blake out of my head. I crawled into bed next to my snoring husband and touched myself, bringing myself almost to climax when I realized the body next to me was warm and belonged to me, so I woke up Glen's cock and rode him home. He was pretty happy about it, judging by the sleepy smile on his face. *Win, win.* I thought, then: *God, I'm evil.*

My period started the next day and once again I was so sad. Lonely too, in my sadness. Glen seemed unaffected by the news, as usual. I ached. I so wanted a child of my own. I wanted a different life. I wanted.

"You need a change of scenery, a completely different world view," Jennifer exhorted that afternoon on our walk. "Seriously. You've been cooped up in that house too long."

"You're right, I need to get away." I couldn't keep going the way I was. The seesaw between Glen and Blake was starting to tear at my foundation.

Wanting the one I could never have kept me from wanting the other. “I need to re-imagine everything. I should go someplace challenging, someplace that demands big dreams.”

We said it almost simultaneously, “New York City.”

I booked tickets the next day. I’d go in May, for a week.

“I’ll never think about my passenger seat the same way,” Blake said the following Monday morning when he called. I’d come to think of the weekdays, when Glen and Cami were at work, as *our* time. “You got to break in the cab.”

“Well, it was my pleasure.”

“I should hope so, little lady. So, thanks much. I appreciate it.” His words seemed strange to me, hollow. Something in the tone of his voice made me think he was distracted. “I’ll see you in two weeks, all right?”

“Okay,” I said hesitantly, trying to put it together in my head. *Two weeks?* I tried to figure out the reference. Was he talking about game night? The past few weeks he’d been calling me all the time, daily, sometimes a few times a day. He’d said he couldn’t get enough of me and wanted to make excuses to come see me but life kept getting in the way. All of a sudden here he was cold on the phone, distant. I didn’t think I’d done anything, but maybe he was having second thoughts about what we were doing. *Maybe it’s over.* A sudden shot of panic bolted through me. *You have to be okay with this,* I told myself. *You signed up for it.*

I let a week of the silent treatment go by. Then I broke down. I didn’t want to be the weak one; but I had to know what was going on. Was it over? Was I reading too much into his retreat?

“What’s up?” he said, still distant. At least he’d answered. His voice wasn’t the slightest bit warm.

Cautiously, I said, "I was wondering what was up with you. It's not like you to go all silent on me. Is there something I should know?"

He was quiet for a moment. "You're worried that I'm breaking up with you." I could imagine his clunky, construction-grade, rubber-wrapped phone cradled in the crook of his neck as he wiped off his hands. "Nothing's changed, Aleah. I'm just busy. And lying low a bit. You know. Ebb and flow. Trying not to get noticed."

"Sure," I said. But I still felt like he was testing the waters, seeing if he could let me go. It would be best for all of us if he could.

"Plus, it's just a tease and it drives me too crazy to talk to you and not be able to do anything about it. It's better to just not talk."

"Sure." Whatever. I was discardable. I got it.

The days dragged on. I refused to call Blake. Instead, I spent my quiet days, afternoons and evenings at home, mostly alone, and got a real sense of how empty my life with Glen had become. When I looked to the future, I saw a wall of fog. I had no notion of what was in front of me, no matter how hard I looked at it. I couldn't believe I was contemplating divorce. I didn't want to be a girl who'd been divorced. It represented a failing, something I couldn't turn back from. It didn't have to go that way. I tried to convince myself we could find our way back.

I felt so empty. I was nothing.

Every time I tried to talk myself into feeling good about a life where I stayed with Glen, I only felt heavier. I found myself less and less willing or wanting to get out of bed in the morning. What the hell was I going to do with my life? With myself?

Surely New York would give me the space and inspiration to figure it out. I only had to make it another seven weeks.

That Thursday, Glen and I returned to the fertility clinic to get the results of our diagnostic tests. Dr. Skanska was to the point. "Your results have all come back within acceptable parameters." She tapped a red mark on the chart in front of her. "Motility is a little on the low side, but it's not something that would support such a prolonged infertility."

I wasn't entirely sure what that meant, but inferred that it had something to do with his sperm. Glen looked decidedly uncomfortable and remained silent.

"What are the next steps?" I asked.

"We could do a few more tests, but given what we're seeing here, I say we put you on a round of Clomid and AI. When are you expecting your next cycle to start?" Her gaze pierced me with its intensity.

I knew this was her everyday line of work. I was still decidedly embarrassed. "First week of April," I said.

"Good. We'll get you set up with the prescription." She spent a few moments describing what to do. I'd take these pills and then a shot of some hormone in the belly to stimulate ovulation. Then we'd come into their office, Glen would jack off and they'd shoot me up with his fresh sperm, positioning it optimally for impregnation. All this for a little under $600, while the next diagnostic the doctor recommended was over $1,200. It made sense to take the plunge.

Maybe it had always just been a matter of timing. Or needing to force ovulation. The reality of all of this started to hit me. I could be pregnant within a month. It would change everything.

I was jubilant. I had something to hope for. And then it hit me. I would have to choose Glen. I would have to be with Glen.

I was sitting at my desk, working on my bloody forms as usual when

Cami called in the middle of my drought from Blake. I wasn't sure at first if I should answer or not. I couldn't think of what she wanted. Then I thought it would be strange if I started avoiding her. So I answered.

"So, I have this really weird question for you," she said after we'd said our hellos.

"What's that?"

"Does Glen keep his dope in an Altoids tin?"

"Umm, Glen doesn't really smoke dope." He had, a few times, maybe twice since I'd known him. It wasn't his thing. Just like beer wasn't mine.

"Okay. So there's no way it would be his..."

"No, I don't think so. Why, what's going on?" Of course it was then I realized who the actual target of her investigation was. Sometimes I was completely clueless. Or distracted. Take your pick, the result was the same.

"Oh, I'm sorry to involve you in all our addiction issues," she said. "I had a feeling that Blake was smoking again—I mean he came home every night smelling like skunk, Aleah—and then I asked him about it and he said he wasn't so I searched his truck and I found this Altoids tin with about a gram in it and when I confronted him, he said it was Glen's. Anyway, I just need to talk to him. He needs to be sober and he needs to be honest with me. Right now he's clearly not either." Her voice was forcedly cheerful. I could tell there was anger building up inside.

"Well, best of luck," I said, not sure what else to say. I mean, Jesus. She was pretty worked up over a gram. I guess I'd be pissed if my husband were lying to me. But it wasn't like she ever made a safe haven for the truth. If she were my spouse, I'd hide things from her too. It'd just be easier.

Blake called me after nine days. I sat down to take the call. My hands were shaking so badly I almost ended the call instead of answering. His first words were perfect, the fucking bastard.

"I've been missing you, baby."

I wanted to hurt him. I wanted to cry. I wanted to laugh. But the sum total of it was that I'd been missing him too. "When can you come over?" I whispered, not trusting my voice.

"Today. Now. Soon."

He came over and it was fucking amazing. There was a feral quality to the way we were with each other, a roughness that sent us tumbling across the bed, onto the floor, growling and playfully biting, licking. I loved it. Hours flew by.

"Damn I've missed you," he said, curling me up in his arms after. "Where you been all my life, woman?"

"Right here waiting for you," I said. "Where've you been all these last two weeks?" I said, poking at his chest.

"I know." He sighed, stroking my hair. "I'm sorry, baby. I got this new guy at work chained to my hip pocket. There just hasn't been any way to talk without the newb right there. All the fucking time. And then Cami at home..." He trailed off. It was a different story from what he'd told me before. "But I think about you every goddamn day," he said. "Stroking my cock in the shower I think of you kneeling in front of me, your soft lips, your hot mouth, sucking, licking, moaning. That magical tongue."

I leaned back against him and his lips brushed the top of my head; he kissed my temple. I'd think his words crude except that I loved every bit of it as much as he did. I didn't care how he expressed himself. He was a man. He was my man. "It's not fair, how good we are together." I said.

"I know. Cami is grossed out by anything remotely sexual. She doesn't have the same sex drive I do and she's got this Catholic streak a mile wide when it comes to a man taking care of his own needs. Just this morning, I'm in the shower and she leans in and shouts, 'What the fuck are you doing in there? You're not masturbating are you?' Like it's something to be ashamed of. And it's not like it's *all that* with her even when she does consent. Can't you just come and be my playmate all the time?" he whined.

"I know what you mean." I sighed. "I love our foreplay. I don't get that with Glen. I'm lucky if he lasts four minutes—that's including the foreplay and him falling asleep after."

"Cami's the same way. It's just stress relief for her. She wants someone to fuck her hard. Insert cock here. Jackhammer away. Wham, bam, it's done." He stroked the length of my hair. "It's all mechanical, and you're so sensual. It's fucked up. Seems like it should be the other way around, like the wham bam should be with the mistress and the romance with the wife, but it's not that way."

"I know, right?" I said. "I'm surprised at how sensual you are, you know. I didn't expect it. Not from you."

"I was surprised by you for the same reason. And for how much of a nympho you are. Hey, you know what?" He turned on the bed so I could see his face. "We should make a video. We could wear masks so no one would know it was us. You can teach Cami how to fuck me. We can show it to Glen to, so I can teach him."

"Not your best idea, Blake," I said.

"Ski masks?"

"Seriously?" I said.

"Yeah," he said. "You're probably right."

"I am right. Still, when I'm old and on my deathbed I'll remember these weeks as the best sex of my life."

He said, "Maybe I'll be there with you, my head buried in your thighs eating you up." He gave me a funny look.

Inside I panicked a little. He couldn't say those kinds of things to me.

I liked him. I liked talking to him. I wanted to be with him all the time. I wanted to fuck him for days and not have to sneak around or apologize or lie about it. I wanted him for my own. I wanted to serve him, to wake him up by sucking his cock. I wanted to take a vacation to the islands and do nothing but eat and drink and fuck, fuck, fuck.

I forced myself to remember his words to me when we started: *"I don't love you and I'm not going to marry you. Even if everything fell apart, I don't love you and I wouldn't marry you."*

Yes, I believed him. Yes, I had to keep my heart locked up in an iron cage. He had to walk the delicate balance between being sweet enough to keep me turned on and not going too far. I had to stay emotionally distant or it would kill me. New York City. I had to get away. New York City.

Chapter Five

"Listen," I told Glen. "I don't want you to feel like I'm stacking the deck against you and if you'd rather find someone else, that's cool, but I asked David to recommend a counselor for us. Apparently she is very good, very expensive, and very booked, but if we want to use her he'll get us in. It's Dr. Auel. I sent you a link to her website."

"Whatever you think, Aleah," he said as he came up to me at the kitchen counter. He didn't take my hands, but he did look at me earnestly.

"Really?"

"Really." It had been Glen's idea. He thought we needed professional help to work out our issues. I didn't disagree.

I had no idea if it was worth the exorbitant cost, but it did make me feel better about the possibility of going forward with an "us." If we were going to have a baby together, we had to figure out how to love each other again. It was the best possible outcome. I started taking the Clomid the same day. We would try to get knocked up that week.

I didn't know what I was doing. If I held still for too long the world started spinning and everything made me dizzy. I kept trying to put on the brakes, but they didn't respond.

Dr. Auel's office was in a high-rise condo in Belltown. There were a few somewhat modern chairs lining the hallway. We knocked on her yellow door. "Come in," we heard after a moment as the door opened from within and a woman, presumably Dr. Auel, let us in. She struck me as extremely clinical, hair shorn short like Annie Lennox, wire framed glasses. The room was warm, though, filled with books and plants, a box of tissues on the coffee table—decidedly more like a living room than a doctor's office. There was another closed yellow door between her office and the connecting suite.

Before sitting down on one of the cushioned, white wicker chairs opposite her, I strolled past the window. She had a nice, though somewhat distant, view of the water, and even though it was mostly gray outside, there were patches where the sun was trying to burn through. The shrink introduced herself and asked if we had any questions. She said, "I find it best to meet separately and get to know you as individuals first, then I'll bring you back together." I hoped she could keep her promise. "Aleah, if you wouldn't mind stepping into the waiting area..." She gestured back to the hallway.

"Not at all," I said and left to take a seat. Part of me wondered if she were such a successful counselor, why was her waiting room the hallway in the corridor of her condo complex? She didn't even have any magazines. Not that it mattered. I pulled up Settlers of Catan on my iPhone. I had just started my third game when Glen emerged, a look of relief on his face. "She's ready for you," he said.

I went in and took a seat opposite the doctor. She asked me a lot of questions about me and my life, about me and Glen, about what I wanted for myself. She seemed to listen with her whole body. I warmed up to her a bit as we talked through what was going on for me. I talked my heart out.

"It must be so difficult to want something so badly for so long and feel unheard about that desire for a child when you thought you were in sync," she reiterated.

"It has been. I mean, I've been really sad." I felt like she was really hearing me. I felt a glimmer of hope that maybe she'd be able to give me what I'd been seeking.

Somehow I had this amazing ability to compartmentalize what I was doing. I didn't feel it was necessary to mention my affair to the counselor. I honestly didn't consider it relevant. I needed to fix my marriage with Glen and that had nothing to do with the sex I was having on the side. That would have to end soon, anyway. I had been in a marriage of convenience over love for so long that the fact that I was getting really hot sex felt like something I'd earned. It was completely separate from the trust issues I had with Glen, the fact that he couldn't follow through on his promises, the fact that we still rarely had anything to say to each other.

"All right, let's bring Glen back in," Dr. Auel said, rising from her chair. "Are you ready?"

"Sure," I agreed. I'd said what I needed to. She opened the door and motioned for Glen to join us. He walked in and sat down next to me. We looked at each other. I'd like to say the looks were meaningful, but they weren't. I smiled wanly at him.

"Wow, it's like someone just turned the energy volume way down in here," Dr. Auel said. "It's almost as if you two are in collusion to depress each other." I thought that was a pretty astounding observation.

"So," she continued, lips pursed. Thin Seattle sunlight came in from the windows behind me, lining her face with slatted shadows. "What I see is a relationship that has stopped functioning well, or maybe never had a mechanism for respectfully handling conflict."

She had that right. I remembered our very first fight, before we were married or even engaged. I'd gotten pissed about something and confronted Glen about it. He'd turned around and left my apartment instead of talking to me. It was like I was on a phone call and he just hung up. I'd walked out after him. "Where are you going?" He'd put up a hand in the air, shutting me down without a word.

I'd called him three hours later, and again an hour after that. He didn't pick up.

I'd called him twenty hours later and left a message saying if he didn't come and talk to me within the next four hours, we were done. He was there an hour later. He told me he had to think about it for most of that hour, but decided the relationship was worth saving. I felt an eerie resonance at the recollection.

Dr. Auel continued, "But I also sense a deep love here, and that both of you very much want to work this out, that we can save this marriage."

What? She didn't hear me at all. Panic took me over; I wanted to bolt. I sat there, stricken at her verdict, stunned at the thoughts in my head. Didn't I want to fix our marriage? I don't think I knew until that moment how much work Glen and I still had to do. I could feel my face flush, my eyes widen.

I wondered if Dr. Auel played poker, and if she'd picked up on any of my tells. Glen never even looked for tells, though he did adopt a stoic attitude at the table to disguise any of his own. He just played his cards.

"So, our time is up for today. I look forward to seeing you both next week." Dr. Auel stood up, extended her hand. Our session was over.

The car ride home was quiet. It was weird to be in the car together after such an experience. I wanted time to process the black pit of hopelessness I felt in my belly. We were scheduled for an entirely different kind of appointment the next day. My artificial insemination.

A baby would change everything. It fucking had to, because otherwise I was facing madness.

Chapter Six

I won't tell you about the strange darkness or the weird electric beeping, the fucking machines that went *ping!* in the examination room that morning. I won't mention the surprise I felt at learning Dr. Skanska had a pimpled, rumpled assistant whose lanky, greasy hair would never make it onto a soap opera, but who would be observing and participating in the entire proceeding in the vicinity of my vagina while Glen sat out in the waiting area—his choice. It was hard enough having one person in here I barely knew, Dr. Skanska. I hadn't anticipated an audience, though. As I sat back on the gynie bed, my feet propped up in the stirrups, the hospital gown provided no real warmth or cover. I felt exceedingly naked.

I'm not going to tell you about the huge, cold, vaginally-inserted wand the doctor stuck inside me without warning to view my uterus and ensure we were in prime position, or the coldness of the goop she spread over the fake penis. Actually, the whole ultrasound wasn't all that different from when I'd been raped at fifteen. My jaw stayed clenched through the procedure. After jabbing around at my insides for a few minutes until I was sure I'd been bruised, the doctor removed the wand just as suddenly. "There," she said. My abdomen clenched, my neck too. "The difficult part is over."

"Check on the specimen, would you, Marcus?" Dr. Skanska murmured to her assistant. The young man scurried out and returned long, quiet, uncomfortable minutes later with a closed urine collection cup. *Not urine*, I corrected myself. Glen's sperm.

Dr. Skanska narrowed her eyes as she looked at the tiny print on the vial. "Confirm the name of the donor for me if you would," she said.

"Glen Clayton."

"Check. Glen Clayton." She read me his birth date. "That's right isn't it?" The doctor looked at me.

I nodded.

"I need to hear it. Company policy."

"Yes."

"Good."

Marcus walked over for my initialed consent to the procedure while the doctor took a quick look at a sample under a microscope to confirm whatever it was she was looking for. Then she prepared a long plastic syringe.

"You won't even feel this," she said as her latexed fingers probed my labia for an entrance point. I winced as she forcefully slid the thing into me, jamming the tip against my cervix. It was over in a moment, though, and she slid it out. "There. Leave your legs up like this on the table for ten minutes or so. We'll let gravity work in your favor, too." She smiled, the first warm gesture I'd received from her.

My phone rang as they were leaving me alone in the near darkness, having thrown the light switch. "Do you mind handing that to me?" I asked of Marcus, who kindly did.

I almost didn't answer it. But then I thought about the irony of conceiving while I was talking to my lover and did.

"Hey, lady," Blake said and I melted all over. "What're you up to?"

"Oh, you know, the usual," I said. "You?"

"It's almost lunchtime and I'm hungry for you."

I laughed. The tension melted from my body. "Does that one get you far at the fast food joints?"

He laughed. "No, baby. Just missing you is all."

"I'm actually in Seattle today. I don't think it'll work out." I knew it was good to deny him now and again, but suddenly my thighs were throbbing, my clit pulsing. I wondered if it would help my conception. "Call me again sometime."

"Do you feel any different?" Glen asked on the way home from our next counseling appointment. It had been a week since the artificial insemination.

"No, not yet, it's going to be another four or five days before we can test with any assurance. I mean, I don't feel PMS-y yet, so I suppose that's good." I'd seen so many negative pregnancy test results, I didn't want to torture myself with a false negative from taking the test too early.

He shook his head. The pervasive mist outside began to splatter in droplets on the windshield. "No, I didn't expect you'd know about that yet. I meant with counseling, with us. Is it working?"

"Glen, we've only been two times. How can it be working already? I mean, I'm glad we're going. Seems like the right thing to do. What do *you* think?"

"I think it all depends on you, Aleah. I don't know how to make you happy."

"You're not supposed to make me happy, Glen." *You're just supposed to be there. Come to the table.* It occurred to me that he had changed, a lot, actually. Just not in very many ways that brought him any closer to me. "How's the meditation going?"

"It's great. You should try it."

"I don't think it's for me," I said. I sat around doing nothing enough as it was already.

"Do you know when you'll know?" he asked.

"When I'll know what?"

"If it's going to work out for us. If we're going to stay together."

Was he really that much of a black and white thinker? Yes, we're together and everything's great? No, we're not going to work out and split? Maybe I needed to be more black and white myself. Maybe it was the not knowing that was killing all of us. "It's a process, Glen. I think we're on the right track, doing the right things. I mean, I feel like we're taking steps I've been wanting to take for a long time."

"It's just that I've been trying so hard for so long," he said.

Since November? We'd been working on our marriage for all of five or six months. It struck me that if it was so hard for him to try to make our marriage work, what would happen if I said, "Okay, we're all better now?" Would he just slip right back into the old Glen? I mean, if it was such an affected and difficult behavior for him, how would he sustain it?

"I know you have," I said. I thought for a moment longer and told Glen, "I want to see if we're pregnant and I think I need that week away in New York to get my head clear before I make any decision about the future."

The one good thing I could say about counseling was that I no longer felt like I was making a colossal mistake on a daily basis for feeling like I didn't want to be in my marriage any more. We'd had short individual sessions with Dr. Auel in addition to the longer couples counseling session. "Have you thought about what your life would be like without Glen in it?" she asked. "Emotionally, where are you when you think about that?"

My mind went to a white-walled apartment, sparsely furnished. Thirty-one years old and starting over. I felt empty. A little hopeless. Destitute. Right now I had a house. I had a husband. I had beautiful furniture. I had really nice laundry machines. Could I walk away from that? I realized it wasn't Glen that I was missing in that dream of my future self. I was pathetic.

"Mostly I just wonder what I'm going to do with myself," I said. "I mean, my job is a job and I could subsist on it. But I still don't know what I want to do with my life. Do I want to move to New York and get into fashion? Do I want to go into philanthropy, find some great cause to get behind? I want more out of life, I know that much."

"So you're considering all kinds of changes. That seems like a lot to take on right now."

"Well, I need to find a way to be happy on my own. I mean, the future is up in the air. I'm not sure I even want to stay in Seattle. I work from home. My home can be anywhere." As I said it, I realized it was true. I could get out from under the gray skies and find the sun. Suddenly that white-walled apartment seemed a lot more welcoming.

When we reconvened as a couple, Dr. Auel asked Glen, "What do you think Aleah would excel at, career-wise? You know her so well, after so many years together. What strengths does she have that she might not be seeing in herself?"

Glen thought for a moment and then told the doctor, "You know, I've always thought she—"

"Glen, why don't you tell Aleah?"

He turned to face me more directly. "I've always thought you'd be so great as a CEO or some kind of executive. You have vision like no one I've met. You're a natural leader. You get things done. I think you should go back and get your MBA so you can lead teams to accomplish great things."

"Wow. Aleah, those are some pretty strong endorsements of your abilities. How do you feel about that? Can you see yourself going back to school for your MBA?"

"Honestly, Glen? I have knots in my stomach just thinking about it. The thought of doing that makes me feel like I do when I have to go to the doctor's." I could feel my shoulders tighten as I spoke, the acidic outpouring of stress from my stomach.

He shook his head. "You are always letting fear be an obstacle. You should get over it."

"It's not fear." I could feel my lips and nostrils curl in distaste. "It's dread. I don't think you could have said anything that would be further away from what I want to be or what I'm really good at. You know I hate the corporate environment."

"You just haven't worked in a good one yet. There are good companies out there."

Sometimes I thought the chasm between us was one no rope bridge could cross. *Could he get me any less?*

The two weeks following my artificial insemination appointment passed like any other, though not as agonizingly slowly as I might have expected. I had mixed feelings when I thought of the procedure, when I thought of how I could possibly finally be carrying Glen's baby, when I thought of holding that little life in my arms, of mothering. I still wanted that. Very badly. I don't know if it was the ambivalence towards my marriage or if I'd just had my hopes dashed so often I couldn't bring myself to be hopeful anymore, but I didn't let myself get attached to being pregnant *this* time.

I kept charting my temps and mucus every morning. Two days before the two week mark, my temperature dropped. Not a good sign. The hormones from pregnancy keep your temps up slightly from normal. A drop usually signals the next stage in the cycle.

Two days later I didn't have to take the test. My abdomen writhed with cramps and when I sat down on the toilet, dark red skeins of mucus-laced blood fell from my uterus. Negative.

Chapter Seven

"Do you know yet?" Glen asked over dinner several days later.

"About what?"

"If we're pregnant." He said it like he couldn't possibly have been asking about anything else.

My period had come and gone. I thought I'd told him. I guess I hadn't. "It didn't work," I said.

"I'm sorry," he said. He sounded like he genuinely was.

We didn't really talk about it anymore than that, though. Neither of us brought up trying again. I felt beyond dejected, like we were broken and just couldn't be fixed.

The blue boxes kept on filling my charts. It didn't matter what time of the month it was. I'd see Blake, hear his voice on the phone, even just think of him, and I'd get wet. He made it so easy to let go with him, to be a sex goddess. He was so fine to me. He risked far more than I did, and with a much less forgiving partner. I worried for him. At night, my dreams were filled with us getting caught.

By day, he just made me smile. "You're always so happy," he said once.

"I'm always happy to see you," I said. It was true. There was no use denying it or even teasing about it.

The weeks bled together. Of course, we were exceedingly careful. We kept up appearances. Game nights. Poker nights. Cami and I enrolled in a yoga class together. She called me before class one day to tell me she wasn't going. Desi had a bad cold and Blake was running late from work. I felt a twinge of guilt. He was running late because he'd taken an extended lunch in my bedroom.

My butt cheeks burned a little from his visit. At first he'd interjected a surprise swat on my ass here and there, but his hands had grown more and more insistent until he'd begun to punctuate every thrust with a delicious slap. The tingling and burning was all tied in with my swollen pulsating clit, our frenzied lovemaking. I'd been delirious with the sensations, the heat of it all. He took me places I couldn't even begin to describe. All I knew was I wanted more.

"God, you're good. I can't get you out of my brain," I said after, and groaned.

"Tell me about it. Every time I hear a goddamn Dave Matthews song," he told me and went on to complain of his whiny voice and sappy ass lyrics, but I knew what he meant. *As well his thoughts should be on me. I'm his siren. I've already trapped his soul.* I'd noticed sweet red welts on my ass when I changed into my yoga pants later. My own personal temporary tattoos. I loved them.

"Oh, well, I'll miss seeing you," I said to Cami, shaking my head out of my reverie. "Hope the kiddos feel better. Do you need anything? I'm running to Costco on my way..." I offered. I ended up getting diapers, wipes, and formula for Cami and drove them up to their house after yoga. I rang the doorbell and let myself in, figuring her hands were full. I walked into the kitchen.

The kids were sniveling, snotty nosed, and strapped in their chairs. Cami was pulling food out of the oven. "Mama. Hungry," Davis said. It sounded more like "huggy," but I got the message. "Hungry, Mama. Hungry!"

Cami whirled on him, her eyes burning. "Hush it. Hush! You'll get food when it's ready. Now, quiet," she snarled. Davis started to cry in earnest. I didn't blame him. She turned to me and said, "I like them to be a little afraid of me. I think it's important for them to have some fear of their mother, some understanding of consequences. They need a healthy dose of respect." I nodded, not daring to speak. That kind of parenting showed in the whites of their eyes, the poor littles.

"I'll just stack these by the changing table," I said, nodding to the diapers in my hands. I melted back into the hallway shadows and spent a minute in the far back bedroom putting the diapers in the holder. As I walked back to the kitchen I heard her voice amped up with bitterness. "I work my ass off, Blake. Day in, day out." Blake's back was to me as I drew closer. He'd made it home. "Where are you when I need you? You know this is the only night I get for myself. You couldn't convince your boss to let you go on time for once—"

"Hey," I said, walking into the hotbed of tension. I figured it was better to intervene than overhear something I didn't want to.

"Aleah would be a better husband than you are." Cami lit back into him as if it didn't matter that I was there. "At least she's thoughtful. She isn't selfish like you are. She just put your kids' fucking diapers away."

I wanted to claw her for treating him like that. Instead, I retreated to their front porch and smoked a cigarette as they fought. I hoped the awkwardness would fade. I wanted to run. It grew quiet for a moment and then someone must have put *Sesame Street* on because I faintly heard the theme song's opening bars and then Blake belted out "Sun-ny Day," his voice somehow devoid of any tension from his wife's attack. It was so him. I felt my whole face shift to a broad smile of happiness. I heard a soft tap on the kitchen window and looked up to see that he was watching me. I knew he'd seen that smile break like a wave on the beach washing over everything. I saw a kind of ease in him I never saw when he was with Cami.

I grabbed the wipes and formula out of the car and walked back into the house.

"Hey Aleah," Cami said, her voice flat.

"Here's the last of it. I'd better get going. You have a good night." I said a quick goodbye.

Blake took the formula off my hands and walked me back out. "Do you have to go?" he whispered. "You just got here."

"I don't exactly feel comfortable right now."

"I know." He sighed. "I'll miss you."

"'Bye, Blake," I said, walking away as my heart did somersaults.

Book Two

I drifted through the rest of the evening, wanting Blake. That night, I played with myself and still it wasn't enough to quench my thirst for him. I woke Glen up with a sweet kiss. "Hi there," I said and slid my hand along his body until I found his dick, which sprang instantly hard at my touch. I moved down the bed and sucked on him for a while. He moaned and writhed until I had him on the edge of coming. He got lost in the pleasure and begged for me. "Come here." He rolled me over and clambered on top, already seeking to impale me.

He hadn't even touched me yet, hadn't even tried to wake my body up so that I could take him in easily. I'd dried up during my ministrations, but let him have his way because I knew from years of experience how much he didn't know about foreplay, and educating him was too daunting a task to tackle just then. He buried his face in my shoulder as he pounded away until he got off in me. I bit my lips to keep back the tears. I just wanted it over with.

I woke up sore and feeling like I'd been split open and then I remembered the ugliness of it all. While Glen slept in, I got up and on the way to the toilet I noticed that the welts on my ass from my lover's hand slaps had faded. Glen would never have noticed them anyway. It's missionary or nothing with him. He never sees my ass.

I called Blake once I'd wiped the sleep from my eyes, knowing he'd already be at work. It would be another half hour before a conscious thought crossed Glen's mind. Still, I went out to the garage to make the call. "Good morning, lover," I said. "How are you?"

"Good morning," he said with such warmth and happiness in his voice. "I'm moving a little slow today. I shouldn't be working out so quickly after such a great workout yesterday."

"Your personal trainer kicking your ass again?"

"You know it," he said. "Kicking my ass on the carpet, kicking my ass in my bed..."

"She sounds hardcore."

"Something like that."

"I can't get over it, how good we are together."

"I know it. I know," he said. I was hardly awake; I hadn't had my coffee yet and we were both half moaning on the phone.

I didn't care if I was gushing. "It's just so good. I don't even know what else to tell you. I never thought it could be this good. I feel like I'm just saying the same thing over and over again."

"I don't mind. It's nice to hear. I'm glad you're happy."

"The way we are together is so good it's not right. How comfortable we are—"

"The way we play," he added. "It's different every time; it keeps getting better." He was quiet for a moment. "You know, in the beginning, I thought we'd take a tumble or two in the sack and I'd get you out of my system. I mean, that was the whole point, to have a little fun. I didn't think it would be like this. I thought I'd be getting you off my mind, not filling it with you." Then he said the dangerous words. "I don't want this to stop, Aleah. I can't get enough of you. I can't see this ending."

I was quiet for a moment, letting that sink in.

"I know," I said. "I don't want it to, either."

No end, no tapering. *He just keeps wanting me.* I didn't allow myself to think about what that might mean. To survive, I had to keep telling myself it was just sex. Crazy amounts of sex. There was the weekend Cami was out of town on business and I spent every possible minute there. I made up some excuse for where I was Friday, then went "shopping" all day Saturday. Sunday Glen actually had a meditation thing that covered for me. Blake came eleven times with me that weekend. I mean, I put eleven freaking blue boxes on my charts. Five Friday, three Saturday, two Sunday and one for Monday morning. He just kept being ready for me and I just kept wanting him.

It didn't matter to me if I came because every moment was so delicious. But it mattered to him and he made sure to take care of me, often. He liked the way I whimpered and moaned with him, the way my body, pliant, melted into him, how everything fit together between us. He liked how soft I was, how I got sensual, how it was more than the eye roll and the, "Okay, you can fuck me now," he said he got from his wife.

"I love your body," he said. "So curvy, and your sweet, small breasts fit perfectly in my hands."

I loved the anticipation with him. I loved how strong he was, that he could throw me around like I was just a slip of a girl, that he wasn't afraid to take possession of me, that he was so full of his own sense of self. But I couldn't say this aloud. Instead I told him, "I love what a man you are."

"It's your being such a woman that lets me," he said like it was the easiest thing in the world. I knew I was glowing. I knew he brought out radiance in me.

This was something I absolutely didn't have with Glen and something I had to have the next time I found someone, I promised myself. Must. Every time I left Blake, I still hungered with want. My whole body came alive with desire, begging to be touched. I'd go home to Glen and my body would turn off. The man I married, the man who said he loved me more than any man ever had, I couldn't get wet for to save my life. Tell me how this was fair. For anyone. But I was still trying.

And so the days went on and while I sought ways to find my way back to Glen, I reveled in my play with Blake. I tumbled back and forth between passion and security, an endless cycle in the washing machine, never feeling clean.

It hit me during Shivasana at the end of Saturday morning's yoga class. All Blake and I ever had were those little moments, secret stolen hours, discreet phone calls. If I listened to Glen, the moments were all that mattered, the now. But more than that mattered to me. Blake and I weren't building up to anything. It wasn't a replacement for anything. He wasn't going to leave his family for me. I knew he would never have what he got from me with Cami. But I would never have what she had, his family, his everyday *everydayness.* And I'd never have the passion I needed with Glen.

And so the most obvious thing to do, I thought, was to leave both of them and find my own way, to find a man who had it all. Right. That was going to happen. I felt unbelievably bleak and the dark clouds of depression rolled closer in to engulf me.

Chapter Eight

I felt myself softly seethe with a hatred that would slowly take over whenever I sat in one of Dr. Auel's cushioned wicker chairs. I dreaded the visit, and tension would build up in my abdomen as we drove over the bridge on our way there. I hated her tropically-patterned fabrics. There was too much yellow. The sessions were interminable and the drive home empty. It didn't feel like we were getting anywhere but closer to financially destitute with all of our trips to specialists of one kind or another. I hated my real life.

Dr. Auel did encourage us to be present with one another, to speak our minds and hearts. At our last session I told Glen, "I need for us to not have sex or even kiss for a while."

Dr. Auel nodded, clinically, while Glen looked like I'd taken away his last hope.

"Why?"

"I can't really explain it. It feels like a betrayal of myself. It's not that I don't want to be attracted to you, it's that my body just won't respond and I don't want to force myself. It feels like I'm letting myself be raped when I do. It's not you, it's what I'm allowing to happen. The attraction has to come first." For some reason it was in that moment I realized that, aside from the Valentine's Day fiasco, we hadn't once gone out alone as a couple since the come-to-Jesus conversation I'd had with him the previous November.

"What can I do?" he said.

"Try taking me on a date first."

He looked at me with narrowed eyes. I wondered if he thou invitations to come to meditation with him had counted. "Okay," he saic

That Wednesday, Cami invited me up to the house to watch *American Idol* after yoga. Blake was going to be late again (*ahem*) and she wanted company. There was a certain kind of adrenaline that rushed through me whenever I was there. For whatever reason, I always felt closer to being discovered when I was at their house. But I couldn't keep myself from going. Anytime I was asked, if I could, I said, "Yes." *Yes, I'll babysit. Yes, I'll watch TV with you. Yes, I'll buy your groceries. Yes, I'll come play games.*

My relationship with Cami was one of the stranger things in my life. We'd always been socially in the same circles. But now that Blake and I were drawing nearer, Cami and I were spending a lot of time together, too. I think she thought of me as one of her closest friends. She was fun and lively. I enjoyed the bright side of Cami. I drew her as close as I could to keep her sheltered, so that the truth wouldn't hurt her because it would never find her. That night, after a Clear Blue Easy commercial, I found myself telling her, "So, our first fertility treatment was a bomb."

"Oh, Aleah. I'm sorry. I didn't know you'd made it that far."

"We didn't really tell anyone." At least, I thought we hadn't. Though Glen had probably told his mom, now that I thought about it. "All the diagnostic tests came back normal. There isn't really anything they can point to that's keeping us from having a baby. It might just be a timing thing." I didn't really believe it was a timing thing. The only thing we hadn't done were the expensive tests on me. It seemed a foregone conclusion that since I was the only one with anything left to investigate, the problem must lie somewhere within me. I was infertile.

I decided I could keep my mouth shut about counseling.

"I'm so glad you told me," she said. I could see an intensity in her eyes, the wheels spinning in her brain. I feared that Glen and I having a baby had just become one of her projects. Cami liked projects that had to do with fixing other people's lives. I found it a repulsive habit born of arrogance, but that was Cami. Although, what the hell. Let her try. I wasn't sure how she'd have any power to affect my fertility one way or another.

Blake walked in before she could say anything else, though, effectively ending the conversation. He looked exhausted, poor thing. The tone of his skin was actually gray. I'd never seen him so depleted. He issued the barest of greetings and collapsed on the couch.

After *Idol*, Cami wanted to watch an episode of *Firefly*. We'd been watching it off and on together, usually at my insistence. "But first we have to get the kids to bed." She looked at her watch. "Shit. They need a bath tonight." She looked over to where Blake was dozing.

"It's okay," I said. "I can help."

Her eyes narrowed. "It's not fair he gets to sleep through all the chores. Blake!" she shouted. Startled, he jolted awake. "I need you to get the kids ready for a bath."

He sat up and rubbed his face in his hands. "Okay."

She nodded. "Thanks. I'll get the bath started." Cami walked away.

"I'll help," I said, and Blake and I walked to the back room where the kids were playing.

"Time to get ready for your bath," I said, kneeling down. "What a cool block tower you have there."

"And there's pwincesses and monsters there," Desiree said, pointing excitedly at her creation. "And the monsters will eat you! So don't put your fingers there."

"Good advice," I said. "Here, let's get your clothes off. Hands up." Desiree obeyed and I lifted her shirt over her head, and helped her with the rest of it while Blake stripped Davis down. I marveled at the leap in her language skills. Even a few weeks ago she wasn't putting together complex sentences like that. I'd have one more pair of eyes to watch for now. We ferried the kids to the tub, which Cami was filling with sudsy water. "I'll get jammies," I said, heading for Desiree's room. Blake followed me in.

"Second drawer," he said as I began to fumble with the bottom drawer on her dresser.

"Thanks." I pulled some Tinkerbell jammies out and kneed the drawer closed.

"Come here," he said, his voice hushed. I walked up to him from behind and wrapped my arms around him for a hug.

He pulled my hands ever so slowly, down and further down still until they rested on the bulging button fly of his blue jeans. I pulled back at the feel of his hard and eager cock—it was too crazy to do this with Cami in the next room. "It's okay," he whispered.

I closed my eyes, began to relax when suddenly Blake shifted in my arms.

I opened my eyes just in time to see Cami's hawkish gaze narrowing on me as Blake slid out of my arms and ducked in front of her. She stared at me, a cold question in her eyes. The world slowed. My heart pounded in my ears, each beat a cavernous moment away from the next one. She didn't take her eyes off me. What had she seen? I forced my lungs to draw breath and quickly schooled my features into a placid look. I began to let a genuine smile build on my face. I said nothing and she walked past me towards the bathroom. I hugged my arms across my chest and bravely followed, struggling to breathe without heaving, my heart suddenly fluttering faster than a hummingbird's. *How much had she seen?* I felt like running. I knew that I couldn't. The only thing I could do was act like nothing had happened. "Need help?" I said.

"No, I got it." Her voice was flat and her feet pounded the wooden floor as she made for the bathroom where Blake was waiting for her.

I walked to the couch to await my fate, my heart pounding.

I felt like running. I mean that I had to literally concentrate on sitting and breathing and staying. Fight or flight? I knew which camp I was in.

I knew that I couldn't run. This was a make or break point. I had to play this one perfectly or we were well and truly fucked.

Blake came out after a few minutes of what was clearly a heated discussion. "She doesn't know what she saw. You were tickling me," he whispered. I didn't know if that was a lie I could pull off, but it was the one he'd already told her, so I had to.

After the kids were in bed, Cami and Blake both came out and sat on the couch. Cami queued up *Our Mrs. Reynolds*. Every one of my spidey senses tingled at the rage I could feel seething out of Cami. It grew, filling the room, until it pressed all over the edges of my awareness; I could think of nothing but the huge anger contained in that woman. I steeled myself for the fight. I thought about what I'd have to do. About ten minutes in, she hit the pause button and turned on me.

"Are we going to talk about the elephant in the room or what?"

"Cami, I can tell you're upset, but I'm not sure why," I said. "I feel like I am about to get eaten alive and I'm not sure I've done anything wrong." I knew Cami. I knew I had to go on the offensive. "I'm sorry for tickling Blake, clearly I crossed a line with you. But god, was the offense really that huge? It feels like you're about to explode on me."

"You're saying nothing happened," she asserted.

"Nothing happened," I assured her. I was exceptionally glad in that moment that I was an accomplished poker player. "My god, you're one of my best friends. What do you think you saw? I mean." I let it hang for a moment. "Who do you think I am? I would never..."

Cami pursed her lips and turned to Blake. "So help me God," she said, her shoulders quaking as she pointed at him. "So help me God, Blake Porter. If I find out otherwise. If I ever find out that you have betrayed me... I will destroy you." She said each word separately, menace coloring her tone. "You know what I've been through." She rounded on him, like he'd been the one to cause whatever tragedy she'd faced. "You know how often men have done this to me. Do not be one of those men. And you," she spun on me. "I know about the apartment all those years ago. I know about you. Don't think I'm not watching you."

I shook my head. "Jesus, Cami," I said. "I have no idea what you are talking about." I really had absolutely no idea what she was talking about. It was easy to conjure disdain in the lilt of my skeptical eyebrow. "I'm tired. Nothing happened. This is ridiculous. I'm going home," I said, and stood. "I thought we were friends. You're treating me like I work for you, or I don't know. Like you own me. Sometimes you are crazy manic. I don't even know what stories you tell yourself. I'm glad the world I live in isn't filled with evil like yours is." My legs felt like they were going to collapse underneath me. I took a step for the kitchen. The walk across the room to get to the entryway was like slogging through molasses. All of the normal energy had left my body and pure adrenaline ran through my veins like acid.

I heard footsteps behind me. "Stay," Cami said. "Please, Aleah. I'm sorry. You've been such a good friend and you're right. I'm way overreacting to what you and Blake are both telling me is nothing. I know you would never hurt me like that. Please stay."

I swallowed and turned to face her. There was nothing I wanted more than to flee for my car.

"Okay," I said. I would stay. It was what a not-guilty person would do. I knew, because it was exactly the opposite of what I wanted to do. I let that be my compass and somehow forced myself to walk back to the couch.

We finished the episode and then I said I really had to leave. Cami hugged me goodbye, and I could tell in spite of her words there was a new layer of distance between us.

The events of the night haunted me on the drive home. She knew something was different, or at least suspected it. She'd be watching me, I knew. Every rational part of me screamed that Blake and I should stop and every part of me that hungered for passion and the amazing feeling of being alive I had with him wanted me to risk it all. The craziest part? I was angry with *her*.

When I got home, I let myself in as quietly as I could in case Glen was asleep. Sadie came up, tail wagging, and licked my palms. I sank to the floor and hugged her, burying my head in her coat. I breathed deeply to avoid sobbing and forced myself up the stairs. It was over. It had to be over. We couldn't go on in the face of Cami's scrutiny. I felt as though I'd been punched in the stomach, like someone had lodged a cannonball there. I'd never be with Blake again.

Glen was asleep. At least there was that. I didn't think I could talk to him and maintain any kind of aplomb.

The emotion of the evening caught up to me and I stayed up half the night huddled over the toilet dry heaving. The loneliness in the bathroom while Glen slept in the next room was staggering. I wanted to be held. By Blake. And after that night, I didn't think I ever would be again.

Blake didn't call the next day. Or the day after. I didn't know if that made the inevitable acknowledgment of our breakup easier or harder.

Glen took my advice on a date and took me to Marrakesh for dinner that Saturday. I loved it there, the inside of the restaurant was decorated to feel like the inside of a Bedouin's tent: tables were set low to the ground, cushions served as chairs, and silk fabric the color of bright ochre spanned the walls and ceiling. We ate with our fingers and stuck dollar bills in the belly dancer's skirt. It was fun; I found myself having a surprisingly good time. Maybe we did just need to rediscover each other. Maybe I wasn't trying hard enough with Glen.

"I want so badly for us to work this out," he said, "but you not being attracted to me... I'm just coming to terms with how you're saying it's a constant. I mean, I had to get over the denial and the hurt." I saw he was actually crying and, for his sake, was glad that the lights were dim. He took my hand. "I feel like every minute we have together is limited. I feel like I've already lost you. I'm trying to find a way to let you go, to let you walk away. I mean, if you don't even want to have sex with me what do we have left? But you're so beautiful and I want to keep you. I'm so happy just sitting here, holding your hand," he said. "You know, I thought we'd have fifty more years of hand holding."

At first I felt sad, too, at the loss of that sweet little dream. And then I thought back to the last time he held my hand. It had been on Valentine's Day, briefly, and only because I'd asked him to. And before that? I remembered holding hands in the car when we were first revealing our attraction to one another. Eleven years ago? It was difficult to feel sad about missing fifty more years of something I'd never had in the first place.

The rest of the weekend was hell. And still, the crazy passion I had for Blake built up like water behind a dam. My body kept burning for him. Everything was in flux and I simply *wanted*. I'd never have him again and I couldn't turn off what I felt for him. It was a private hell of my own crafting. I told myself I deserved it. My trip to New York was only a week away. It couldn't come fast enough.

Chapter Nine

My relationship with Blake was clearly over, I reflected as I filled my suitcase in preparation for departure to New York the next day. I had cried during the lonely days that had passed since the night Cami had gone ballistic on us. Now, I resolved to look forward. As I considered what to bring, I filled the compartments with clothes I felt good in, daring clothes, the closest I could get to New York clothes with my boring Seattle wardrobe. I had black covered.

The trip had started on a whim, as an excuse to clear my head and I found I needed that more than ever. What the hell was I going to do with myself? With my marriage? I needed to lift myself out of the endless loop completely. I tried not to think about Blake. I tried to think about how fun it would be to visit my friend Aimee, to go to museums and eat in restaurants and go for long walks and get lost.

My phone rang and I almost hung up on the call in my eagerness to answer it.

"Good morning sunshine," Blake said and I could hear him smiling. My whole body felt warm in response, like he'd chased all my cloud shadows away and I was bathed in sunlight. "God I've missed you this week," he said.

"You have?" I needed him to say it again.

"Yes. My wife is a complete and utter fucking tyrant and I missed your sweetness. I missed your muchness, milady," he said, like I was Alice in Wonderland.

I was sweetly touched. Sometimes he surprised the hell out of me. I almost started crying. "I thought we were done. I mean, we should be done, Blake. We have to stop. It's too much with Cami. She'll be suspicious now."

"We can lie low. But I'm not done with you, not yet. I'm just getting started."

Zing. Zing zing zing zing zing! I forced myself to breathe. "Blake—" I'd had the best intentions. If we were caught, it would affect so many people. I'd had time to think about it. "After what happened last week... We can't."

"Let me be the judge of that. She's not your wife." He exhaled sharply, I could almost see the smoke streaming from his lips and suddenly I wanted a cigarette. "I'm coming over today, if you'll have me."

"That's your definition of lying low?"

"That's exactly my definition. We've been lying low. And now I ... I haven't been able to taste you for almost a week. I need you, Aleah."

Oh.

"Okay," I said. "If you're sure." My eyes closed in relief. I was pathetic. I had no resolve. And I felt so happy.

"I'm more than sure," he said.

When he arrived I shuddered in his hug until everything that had been building up exploded. I sighed and moaned a little in his arms. "Did you just?" He looked at me funnily. "Did you just do what I think you did?" I purred in his arms. "Oh, little lady, I think you are in need of a spankin'," he said, smiling. "Get on up with you." He pointed to the staircase and issued the first of many delicious slaps on my ass that day.

We romped on my bed a little. He crawled to me, nipped at my neck. He bit a little too hard and I pushed him away and slapped his cheek. Just a little. My hand caressed him on the recoil, and I started pulling at the button holes on the collar of his Polo.

"Last week, with Cami. Before she saw us. I told you it wasn't safe. I trusted you. It wasn't safe, Blake."

"I know. I know. I'm sorry. I was stupid. We got out of it all right."

"It was brutal."

He snorted. "That was nothing. You haven't seen her when she's actually got evidence. Then she goes on a rampage like a tornado through

Oklahoma."

I tried really hard to imagine that.

"You played it perfect, by the way," he said. I resisted the urge to add an *-ly* to his *perfect.* My mind was still trapped in the image of Cami on an actual tear. "Attacking back like that. She respects that. You have to be strong or she'll flatten you. You did perfect."

What I should have said was, *What are we doing? We have to stop.* Instead I said, "Blake, how can you live with her? She is always looking for ways to persecute you."

He sat back on my pillows and a shadow of sorrow deepened the color in his eyes.

"It's my kids. She'd get them. You know how the laws are. Even without my conviction... The deck is stacked against me."

He'd served time for statutory rape. He'd been eighteen. She was seventeen and his long-time girlfriend. It was consensual, but that didn't matter to her big Texas daddy. The law being the law, Blake had done some hard time. And he was right, Cami would spin that for all it was worth.

Blake had celebrated the end of his parole with a party at our house, ages ago. I smiled, remembering our laughter that day.

"What?"

"I was just thinking of your parole party."

He smiled and really looked at me, his eyes found their glow and his smile cracked into a grin as he pulled me to him, kissing me in between his words. "I wanted you, so badly, that day. You in your little, black bikini. Flitting in and out of that hot tub, waving your sweet little ass in my face." He enveloped my whole body in his kiss, wrapping his arms around me, his legs around mine. We melted into each other. "You're my sweetness, Aleah. That's what you are."

I didn't know what to say to that. I just smiled. I couldn't help myself.

"When am I going to see you again?"

"Probably at poker. Unless you're going to pick me up from the airport."

"I could do that, yeah. Or I could get on the plane with you." His voice grew husky. "You could go to the bathroom and forget to lock the door and I could walk in on you. *Oh, excuse me, ma'am,*" he drawled.

"Don't call me ma'am," I said. "You're two years older than I am. You better not slam my head against the wall either." My voice grew lower, softer. I couldn't help it. I was a total sex kitten with him. "Those stalls are so small you'd have to hoist me up against the sink, lower me onto your hips, ride me against the mirror."

"Yeah." He cleared his throat. "So I'm going to go now," he said. "I guess I won't talk to you for a week."

"Why not? I'll have my phone with me."

"But now I've said it and it's the principle of the matter."

I groaned. "You can't go a whole week without calling me," I said, but I knew he would. Maybe it was a good thing. I reminded myself I was going to get my head on straight. I could use a week without the mesmerizing fog of Blake.

There's something about traveling; when you're in an airport you have that freedom to be the person you dream of being. No one knows you at all. It's all image. When I'm in a new place I shine. I carried my head high as I walked tall down Sea-Tac's long corridors of glistening white tile. I knew people saw me. I knew they were watching.

When I got to the gate, I did yoga on the blue Berber carpet while I waited for them to call my rows for boarding. I knew that every male in the vicinity wanted to have sex with me. My hip-opening lunges were the stuff dreams are made of. This confidence was something I rarely carried with me in my real life. And yet I persisted, reaching for the sky, the floor. Displaying my ass. Who was this girl? Was I doing it to prove something? Because I was free of Glen's gloomy presence? Was it because of how Blake made me feel? *Downward dog. Lunge.* My row was called. *Downward dog, jump to forward bend, slow spine roll up, mountain, Namaste.* I gathered my things and heard someone sigh.

Once on the plane I unbelievably had an entire row to myself. A traveler's luxury. I spent the flight journaling and dreaming. What should I do with my life? I asked myself until it became a mantra. *Damned if I know.*

I didn't want Glen. Didn't want to touch him. Didn't need him. I thought of my life with only Glen in it and I couldn't lie to myself any more. The only reason I was able to stay with him was because I was getting that passion fulfilled outside of the relationship. But take Blake away and what I had left with Glen was emptiness, like cracked eggs put back in the container. I didn't want to face that our marriage had moved into a place that was beyond fixing.

It wasn't about blaming Glen. I was angry with myself. It was all about how I had always chosen to abandon my own true desires. Time and again it got so I didn't even know how to listen to them anymore. Maybe I never had.

I felt that if I left him I'd be leaving my entire life. I didn't want to leave poker. I didn't want to leave my proximity to Jennifer. I didn't want to leave my house. And I still wanted—far more—the one I couldn't have. But Blake wasn't mine. Not now, maybe never. Travelling over Minneapolis at nearly 600 mph, it seemed easier to go on without him. I could see he was only a distraction; he wasn't willing to do more than play. Someday, maybe, I'd be worth more to him. But I wasn't his first choice and he only got to pick one. I wasn't the mother of his children. I needed to walk away. I put my headphones on and Bob Marley told me everything was gonna be all right. No woman, no cry.

Chapter Ten

My dear friend Aimee picked me up from the airport. She'd been a regular comrade in our book club before moving to Brooklyn. We'd gone out for coffee and walks, gone to bookstores together. I missed her. She picked me up in a little blue sedan. I was surprised, actually, to know that there were cars other than taxicabs in the Big Apple. The place was just teeming with humanity, with energy, noise and light. The smells, most of them disgusting. And so many people.

Aimee sprung out of the car, a little pixie of a thing with huge attitude. She threw herself at me in a giant hug. It felt so good, like a haven.

"Aleah! I'm so glad you're here. We are going to party, girl!"

Glen called shortly after we made it back to her apartment. "Aleah, I need to start talking to my parents about what's going on," he said without preamble. "You know, between us. So I can get their wise counsel. I don't know anyone who's been married longer than them and I need their support. I need to know if what we're going through is normal."

"Okay." I knew there was nothing I could do about it. I was being informed, not asked. I understood his reasoning, but also had an impending feeling of total shame, sure his story would be lopsided. There was a lot leading up to this point in our marriage from my perspective that he would conveniently not mention. I wanted to be fairly represented. He was controlling the message. But I said none of that. Instead, I opted for, "Somehow this feels like a step towards the end." By the same token, I'd been talking to my family, so it was only fair. I guess the difference was that my family was four states away. His lived fifteen minutes away and we saw them all the time. I'd have to face them soon.

After the call I told Aimee my fears. She said, "No matter what he says, or even if you had a chance to be there, it will be your fault in their eyes. He is the golden child. That's been part of the problem all along, hasn't it?" Damn, she was intuitive.

That night I put on my Catholic school girl skirt, a black T-shirt, and black boots. I felt like a total sex goddess. My period was going to start and all I could think about was Blake. But then we went out into the wash of people on at Times Square and I let myself go in the moment. I wanted to ask everyone I met what *their* story was.

As soon as we got off the subway, I got a huge "Woohoo, love it girlfriend," shout out from a flaming bicycle cabbie. Later, I was having a smoke outside Roxy's diner. I leaned back against the building and kicked one booted foot up on the wall behind me, bending at the knee. A freaky looking short man walked up to me. "Are you working?" he muttered.

Confused, I said, "No."

"You're standing here like that dressed like that and you're not working?" he snapped.

It dawned on me what he meant. My catholic school girl skirt. I was attractive. I was flaunting it. He wanted to pay to fuck me. That was a first. "No, I'm having a cigarette waiting for my friend."

He scowled at me. I thought he was going to spit at me, but he just walked away.

We walked all over Times Square, to Grand Central Station, the NY public library, a park. I loved just being there. I drank it all in. The dirty, glorious humanity. The lights.

The next day we rode the subway to Union Square. We saw Jean Reno on the street, had pizza for lunch, went to Forbidden Planet, saw the Strand. I didn't want to go in. It's not that I'm not in love with books, but I just didn't want to cart any more home. I thought about the two guidebooks and three books I'd brought weighing down my luggage... I really needed a Kindle.

Aimee laughed when I told her I wanted to go to the museum of Natural History. "I thought that was for fifth graders."

"I've never been," I shrugged. We tried to go but it was closed by the time we got there. I felt like we spent all day riding the subway. My period was a day late. Interesting. I decided to wait a few more days before saying anything to anyone. It wasn't like I was ever that regular.

Glen called again the next day.

"So, what do you think?" He asked. "Are you moving to New York?"

Was he actually asking me what I thought? Who was this man and what had he done with my husband? I said, "I don't think it's quite right for me. I'm having a great time and all, I mean, I think I'm actually enjoying it here more than I thought I would. All the energy, the rush of people everywhere, doing everything, anything. It's been crazy." I told him about my experience with the man looking for a hooker.

"Why not move there? Sounds like you already have a job."

"Fuck you."

"See, you already sound like a New Yorker."

Asshole. Suddenly I just felt sorry for him and let go of the fight in me. "Nah. It's wrong for me. For the long run. It's stressful. Constantly. It's also strange how dry it is here. I mean, for a place that is surrounded by water it feels like the concrete obliterates all of it. I know there are richer, more beautiful parts, but, I mean the income it takes to maintain that lifestyle..." Aimee had bragged to me about New York's environmental bent, how small her personal carbon footprint was, but her grapes came wrapped in plastic on a Styrofoam tray. "I don't think I could move here. I don't like what it would do to me."

"Like a city could do anything to you." He sounded really bitter.

"It could. Have you been here?" I knew he hadn't.

I hung up, knowing that I loved Glen, but not the way I need to. Now all the other hard shit would start. Separation. Divorce. Moving. Fuck. I was just so sad it'd come to this. I'd have to leave both the men in my life at the same time. Fuck.

Book Two

Aimee had to work the next day. My period started and I took myself to Manhattan on the subway, trying to do some bigger dreaming while the lights flashed by. Where did I want to live? Work? I watched people, wondering where they were going, what made them happy. I was surprised at how few blondes were around. I wasn't exactly comfortable, but it felt good to be moving, even the weird chugging sway of the subway was comforting, the horrible smells made me feel alive. At least it was new. It felt good to be alone on the subway surrounded by people. I wanted a life with more sun. I knew that much. Seattle depressed the hell out of me.

I got off in the East Village. It felt like desperation there. Frenzied. I walked for blocks trying to find anywhere to sit down. It was hot and all I saw in all directions was cement and buildings crammed together with no space to breathe.

I saw a neon sign flashing "PSYCHIC" with an arrow pointing up some cool, dark stairs. *What the hell*, I thought, and trudged on up. It could be fun. I would see what story the psychic made up with absolutely no help from me.

The madam sat behind the reception desk playing solitaire in what turned out to be a room ornately decorated with luscious red velvet curtains crawling with a gold floral pattern, crystal beads everywhere, plants teeming in places like a little jungle, ochre-colored silk shades on the lamps. It was dark and light at the same time with the lushness of the fabric while sunshine poured into the center of the room through a skylight.

"I can help you?" The woman asked, her accent thick and difficult for me to place. She wore blue jeans and a blouse. She looked perfectly ordinary.

"I wanted to get a reading done," I said.

"Tarot or palm?"

I thought for a minute. I'd never had my hand read. "Palm."

"Come to my table." She got up from the desk and ushered me to the round séance table in the center of the room. "Stand here a moment." I watched her light a sage bundle and pick up a feather. She knelt and worked the smoke up and around my body, fanning it with the feather and chanting under her breath. "Good," she said at last. "Take a breath. Ground yourself."

I did.

"You did quickly. You are good at this. You do this before. You know this. You do yoga," she said rapidly.

"I do," I said, kicking myself for already breaking my commitment not to give anything away.

"Well, sit, sit. Make yourself comfortable." She sat across from me. "When you are ready, show me your hands."

I held them out together in front of me and reached across the table, palms up.

She held them and looked at them for a brief moment. Her hands were dry and slightly leathery, soft and callused at the same time. Her smile, when she looked up at me, was surprisingly genuine. "I like you already," she said. She was beaming.

Everything about her surprised me, actually, from her unassuming dress, her short straight hair, to her openness. She launched into a litany of my attributes. "I can see that you are the one that is good with money; you manage the finances. You are extremely organized; you know the details. And you are also very creative—see the size of the mount of Venus, here." She pointed to the fleshy base of my thumb. "And here though, I see—" Her finger pressed lightly at the base of my index finger. "You passed by the visual arts. You like music. You played... The flute," she said. "For a long time. You were very good. You are good at a lot of things. But you stopped. Suddenly for some reason."

It was a lot to digest. I found myself thinking yes, yes, yes, like I was checking off boxes. Not one thing she said was the slightest bit incorrect, right down to the fucking flute. I was trying to convince myself that the things she was saying were generic and could be said to anyone with reasonable success. But I knew they couldn't. The thing was, they were dead on for me. I did the finances. If Glen did them, we'd be bankrupt by now.

I'd never taken an art class even though I'd wanted to. I'd been a dedicated flutist for eight years. I'd been in the youth philharmonic. I stopped suddenly when I figured out it wasn't what I really wanted to be. I wondered how the hell she was telling all this from my hand. I wondered what any of it mattered. Then shit got real.

"I'm looking at your life line now, the chronology. You have a big loss here," she pointed to a long line crossing my palm, "in your early twenties. Someone you loved deeply left you." That was completely generic, I thought. "Your father," she said. I blinked, revising my criticism. I didn't let myself think about my father. His life was buried in alcohol, but he was sweet and smart and kind. He never seemed drunk, just happy and productive. And then they discovered liver cancer when they went in to remove his pancreatic tumor. By the time he'd acknowledged the pain, he'd only had three weeks to live. He'd died when I was twenty-two.

She might actually be the real deal, I acknowledged to myself. I kept up my poker face.

"Your life is pleasant," she said. "You don't have any major —well, until you get here," she pointed to an oval surrounding what she'd called my lifeline. "You have an oasis of pain, here. Like an island. You will be alone and you will have to get through it alone. But you will come out on the other side. When you are in your early thirties." I was in my early thirties now. It didn't take a genius to figure out what that island of pain was going to be.

"And then it looks like happily ever after. You will live a long time, into your eighties at least. I see a comfortable future. You won't have to rely on your children or family." My breath caught at "children."

"Here," she pointed to a place where a long line diverged from the main. "I see that you will start some sort of endeavor by about the time you are forty. It will power you through retirement. Some kind of business or trade. *Right. Because I am going to make an awesome CEO.*

"And look," she said, pointing to a small intersection of three lines on my hand. It looked like an asterisk. "A star," she said, "Here, here, here, too. All over. Oh! You have lots of them. Lucky!"

She smiled at me and clasped my hands within her own, the session seeming to come to an end.

"Anything else I can answer for you, my dear?"

I hesitated. But, why not? "You said 'children'?"

"Yes, I see them."

Them? "How many?"

"This is not so accurate. It can be off." She shrugged as she turned my hand to the side and curled it into a loose fist. "Maybe sixty percent accurate." It would do. "Three," she said.

"Three children?" How the hell was that going to happen?

"As I say... Not entirely accurate this part the reading. Too many variables, you know?"

I knew. She was completely full of shit.

I paid the woman and tipped her. When I walked down the stairs, back to the concrete, I felt lighter. I turned the corner and found this charming little garden with benches that was open to the public. I sat in the shade and wrote down everything she'd told me, just for ducks.

I took the subway to MOMA, debating whether or not to call Blake. I decided not to. I didn't want to end it, not yet, and I knew that was the next step for us. For me. I couldn't move forward if I were still attached to him.

The museum was airy and spacious. The guard in one of the first rooms I entered tipped his hat to me and said, "You look nice." I was wearing a crisp cotton dress with a floral print, sort of a '50s garden dress. I smiled and felt like my whole afternoon was buoyed by those simple words from a stranger. Serenity flooded me as I looked at all the art. So many people were stuck behind their cameras, taking pictures of the pictures. I wanted to wrest the cameras from their hands, tell them to be present, just experience the actual wonder of it all. I was blown away by the sheer magnitude of Monet's Water Lilies; I'd no idea it was so large a canvas.

I broke down and called Blake once I got outside the museum. I wanted to sever the tie while I was still in a place I could imagine happiness. "Hey there," I said.

He laughed. "I win," he said.

"Sure," I said. "Whatever. I called you first. You win. Listen, I'm calling because I have to tell you something, Blake. And I think I have to say it before I get back, before you call me again. We have to stop what we're doing together."

"Aww," he said. I could tell he thought I was bluffing.

"I'm serious. You can't lose her trust. We should stop." I thought I should step away out of some sort of respect for Glen, and Cami, too. "We have to stop."

"I don't think I can do that," he said. "I think about you all the time." *About me*. "I'll let you know when I'm done with you."

I was angry all of a sudden. *Like I'm a fucking dish towel. All this means is someday he's going to hurt me very badly.* "I don't know, Blake." I didn't know if I was strong enough to pull away with everything else that was going on. I had to try, though.

"There's something you don't know, Aleah. She's going away. For a week. She's taking the kids to her mom's. In New Jersey. For a week. Please, just give me that with you. Please."

"I don't know what to say."

"Say yes," he breathed, suddenly vulnerable.

"When?"

"In three weeks."

A week together. A week.

"I'll think about it."

I'll admit, it didn't take me long before I was scheming. *Where could I ship Glen off to for a week? Where could I pretend to go?*

I headed back to Aimee's just as the sun was setting on the giant buildings. I stared at the Statue of Liberty through the iconic columns and wires of the Brooklyn Bridge. I felt disembodied.

By the next day, the smell of the city had started to make me sick. The stench of urine and vomit at the station on the way home that day was so strong I puked a little in my mouth. It was hard to feel safe. I left the next day for home, or what was feeling more and more just like a house.

There was no one to pick me up at the airport.

Book Three

Chapter One

I'd felt so clear in New York, but as soon as I nestled back into the familiarity of home I felt the cloud of indecision settle back over me. I sank back into my routine of long, empty days. A few hours of spreadsheets and email. Phone calls from my lover. A week floated by and I got all jangly in anticipation of seeing Blake at poker. And then, when I got there, he was utterly cold to me. It was infuriating, his on and off switch. I didn't have one of those. He barely looked at me, not even a smile. It was so disconcerting I threw my game so I could go home early.

The following Tuesday Cami called in the middle of the day to ask if I could watch her kids. "I've got this emergency meeting and I know it's going to run late. The nanny can't stay today and I don't know when Blake's getting home; he's been working late a lot lately. If you could it'd be a lifesaver."

I was so pissed at Blake for having ignored me at poker I almost said no. But she was my friend. And he wasn't the one asking. He didn't even have to know I was going to be there. "Sure," I said. "What time?"

Shortly after I arrived, Flanders, the Porters' neighbor, knocked on the back of the sliding glass door. I didn't even know his real name. It's just that he's such a *hi-diddly-o neighbor!* kind of guy that everyone called him Flanders.

"Hey, Cami mentioned you were going to be over and Laurie and I wanted you to have this." He handed me a Clear Plan Easy fertility monitor. I was mortified. This wasn't the first near stranger connected to us through Cami who'd approached us to "help" with our problem. Who had Cami *not* told that we were trying to conceive? Jesus. I managed to stammer a thank you. He was clearly uncomfortable and made a quick exit. I set the kids up with some finger paints and started cutting up fruit for a snack.

Half an hour later I heard the crunch of gravel under tires in the driveway. Blake found me in the kitchen.

"Cami just told me you were babysitting. You weren't even going to tell me you were here, were you?"

"Nope." *Fuck you*, Blake Porter.

"You sure looked fine at poker the other night," he went on, undaunted by my coldness. "That green T-shirt and no bra, those tight jeans and the evening sun glinting off your hair."

"You couldn't even spare me a *hello*. You made me feel cheap. For the first time, you made me feel cheap. You completely ignored me."

"I couldn't even talk to you, you're right. Not around them," he said, his hand drifted from my shoulder to the small of my back as he caressed me. "Had to avoid temptation. I had to force myself not to chase you and slam you against the wall, to devour you utterly every time you stepped out that door for a cigarette." His eyes trapped me in their intensity. "Erik caught me checking you out a few times. He gave me weird looks. He started watching me like a hawk." He lifted my hair, plied the nape of my neck with kisses. Given how much their language skills were improving lately, I was glad the kids were in the other room. "I think about you every day. I think about you all the time."

He was so smooth. He erased all the hurt with a few small words. I was paranoid beyond belief, knowing that Cami could be home at any minute without warning. I kept having to slap his hands away from me. I did not give in to his desire for a quick fuck. I wanted hours and hours with him. Days, a week, forever. A week. We had a week.

"She's really going to New Jersey?"

His eyes lit up. "Really." He told me the dates. We schemed a little.

The frogs were singing in full force and the stars were shining brightly when Cami got home. "Hey lady," I said giving her a quick hug. "Blake's inside," I said, knowing she'd be wondering why I was outside smoking while her kids were alone in the house.

"Ah, thanks for your help. You're a lifesaver as always. Come in for a bit?"

"Nah, I'm going to get home. Thanks for the offer, though."

Everyday. I think about you all the time. Blake's words echoed in my head as I drove home. But all I was to him was a body; I knew this. I knew he'd break my heart. He bought presents for his wife, treasured his children. All I'd ever have, I had already. I wanted more. I was addicted to being so alive.

The next day I found a week-long Zen meditation retreat at a center a few hours outside Portland. It was to be held the same time that Cami would be with her family. They still had a few openings. I signed Glen up and presented it to him as a surprise gift, a reward for his hard efforts working on our marriage. I showed him the brochure and told him he was going. I almost felt guilty when I saw the pleasure on his face.

"Wow! Thank you!" It was more joy than I'd heard in his voice in ages. He seemed genuinely touched.

I dreamed my way through the next week. I imagined packing my bag of toys and lingerie over and over, memorizing the list so I wouldn't leave anything behind. I didn't dare write it down until after Glen left. I was just a body, I'd tell myself. I was just sex to Blake. I told myself it was just sex for me.

The morning Cami left for New Jersey, I shaved all the hair off my pussy. I decorated myself. I put on a temporary tattoo of the sun, and stuck tiny costume gems along my cunt, like stars. Vajazzling. It was just sex. It was just fun.

Chapter Two

It actually happened. Glen left for his retreat. Cami took the kids across the country. I loaded my little VW bug with a shoebox packed with toys and a suitcase full of lingerie. I decided I would go over to the Porter's dressed as Blake's little school girl. I liked it when he played teacher. I dressed up in my short flannel catholic school girl plaid mini. The black lace threaded through my bra subtly showed through my cream-colored cashmere sweater. My legs went on forever in white thigh-high socks and black pumps with ankle straps. I styled my blonde hair in short braids.

The back country roads seemed longer than usual. I crunched up the gravel drive in my heels and found Blake waiting for me on the front porch. His grin threatened to crack his face in half when he saw me. He knew I did this because he loved it. I felt a reverence from Blake I'd never felt the like of, just from bathing in the light of that smile.

As I stepped up the porch stairs, I felt the lingering ghost of Cami's threatening anger lurking, a shade in my consciousness. Blake took my face in his hands, softly kissed my forehead, my lips. "You're really here," he said, taking the suitcase from me. "Pack light, do you?" He laughed as he hefted it. I had rarely seen him so happy. He was glowing.

"I'm feeling a little gun shy."

"Don't worry. I'll take care of you. C'mon." He stroked my back, then took my hand and led me inside to the kitchen, which smelled decidedly skunky. He passed his little pipe to me, offering me a hit. I smiled that he had it out on the counter, at how free he felt to be himself with Cami out of town. I accepted the pipe and took a deep drag.

I exhaled and he pulled me to him. "Come here, baby," he said and slathered me with kisses, leaving a whispered trail down my neck to the swell of my breasts.

"I can't wait to have you again," he whispered. "It's been far, far too long." He began to tug at my skirt and rushed me into getting my clothes off. I let him. I wanted him to see my decorated pussy. The little press-on jewels sparkled in the late afternoon sunlight streaming in from the window.

"Whoa. You did this for me?"

I didn't deny it. He sank to his knees, his tongue deftly navigating my nether lips, and he licked me softly, eyes cast up from where his face was buried in between my legs, surrounded by my little glittery fake jewels.

"I like your shaved pussy," he murmured.

"Yeah?"

"Yeah."

"I think I do, too."

He pushed me against the small kitchen counter and sucked my breasts, put his hot, hard cock inside me and I gasped with delight. It was always so good with him. Somehow I'd forgotten how good—it was always a complete surprise. He pounded me against the counter until I complained of the bruise I'd have the next day. I followed him to the bedroom and sucked him, licked his balls, rode him. Our playfulness was so fine to me.

His hands were a ghostly whisper caressing my ass, travelling up my back to lift my hair off my neck, which he then brushed with his soft lips, the tease of his goatee. He was alternatively rough and tender. Such a turn on. My body flooded with desire for him, it crashed through me.

He said, "I just love being with you," and I melted. I waited as long as I could.

Maybe a minute.

"I just love being with you," I said.

He fucked me hard, from behind, from the front, and I reveled in the pleasure found in a little bit of pain. He came hard, crying out in such abandon I worried about the neighbors hearing.

I kissed the sweat off Blake's forehead. "I'm going to go put my things away." I slipped back into my panties and headed to the kitchen to get my bag. I intended to go into the spare bedroom to slip into something I could lounge in, but I didn't make it all the way. I heard his footsteps behind me and decided to tease him. I stopped in the hallway and stretched into a forward bend, then down dog. He grabbed me and pushed me into the bathroom, my face pressed up against the towel bar. He yanked down my panties and fingered me.

"My god, you're dripping wet for me. Again." He groaned.

"All day," I said, turning to him. I sucked him off and he stripped the rest of my clothes off and guided me into the shower, hot water beating on us as he pounded into me against the back wall.

We finally made it to the bedroom and he put on a little black cock ring—my eyes fluttered in ecstasy with its insistent rubbing on my clit.

"I knew it would be like this. We'd fuck like rabbits until we collapsed." Blake said, after we'd made it through the initial round of crazy good sex. "I've been dreaming about this time with you for so long. So many things I want to do with you. To you."

"Well, you've just got four of them down," I said.

"You're keeping track?" He laughed. "You would. It's your nature."

The first night I kept trying to get him to go to sleep. He had to work in the morning. But he kept getting hard for me. Unbelievably. Lying against his heaving chest, I thought after eight orgasms maybe we'd reached the end of his stamina for the night. *Battle of Evermore* came on the radio. I told him, "I love this song."

"I know."

"How do you know?"

"'Cause I dig it."

"And you think because you dig it, I'm going to dig it?"

"I know you will." He had this sleepy, sweet, self-satisfied smile that just made me want to eat him up. "You always do."

"Nice," I said, intending only a little sarcasm.

"I've always known that about you and me," he said. "It's the coolest. You actually like what I like. Or you do a damn good job pretending. You never make me feel small." He looked at me with a lion's smile and I knew the night wasn't over yet. By morning, he'd had little sleep, but we'd racked up twelve orgasms before he had to go to work. That's about where I started to lose count.

If I was really honest, the only real reason I wanted to make things work with Glen was so that none of this would end. It seems strange when I say that now, but at the time the two were inextricably linked for me. Leaving Glen was akin to leaving my life. I guess I knew if I was leaving Glen, I'd have to leave Seattle.

Blake called me on his lunch hour. I'd slept in and was still lounging in the sheets.

"Is this my naughty little teacher's pet?"

"Of course."

He laughed. "Oh, girl, you are so much fun. I left you a present," he said. "It's under my pillow. I want you to put it on for me. Now."

My body tingled with anticipation as I reached over to his side of the bed and lifted the pillow. I recognized the pinkie-finger-sized ass plug for what it was, though I'd never actually put one in before.

I must have made some kind of noise. "I take it you found it?" he said.

"Yes."

He lowered his voice. "Good. There's lube in the bathroom under the sink. Enjoy yourself. I can't wait to get home. I'm trying to get out early, but the boss's son is here watching my every move."

I took my time in getting ready. I made coffee first, ate some fried eggs and bacon. I took a shower. And then I went and found the lube.

It was a distinctly uncomfortable sensation, sliding the little jellied plug into my ass. I took it millimeter by millimeter at first. The plug tapered slightly, so that the deeper it went, the wider it got. Just before the end of its pinkie-length, it contracted to a skinny neck and then flared out big, flat head. I slid it in slowly until I was on the edge of pulling it back out, the stretch was so uncomfortable. You wouldn't think something so small could be so commanding, but all my awareness was on that strange sensation of discomfort. I wanted to pull it out but I pushed instead and was rewarded with a sudden sense of rightness as the widest part passed and the neck slid into place.

That's when the fun began. Every time I moved—got up, sat down, walked, or stopped—I felt the little nudge of pleasure and pain combined in the pressure of that plug. Goddamn Blake Porter. He put me in that place of dizzying sensation for three hours before he got home. And when he got home, he wasn't alone. He brought the boss's son, Peter, with him, ostensibly to borrow a tool. And so Blake and I pretended to be just friends hanging out, all the while I could feel Blake's eyes on me. I knew he loved watching me walk, knowing I was feeling the constant pulse of sweet pain at his bidding. My knees quaked with every step I took.

We hung out in the backyard, at the pool. I found it was much easier to bend at the hips than at the knees. I gave them both a juicy view of my ass when I went to the cooler to get us all fresh brews. I was wearing super short denim cutoffs and my bikini top. When I rose up, I flipped my hair over my shoulder. I felt like a girl in a Corona commercial.

Everything was an escape, I realize now. I could never be a girl in a beer commercial; I was the brainy one. God, though, it was fun to sink into that fantasy. We hung out. We chatted. We smoked, swam, and drank. We had a rare, relaxing summer day by the pool. But three was a crowd. I'd waited for hours, all day, for Blake to be home. Mine. Alone. This was *our* time together. Blake began to hint that Peter should go. At last he did, after turning fifteen minutes into two-and-a-half anguishing hours.

Blake circled my body with his arms from behind as we heard the tires retreating on the driveway gravel. He lifted my hair and kissed the soft hollow where my neck met my shoulder. I moaned a little, sank against him.

"Peter said you were hot," he whispered in my ear. "He asked if I was fucking you."

"And you said?"

"I said 'Of course not.' Then he asked if you were single."

"Interesting. He's not exactly my type."

"That's what I told him." He laughed. "Then he asked if you were the type to like two cocks in you."

I shook my head. The lanky, mustachioed, mullet-haired boy was definitely not for me. "And you said?"

"I said, 'Dude, she's my friend's wife.'"

"Oh. Maybe I shouldn't have been wiggling my ass so much."

Blake laughed. "You wiggle that sexy little ass any time you want, okay?"

He was tender with me that evening. I mean, first he fucked me on the grass, with that ass plug in... Delicious. I even thought, *maybe I would like two cocks in me*. Blake helped me get the plug out, touched my back softly as we slowly walked to the kitchen. He wiped me clean, transforming every stroke of the damp towel into a caress, and we made dinner together. He found every excuse to brush his hand across my ass, reminding me of the deliberate pain, the pleasure in the bruised absence of the plug. He grilled up steaks and I made garlic butter green beans and cauliflower mash.

I'd think of Cami, so far away in Jersey, at odd times. Like when I was looking for something in the kitchen and it was stored in the last place I would ever think to put it. Measuring cups in a cupboard? Plates under the counter? Who did that? Maybe she ordered in a lot. I thought of how different we were. And then I decided not to think of her at all. It was easier not to dwell on the ramifications of what we were doing. Blake and I existed in a space outside of time, removed from normal life, unaccountable.

When I think of the days that followed I think of so, so, so much sex and all of it really good. We agreed on this. Beyond that, everything blurred together. I have moments in my memory, but I couldn't tell you what happened when, or what was in between. I reveled in the power of our melded bodies, in the rush of life flowing through me.

"You're so hot," he would say, over and over. I didn't get tired of it. The depth of our hunger for one another continued to be a revelation. In the candlelight he ran his hands over my shoulder, the curve of my thigh, down my leg as I lay there next to him. "You have such an intriguing figure, Aleah. Long torso, lithe legs, curvy hips, a small pot belly of definition, here—" He pointed to my abdomen. "In your sacral chakra." I could feel the energy he funneled in a swirling mass toward the root chakra. This was poetry to me. I felt every bit of it. The way he moved the energy around in my body, powerful and magical. The fingers and waves of energy as he pulled it from his heart to mine, down through my back and then channeled it into our center as he thrust into me. *Ohmygod powerful.* Did he know what he was doing to me?

"I love you," I breathed in his ear and my eyes flew open. I couldn't believe I'd said it. Quickly, I followed with, "I love you pounding into me."

As he slipped inside of me again he said, "I love you..." The space after those words was long enough for me to catch my breath and hold it; I froze with the tension. "Inside," he amended. I was on a plane of pure bliss and surrendered as he came. It felt like a sheaf of heavy velvet blanketed me. I lay back in a stupor. Blake shook his head, kneeling beside me as I lay on the bed.

"What?" I said.

"These orgasms are so powerful. If one of those doesn't make you a baby, I don't know what will."

I sat bolt upright and looked at him, startled. "What?"

"You heard me."

"There's no way I'm pregnant," I told him. "Even if I were fertile it's the wrong time of the month." And then I wondered, was he trying to give me the present I most desired? Or testing me to see if I was honoring his parameters? We were both on the tightrope, a balancing act, trying not to fall. "Why are you even talking about that?"

"Just thinking about what it would be like if you were a mom," he said. "You know, if you have a vaginal birth it will loosen everything up down there."

I looked at him. We weren't using birth control, hadn't for months. I hadn't used it with Glen for... well, ever. I clearly wasn't fertile. "It's kind of a moot point," I said.

"I just meant it was really good, Aleah. Don't make it into more than it is. This is the best sex ever. You're like a virgin down there, every time. A virgin who gives good head."

"Does it make you want to sing Madonna songs?" I asked and laughed. The next song that came on the radio was *Like a Virgin*. We howled. I felt at one with the universe.

"See, if we were together we'd never get anything done," he said the next afternoon. We were still in bed.

"Sure we would," I said. I knew myself. I couldn't sit still doing nothing for too long. "We would," I insisted. *If we were together?*

"You don't think we'd just fuck and fuck? I mean... About the last ten orgasms have really blown my mind," he said. "So amazing. This is more than just fucking or even making love. This is primal, transcendent. You are the perfect drug."

"That something is still there—" I gestured back and forth between us.

"Crazy ass pheromones."

"Crazy ass something." I ran my hands over his nipples and he shuddered.

"No," he said. "We both know it's more than that. I still don't know what to make of this. I don't know what this is." He mimicked my gesture.

"I don't have an answer for you. I just accept it," I said. "What is there to know?"

"I know you're my every fantasy come true."

Shutup shutup shutup. I blinked. I stopped breathing. *Unfuckingbelievable.* These were the kinds of things I desperately wanted him to say and that he absolutely could not say to me. My toes jutted out over the imaginary abyss. I didn't want to fall. I could imagine myself so easily, bones shattered, my body unrecognizable. I was just his fantasy, I told myself. None of this was real.

Days slipped by. Days and nights full of sex. It was Friday before we wound down at all. "Let's sit outside awhile," Blake said, picking a robe out from his closet. I expected him to put it on himself, but instead he turned to me and slipped it over my shoulders. "It's cold out. You're not dressed for it." His hands slipped into the folds of the flannel robe and stroked the white satin of my lingerie. I shivered with goose bumps in response, my nipples perking up.

"Oh, you're sweet," I said as he wrapped it around me.

"It's just treating you the same way you treat me." He paused, his gaze steady. "You are always considerate, kind, compassionate, passionate... "

He would have gone on, but I kissed him softly to shut him up, so that he wouldn't see the soft tears of happiness glistening in my eyes.

We sat under the stars on the back porch talking for hours, sharing stories. Amidst our words we couldn't stop touching. We couldn't go twenty seconds even, there was such an urgency between us to be close. When he got up to refill our drinks I yearned for him, the absence of his body was that noticeable. I felt like when he walked away, so did my joy.

He came back and straddled the bench behind me; I nestled back against him and stared up at the stars. "I'm jealous of Cami, you know. Her ability to be with you, like this, out in the open." I laced my fingers through his.

"But she never is like this." His thumb stroked my palm.

"Doesn't matter. She can be. I can't. I wish I could sit alone with you in a restaurant and not draw suspicion. I want to be able to be with you without hiding."

"I know. I'm happy, too, Aleah."

Something about the darkness, maybe because I couldn't see his eyes, his face... I got brave. "I know why you stay with her... I understand the kids. It's just that... You don't seem really happy. How is that good for them?"

His thumb stopped moving. "Make no mistake," he said. "I'm with Cami until the end."

"I know," I said.

"I'm not going to marry you. Even if everything fell apart."

"I know," I said.

"I know you know or this would not be happening," he said, moving his fingers back and forth between us. "But you're right. I've told her from the beginning, I have a hierarchy of happiness. It's me first, then her. She's the same way."

In his own way I knew he was searching for a way to justify what we were doing, what we'd already done. This was his happiness. He'd told her it came first. I knew he felt guilt in a way I didn't. He was trying to find a way to make it all right; I knew he needed what we had. Without it, she'd flay his soul to shreds. I gave him what he needed to survive. "I would never do anything to damage your relationship."

"I know."

"But if something happened... You might call me."

"Who else would I call? Duh." He seemed not to realize he'd said something completely the opposite just moments before.

His phone rang. "It's Rex," he mouthed as he answered it. "Hey, Dad."

They talked for a while and I heard Rex ask about the family, the kids, and Donna, Blake's sister. I hadn't seen her in a while. Blake pointed to me and to the phone. He covered the speaker and whispered, "He's asking about you." I didn't know what to think. It was nice that Rex thought of me but I didn't know I was even a blip on his radar.

"You know, she's just trying to figure out what she wants to do with her life, I think."

I heard Rex's response loud and clear. "Well, tell her to settle down and quit thinking so much." I liked the advice.

"All right, Dad. Well, I gotta go. Love you, too."

Blake went in to get us some water and came back out on the front porch, a candle burning in his hand. "I'm having a good time," he said. We'd been talking for hours.

"Me too," I said.

"No, I mean I'm having a really good time just like this, just sitting here talking to you." He seemed a little surprised. "I thought we might run out of things to say."

"I know," I said. "Me too. I mean, I'm having a good time, too."

"I wish my honeymoon had been like this. I don't even remember the sex on my honeymoon. What I remember is that I didn't want to be alone with Cami. You know me, go, go, go, do, do, do. I couldn't stop and just be with her like I can with you."

"Me too," I said. "This would have been a perfect honeymoon. I couldn't even get wet for Glen on ours, even then. I remember him turning to me at one point and asking what the fuck was wrong because he was randy as a goat and why wasn't I? Let me tell you how attractive *that* was."

"I'm sorry."

"We all lie in the beds we make," I said.

Later, Blake guided me back to the bedroom and we made sweet, gentle love. Our energy was so alive. I could feel him everywhere, all the way through me. I drifted off, exhausted and awoke to him staring at me. I told him, "I can so imagine living somewhere close to the beach with you. Someplace with fine white sand and the kind of turquoise water you can see straight through to the ocean floor. We'd live cheap and spend the rest of our lives being happy together."

"Yeah, that would suck," he said. We laughed. "I feel so at peace right now." He had a sleepy smile on his face and I knew he didn't feel that way often.

Around 4 a.m. Blake rolled over and propped his chin up on his hand. "This is about the time in the morning I'd tell a girl I love her. But that was before I knew better." We were so tired. Blake kept saying words that were disconnected to other words, like half of the conversation was only in his mind.

"I could fall in love with you so easily," he said. "But..."

It felt like we'd been dancing around this all weekend. I was a little tired of the game. "But what?"

"But I can't let myself feel that way."

The truth is there is no such thing as no strings attached. I mean, that's something you agree to, sure. I could hold to it in the beginning but not anymore. "You either feel that way or you don't," I said. "You can't control it."

He looked at me wistfully, his sleepy green eyes tinged with gray, and yawned. "You know. I don't have to say it."

"It would be nice if you did," I whispered and a long moment later he responded with a snore. I don't know if he'd heard me. *Poor, tired man.*

Being with him was so satisfying. Sometimes I thought it was the only way I was going to be able to keep myself sane. I realized, though, as I lay there looking at the man sleeping next to me, I was living a dream that had to end. I resolved that when the weekend was over, everything would be over. I'd never be his wife. He didn't love me enough; he loved his kids. I had to step away.

In the morning, he followed me into the bathroom and said, "I didn't tell you I loved you last night, did I?"

"No, you didn't," I said, a chill in my tone. Did he feel the need to rub it in? I turned the water on in the shower and adjusted the dial.

"Good. Because that would complicate things," he said.

"Would it? Seems like they're pretty complicated already." I stepped into the shower and let the hot water pound on my neck. I turned into it, letting the streams hide my tears. When I got out he was still standing there. He wrapped a towel around me and held me to him. I couldn't stay angry, couldn't keep from touching him. "Stop telling me what you think I need to hear," I said. "I just want you to be real with me."

"Aleah." He spoke my name with his lips buried in my wet hair. I could feel him shaking his head. "Let it be for now. Come play with me." It was our last day together. Glen would arrive the next afternoon and I needed to be there when he got home.

We played.

I woke the next morning, our last morning, to see Blake propped up next to me, watching me.

"You don't sleep much, do you? Been watching me long?"

He smiled a slow smile and took the time to breathe before saying, "I could watch you forever." He loved me with his eyes, as if he were memorizing every strand of my hair, my eyes, my lips, my chin. He kissed me softly on the lips. "Good morning, lover." And then, stroking my hair, he said, "When it's time, you should just leave. You know. No goodbyes, just slip out." He was quiet after that and so was I, as his words slowly hit me.

I started to cry. "That's not going to happen." It was over. He looked at me through clear gray eyes clouded with misery. He was crying. "Are you telling me it's time now?"

"Yes. I think you should go." His words came out in a hoarse whisper.

I slipped out of bed and started crying in earnest as I got dressed.

It was over. I don't think he knew it yet, but for my part I was resolved that it was over. I was done playing with fire, fucking up his family. I managed to make it out the front door, load up the bug and then realized

I'd left the car keys behind. I went back in. Blake came up behind me. "I miss you so much already," he whispered into the back of my neck. Glittering energy soared through me. He breathed into my neck through my hair, clutched me to him. I melted. A lead anvil lodged in my heart; a tear slipped down my cheek. I walked back to the car and drove away.

Chapter Three

I unpacked the moment I got home Sunday morning, smelling everything as I pulled it out of the suitcase. If it smelled like Blake, I stashed it in the back of my closet. The rest I washed. A lot smelled like him. My Bambi T-shirt ("That's your porn name," Blake told me when I wore it), my black vinyl corset ("Needs a dog collar," he'd said. I told him I'd brought a fat black ribbon to tie around my neck. "Yeah, that's hot."), and my pirate outfit (blousy poet's shirt and tight black vinyl pants), among others.

I was deliriously tired. I'd kept an inventory of what I packed, to make sure I brought everything back with me. I crossed things off the list as I unpacked them, eradicating the evidence. There was one item I couldn't find. I called Blake in a panic.

"Hey, I need you to look for my brown belt. I think I left it by the couch. It's not in my bag."

"All right, lady. But I already vacuumed. I don't think it's there."

I looked down and saw the buckle on my jeans. "Damn, I'm tired," I said. "I'm wearing it."

He laughed. "Take a nap, woman."

"Good idea. I think I'll do that." My bed looked decidedly inviting just then.

"Sweet dreams," he said.

"You too."

"Oh, they'll be sweet. I'll be dreaming of you."

Ahh. I missed him, and my body still wanted more. I took a few minutes to color in thirty-six blue boxes on my fertility chart, roughly spacing them across the week. Then I crawled into bed and played with myself for a long time, finally succumbing to sleep a few hours before Glen got home from his retreat.

Sadie barked excitedly when the car pulled in the drive. I woke up and pulled on a T-shirt and leggings, made my way downstairs. Glen came into the house, suitcase in hand, wearing a baggy sweats and a T-shirt that hung loosely and accentuated the paunch of his seemingly more and more ape-like frame. I don't know that he was actually getting more out of shape, but in comparison to Blake's physique, Glen was a slouch. Glen beamed when he saw me; he seemed really happy. I was glad for him.

"Hey," I said. "Welcome back. You have anything else in the car?"

"Yeah, my meditation pillows are in the back." He smiled, but he didn't move in to hug me. He didn't offer even the slightest kiss on my cheek. I helped him unload.

"How was it?"

"Good," he said after a quiet moment.

"Yeah? What was it like?" I don't know if he was feeling quiet or just ignoring me, but it took him twenty minutes and two reminders to tell me anything else of his trip.

I actually felt angry that he was home, that he was in my space, taking my time, investing nothing in talking to me. He didn't even ask how my week was. I mean, I'm glad I didn't have to answer, but it was weird that he didn't ask. I wondered if he was lying to himself about how much he loved me. Or was I just so easy to take for granted?

It was completely unfair that I was attached to a man who didn't know how to love me and that I had to leave the one who did. I wished for a distraction from the searing pain; it was like a sunburn on my heart. I managed to pass the time and make it through the day. I took another long nap. I took a shower. I went for a walk. I called my mom. I called Jennifer. I ordered pizza and streamed something from Netflix on the TV. I had some work to do and brought my laptop and paperwork to the couch. Glen sat near me and eventually fell asleep. I helped him to bed and crawled in next to him. It was 11:40 p.m. and I missed Blake so much my heart actually ached, fingers of energy radiated out from my center to my nipples, belly, and throat.

My cell phone vibrated on the nightstand, waking me at 12:40 a.m. It was Blake. I picked up, walking to the bathroom with a glance over my shoulder to make sure Glen hadn't woken up at the disturbance. I told Blake, "I've just missed you so much," before either of us said hello.

"You think you've missed me," he breathed. I could hear the hunger in his voice.

"I just want to come over," I said before I thought. I ached for him; my whole body throbbed.

"Come on over," he said with that delightful twang.

"Really?"

"Come on," he urged again, huskily. "Cami's not home until tomorrow."

I told myself, *It's still the weekend. I'm not breaking my promise to myself. It will be over when the weekend is over. But it isn't. Cinderella's coach hasn't turned into a pumpkin, not yet.*

The roads were empty and I made very good time. Before I knew it, I was pulling into the gravel driveway. It was so dark, I didn't see him at first. I got out of my bug. I could barely see the outline of his truck in the blackness of the night. The driver-side door was open and the radio was on so I poked my head around and looked for him in the cab. He wasn't there. I turned to the house and saw the intense orange glow of a cigarette in the dark. He sat on the stairs.

"Hello," I said, moving toward him.

"Hi," he said, rising. When I drew near enough he pulled me close, holding me tight to him. I was so happy to see him I was almost crying. The crisp racket of crickets filled the night.

"I know," he said. "I know."

I was still so tired. All I wanted to do was be near him. I bummed a cigarette off him, and sat on the stair next to him.

"Did you get any sleep?"

"No," I said and realized it wasn't true. "Well, some. Not nearly enough."

"Me either," he said. "I couldn't sleep."

I tried to tell him about my day, "It was weird when Glen got home, the emptiness of it, the hollow place in my heart. He wouldn't even talk to me." The words coming out of my mouth stopped making sense even to me. "Like the, like there wasn't any, like—"

"Here's how it was for me," he said, rescuing me from drowning in blather. "I spent the whole goddamn day cleaning up. I worked my ass off. The Flanders came over and Penny entertained their kids in the pool while Flanders and I barbecued. I'm exhausted and... And every fucking place I look, *every fucking place*, Aleah, I see you. On the couch, both couches, in the hall bath, in the office, lounging in the kitchen door frame, bending down in front of me in the hall, on my bed, in the shower, in the kitchen, in the pool, on my front porch. I see you and I miss you so goddamn much. And then I see the phone and all I want to do is call you and the Flanders just won't go. They're hanging out forever. Finally one of the kids has a complete meltdown and they realize they should go home and finally—*finally*—they leave. But it's freaking late. I think of crawling into a bed you aren't in and I think of you feeling the same anguish that I do. So I called you... And now you are here."

I felt like a goddess. I was speechless.

We went inside and snuggled. I told him, "I don't care if we fuck, I just want to be with you."

"I know." He said it a lot that night.

We did fuck, though, and it was sweet and wonderful and primal and hungry. I was wet for him and he was still hard for me. "Your stamina just amazes me," I told him.

"So does yours." We snuggled and he kept trying to cover me with a blanket to keep me warm. He seemed determined to take care of me, protect me, even though I told him I was plenty warm now that I was with him.

We fell asleep and half woke up around two. He said, "You know we're just going to fuck all night."

I was reminded of the first night together, when he'd said the same thing. "Do I?" I said. "I'm not sure I do."

He grinned a wicked grin and plied me with kisses that led to more.

We were giddy in our exhaustion. Most of our sentences started with "I love..." and ended with anything we could think of to say to fill up the end of that sentence as long as it wasn't "you." *I love ...what you do to me ...how you feel ...your skin against mine ...the way you kiss me ...the way you hold me ...being with you ...the color of your eyes ...how hot you get for me.*

At 5:00 a.m. I told him, "I have to go." I wanted to be home before Glen awoke. Thankfully he was a sound sleeper and Sadie knew better than to bark at me.

Blake pulled me close. "No you don't."

"I really should."

He shook his head.

"You're so beautiful," I whispered to his resting figure, holding his hand and softly kissing him at the temple. I got up reluctantly and started pulling my clothes on to leave. Blake lay prone on the bed, staring. "I love being with you, Aleah," he said with a conviction that caught my attention.

I held back from returning his words this time, knowing that I could go deeper, but if I did, and he pulled away, I'd be deep in love with no hope of return and no ability to move on with my life. I couldn't do that to myself. I couldn't dare hope this would have a happy ending.

"It's pretty amazing with you," I told him instead. "You blow me away, the way you connect with me and move all that sparkly amazing energy all through my body. It blows me away how I feel you everywhere."

He stared at me. "No one's ever been able to feel that before. No one's ever even noticed."

"Well, I did. I didn't know you were doing it consciously."

He stared at me, disbelief and reverence shining in his eyes. I looked at him, knowing I had to end this. It was all or nothing time for me. "Relationships aren't static, Blake. We can't stay in this halfway place. We can deepen or pull back, but I can't stay here emotionally. Not anymore. We're teetering on the brink and you know that can't last."

"Stay here," he said.

"I can't," I said. "Not possible."

"So, are you breaking up with me?"

"I don't know," I said. "Am I?" And then the conversation was full on.

"I know," he said. "I know what you're thinking. I'm thinking it too. This week with you... You know how I'm the doer, always on the go. With you, there was such peace. It was the first time I've ever felt like I could just be. What do you call that?"

"Bliss?" It was the closest word I could find.

"I call it love. To me it felt like love. We talked our way around it all weekend. I knew that first night something was different. I just wanted to be with you. The whole next day at work I couldn't stop thinking about you. Don't think I haven't lain awake nights wondering if I shouldn't give it all up and take a chance with you. Don't think I don't think about you all day long. I envy where you're at right now, with your marriage. Free to start over. Free of kids and family."

"I don't know, Blake," I said. "All I know is I've never felt anything like this. I'm scared I won't find it anywhere else."

"I know. I never have either. Not even in the beginning with Cami, not ever. But I'm not going to leave my kids. I'm not going to do that to them. And, it's one thing when it's just sex. I mean, Cami doesn't deserve to be cheated on, but she certainly doesn't deserve to be cheated on and then have me fall in love with the other woman. It's starting to spill over and I can't keep it separate any more. It's starting to affect my marriage."

"Then it's over." I laughed a little. "I've never had anyone break up with me because it was too good before." We laughed hard and I started to hyperventilate.

"No tears."

"I'm not crying," I said, silent fat tears dropping from my eyes.

"I'm going to hate every minute of it, Aleah. I'm going to miss the hell out of you. I'm going to be aching every day." He caught his breath. "No tears," he said again and I realized he was talking to himself. His eyes had changed to a soft gray, milky with tears.

He went to the bathroom and rifled through something on the counter, then came over to me and placed a large ring in my palm, a men's ring. "A memento," he said as he wrapped my fingers around it, but not before I saw that it was heavy silver with a giant clouded red stone. "My mother gave it to me," he said. It was heavy in my palm. "I want you to keep it."

I slipped it on my middle finger.

"It fits," Blake said, astonished. "Wow." He rummaged in the closet for a bit and pulled out my favorite dark blue T-shirt of his. "Take this, too," he said. "It's my favorite shirt." Of course it was.

We went outside and just held each other for a while. I buried my face in the hollow of his shoulder, tried to memorize the way he smelled, the solidity of his gorgeous muscles, the warmth in his grasp, the tenderness of his caress. I knew he didn't want to let go. If he felt a tenth of what I was feeling, he never wanted to let go. I made myself pull away a bit.

I looked up and met his eyes and said, "I love you."

"I know," he said.

I waited, but there was nothing else.

I gave him a quick hug and a final sweet kiss and said, "Goodbye, Blake Porter."

"Goodbye, Aleah Clayton," he said.

I turned and didn't look back.

Wanting nothing more than to run, I took each agonizing, crunching step on the gravel as slowly as I could. I got in the car and started driving. I made it to the end of the drive before I started crying. Hell, I was shaking, sobbing. I pulled out onto the empty country road and pressed the gas pedal. My mind raced with all of it. Not just the last half hour, day, week. No, I thought of every time he'd been over, every time we'd loved each other, every blue box I'd put on my fertility calendar. I remembered and I cried. I screamed out the anguished love songs with Florence + the Machine, a permanent fixture in my CD player. The dog days were over.

It couldn't have just ended. Not like that. I made it down the hill and maybe half a mile down the road before I turned around and drove back. I managed to dry my tears as I navigated the curvy back country road and pulled back into the drive. I deserved a better ending.

I let myself in and Blake found me in the hallway, smiled that goofy ass "heh" smile of his, and grabbed my hand.

"C'mon. I was looking for the phone to call you," he said. "That wasn't supposed to go down like that." He led me down the hall and fell back on the bed with me in his arms and we kissed and kissed.

"You know, I was figuring out in the car, what our track record was. You know, just how crazy we've been."

He laughed. "Of course you were."

"You want to know, don't you?" I looked at him, waiting.

"Go on," he said.

"We have fucked an average of once every thirty-six hours since we started."

"How many this week?" he said.

"Thirty-six. About."

"Plus one," he said and I raised my eyebrow. "No," he said. "You're right. I can't. I am spent." He sighed. "All I could think about was you, when you were gone. Everywhere I went, I saw you. I missed you." He held my face close, kissed me. He started to cry, turned away. I pulled him toward me and kissed his tears away.

"I love you," I whispered against him.

"I know," he said. I shook my head softly in his hands. "I know because I can feel it; I see it. It's so clear. Everything about you tells me that over and over. I know, Aleah."

That's when I realized he wasn't being a smartass when he said this. I'd been reading him wrong all this time. When he said *I know,* it meant *I love you.*

"Is it so hard to say?" I asked as he pulled me in close.

"Look at me," he said. "Look at me." His eyes were gray and clear. Tears streamed down his cheeks. "I love you," he said, the words filling me with wonder. I felt him shudder against me. I knew it cost him to admit his feelings to me aloud. He buried his head in my shoulder.

I nodded. He kissed me again in the hallway and again at the door. He walked me out and I said, "Goodbye," and walked halfway to the bug, my head held high and my hand in front of my face to cover how my bottom lip was trembling. I turned back and blew him a kiss. He reacted visibly to it, closing his eyes and rocking back as if hit.

I made it back to the car before my shoulders shook uncontrollably and the pain rolled through me. It was over. It was over. I drove a mile to be sure he couldn't hear me, then rolled down the window and screamed my sobs into the wind on the lonely country highway.

Chapter Four

I drifted through the next week in a cloud of aimless sadness. I couldn't keep the gray from seeping into my day-to-day. I managed to wake and eat and work and sleep. My life was not what it should be. And yet, I didn't know how to fix it. I wanted to hit the rewind button by ten or eleven years and start things over. I wanted to be with Blake even though I knew I couldn't. It was slowly killing me. It ruined me for Glen. I hated that. Glen was so good to me, I told myself. Understanding, encouraging, compassionate, unendingly patient. He was a good person. I struggled to find contentment. I didn't want to settle. Everything sucked. I found myself sinking back into a strange kind of despair that matched the constant gray weather of a timid Seattle summer.

I did what I could to move on. I looked into what it would take to go back to school and change jobs. I really tried with Glen. What else could I do?

Blake called me on Tuesday. I lit up, pulses of an achy desire throbbing through me when I saw it was him. But I didn't answer the phone. I was Glen's. I had to try. And then that night we had awful, awful, unfinished sex. It wasn't fun from the start. I was tired and he said he wanted me in the driver's seat. I just wasn't into it. He grew soft and I was dry and no one went home happy. I ached for Blake. I ached for his voice, his touch, his laugh.

I shouldn't be in a rush to end things. I don't need to make my life harder, I told myself. I knew I had a roof over my head, food to eat. But every day I wondered why I was still in the marriage. Yes, I was selfish. Yes, I wanted to maintain the comfortable lifestyle his salary afforded. On my own, I'd struggle to make my ends meet with my meager paycheck. It would be like I'd just graduated college all over again. Days grew bleaker. It became more and more apparent to me that everything would be better if I just went away.

The days bled together, a constant gray miasma. I took showers. I made dinners. I filled out spreadsheets and answered emails. There was nothing I was doing that couldn't be done by someone else. No reason to be. I didn't really think of how I would do it, not yet.

Sunday morning I went for a walk with Jennifer. It bothered me that I couldn't think of anything that I could give her. My collection of first editions she wouldn't care about. My clothes wouldn't fit her. She had cats, I couldn't give her my dog. But jewelry, maybe... We had different styles but I thought she would like the memento of me.

When I got home, Glen was waiting for me at the kitchen table. He could have my father's clock. He would do right by it. "I want to talk," he said, his voice hard.

"All right." I could tell he was angry. All I wanted to do was crawl in bed and cry, but I had to stay and allow him to be angry with me and blame me.

"I can't hold out without the hope or sight of change any longer."

I started crying. "Glen, I think I need help."

"Oh, I definitely think you need help."

"No, I mean, I need help with depression."

"Yeah, I'm worried about you. You need help. I want a divorce."

Just like that.

"Really?" I said. "I want to go back on the meds. Maybe it would be better if we waited 'til after that to make this decision. I'm not ready to pull the trigger yet, Glen," I said. I wanted to try. I couldn't be a failure at everything.

"I'm ready," he said. "I can't go on like this. I want a divorce."

"Oh." I sat with that for a while. "You sound pretty certain."

"I am."

"Oh. Okay." I wanted to melt away. I wanted it all to end.

I was a failure at everything.

Chapter Five

"I have to go," I said, picking up my phone and wallet. Glen didn't try to stop me. I walked out the front door and kept on walking. I didn't need to cry. My system flooded with its own version of Novocain. I didn't feel relief. I didn't feel anything other than the dull ache of the constant pain I'd grown used to. I knew I was sick. I had been there before, the place where you can't remember what happiness feels like. I'd rigged little red flags to go up to tell me I needed to ask for help. They'd been popping.

I called Jennifer. "Jennifer, I need help."

"What's wrong?" Her voice was instantly calming and concerned at the same time.

"Depression," I said. "I'm really fighting it right now."

"Where are you?"

"Walking to the grocery store. I'm going to get a mocha and a donut."

"Okay, hon. I'm on my way."

No questions. Just, *I'm there for you.* That was the difference between Jennifer and Glen. The difference between a best friend and my husband. I wished I could have married her.

Jennifer found me at the coffee counter in the bakery. The darling little gran-lady who always made my mochas asked how I was. Jennifer patted my shoulder. "I've had better mornings," I said, swallowing back tears. "My husband just asked me for a divorce."

"What!" Jennifer said. Her eyes flew wide open and she squeezed my shoulder.

"I'm so sorry, hon," the mocha lady said, sliding my drink towards me. I dug into my back pocket. She waved my money away. "Oh no, no. Men are bastards. This one's on me."

"Thank you," I said. There was so much kindness in the world. I didn't deserve any of it, but it tasted sweet all the same.

Jennifer led me to her car. "You're coming home with me," she said. So I did.

She made me food and I ate. After an hour she made chai tea for us. I held the cup in my hands, letting the warmth seep through me.

"So, he asked for a divorce?" she prompted at last.

"Yes. I told him I was struggling with depression and needed help. He agreed that I needed help and said he's tired of waiting for us to work out and he wants a divorce."

She nodded. "So, you've been struggling to come to that yourself, right? I mean, how do you feel about it?"

"I don't feel anything. Numb. Empty." I thought a while longer. "It's funny, I don't really care. I mean, I think I have spent the last seven months agonizing over whether or not I should end my marriage. I couldn't find a way to leave and I couldn't find a way to stay, not really. And now I'm just numb and I don't have the energy to figure out what to do next. I just... I don't have anything to hope for, Jennifer."

She looked at me with the calm and compassion of the ages. "Stay with me tonight. We'll get you to the doctor's tomorrow, get you back on the meds. One step at a time, Aleah. It'll be okay."

"Okay," I said, not believing but choosing to trust her nonetheless.

I managed to wade through the hours between then and the next morning. Jennifer took me to the doctor's and to the pharmacist to get my prescription filled. I popped the first pill on my way to normalcy. They tell you it takes two weeks to kick in, to experience the full effect of the meds. But there must have been a placebo effect, or maybe they just work super effectively on me. I knew from before it would only take a day or two to feel the difference, for my brain to start making connections, to start believing I might again have a worthwhile future.

That afternoon, I went back to my house. I looked around and realized it wasn't a home and it never would be, not for me. When Glen got home from work, he didn't ask where I'd been. We talked about our separation and what steps we would take. We talked about how it would be okay to see other people. He was surprisingly calm, kind even. He had already moved into the guest bedroom. We'd be roommates until we figured the rest out.

I ached for Blake. I ached for the loss of him. I cried for hours at a time. I let Glen think I was crying for the death of our relationship when really it was for having left Blake. I can't believe how much my heart ached. The days were long. I felt myself cracking in two.

I needed to move somewhere hell and gone from Seattle. Someplace where the sun shined on a regular basis. Jennifer had suggested Austin. It fit the bill in a lot of ways. Plenty of sunshine, university town, cheap real estate, young population. Besides, I'd always told myself I should move to a red state and keep voting blue. Why not?

I went to bed early and cried myself to sleep. With everything else that was going on, all I could think about was how much I wanted the one I couldn't have. I wondered how Blake was doing, how life had been for him since Cami had returned.

The phone rang early the next morning and I picked it up before I was fully awake.

"Hey pretty lady," Blake said, his voice ragged. "How you doing?"

The spark within flooded my body with the warmth of a ski lodge after an icy day on the slopes. I remembered what it felt like to want to be alive.

"Oh, you know," I said, breathless. Tears fell down my cheek, hot with joy.

"I can't do this anymore is what I know."

"What?" I felt stupid. This wasn't happening.

"I want to see you. Today. I can't do this anymore. I don't want to be without you. Okay?"

"Okay," I said and almost started to sob, so deep was my relief. "So much for my resolve." I really had intended to leave him alone, let him get back to his life. Again. Quitting Blake was like quitting smoking. Apparently I had to do it twenty times before it stuck.

"Oh, I knew," he said. "I knew all I had to do was call you." I could practically hear his goofy smile. "So, yes?"

"Yes," I said, tired of being sad. Besides, I told myself, Glen and I had agreed it was okay to see other people.

"Good. I'll let you know when I'm on the way," he said.

"I've missed you," I said.

"You don't know the half of it, pretty lady."

I took a hot, hot shower, shaved my legs, and slopped on lotion. All over, just as he liked it. Gardenia. My body ached for him all day. It took him hours, as I knew it would. He had to at least show up to work, put in some time.

And then he came to me.

Blake knocked on the door and let himself in. He walked up behind and held me, his goatee softly tickling the back of my neck and I burst into tears. "I missed you so much," he said. I nodded, still crying. He kissed the nape of my neck, parting my hair to brush his lips against it, breathing warmth onto me. I sobbed.

He pulled me closer. "That's not the effect I was going for." It felt so good just to be held by him. I turned into him and we started kissing, soft at first, rediscovering each other, and then we took each other's kisses like hungry animals. The best kisses. Oh my god, the best you can imagine.

Trembling, I said, "You're actually here."

"I'm here." He took me in his arms, breathed in deeply the scent of my hair. He held me close, rocked me against him. I don't think I knew, until that moment, how lonely I had been. My body shook and he held me tighter. "Shh, it's okay," he said. "I'm here."

"I know," I said. I felt like I was home and not because I was standing in my front hallway. "I can't get over how much, how incredible our week together was. Every day is so long without you."

"You're telling me?" he said and looked like he really meant it. There was an intensity in his eyes. This wasn't bullshit. He pulled me close and kissed me and we kissed and I couldn't get enough of his kisses. He pulled his pants and briefs down so I could suck his cock. I knelt and pulled his briefs back up and rubbed my face in the thin, soft cotton all over his hard cock, breathing hotly, teasing it. I tugged the elastic down and nuzzled his cock softly until he groaned. I took him in my mouth and lost myself in the pleasure of sucking him off.

He lifted me to my feet and we kissed and kissed. He was by far the best kisser I'd ever known; I could spend eternity like that. I knew if it weren't so good with him, I'd be able to let go. If I didn't feel so close to him, if I didn't adore every inch of his body, every crack of his smile, the light in his eyes... If it didn't feel like the way the universe meant it to be.

"I want you," he said. I nodded. We still hadn't made it past the front entryway. I took him upstairs to my bedroom and helped him take off his shirt. I put it on the floor, right side out as always, ready to run. I ran my fingers over his solidly muscled chest and let the energy build between us. Incredible.

He clutched me to him and we scrambled out of the rest of our clothes. I fell to my knees and sucked on him, so ready and warm for me, until he could barely contain himself.

"Please, Aleah," he tugged on my arms. "Please, I need you."

"Take me, then," I said and he obliged, throwing me on the bed. He surged on top of me, sliding along my body until I felt every inch of him, along me, inside me, like we were built for one another. He took it slowly, sucking on my breasts while I played with myself, feeling the length of him deep inside me. "Please," I begged, "Please, stop." I didn't want to come, not yet, but he didn't stop or give in until I became a writhing, squirming cataclysm beneath him. He felt me pulsing and rode me hard, rocking my body into the bed, harder and harder until he spilled his seed in me, grunting with the release.

His brow was slick with sweat. I licked his forehead and laughed.

"That is so sexy," he said.

"Really?"

"Really. You have no idea. The way you accept everything about me, the way you show me, over and over, that you're into me, that I don't disgust you..."

I must have looked confused.

"Cami would never have licked me like that. It's her Catholic upbringing. Everything is dirty to her." He shook his head. "That's all." He looked at his watch and moaned. "I have to go."

I nodded and went to the bathroom to get him a wet washcloth. I handed it to him and lounged naked beside him, running my fingers in trails down his chest while he scrubbed up. He rose and put on his clothes. I leaned in to kiss him goodbye, felt the length of him along me, the warmth of his body.

"It's so strange," I said in between kisses. "As soon as we're done making love and you've left, I just want you more. It's like I can never get enough of you."

"I know." He sighed. "I know."

He leaned back against the footboard and unzipped his fly. His soft, well spent dick lay exposed. "Suck me," he begged me softly.

"Yes," I breathed and knelt before him, wrapped the whole of him in my hot, wet mouth. He gasped and threw his head back. His cock sprang to life, instantly hard.

"I want to fuck you," he said.

"You have to go." But he was the master of the quick after-fuck and it shouldn't have surprised me that he bent me over the bed and took me fast and fierce from behind. A delicious dessert. "I wish you didn't have to leave," I whispered.

"I know," he said, but what I heard was: "I love you."

I let him go, trusting he would come back to me.

Chapter Six

While Blake and I fell back into the habit of seeing each other a few times a week, other than not sleeping in the same bed, Glen and I carried on with life as usual. He wasn't in any particular rush to push me out of the house and I wasn't in any particular rush to leave. It was as if we'd tacitly agreed to a period of disengagement to mark the end of the marriage. It felt natural. By the same token, I knew my life would remain in purgatory until I actually moved on.

Mostly, I think Glen and I both felt a sense of relief that the pain of not knowing our future was over. Part of me had thought he'd wait patiently, forever, for me to come to love him again. It had come as a surprise to me that he'd reached the end of his rope, that he'd been the first to take action. A surprise, and a relief that I no longer had to try to love him better than came naturally to me. He didn't have to keep trying to change himself to make me happy. Why hadn't we come to this ages before?

He did keep up his meditation practice. Good for him.

I met up with Glen at the local pub after his meditation session. He didn't bother to mention when he called to invite me that he'd run into a bunch of our poker friends there. Everyone was a little weird when I arrived, tossing me funny looks—evaluating, not smiling. At first I thought it was just me. Glen went to buy me a drink and I looked around for a seat. Jack patted the seat next to him and when I sat down he leaned in close. "So it's the end of your era, eh? For real?"

"Apparently," I said.

"Well, for what it's worth, I'm sorry."

When he returned to the table I pulled Glen aside. "You told them about us?"

"Yeah, I told them about the break up," he said, like we'd just been dating and it wasn't nearly a decade of marriage we were abandoning.

I said softly, "It's not cool that you let me walk into that blind." A few weeks earlier, at Erik and Donna's I'd gone to the bathroom and when I'd come out they were looking at me strangely because Glen had just told them we were having severe marital problems that might end in divorce. "I feel like I keep stepping on a rake with you."

"Whatever. It's not like it changes anything. What does it matter who breaks the news?"

"I'm just asking for a little respect. There's no reason we couldn't have told people together. At Erik and Donna's, too."

"I'm sorry, but I'm out of here." He stood up, leaving most of his beer on the table. I wasn't sure what he was apologizing for and I wasn't going to hang out on my own with the guys, who were probably full of venom for me at the moment. Who knows what Glen had told them? I gave my beer to Johnny and left as well.

A few weeks after he'd asked for the divorce, I spent a Saturday in my office, looking online at real estate in Austin. I called my mom and asked if I could stay with her in Tucson for a little while, to get my financial footing before launching out on my own again. I'd considered asking Jennifer, but there's only so much the bonds of friendship could take. For this I'd resort to family. My mother and I didn't always see eye to eye, and she was horrified and devastated that Glen and I were divorcing. But she promised to take me in nonetheless.

"When do you think you'll move?"

"I don't know."

"Well, what's holding you back?"

"Oh, you know, do we sell the house, do I need to be here for the paperwork, packing, divvying up our stuff, all that."

"But you can take care of that pretty quickly, Aleah. You don't have to be there for the house to sell. Don't you want to move on with your life? What's really holding you back?"

"I don't know." But of course I did. It was Blake Porter. When I left Seattle, I wasn't just leaving Glen and my old life. I was leaving love. And Jennifer. I'd miss the hell out of Jennifer. "I guess I'm still figuring it all out. Give me a week? I'll get back to you."

"Okay."

"Thanks, Mom. I mean it."

Shortly after I hung up, Glen popped his head in the door. "Are you ready?"

I had no idea what he was talking about. "For what?"

"Dinner. I made reservations. Did you forget?"

"Forget what?"

"Aleah, it's June thirtieth."

I stared at him, waiting for some kind of clarification.

"Our ninth wedding anniversary."

I think my jaw literally dropped. He'd made reservations. He had a prettily-wrapped package tucked under his arm, flowers even. I was stunned.

"I completely forgot. I'm sorry. With everything going on..." I held up my hands and shrugged. "I'm so sorry." Then the abnormality of the situation sunk in. Where had *this* Glen been all my life? Seriously. He had never once made reservations for an evening out before. He rarely remembered flowers. "It does seem like kind of a weird time to start celebrating our marriage."

He sighed. "We've had a good run together, Aleah. I still love you. I want for us to be friends. I think we should do this."

"Okay," I said, glancing at my phone to see the time. "When's the reservation?"

"It's okay. We have time. Go get dressed."

I went and changed into a dress, applied fresh makeup. We chatted of this and that on the drive, nothing substantial, no pressure behind the exchange. We remembered how to relax and have fun around each other.

Dinner was exquisite, fresh salmon, caviar. His card to me was really sweet, full of forgiveness and letting go.

Nine years together and while not all
of them were happy, I wouldn't trade my
time with you for anything. Here's to a beautiful
future, Aleah. I hope you find happiness.
Love always,
Glen

He got me a box of Godiva chocolates. Ugh. As if I hadn't told him every time he got them for me that I don't like Belgian chocolate. If he's going to spend that kind of money on chocolate for me, it should be my favorite. Or at least one that I don't want to spit out. I smiled as best as I could and said, "Thank you."

"I know they're your favorite," he said.

I blinked my eyes shut a moment, nodded, and managed to keep smiling. Soon it wouldn't matter, none of it would. I breathed it out, let it go.

"So, are you ready to get out in the dating world?" I asked.

"Not really, no," he said. "But I will be. Soon enough. Why? Is there someone you're thinking about?"

I shook my head. "No one," I said. It wasn't the first time I'd lied to him; it wouldn't be the last.

"Well, why not? Who's your type?" he said. "I mean, if you had to pick among our friends, who would you fuck?"

"Seriously?" I said. "You first!" I laughed. A tiny part of my flared up in alarm. Why was he asking?

"Come on," he said, a gleam in his eye. "You know you're closer to dating than I am."

It was true. I thought it very mature of him to recognize that. "Okay," I said. I didn't know where this was going, but our impending divorce let me be free and honest. "Who do you want to know about?"

"Erik?"

Donna's husband. "No. Erik's too short."

"Jack?"

The bass player in his band. "Jack's too old at heart."

"Adam?"

One of our poker friends. "Umm... Maybe I'd fuck Adam—except, no, no I wouldn't. Because of his teeth." They looked like they'd smell bad, yellowed and dark at the gum line.

"Johnny?"

Another poker friend. "Johnny, maybe, for curiosity's sake but I'd probably regret it. There's not really any attraction there."

"Trevor?"

An old friend of mine; we'd both moved to Seattle after college. "Trevor, uh, yeah. Except the attraction now isn't anything like it was before I met you. And he's got that puritanical born again streak now. So, maybe not, actually."

"Blake?"

I felt my face flush and hoped he hadn't noticed. We were sitting next to each other on the bench so it was at least difficult for him to take in my face. "Blake?" Might as well be honest. "Yeah, I'd sleep with Blake."

He looked at me appraisingly. "Well, I think you'd be good together." He paused, drumming his fingers on the Formica and considered his words. "In fact. I think if you have the desire and the opportunity you should totally fuck him."

I blinked. "Excuse me?" I felt completely disoriented.

"You heard me." His grin lit up his bright blue eyes.

"I think I need you to say it again."

"I said, if you have the desire and the opportunity, I think you should fuck Blake Porter."

Whoa. "Why would you say that? He's married."

"She's a bitch and everyone knows it. She's especially been a bitch to you."

I didn't disagree. Of course, over the last several months I had spared no mercy in my stories of Cami's demonic tendencies. Glen knew mine was a complete love-hate relationship with her. Or something like that. Even if Blake and I hadn't been lovers, it would have been difficult to be her friend. I'd always had to work at it.

On the way home the conversation drifted and turned. We were talking about our food when Glen got a silly grin on his face.

"What is it?" I said. "Why are you laughing?"

"I'm not laughing. I was just thinking about you and Blake together and it was turning me on." I didn't know it at the time, but my world had just changed. I mean, shit got crazy.

Book Three

Chapter Seven

It rained on the fourth of July and we canceled our plans for a barbecue at the Porter's. Cami called the Friday after as I was tidying up my desk at the end of my work day.

"Hey lady, I heard about your split from Glen. I'm so sorry." Word traveled fast. I wondered briefly why Glen was talking to Cami, but let it go. "How are you doing?" She sounded actually concerned.

"Surprisingly, I'm doing all right."

"I'm glad to hear that. Listen, I'm actually calling to see if you'd go out to the bars with me tonight." Of course she was. She was only concerned because she wanted to know if I was healthy enough to come party with her. "Glen can come over and hang out with Blake and we ladies can go out for once."

"Sure," I said. I knew I had to go into the dragon's den every once in a while to keep the fire of her suspicion at bay.

"Oooh, good. We can totally scope out the market for you and find you a man to take home if you want."

"Oh, Cami. I don't know if I'm ready—"

"No, don't say that, you should totally take advantage of having me as your wingman. I want to go out and flirt for you, find some guys and give them to you. We are totally gonna hook you up tonight."

"Sure," I said. It was no use fighting Cami when she had a purpose in mind. A sick image popped in my head of a hawk dropping a disemboweled mouse in front of me. I told myself I didn't have to accept whatever offerings she laid at my feet.

Blake called an hour later. From the way he asked how I was doing I could tell he was stoned. We chatted about nothing for a bit and then he said, "Listen baby, if you get a chance, you should hit on Cami tonight. Get her all turned on and bring her back here. We'll have a foursome." Was he drunk and stoned?

Did we all have sex on the brain? All the time? It was starting to feel that way. Like cherry pie to someone on a diet. I knew I thought about it all the time. Still, I felt a great deal of resistance. I wasn't attracted to Cami; I'd never been with a woman or had any interest in women. The whole suggestion just seemed like too much of a Pandora's Box.

"I don't know, Blake," I said. "That sounds a little dangerous." Cami was a massive wildcard for me. Maybe she'd be happy in the moment. But I had a feeling she could twist anything however she wanted to suit her purpose in the aftermath. "I mean, why would you want to play with fire?"

"I guess I was just hoping. Cami's been pushing me to have an open relationship."

Oh, I thought, and I hated her a little more. "How did that come about?"

"She started partying with this bunch of swingers up the road, friends she met at the bar, and they all convinced her it was a good idea. She says it will help our sex life if we bring in new blood."

"But she doesn't know about you and me."

"Of course not. You're the only person I'm not allowed to sleep with."

"Of course."

"I couldn't exactly forbid her from it when she brought it up, you know." I felt like I could hear his shrug.

"It's just that she's so possessive of you; it seems weird."

"You know Cami. The rules are there for everyone to keep and for her to break. And, if it feels good, do more. She wants to sleep with other men and wants me to sleep with other women—as long as it's not you."

"She actually specified that?"

"Yeah. But if you hit on her... Maybe she'd bend the rules. Then maybe we could stop all the sneaking around and just enjoy life. Please, Aleah, please? Do it for me."

That was a lot to digest. If Cami was pushing for an open relationship, maybe they had bigger marital problems than either of them were letting on. It sounded like an act of desperation. "Maybe," I said, not wanting to talk about it anymore. "We'll see how drunk I get."

Knowing I'd see Blake, if only for a few minutes, I got dolled up for the night out—I wore my black vinyl corset under a sheer black pirate-style blouse and tied a black ribbon around my neck. This over skinny jeans with black, knee-high boots. Glen came along to hang with Blake, drink beer, and play darts on the back porch. The kids were already jammied up and in bed when we arrived.

"Looking sexy!" Cami exclaimed, giving me a hug at the door. "Oooh, I'm so excited! C'mon back." She motioned for me to follow her to the back bedroom. Cami passed me a full pipe and a lighter while she rolled two joints to take with us. Apparently she'd moved out of her abstinence phase.

I lit up, suddenly nervous around her and grateful for the dope. Cami nattered on about her days selling dope in college, paper crackling as it rolled in between her purple acrylic fingernails and I reflected on how surreal the whole night was. She was like a little dictator in her own world, I realized. She would make sure everyone else had to follow the rules, but she could break them at her leisure—or pleasure. Would I try to hit on her? I honestly didn't know. At this point I was taking everything one moment at a time. It felt like everyone and everything was in flux.

Cami drove us to nearby Woodinville, to a bar called Willie's. We'd hung out there on occasion in the early days and played our share of darts, saw amazingly mediocre metal bands. Tonight was no different, except for the caliber of the band. The house throbbed with the dark, heavy bass, relentless in its pursuit of a new standard in war ballads. I slammed a pint and found myself awash with feelings of nostalgic joy. I mean, it was fantastic. I made my way into the mosh pit. All day I'd been silently screaming with trapped sexual energy; I could feel it pulsing from my cunt to my toes to my head and back again. I had such a buildup of desire for

Blake. Overload followed by drought. I was a total nympho. I wanted to be fucked. Plain and simple. My body was begging for it.

The band really was excellent, but Cami was barely into them. She hung on the outskirts of the crowd, pouting. The band utterly rocked it, such a deep, good groove. I promised myself I'd buy their demo. Cami used to be a band manager. She should have been able to recognize their talent. But whatever. I floated back through the crowd to her. There's an art to it, to finding the hole, watching for toes, catching people's eyes, smiling. A smile is extremely disarming, I've learned. I wanted to stay, to rock myself into oblivion, but I moved on out. Cami and I were supposed to be hanging out together, after all. And it was kind of hard to meet guys in the pit. Then again, maybe I should have stayed there.

"I'm going to get a pitcher and play some pool," she shouted when I reached her.

"Okay," I shouted back. "I'll go with you."

We started a game of pool and in two minutes she had two meat hunters on her. Both in their mid- to late 30s and actually sporting mullets and plaid lumberjack shirts. In spite of this, Cami laid on the charm, flashing her huge white teeth, leaning in close to talk with them. I wondered how many beers she'd downed while I was in the mosh pit.

It wasn't long before Cami had me on the rails and called her eight ball pocket to finish the game. Pool isn't my game. She put her cue down and draped her arm around me. I could smell the beer.

"So they're kind of cute," she started, nodding at her new friends across the table.

I snorted. "On what planet?" I said, confident they wouldn't hear me over the din of the band.

"Ohh." She sighed. "Strike. Out." She seemed disappointed more than was warranted—I could actually see her deflate, her shoulders slump, her smile fade. "They said I was pretty."

"Of course you're pretty." I reached up to pet her hair, sweep her bangs to the side. "What the fuck, Cami? Of course you are." What the hell, maybe I would try to pick her up. Pour some more alcohol in me, let's see what would happen. I downed the last of my beer. I stroked her arm and leaned in even closer to her. "Let's go to MacDub's," I said. It was her neighborhood bar and I knew from Blake that lately she'd been hanging out there a few nights a week until the wee hours. I wanted to get her away from this place.

"Okay!" she said and her energy instantly soared through the roof. "Should we ask them to come with us?" she motioned to her pool buddies, one of whom I noticed had left.

"No," I said firmly. "I don't think so."

"Oh, but they're getting us tequila shots!" *To kill ya*, I thought. *Gross.*

"Well, drink 'em and let's go, then," I said and we did. Or, she did. I didn't drink. I drove.

We got there and I opened the sun roof and turned the engine off in her Jeep. This was a country bar, and the parking lot was pretty dark, ringed by tall firs. I turned to her and set my elbow on the maroon leather armrest. "Let's smoke one of those joints you brought," I said.

"God, I thought you'd never ask!"

"You were waiting for me to?"

"Yeah." She looked at me as if calculating how much to say. "It's better if I don't push it. You have to ask if you want it. I mean, I usually have it but I'm not going to just offer it. You have to ask me for it. That way *you* control your addiction."

I actually snorted. I had to fucking beg her for it? The dope she got for free from her father-in-law that she smoked with impunity? Unbelievable. Something about the tone in her voice, the narrowing of her eyes... I flashed on the first time I'd experienced the wrath of Cami. Why did she have to be such a fucking tyrant?

"You know that makes me feel like a complete beggar. I know you get it for free. If you feel like sharing, cool, and if you don't, then don't. I feel like there are always deeper issues with you, though, Cami. I feel like it's not about you, it's about your perception of me as having a problem. You know, just about the only time I smoke pot is when I'm with you and Blake."

"Oh. That surprises me." She sat back in the leather seat and dug a joint out of her purse, lit it. "I think that makes me feel a lot more comfortable," she said after she inhaled and passed it to me. "I thought you smoked it all the time."

It was a little deceptive. I mean, I was with Blake a lot more than she was aware. I was okay with deception in this instance. Her and her addiction and control issues were a combination that equaled total bitch. I didn't need her attitude. Who did?

"You didn't tell those guys where we were going, did you?" I passed the spliff back to her.

"No," she said, sucking hard on the little paper joint. The silver air seemed crystalline in the moonlight. I leaned back to see all the brilliant summer stars piercing the fabric of the night. "I didn't. Men are all liars."

"If you train them to be," I said before I could stop myself.

It was as if I'd triggered her internal alarm system. I could almost hear the *Warning! Warning!* going off in her head. Her eyes instantly narrowed and she squared her shoulders to me. "What do you mean?" she said, looking exactly like a cat about to pounce.

I took a deep breath. "I know you have trust issues with Blake. The thing is..." I stumbled a little. "I think you might inadvertently set him up to lie to you." Might as well face her head on.

"I do not! All I ever want from him is honesty and if he gives me that he's golden."

"I don't think you even know you do it, Cami."

"I can't even begin to imagine what you're talking about." She crossed her arms.

"So," I paused, catching her gaze and trying to look reassuring. "By way of example, you don't want Blake to smoke cigarettes."

"Right."

"But you say it's okay if he does, as long as he tells you about it first. So you can keep tabs on how out of control it is."

"Completely, totally." She relaxed and leaned forward a bit, like she was going to bet out, like she had aces. Someone finally understood her.

"So, your husband has to come to you and declare his intention to have a cigarette, and essentially get your permission."

"Right, and if he does that I'm fine with it. That's upfront. That's *honest*, right there." I think she really believed her own bullshit, she was so earnest.

"So, like at that barbecue a few months ago when we were over he came to you and said, 'Cami, I'm having a cigarette.'" It had been a rare, hot, late-April day in Seattle and we'd spent the day on their back porch, grilling up chicken and dogs, and watching the kids play in the pool. I remembered Blake's smile from that day, the broadness of his strong shoulders, his silly hound dog grins. I suddenly felt lustful again.

"Right."

"And you said: 'You don't need to have a cigarette, Blake Porter. Stare that demon down, fight it. See how strong you can be.'"

"Exactly," she said. "Because he's better than that. He doesn't have to give into his demon addiction."

"Okay, and then when he lit the cigarette up, your face clouded over and you stormed away, pissed."

"Right, because he's saying, 'Fuck you, Cami, fuck you.' I'm doing everything I can to support him. I'm helping him quit."

"Except that's not what he's saying, Cam. Blake doesn't want to quit. He's cutting back on it for you. And he's going to indulge every once in a while. He loves you enough to follow your instructions—he's doing exactly as you asked, informing you of when he's indulging in his habit so that you know how much of a smoker he actually is. Then you come at him with this serious Catholic guilt trip and try to get him to change his mind. You punish the hell out of him when he doesn't do what you want."

"Of course I do. I'm pissed at him. He has no strength."

"Do you see how you're breaking the contract you set up with him?" I tell her again, because she's clearly not hearing it. "Think of it broadly, from his perspective, you tell him there are no consequences for being honest. He takes you at your word, he trusts you, he's honest. Then you lay into him. You remind him of it for days. You make the punishment so much worse than the crime. Worse, you don't keep your word."

"Because he's saying, 'Fuck you, Cami.'"

"But he's not. He's saying, 'Cami I love you and I'm following your instructions.' But then you make it so hard... Why would he want to tell you the truth again? Why would he want to do anything other than go have his fucking cigarette in peace and hide from you? Not tell you about it, deny it if you challenge him? You give him no reason to be truthful with you."

"Oh," she said and sucked hard on the joint, revelation dawning on her face as she considered my words. She relaxed back against the leather and blew smoke out the sunroof. "I never realized that."

I figured it was not the time to get into why having to be accountable to your spouse for your vices is a shitty thing to implement in the first place. I mean, you trust your husband or you don't. You let him be who he is or you're miserable. If you can't trust him, get out of the relationship. I knew Blake and I didn't think any of his habits crossed the line. I mean, I didn't think he had any real problem.

"Thanks for telling me," she said. It was not lost on me, the irony of me giving this woman marriage advice.

I picked up her hand and kissed the back of it. "Let's get a beer."

"Okay," she smiled, her face brightening.

At the bar, she squealed and came up behind one of the patrons, running her long fingernails through his curly mullet. "Carter," she gushed. "I didn't know you'd be here." She winked at him, one of those giant comedic winks. Maybe she thought I wouldn't notice. She introduced him as a friend, but I saw his hand float to her ass and stroke it. She pushed it away, but with a caress not a slap. I found it interesting. Apparently, the rules only applied to Blake. She was her own little queen. I wondered how far she'd gone with him. Had she fucked him in the bathroom?

I carried the pitcher and two stacked pint glasses outside and stood for a moment, scoping the place out before traversing the treacherous gravel to a bench in the middle of the courtyard. The stars were sparkly pinpricks, a web of faint light in a black sky; the blacker shadows of fir trees sheltered my face. The well-worn wooden benches were hard and soon I found myself shifting often in my seat.

Cami took a seat across from me. I reached over and caressed the back of her hand. She looked at me slantwise.

"Blake and I are so in love, more in love than we've ever been. We have no secrets. Plus we have *rockstar* sex."

Not really knowing where to go with that, I nodded and cleared my throat a bit. Thankfully, the waiter stepped in and saved me.

"You know what he told me?" Cami said after ordering another pitcher. I shook my head. "He said we're stuck together. How's that for romantic, eh?" I heard a bit more of her Jersey girl seep into her voice, her mannerisms. I imagined her in a faux leopard skin vest with tassels.

"Oh, nice." I groaned, wondering how he'd been so brave. Any indication of dissatisfaction was a direct ticket to the danger zone with her.

"Then he said that we had two beautiful children and we would always be together for them." I doubted she knew anything of the undertones on his side, of the unhappiness stored in those shackles.

I heard her message clearly, though. Cami thought she was telling me of his undying devotion to her. Of their very happy marriage. She'd watched me like a hawk at every gathering since that night she'd nearly caught us. She thought I flirted with her husband. She'd invited us over less often since then. I knew what she was saying was, "Back off, mine!"

I knew what Blake had been saying, too. Without the kids, he wouldn't be with her. Without the kids, he'd be with me. I look down and saw the pitcher was already three quarters empty. Damn, she could drink. From what I'd gathered from his comments about stopping at the corner store for a six-pack on the way home, Blake'd been drinking a lot lately, too. They clearly weren't happy, but seemed comfortable living in a state of deception.

"Aw, that's sweet," I said. We chatted, things got less serious. I'd almost forgotten, for all of her scary energy, Cami had an equal amount of fun inside her. I hadn't given up on the goal Blake had set of getting us all into bed together. Plus, alcohol. That was going to be necessary. The conversation turned to me being back on the singles market, looking for another relationship.

"Not that I need one, *at all*," I said. I realized that I had absolutely no idea how to flirt with her. "You know, sometimes I feel so naïve. I've never even had sex with a woman before. I just want to play a little. I mean, isn't that one of those things that you try in college?"

"Usually!" She laughed. "Well, I did." She looked surprised, appraising. "You haven't?"

"Nope. And coming out of this nine-year-long monogamy, I'm feeling... Adventuresome." I smiled at her.

"We can do whatever you want," she said, a strange smile spreading on her face. "We just can't tell Blake. We'll have to do it in the car."

"Why?"

She looked at me, calculating. "Because if we tell him," she said it slowly, enunciating each word carefully, "he will want to watch. And... I don't want to share him."

Well, that was honest. "I don't care about Blake," I said, stroking her hand, embracing the role of seductress. My thighs were throbbing under the table. I could get her home. I could get her to Blake.

She very conspicuously looked at each of the tables around us, taking in, I'm sure, as I'd done, the predominant heterosexual male—one might even say redneck—population. While most of them probably would have enjoyed a display of affection between us, there were enough who might just get a little *too* turned on... Cami seemed to come to the same conclusion and lurched to her feet.

"Come with me to the bathroom," she said.

I didn't know how drunk I was until I tried to cross that gravel. I stumbled forward and clutched at her hand, laughing. I was such a lightweight.

I was excited. Not because I was particularly attracted to Cami; while I'd often admired a beautiful woman, it was hard to think of a time I'd felt sexually aroused by one. Sometimes, sure. Watching porn or whatever. But not in real life. Not by a real female. I think I was as much or more excited by the notion that I'd be doing something new, something I'd never done before.

We walked faster and burst through the dark gray metal door. It was a typical bar bathroom. The mirrors had never actually been glass and were so fogged and scratched over it was impossible to see your own reflection. The place stank like old urine and vomit and the best you could hope for was a healthy dose of air freshener to cover the reek.

She kissed me, then, pushing me up against the tacky wall covered in posters and *oh my god.*

Okay, first, the good: those amazing soft lips. Men don't have soft lips like women do. Now I understand, a little, their drive to protect the innocence we represent to them, what their wives must mean to them. That softness was better than a pillow after a hard day's work.

Beyond that... I should have known there'd be no collaboration in a kiss with Cami. She rammed her tongue into the back of my mouth like she was drilling for oil and spun it around like crazy. It didn't matter that I was there at all, she was going for China. It was painful. My jaw started to lock up. It was as if someone had taught her how to kiss, this one way, when she was in fifth grade, and she'd never changed it up, not once. I felt like I was suffocating; it was a struggle to find room to breathe under her assault. I pulled back from the relentless pursuit, tried some give and take but was met only with the reasserted thrust of her tongue, circling. I tried to soften, to turn from her a bit, to engage her differently. Hell, to feel my lips. It wasn't working.

I understood, suddenly, why that first kiss with Blake had been such respite for him, why the combination of the softness of my lips, the pliability of my kisses might have been beyond intoxicating.

Cami was a horrible kisser.

If we'd both been single and I'd have been interested in her, it would have ended right there. There would never have been a second date. I mean, it was that bad. I didn't have the slightest bit of attraction for her; suddenly everything felt awkward. I guess I'm not really into women, except maybe as accessories in an orgy. I did it for Blake, because he wanted so badly for her to learn from me. I did it because I knew I was leaving. No holds barred.

I did it because you only live once and why the fuck not?

I endured another of her suffocating kisses before I managed to slip from her arms, professing a need to pee. "It's almost two, Cami. Bar's closing. We should go," I said from the stall.

I managed to get us in the car and drove her home. She'd had four times as much beer as I had and I'm not sure I was any less sober than she was. But we knew my blood alcohol level was lower.

We should have called a cab. I know. We were stupid.

But we didn't die that night, or have anything untoward happen, actually. No deer, no cops, no accidents. The lights were on all around the house when we pulled into the drive.

"Wait, wait," Cami said, pulling the second joint out of her bag to show me. "Let's smoke it before we go in. I don't want to share with them." I was picking up on a theme with her.

"Okay." We stood out in the front yard and smoked it.

The boys were out back playing darts on the porch. We got some beers and joined them for a game of cricket. Glen won.

"Getting a drink," Blake said, striding through the sliding glass door.

"Oh, me too," I said, following him.

I went in the kitchen where Blake was.

"Hey pretty lady, what's new?" he said quietly. His voice sent lightning up my spine.

I tugged at the cuff on my blouse and shoved the sleeve up my arm to expose my tattoo. "This is new," I said. I'd spontaneously decided it was time for a tat as I'd been walking downtown earlier in the week. The design was a giant sun, with the words "to thine own self be true" written within the ball. The outline of the sun was Celtic knot work. I know, not original, but appropriate for me, something I needed to be reminded of in the face of my impending divorce.

"Nice," he said. "Did you have any luck with the foursome? Glen and I can't wait," he said, hands darting towards my hips in the semi-dark.

I slapped his hands away. "You told him?" I hissed, my eyes darting to Cami. I had no desire, not the slightest bit of any kind of lust for that woman.

Those atrocious kisses... I couldn't bring myself to get into bed with her. "It's not going to happen, okay? So drop it."

We walked out to the back porch and Cami flipped out. I mean, she *flipped out*. She was emanating black energy, glaring at us, at me. She waited less than a minute before storming into the house, slamming the sliding glass door shut behind her. Blake just watched her go.

After a few moments of debating with myself, I went in after her.

I found her in the bathroom, wiping makeup off her face where the tears had streamed it down. "I'm checking in on you," I said, opening the door. "Are you okay?"

"Yeah, why?" she glared at me with hawk eyes.

"You seemed upset when you left," I said cautiously.

"What were you and Blake talking about in the kitchen?"

"I was showing him my tattoo."

"Is that all?"

"Yes," I said, schooling my face into puzzlement.

"'Cause you looked at him and you both looked at me..."

"I don't remember looking over at you," I assured her. "Cami, you're making this up." I met her eyes and looked at her expectantly. She was beyond drunk. She needed an iron hand.

"Oh, okay," she said. "I'm sorry. I didn't mean to make something out of nothing..." I hugged her. "See how much easier it is to deal with things when you handle them right away?" she said, as if my following her to soothe her riled up ego had been her fucking idea. She put her face to mine and held my cheeks fast between her palms. I endured another oil drilling expedition from her violent tongue and got away from her as quickly as I could.

"It's time to go," I said to Glen when I got back outside. The night was spent. It was 3:30 in the morning.

"Bye guys," Cami said as she dragged Blake to bed.

Glen and I went home. He sat on the couch and watched porn, jacking off in front of me. This was new behavior, even for Zen Glen. He was really drunk. We both were. What the hell did I care what he did now?

"You were really flirty with me tonight at Blake and Cami's," I said. He was quiet. "Were you trying to tell me you want a fuck buddy?" I ask. "Because that's all it would be, meaningless sex. I don't want you back, Glen." I was trying to be straight with him but instead I was drunk and mean. I don't think it mattered, though. I had him at "fuck buddy."

"Yeah," he said, looking at me with glossy eyes. I was suddenly sure I didn't want to fuck him. I didn't know why I'd even offered, but I didn't take back my offer. Glen told me he and Blake talked all night about how hot I was, and about sex and how he likes it and... *Ugh.* What the fuck was Blake doing, even having these conversations?

I clutched at my mouth and belly as if I had to throw up, widening my eyes at Glen before I darted for the staircase and the upstairs bathroom. I pretended to throw up, coughing into the toilet and then my body obliged me and I hurled what felt like an entire pitcher of beer into the bowl.

After, I stumbled to the top of the stairs. "Sorry, Glen," I called down. "I'm going to bed."

I got no response. I peered over and saw he was asleep on the couch, limp dick in his hand.

Chapter Eight

My phone shrieked the next morning, jerking me out of blissful sleep. I sat up in bed, squinting in the harshness of the morning light and saw that it was Cami. Not even ten o'clock yet. Bitch. After the night we'd had before, I knew I had to pick it up. "How are you doing, sunshine?" Her voice was far too cheery.

"Good," I croaked. "You?"

"God, great. I was horny as hell last night, you turned me on so much Blake and I had sex like four times in the last eight hours."

I nodded, and said nothing. If she wanted to post her scorecard, it was fine by me. She had nothing on my record.

"But I wanted to check in with you after last night. I mean, that was very different for you. Are you okay?" She sounded almost aggressive, a bit cold.

I blinked hard against the bright light and wished she would talk a little more quietly. What was she talking about? Then it dawned on me. Kissing her. Ewww. I panicked, trying to think of what to say.

Apparently I took too long to respond. I never was a very fast thinker. "Aleah, it was cool and all and I was very happy to be a part of your new sexual awakening but I'm not sure something like that is right for us—"

"Cami, it's okay. You don't have to worry about me coming on to you again. I mean, as much as I totally appreciate your willingness to go down that path with me, you're right, it's an experiment best left in the past."

"So I guess Glen and Blake are fixing your fence today?" She changed the subject without missing a beat, sounding relieved.

"Are they?" It was news to me.

"I guess that's what they decided on last night."

"Huh." The fence did need staining.

"I was just wondering how much lunch I should send over."

"Cami, I'm sure we have food here. Better yet, Glen can buy lunch for Blake." I almost snorted. "It's the least he can do." Everything always seemed contrived with her. I knew she was just calling to see how much of a threat I was. "I'm going to the Mariner's game with a girlfriend," I said to sate her fear. "I won't even be here." Although, I'll admit I suddenly didn't want to go.

"Oh, okay," she said cheerily. "Well, I'm glad we got that all cleared up." I hung up, knowing she was feeling like she'd won that round, but knowing in reality I had. She'd told me once that there was nothing she hated more than being played for a fool. It dawned on me that she would well and truly hate me, if any of my affair with Blake ever came to light. I thought that underneath her shiny veneer, she probably did already. Still, I hoped the veil was never raised.

Blake came over to help stain the fence. I *was* supposed to go to the Mariner's game with a girlfriend, but she was going with a large group and wouldn't miss me. However, if I went I'd miss him. I didn't like the idea of missing him. I hadn't seen nearly enough of him the night before.

Collectively, we were a bit hung over and we were all having a hard time getting started on the task at hand. I made a third pot of coffee and we all went out for a smoke. Cami may have gotten her fix, but I was still feeling cunt-throbbingly horny.

I started talking about sex, about how aggressive a kisser Cami was, about how I kept trying but she wouldn't soften up. Glen leaned in, eating up every word.

"Whoa... What? Where? When?" Blake sputtered. They demanded to know more.

"Four times in eight hours, eh Blake?" I said, looking sideways at him, quoting Cami's statistic from her phone call earlier. "Is that like a record for you?" I smirked at him, knowing we done twelve in eight hours more than once.

“Yes, I am a stud,” he declared. “But damn, I’m tired now. I need to rest.” We all did.

I knew I had Glen’s full permission to fuck Blake Porter. I knew we had an agreement that it was okay in the house as long as the other person wasn’t home.

“So, what do we need to get this show started?” I said.

“Stain,” Glen said. “I have to run to Home Depot.”

“Cool. You need help?” I stood up from the table to go back inside.

“Nope.” He smiled at me when he left, like he was sharing a secret. Like he was wishing me luck.

I took Blake upstairs and loaded the bong. It felt so good to be alone with him.

“So, she’s bragging to you about her sex life?” he said without preamble.

“A little. Apparently you have *rockstar* sex.”

“She feels threatened by you.”

“I know. I don’t know why. It wasn’t very fun watching you fawning all over her while we played darts last night. I kept wishing it was me.”

“I kept imagining it was you.” He leaned in close and kissed me softly. I was his again. “How much time do we have?”

“Enough for you to fuck me.” I figured we had at least half an hour, maybe forty-five minutes.

“C’mon,” I urged, tugging at his white T-shirt. “I want you inside me,” I growled. He took me and threw me on the bed. He was rock solid and wasted no time sliding into my slick, tight pussy. It was beautiful to be with him again. We fucked each other hard and I felt satisfied for the first time in too long.

He was in a hurry to get dressed again. “I don’t care what he said, I don’t want him to walk in on us. He doesn’t need to know about this.”

“It’s okay. He and I have an agreement.”

“You don’t understand... It’s the man’s wife I’m fucking.”

“Now you tell me,” I mocked.

"Ha ha," he said. "I don't need anyone telling Cami. It's better if no one knows."

"Totally understood. Believe me. But what you don't know is that he has actually encouraged me to sleep with you. I think he actually wants us to."

"No way. He does not."

"I know it sounds crazy but I'm not bullshitting you." I told him about our anniversary dinner conversation.

He looked at me, a question in his eyes. Could he trust me? Could he trust Glen?

I had always trusted Glen. I kept on trusting him, no matter how often he didn't keep his word to me personally. He was loyal. He was a stand-up guy and so good at heart.

On the way downstairs I stopped and brushed my fingers along Blake's arm. "You'll find me? If anything happens?"

He pushed his breath out. "Where else am I going to go?" His eyes clouded with love.

Glen returned shortly thereafter. He and Blake got busy working on the fence and I curled back into bed to shake off the rest of my hangover. I woke up a few hours later and checked in. Glen and Blake had just finished working on the fence. They cleaned up their equipment. I brought them ripe, fleshy peaches to eat on the back porch while they kicked back with a beer.

"I'm going to need help getting the stain off my back," Blake said. "Seriously. I can't reach it all in the shower and I can't drive home like this." We didn't need to talk about who was going to help him. It was understood.

"You two have fun," Glen said before I even stood up.

"Did he just say what I think he said?" Blake asked as we headed up the stairs.

"Uh huh."

"Does it mean what I think it means?"

"Yup. I told you."

Blake stripped and got in the shower. I got out the loofah and scrubbed and scrubbed. I loved his back, the taut muscles so beautifully defined underneath his skin, his tan, how smooth his skin was. He sprayed me with water so that I needed to take my clothes off and join him in the shower. We started kissing and I think I pretty quickly went to my knees. I could never get enough of his cock.

After a few minutes Blake said, "You should ask Glen to join us."

"Really?" I didn't want to.

"Yeah, I feel weird, being in his house, without including him. I mean we talked about it last night... He might be expecting it. You're his wife, after all."

"Not for long," I said, but dutifully got out of the shower and wrapped myself in a towel, then went to find Glen.

He looked up at me from the couch, surprised to see me.

"That was fast," he said.

"Blake wants to know if you want to join us."

"Oh." He blushed. "Sure." Of course he did. Followed me up the stairs like an eager puppy.

"Whoa," Blake said as I let my towel drop and got into the shower with Glen watching us. Blake moved to the back of the shower. "You are so hot." His hands were on his cheeks as if he were in a strange state of disbelief that he was seeing me naked, pouring on the Hollywood for Glen as my husband slid in the shower behind me. Exactly what you'd do to conceal your pocket aces.

I leaned in and kissed Blake on the neck, lightly. He whispered, "Go suck his cock," and pushed me gently away. I did as I was told, but not for long—Glen was too excited and came early; he already needed time to recuperate.

I turned back and sucked on Blake for a good while, on my knees, his slick hard cock a remedy for all the awkwardness with Glen, looking up at Blake the whole time. So hot, so tasty. I could feel the echoing pulse in my clit in response to his throbbing cock. Our eyes locked. I didn't care how fun a threesome might be, I only wanted him.

We chased the dial into the hot zone, but eventually the water grew cold. "This is your show, Aleah," Blake said. "Where do you want us?"

"On my bed. Not original, I know, but it's comfortable and big."

"Lead the way, woman," Blake said. Glen flipped the water off and went to get enough fresh towels, leaving Blake and me alone for a few minutes. I dried him off with the only towel we had, kissed him along his neckline. He seemed distant and I asked, "Are you okay? Is everything okay?"

He looked at me with glazed over, lustful eyes. "Stop talking so much and just fuck me. Fuck me hard. I can't think about this too much. Gets weird."

"Okay," I said.

Glen brought the towels and we walked to the bedroom. Glen started queuing up porn on the TV. As if we needed it. I told him I didn't want to watch that and got on all fours in front of the stereo to put on some music. From the corner of my eye I could see Blake framing my ass with his hands in the air, like it was a piece of art, Glen nodding.

I got up and turned to see them both wearing their towels around their waists. I yanked the towels off. Glen was so erect his cock was practically pointing at his nose. Blake wasn't as hard as I was used to seeing him. Maybe because Glen was there; he had spent so many months being paranoid of Glen finding us and now, here we were, exposed. It didn't last long though. I knew how to use my tongue. I slid to my knees in front of Blake and it was on.

For the next several hours we were a tangle of limbs and fucking. I know I focused ninety percent of my energy on Blake. In one moment of delirium I rode Blake and just breathed with him, staring into his eyes. He met me in my intensity, moment for moment; he was there with me and the kissing was so dreamy good. I checked in with Glen occasionally, but he said he was okay. Actually, he had a goofy, kid-in-the-candy-store look on his face the whole time.

"It's better than porn, isn't it," Blake said to Glen, his cock thick inside me. He pulled me back off the bed, turned me around and pushed me down, slid his cock in my pussy and spanked me. Harder than normal. I knew he was nervous.

I yelped. "Hey, no hitting!" I said. I'd be sore enough later without a welted ass to boot.

As if goaded by my plea, Glen went and found the cat o'nine tails in my toy box and started lashing me all over. Not hard, but not lightly either. Fucker. Did he never hear me? "Really," I said, not bothering to mask the irritation, "I don't need or want to be hit."

Blake flipped me on the bed so my ass was out of Glen's reach and fucked me with my legs around his neck.

I tumbled on top of him and he let me ride him. Glen came up behind me and jammed his little pencil cock into my ass. I screeched at first—he'd completely neglected to use lube—but then his own natural juices sufficed and I fell deep into the delirious joy, the crazy hot sensation of two cocks plunging into me, feeling them pulsing against each other through the thin membrane separating them within me. Wow. The three of ourselves got lost in the pinnacle of that heat, Glen climaxing first, and then Blake in quick succession, the three of us screaming together in release. Though I hadn't come yet, I felt a kind of contact high with them, the collective miasma of sweat, friction, satin, hair, pheromones, and skin was enough to put my senses on overload.

We all stared at the ceiling for a while after that, but then hands started roaming.

Glen found a towel, cleaned up, and got me back in missionary. As always, he buried his head in my shoulder, pumping into me like a dog in heat. There was never any collaboration in our lovemaking. I looked over at Blake, and said with my face, my eyes, "Help me." I knew from his expression of horror that Blake finally had some understanding of what it'd been like for nine years. He nodded at me and hunkered down at the foot of the bed. I felt his hot, wet tongue envelop my toes. My eyes went wide with the shock of the sensation. God, it was amazing. "Baby, you can suck my toes anytime," I said. Glen plunged harder and groaned, spilling his cum inside me. Blake moved up alongside him and they both sucked my breasts and Blake fingered me until I squirmed and squirmed against them. I didn't want to come, I didn't want it to be over for me.

In another moment I was on top of Blake and his fingers were digging into my shoulder. "You can mark me up." I urged in a whisper near his ear. "Go ahead, mark me up." He'd never dared to before, not wanting to court Glen's suspicion. He couldn't bring himself to this time, either. Instead he flipped me over, put his warm hand on my throat leaving me with just the barest ability to breathe. God, that was *such a turn on.* I trusted him so much; I loved to surrender to his power. There were long segments where I just lost myself to the sensation. They took turns, had time to rejuvenate, but for me it was two and a half hours of constant fucking.

At the end I was sideways on the bed. Glen stood at my head, playing with my tits and kissing me upside down. Blake slipped his cock into me *again* (God, his amazing stamina) and he'd somehow found my purple vibrator friend, too. He plied my clit with it and came in me again before burying his face in my pussy. He lapped at my center. He knew exactly how to turn me all the way on. All this at once; all this at once.

Given the orgasms I'd experienced in my life, I hadn't expected anything beyond a weak orgasm—swift, quiet, sweet relief in the wake of all the stimuli I'd been subject to for the last several hours. But something in the sheer quantity, the overload of fucking affected me. When I came, I came hard, I mean really hard; I shook through and through. I moaned, sinking back, ready to be done.

But Blake wasn't having it. He wouldn't let up with his tongue. He licked and played, teasing me, loving me, until a violent explosion of rolling ecstasy shot through me and my body exploded in an orgasm the likes of which I'd never known. I clamped my legs around his head and writhed on the bed. I threw him from side to side, locked in the clench of my legs but still he wouldn't let up against the tide of my release. He kept at it. My orgasm intensified, rippling out, spreading through the room, through the universe. Everything was *rainbow, rainbow, rainbow* and I saw a multitude of stars. They streaked across my vision, sparkly, as my body squirmed and convulsed beyond my control. So beautiful. I sailed on that high for long, long minutes. I actually passed out for a few moments. Oh my god. I'll never forget that. Never.

Book Three

Chapter Nine

Eventually, the three of us got cleaned up and went down for a smoke and a beer. Blake talked to Glen about fucking me like I wasn't even there. "You've got such a sexy lady in her," he said to Glen conspiratorially. "You know, I pride myself on this. I like to figure women out. I think I got your gal here figured out."

I was all ears.

"Yeah?" Glen said. He hadn't been able to remove the sloppy dog grin from his face since this whole thing had begun.

"In Aleah's case it's AA BB C—C-C-CCCCC!" His voice crescendoed. "I found the magic combo. Yes! I win!"

We all laughed. He told Glen how small and tight I was compared to Cami, and how to find my clit. As if it mattered at that point. As if it would make a difference in the death of our marriage.

We smoked our last three smokes and then Glen volunteered to go to the store for more, leaving Blake and me alone in the sun. I fed Blake a yogurt bar that was warm from being in his car. It went limp in his hand after he unwrapped it. "I know how you feel little buddy," he said. We laughed. He ate it, but still seemed low so I got him another peach and he ate it; I licked the juice from his chin. After, he looked at me gratefully and sighed, said, "That was exactly what I needed."

"You want to go snuggle on the couch a bit?" I asked.

"No, I need sunshine right now," he said.

"Okay."

"You were a good actor," I told him.

"You were too... Until you started looking me in the eyes. I can't hide when you look at me like that. Oh, and then with the growling and the biting. That might not have been the best acting."

"I was growling and biting?"

"Yes milady, yes you were," he nodded, a twinkle in his eyes.

I didn't—except for a glimmer—remember growling and biting Blake.

I ran my fingers lightly over his forearms, watching his little dark hairs ruffle in the breeze. I smiled at him.

He sat there for less than a minute, then stood up and looked at me. "Snuggle on the couch?"

"You want to now?" I said, surprised at his reversal.

"Yes."

It felt perfect there, relaxing into him. "You know I've never done anything like that," I said.

"I know."

"It was fun."

"But..."

"But I'm not Cami and I don't care about having more than one cock in me. I only want you."

We sat with that for a while. "So, Glen does not know how to fuck," he said.

"You're telling me?"

Blake went off. "You can't just smother a girl, bury your face in her neck and move your hips a little."

"I know," I said.

"And you don't ask permission to kiss someone, not with you. God does he know you at all? Someone needs to tell him."

"I've told him," I said.

"And you can't just ram in," he continued. "You have to do it tenderly, lovingly. With lube. He's not a lost cause, though. Just needs a little schooling." Was he still trying to save my marriage? Or had Glen just turned into a charity case?

And then Glen walked in. Blake was so comfortable, finally, he didn't try to shed me from his arms.

"Aren't you two cute together," Glen said. "Awwwww." He seemed sincere, actually. My snark detector wasn't going off at all.

Blake had to go. I walked him to the door, hugged and kissed him softly goodbye. I told myself again, *I have to leave this man. We can't keep this up.* I knew I was the one heading for heartache. I needed to get away, rip the bandage off, move on with my life, staunch the wound before it became gaping.

Glen stood up from the couch and casually stretched his arms to the ceiling. "I don't know why Blake has such a hard time," he says. "I've come four times in the last twenty-four hours and I'm not beat like he is." I smiled, nodded, and said nothing. Whatever he needed to boost his confidence, he could have it.

Glen headed out to meditation, a happy kid look on his face. "How are you doing?" I remembered to ask before he left.

"Great!" he said, "I feel so... Free. Just free." I hadn't seen him so light-eyed in ages. Maybe ever.

Chapter Ten

The next morning Blake called me at 9:30. I'd barely downed my first cup of coffee and was just starting to contemplate how to fill the hours of my morning. "Cami and the kids are gone for the day. Do you want to come fuck me?"

Why yes, yes I did. "I'm on my way."

I told Glen I was going. It didn't feel right to hide from him after the three of us had been together. His eyes lit up with a gleam of freedom remembered from the day before. "Have fun," he said.

I blew him a kiss on the way out. He always had been a good friend, I reminded myself.

I made it to Blake's and let myself in. I found him on the computer.

"Aleah." One word and I was trembling.

"I love it when you say my name."

"Aleah," he said again and the electricity pulsed just under the surface of my skin, fingers to clit to toes. "Aleah," he said again, every other sentence while he fucked me. Then he buried his face in the sweet depths of my cunt and licked me until I pulled him up to kiss me. He got up to go to the bathroom and I slid off the bed and landed in a sprawling jumble on the floor, limp and delirious. Happy. He laughed and helped me up. We got a hit and went out for a smoke. He said, "Yeah, I'm a stud." He counted fifteen times since Friday night. "Oh, is that a record for you?" I said, knowing full well it was nothing of the sort.

He laughed. "God, do you know how hard it was?"

"I probably do," I said, "But which time in particular?"

"No." He laughed. "You're funny. Ha, ha. No. It was hard to pretend it was the first time with you. I just wanted to pull you close, grab your hair, and tell you that I loved you..."

My breath stopped.

I got real still and stared at him. Did he have any idea how much he was fucking with me? Sometimes I wondered if I had any self-respect left at all. Except that he loved me so well and I knew I didn't have much time left with him before I left for a new life. I was having the best time and I didn't want it to end just yet.

"What do you want to do now?"

"Watch NASCAR."

I laughed. I'd never watched car races before. "Okay," I said. I didn't really care what we did, I realized. I only cared about who I was doing it with.

We snuggled on his couch, my head in the crook of his chest and shoulder. He told me about the cars and the drivers, about Kasey Kahne from Enumclaw and how the season qualifying round went and so on. I was interested and it was fun to watch it with him, he was so excited about it. I loved the way he rubbed my back, my side, settled his hand on the curve of my thigh. So nice.

During a commercial break, I stretched out on the floor. I got in bridge pose—I lay flat on the floor, arms at my sides, and slid my flat feet on the floor toward my ass until my knees were at a ninety degree angle. Then I raised my ass up so that a flat plane existed from my shoulders to knees.

"Ooh, stay there," Blake said.

"I can't hold this forever," I said, knowing what he wanted. He looked around the room and hurried to slide one of the kids' bean bag chairs under my back for support. He slipped my panties down and slid into me, delicious as always. Firm and hard in my slipperiness, so good.

After, he stood up, patted his six pack abs. "Yah, I'm a stud," he said.

"I know," I said. He was, too. I'd never known a guy to have stamina like him. I'd never even heard of a guy to have stamina like him. He had a gift.

"Did it hurt you to see me with Glen yesterday?" I asked, not sure where it was coming from.

"Yeah," he said, and looked at me tenderly.

"It hurts me to see you with Cami, too."

NASCAR was back on. "Do you want me to suck you while you watch?" I asked.

"Not just yet," he said.

"Oh, closed for business?" I teased.

"No," he said. "It's just that I want to hold you."

Oh.

A while later he pulled his cock out of his zippered pants and invited me to suck. I did, and soon I was riding him on the couch. So good, so much fun. After, I stood up and stretched, showing off the line of my body. I was feeling cocky and beautiful.

"It's a travesty, isn't it?" I said.

"What is?"

"That someone with this body and my appetite for sex is with someone like Glen."

Blake got up and kissed my temple, my neck, my lips. I thought he'd get sarcastic, instead his voice grew worshipful, reverent. "It is," he said. "You are a goddess. Your body just cries out to be touched, all over." His hands stroked my breast, my arms, my back, my ass, my pussy as he spoke. "You should be held, stroked, fondled, teased. Everything about your body cries out to be worshipped, adored, fucked. And you deserve it, Aleah. You deserve all of it because you give every bit as good as you get. You give it all back and then some."

Oh.

Blake checked in with Cami and found out she was just getting off the ferry to come home. We had just shy of an hour. "One more cigarette and I'm out of here," I said. "One more hit first, though."

He obliged me with a toke and ran his hand through his hair. "Oy," he said, looking around the bedroom. "Now where all did we fuck so I can find all your blonde hair?"

I smiled, my zealous brain having categorically stored everything. “Here,” I said, patting the floor next to me. “In the bathroom. On the bed. On the couch. On the floor next to the couch. On the beanbag.”

He gave me a look I interpreted as pleased disbelief. Like, *how can you do this to me?* and *please don’t stop* all at once.

We went out for a smoke. “Does Glen know you’re here?” he asks.

“He does.”

“Does he know that it’s because I called you?”

“He does.” I could have lied to ease his conscience, but I didn’t. “I don’t want to play games with you, Blake. I don’t ever want to lie to you. If we ever get to a point where we’re lying or playing games, we’re done,” I said. I knew it wasn’t what he wanted to hear.

“God, I feel like he should be here,” he said.

“Ugh. Why?”

“Because I’m fucking the man’s wife and he knows it.”

“Blake, it’s not legal, but you know it’s over between me and Glen, and it was his choice. He wanted to leave me. He asked for the divorce.”

“Still...”

“We don’t have an agreement that we have to be there or watch like you and Cami are supposed to. Quite the opposite. We agreed that it’s okay to see other people, be with other people as long as he isn’t around.”

“But I care for the guy and I still have to relate to him.”

“So do I.”

He stood up on the porch and walked a few steps away, took a swig of beer. “So, are you going to change your name?”

“I think so. I don’t really like Glen’s last name.” I thought for a minute. “I don’t know what I’m going to do. I don’t really want my maiden name back. I’m not that girl anymore.”

“My name has always worked for me,” Blake said. He was quiet a moment, walked down off the porch and onto the gravel driveway, in the sun. “Aleah Porter,” he said.

My eyes fluttered wide at the shock. My whole body went still. I think my heart stopped a moment. I slapped his cheek. Hard. He caught me up in his arms.

"Don't even," I said, tightly. "Asshole." I hit his chest. He kissed me. "Don't even," I said again.

"Okay, okay, I'm sorry."

"You're not sorry."

"I'm not sorry," he said and I kissed him. I looked at him, a question in my eyes. "You think I don't think about it, every day?" he said. "Throwing it all away and starting fresh with you?"

"I'd make you happy," I said.

"I know," he said, resting his hand lightly on mine. "But I will absolutely not leave my children. And I'd have to."

"We could fight for Davis," I said. "Cami's drug problems, her nights at the bar; she's not exactly an exemplary mom. All you have to do is start documenting it."

"No. He would go to her because the court system is biased and they wouldn't break up the kids." He looked so sad as his fingers traced my cheek. "You would make a wonderful wife."

"I'm not getting married again." I kicked at the gravel.

"I know. I was never going to get married. I don't need a piece of paper to tell me that I love somebody. Look at me now. I envy you. I envy your fresh start with nothing to hold you back. I think about that, about moving somewhere like Vegas. And then I hear Desiree's sweet voice in my head, asking 'Mommy, where's daddy?'" He shook his head. "I will never leave my children."

I would never be able to compete with the beauty of that. "I know. And I love you more for it."

I got home and found Glen very stressed out on my behalf. "Oh, thank god," he said.

"What?"

"I was just going for the phone to call you when I saw the car pull up."

"Because?"

"I was worried you'd get caught."

"It's okay. Blake and I are big people. We can handle it."

"I know. I know. It's just that I kept having these images of Cami walking in on you and I was freaking out."

"Well, she didn't," I said. "It's okay. It's also not your concern." I felt intruded upon. I realized, far too belatedly, I shouldn't have told him where I was going.

I told him how upset Blake was because he thought he was damaging their friendship.

"He's not."

"I know. I told him that. I told him I wouldn't have told you about going over there if you weren't cool about it. But I need to be honest with you if we're going to be able to move on and have any kind of real friendship when our marriage is over."

I will say this, after all those hours (and hours and hours) Glen spent in daily meditation... For the first time I very much appreciated his practice of non-attachment.

I went to the coffee shop with Jennifer the next morning. I was in the bathroom when Blake called and I broke my cardinal no-cell-phones-in-public-bathrooms rule to talk to him. What was wrong with me? I was kind of short with him, though, because of Jennifer waiting and because bathroom.

"What's up?" I said.

"I was just thinking about you." I didn't really say anything, just let my heart zing. "Glen called me this morning to tell me everything was cool with you coming over yesterday."

"Oh, he did? That was nice."

"All right. Well, I have to get back to work."

"Okay."

"I will talk to you la-ter," he half sung.

"Bye-bye," I said. The call lasted less than ten seconds, but it made me happy all day long. Float on.

Later, Glen was at work and I sat on the back porch cradling my coffee mug for warmth in my hands, musing. It was mid-afternoon in the middle of summer. It was overcast, cold, gray and rainy out. *Fucking sixty-five degrees in July. I hate this town.*

There I was in this strange tangled web. We were in love with each other, married to different people. He had children. I was the fucking other woman, the bitch, the evil whore, the menace to society. Everything about this, when I looked at it intellectually, screamed for me to leave. But when I acted from my heart I knew I couldn't, not yet. I knew the pain when I left was going to be devastating. I knew it was worth it. Every second with him was worth it.

Friday night was poker at Erik's. I painted my nails a glossy blood red. I put on red thong panties trimmed with black lace at the edges and a black corset atop skin tight jeans and a form-fitting scoop neck black knit top. I snapped the black studded dog collar to my neck and slung my '80s rocker jacket over my shoulder.

I drew no shortage of attention as I settled in at the poker table. My head was bent; I was counting chips when I heard the door open and then a wallop of energy hit my sacral chakra and exploded, a swirling maelstrom of endless sparkly energy channeled through me, like a thousand stars at once, connecting me solidly to Blake. I looked up and saw him in the doorframe. *What the dreamy fuck was that?*

The first moment we had alone he whispered, "That's evil."

"What is?" I asked as innocently as I could muster.

"Your collar."

"This little thing? I just wanted to torture you all night."

"Of course you did." He shook his head, eyes sparkling. "You would say that."

I was out of the game early and Blake never really got in it. Glen was one of the chip leaders and I was most likely in for a long night of waiting. Glen was an extremely patient big stack.

"Hey Glen," I said on the next break. "Blake and I are both out and he's thinking of leaving. Mind if he gives me a ride home?"

"Do you?" He looked at me pointedly.

I thought I'd take the opportunity to throw Glen off the scent. "Yeah. I mean I don't mind. I need to talk to him. He's been coming on to me a bit too much. You know? I just think it's time to tell him to back off."

"Do what you need to do." He was very understanding.

"Take me home?" I said once I found Blake.

"Sure, let me call Cam."

He did and I could tell through the sliding glass door that they were fighting and that he was pissed. He flipped his phone shut and came inside, nodded at me. "C'mon. Let's go." I said my quick goodbyes, grabbed my bag, and followed him out the door.

"What's up?"

"She told me I wasn't allowed to take you home."

Fucking selfish bitch. I did so much for her: free babysitting, I picked up groceries for her when I was at Costco, I did her fucking dishes when I was over there. I asked for this one little thing that removed absolutely no skin off her back... Whatever. I was done with her. We had pushed our friendship past the limits of its bounds. "But you're going to take me anyway," I said, surmising.

"Yes."

"Why?"

"She wants me to get home fifteen minutes faster so she can go out to the bar and fuck Carter. Fuck her."

He stopped to light a cigarette. I could see his teeth clench, outlined in moonlight. I didn't know how I felt about that.

"You know, poker nights are no good for me like this," he said after he'd we'd made it past the front gate.

"Why's that?"

"I just want to play and not be distracted by how sexy you are."

"Uh huh," I said. "It's okay. This—" I gestured to my outfit, "— was a one-time deal."

"Good. Erik kept catching me checking you out. It was awkward."

We got to his truck and he pushed me against the passenger side, lifted my shirt, kissed me right where I'd felt the blast of energy when he first came over. He looked up at me like he was waiting for something.

"I felt you there, when you came in," I said. "What was that?"

He smiled again. "Yeah, that's where I hit you."

"Seriously?"

"Yeah."

It hadn't occurred to me this was something he was engineering. Spiritual Blake was still new to me. It was better that way, engineered rather than just being the manifestation of our attraction; it was a tangible force he wove, holding us together. Its radiance was so strong, so sparkling and alive that even now as I write this I can feel the dampened echo of that energy as it echoes through the universe.

I guess part of me still didn't believe he loved me. Mostly because the psyche is confused by the circumstances of real life. It said, *If he loves me, why isn't he with me?*

On the way home he stopped at the railroad graveyard on Main Street, parked behind one of the rusted old boxcars so that we'd be shielded from any sleepy traffic. I'd been so hot for him all night. We kissed and I told him I wanted to suck his cock. He didn't stop me. I really enjoyed it. I lost any concept of time. I sucked and kissed him until I heard his husky voice say, "I want to fuck you," and I kept sucking until he said it again and lifted me off of him.

I took my clothes off—except for the dog collar and corset—and everything became a tangle, straddling him in the cab, riding him hard for a long time, sliding on and off, teasing the head of his cock with my pussy, almost peaking so often, him saying, "Stop!", "Don't stop!" so that I never knew which he meant. Crawling over him to suck his cock again, him spanking me, hard, over and over and over, on my ass, on my pussy.

I haven't been especially fond of his single slaps here and there... They were always a surprise that took me out of the moment. But this—I didn't want it to stop. The simple rain of slaps and spanks became its own crescendoing mantra crying out for climax, satisfied by our shared release as he shuddered hard into me.

I began to clean up and pulled my clothes back on.

"I want to fuck you again," he said a moment later.

"You have to go," I said, thinking of Cami. Knowing she was waiting for him, counting the minutes.

He tugged at my pants and I took them off. Somehow I ended up on top of him again. He trapped my hands behind my back with one hand and held the back of my collar with the other, pulling it against my windpipe.

"You will bring a leash for me next time," he growled.

My breath came raggedly as the collar bit a little deeper. My vision haloed and my world centered in on the moment. Everything collapsed in on itself, the intensity of the fucking, the sucking, hungry kisses, my need for oxygen. He let up and all at once I was consumed by my passion, like a pool of gasoline just lit. It was so fucking wild. I surrendered to it completely.

He screamed as he came, plunging deeply into me, rocketing his seed into my womb. We sank against each other, panting.

He drove me home and before I got out of the cab I said, “So, poker nights aren’t any good for you, huh?”

“Yeah,” he said, grinning. “Not at all.”

“I wish you could just crawl into bed with me.”

“I know.”

Chapter Eleven

I slurped at my too-hot coffee the next morning while Glen agitatedly shuffled real estate paperwork on our kitchen countertop. I could tell he was having a hard time. It had been three weeks since he'd asked for it and now it seemed like he was racing for the divorce, like he couldn't leave me fast enough.

"After we get the house on the market, I'll file the separation paperwork. I talked to a lawyer. She says we can convert it to a divorce after six months and save a lot of money in court fees."

"Sure," I said. Then it occurred to me. "What about Black Butte?" I didn't even know how I felt about Black Butte, if I wanted to go. It would be our last vacation together, if we did go. We were supposed to leave the next day. "I don't have to go with you if you don't want me to."

"We should go. You love it there. We both do."

I nodded. "I'd like to. One last time." Upon saying it, I knew it was true.

"One last time," he agreed. "And then we move on."

"Okay." I understood. I needed to get my act together. I started to go through my closet and figure out what I was taking with me in my new life, what I would leave behind. I still planned a stopover at my mother's before heading to Austin. For now, at least, that was the plan. I just didn't know when I was leaving. I was supposed to be helping Glen get the house on the market. In truth I wasn't really doing all that much.

Black Butte was empty without Blake.

Let me back up. Black Butte was a desperately remote river resort in Oregon. The scent of cedar assaults you when you first arrive, the air so clean it almost hurts to breathe deeply. But you do, because of its richness, so fresh, crisply full of everything left out of ordinary city life. Our cabin backed up to the river and we spent our days hiking through thick fir forests, swimming in crystal clear pools, and lounging on wide, flat rocks in the late summer sun. At night, we slept on the porch; the constant churning white noise of the river was the best lullaby in the world. Glen and I had been going for a week in high summer every year since we'd been married.

And now I didn't want to be there without Blake. I wanted so badly for him to be there, to share the experience with him. I knew he would love it. *Someday*, I let myself dream. Somehow, we would.

On the second morning I got up early, clutching my coffee in cold hands as I sat on our picnic bench and listened to the birds welcoming the day. I sucked down the coffee and clambered back into the cabin to make blueberry pancakes. Tears streaked my face when Glen found me with a stack larger than we'd ever eat. He knew I was struggling.

He put a hand on my shoulder as he stood behind me. "You were beautiful together, you and Blake," he said, almost like a brother. It was the strangest thing for my husband to tell me. Over the next few days, he repeated it, often.

Blake was constantly on my mind. I throbbed for him, tingled all over at the thought of him. Wished he were there. I thought about writing a letter but realized he'd just have to burn it. I thought of all he risked to be with me. I wondered if he risked it on purpose. I thought somehow that he had, that he was in complete control. I thought part of him wanted his family to self-destruct so that all he would have left was me. Every time we tried to leave one another we were drawn back together. We kept pushing at the boundaries. A little more. A little more. We couldn't seem to let each other go.

I loved that he loved to see me get off and he was always so eager to help. I loved that he spilled his seed deep inside me, powerfully. Yes, I wanted his child. I didn't care how crazy that was. I was always so happy when I saw him. I knew he responded to the safety I gave him with an open joy in the moment. I knew what I offered was better than what he had. We were happy together. I didn't care how long we had. I mean, clearly the longer the better. I'd take him forever, but I knew it was much more likely to be short, especially since I was soon to be moving out of state.

I kept hoping Cami would go completely psychotic and either leave or cause him to say, "Enough!" He had been telling me of her more and more frequent trips to the bar, the boys she was bringing home. Sometimes more than one so that she could have her husband watch and jack off as she had two strangers fuck her at the same time. So weird. I mean, when that girl jumped off the abstinence train it was apparently a huge fucking party. She swung hard the other way.

I wished Blake and Cami would self-destruct without me in the middle, but I didn't know how likely that was, sure he felt the loss of me as deeply as I did him after only three days away. I ached inside, my heart actually hurt, my sacral chakra pulsed, my pussy, my legs and arms yearned for him. I wanted to share this with him. I wanted to share everything with him. I wanted to make him pancakes.

After a while, my attitude wore on Glen. I knew I was being completely self-involved and callous. Mostly, I didn't know how to care and I didn't know how to fix it. I knew he was frustrated with me. Maybe it was my constant presence, my sexuality, my yearning... Probably all of the above. That, and of course, everything that was us was ending. It was already over. I made an effort to enjoy our sweet little cabin. I savored every last moment because I knew I wouldn't be coming back anytime soon and if I ever did it wouldn't be the same. Glen and I filled our nights with small talk, board games, barbecue, and s'mores.

Out of the blue Glen sincerely asked, "Hey, Aleah, how are you doing?" He looked concerned. He put his hand on my arm, seeking reassurance.

"I'm fine," I said. "Good." Automatic pilot. I realized I was giving him the standard American fake answer. I thought about it for a minute, because

I knew the truth wouldn't be pleasant for him, but I thought, *I can stay real with him and maybe keep a friendship or I can go plastic and lose that, too.* So, I said, "I miss Blake."

I couldn't read Glen anymore or maybe I never could. He grew sullen. "I've had enough of hearing about that. If I'd known you two were going to fall in love, I wouldn't have encouraged you in the first place," he snapped, still under the illusion that he had something to do with us coming together. It had to be hard on him. Sometimes I was unbelievably cruel.

I decided to be fake with him from then on. Being real just hurt him and then I'd have to spend the energy to bolster him back up when I was already spent myself. Fuck that. He probably had difficulty assigning any kind of validity to me and Blake. He didn't know that Blake had been harboring this passion for years, and that the affair had been going on for most of the year—not just the last few weeks. No wonder it was difficult to believe we actually were in love.

The future seemed so far away, the one where I would pick up and move in with my mom, and yet it was in actuality right around the corner. I'd picked a date. I was leaving two weeks after we returned from Black Butte. I was leaving. Moving to the sunshine. Putting it all behind. I reminded myself that it was always going to end one way or another.

I found myself daydreaming that when I returned home with Glen, I'd come to find Blake and Cami had split. Wouldn't that have to change the course of things? I told myself to pull it together. I needed to come to grips with the fact that it wasn't going to happen. I couldn't even begin to let myself believe that it would.

Blake's words haunted me. *Do you think I haven't lain awake nights wondering if I shouldn't leave what I have and start fresh with you?* I don't know if he told me those things to keep me hooked, to share his torment, to assure me of his love, or if it was any of that. He really fucked with my head a lot. More and more it seemed. Enough to make me wonder what was under the surface. Would he believe in our love enough to make a life together happen? Would he take that leap of faith? What would his future be then, with his heart ripped out because he left his kids behind? Could he be happy if it were just the two of us? What if I couldn't ever have children?

God, why did even I let myself dream? The hole in his heart would eat him alive.

I fixated on the words he told me the first time. *No matter what happens, I'm with Cami.* I'd been feeling protective of myself, and also quite strong. I knew he made my heart joyous. I knew I radiated when I was with him, I embodied love. I was happy when I was with him.

I felt the truth deeply, perhaps for the first time. It wasn't enough. It wasn't enough if I were the only one happy with the outcome. I wasn't enough for Blake by myself. I didn't come with his kids. I shifted a little, mentally; I prepared to move on. It was the only thing to do.

I thought more and more what a challenge Austin would be and how exhilarating it would be to start over. I was a little excited to change everything about my life, about how my song was sung. I dreamed of Austin and I don't deny my dreams often included a vision of Blake's smiling face in the sunshine. I imagined meeting him at the airport, him swooping me up in his arms, the first sweet kiss of reunion, our eyes locked, smiles plastered all over our faces. Taking him back to my place and trying to give him a tour but not getting very far because he would be so insistently kissing every inch of me, peeling the clothes from my body and strewing them all over the apartment. He'd lick my pussy and discover once again how wet I am for him. "God damn," he'd say. "You taste so sweet."

He'd leave my stockings on, but otherwise I'd be nude. He'd scoop me into his arms like I weighed nothing and carry me to the bed, the rest of the tour forgotten. I'd almost be surprised we made it as far as we did. He'd strip and lie down alongside me. Our bodies would open to one another. I'd drink in his masculinity, relax into it. In response I'd be a blooming flower, fragrant.

I could see through Glen's pain that he was trying to hide the remnants of his love for me. I watched him struggling with the fact that spending so much time with me made it harder. But I wasn't myself when I was with him and I couldn't pretend to be. I couldn't keep living that lie.

Even though he'd started the paperwork for the divorce, Glen was still figuring out that we were over. He started questioning everything again. He asked me under the stars, the river running alongside our cabin, pine trees rustling in the wind, "Is there any hope for us, Aleah?"

"What?"

"I'm trying to figure out whether or not I should fight for you."

He was trying to figure it out? "No, Glen," I said. "Don't bother."

"I need you to tell me to leave you alone."

"Leave me alone. There's nothing for you here." I knew swift and sure was best.

"Okay."

I wished I could cauterize the wound. I also knew that when the right man loved me, telling him to leave me alone wouldn't suffice as deterrent.

We went boating the next day and I was playing that over in my head, wondering if I'd handled it right. The radio was blaring and three of the songs Blake said he could have written for me came on, back to back. I don't think the universe could hit me on the head any harder. I took it as a sign that at the very least I'd done the right thing with Glen and if I kept following my own path in spite of the obstacles, I'd somehow get to lasting happiness.

Being cut off from all external communication did strange things to my brain. No Wi-Fi, no news, no cell phone. I couldn't help but also play all kinds of *oh shit* scenarios in my head: Cami talking Blake's boss into divulging his work phone records, something like that. I imagined going into town and getting cell reception, having a bunch of phone messages to respond to. The first would be from Blake asking me to call immediately. He'd tell me he and Cami were done, that he wanted to come see me.

Other times I thought about him forgetting me, being okay with me being gone, not missing me at all. I thought about not calling him when I got back and him not calling either and us letting each other go. Maybe his world would heal and it would be for the best. But then I didn't want to think about it at all.

When I let myself sink into the surroundings, I enjoyed the moment, the white noise roar of the river, the shivering trees. I wished he were there to share it, imagined a cabin with him.

Glen asked, "What's wrong?" and I couldn't tell him it was the pain of separation from Blake.

"Nothing, just sitting here," I said. I couldn't be the only one feeling the pain. I imagined Blake to be acutely aware of the strength of our connection. I trusted what I felt in my body. I felt my heart open and yearning to be love. I was love. I was in love and imagining a lifetime of it. I knew it would become torture for me later. I knew I was dreaming my life away. Goddamn it.

A bear came by the cabin one night. Glen saw the shape of it and found its huge yellow eyes with the flashlight's beam. I couldn't make out the beast, only heard his chuffing noise, the destruction of his paws just from treading earth. I was content for that to be close as I'd ever get to a bear sighting.

The last few days I spent a lot of hours walking on the riverbank, looking at the rocks. I'd always searched for true heart-shaped rocks. But this time I looked for rocks the color of Blake's eyes, soft mossy green, lit up from within by desire. Usually his eyes were just gray with tinges of brown. For other people, that is. He told me they were only green when he felt passionate. His eyes were almost always green around me.

"Your eyes get real light, like dark amber, like a jar of honey held up to the window in the morning sun," he'd said once.

"Yeah?" I'd smiled.

I'd dream about him running his hands down along the side of my body as he's lying next to me. "God, your body is just perfect," he'd say, reverently. It hadn't been, before. Maybe it was all the exercise, or maybe my body just wanted to please him. The pounds I'd wanted and tried to lose for years had just melted away over the months with Blake. I felt lithe, like a cat. I stretched in the sun.

By the end of our week there I felt like I could leave Black Butte the next day and be at peace with the time I'd spent there. I could always return someday if I wanted to, I told myself, but I knew there were other places in the world and only so many years in the life.

I thought about traditions and how this was really the only one we had built together, Glen and I. It'd been one of my minor complaints, how anti-celebration Glen was. Christmas sucks when you're the only one into it and you have to do all of the work.

I hit day thirty-four in my cycle as we packed for the long drive home. I craved meat; I started to get even more emotional. God, I missed Blake. I hoped my period wouldn't start this time, in spite of how crazy that would be. My cycles were always erratic to say the least. I feared it would start at any time. But it didn't.

"What is going on with you?" Glen said, disdain smeared on his face as we loaded the car.

"My period is late," I said. "Not much. But late."

"How late?"

"It's hard to say. Maybe a day or two."

His face drained of blood. "You think you're pregnant?"

"No, probably not. You know me." I swallowed hard and shoved a green suitcase in the trunk. He shook his head.

He was characteristically quiet for the first several hours of the drive, but then he picked up the conversation as if there were no miles between us. "The worst part is—" He cleared his throat. "If it is true and you are pregnant, I won't even know if it's mine or my best friend's."

His best friend's? "Blake and I have always used protection," I quickly lied. "I don't think I'm pregnant, anyway." Since when were Blake and Glen best friends? Erik had always been Glen's best friend. The best man at his wedding. The one he hung out with when there was hanging out to be done. WTF?

Book Three

Once I was back in Seattle I tried to face up to the fact that everything was ending. Black Butte. My life in my sweet little home. My marriage. I didn't even want to think about it, but I knew my time with Blake was ending too. We had almost no time left. I was leaving in two weeks. At night I dreamed he came to me because Cami had left him. Shit, I was in trouble.

The only thing that started was my period and even that was the end of a hope.

I was sitting on the toilet in our master bath when the phone rang a few times, scooting across the counter as it vibrated. I'd learned the hard way not to leave it in the back pocket of my jeans as I sat down on the porcelain bowl. I glanced at the screen and saw Blake's name. It was Tuesday. Glen and I had been back since Saturday. I let it ring until the tone went dead. So far, I had unpacked and finished all the laundry from our trip. I'd done most of the packing for Arizona, figuring out what I could live without for a few months. Almost everything, it seemed. I was grateful mom was going to let me stay with her while I saved up for the big move to Austin.

I zipped up my pants and started rummaging in the remains of my closet's contents. My phone rang. I looked down to see that it was Blake again. I let it ring. Crazy, the whole time I was gone it was all I wanted, to talk to him. But once I was back, I knew I had to try to let him go. I kept thinking about how if I took his kids from him, if the destruction was in any way my fault, he would hate me forever. I needed to give him an out. I had to try to walk away. Somehow, everything had changed.

The fifth time he called I knew he wasn't going to stop. I picked it up.

"You're home," he said. His voice, *ohmygod his voice.* I reeled from the impact of it. I felt my face flush, my cunt, too. My heart cracked wide open. All my resolve gushed out. I was hungry and sad and happy all at once. And desirous. So desirous. I almost moaned. I swallowed against my suddenly dry throat, felt the slickness in my nether lips. "Uh huh," I said.

"You were gone forever."

"I know."

"I kept asking when you were going to get back. Had to come up with some reason to tell Cami why I was so excited to see *Glen* and you."

"I'm back now. We got back a few days ago."

He let out an exasperated breath. "I'm kind of pissed at you, woman. Why didn't you call me the minute you got in?"

I didn't say anything right away. "It's because I wanted—"

"I know. *I know.* I can read you. You don't even have to talk. You wanted to give me the chance to choose my family."

"Yes." That was it. But he had called me. And called me and called me.

"So how was it?"

"It was fine," I said. Except I'd missed him so much. "Except—"

"I felt you missing me really hard at first, and then it went away."

His spiritual side didn't surprise me anymore. I trusted in our connection, because I felt it, too. "Yeah. I came to a kind of peace with it. I love you and it makes me happy to love you and I need to get the fuck out of your life. And I am. I mean, I will."

"That's what I figured. I came to pretty much the same conclusion."

I caught my breath. "So you're calling to break up with me again? Is that what this is?" *Not yet, please. Not yet.*

"No. No, I don't want to. But everything's really sticky right now." The phone started crackling. I knew he was driving close to a dead zone in the hills and I was going to lose him. "I had a confusing night last night," he said and the phone went dead. I managed to get myself all worked up in my head about what he might mean by those last words.

The next five minutes lasted hours. Finally we were able to reestablish the connection. "So," I said. "A confusing night?"

"No." He laughed. "I said *I'm gonna come see you tonight.* Well, this afternoon."

I loved how he claimed me. He didn't ask permission. He trusted me to tell him if he was asking too much. "Yeah?"

"Yeah. I need to see you."

"'Kay." I was smiling and I knew he could hear it. So much for my resolve. I had none when he called me. I could stay away, but if he came knocking... He had me.

He groaned into the phone. "I will talk to you la-ter."

And then I managed to dredge up my resolve. Even if I couldn't enforce it today. I told him, "You know we have to stop."

"No, I don't know that. Why?"

"Because with all the shit going down with my divorce and me leaving and everything weird with Cami... All I am is trouble with a capital 'T'. I'm no good for you or Glen or Cami or even myself. We should quit while we're ahead." I wasn't all that sure we were ahead, actually.

"Aleah." He said like it was the end of a sentence. "Listen. This is my choice. My risk. And I'm choosing to take it. You let me decide when it's too much."

He passed every test I threw at him, whether I realized I was testing him or not. "Okay. I just think you should choose to stop."

"Don't push it, Aleah."

"Okay," I said. I hated myself. I had no backbone. "What do you want me to wear?"

He was quiet a moment. "Good girl exterior, bad girl underneath."

"You want to see your little school girl?" It had been a while since I'd broken out the Catholic plaid.

"Yeah. Maybe. This might sound weird, but, do you have a longer skirt?"

"Sure."

"Pigtails," he said. "Stockings. Lace up shoes. Sweet outside, naughty underneath. Your green neon mesh is my favorite."

"Yessir."

"And if you were to be walking home from school after I arrive, that would be good. You might come in and find I'm already there... I might jump out of a closet and take you by surprise."

Such a turn on. "I'm wet," I said. I felt like I was living at the edge of my skin, waiting to burst.

"Yeah, I'm going to spend the rest of my day thinking of baseball and dead puppies just to make it through work."

I bathed dressed carefully. Pigtails as requested. I'd put my glasses on over my contacts at the last minute for effect, so that I could take them off and still see. Light makeup. Neon mesh set. It took me almost two hours to get ready.

He called at 2:45 to tell me I wouldn't need to be out for a walk, I could just wait for him in the garage and pretend to be coming in from the school bus.

"Or I could be doing my homework in the kitchen," I said.

"You choose," he said. "I'll be there in fifteen or twenty."

I called him back five minutes later. "Which one do you want?"

He groaned. "Now I've been fantasizing about both." A moment later, "Garage. Give me a few minutes alone in the house. Wait for my rap on your window." Our garage was detached, at the back of the house with a small patio separating it from the house. My bedroom was on the second floor overlooking the garage.

And so I did. I grabbed one of Glen's huge calculus books and waited until I heard a rap on the window from the house. I slipped my glasses on and stepped out on the patio in my Franco Sarto heals, pink satin pleated knee-length skirt, and white cashmere top. I paused for effect where I knew he could see me if he was watching, pushed my glasses up higher on my nose and clutched the book in tight to my chest. I didn't dare to look up. There was no need to act nervous—I had that down. I peeked around the side yard, a little confused because I didn't see his truck and for a moment I thought I'd imagined the knocking.

I walked in anyway, heels clacking on the hardwoods, and peeked through the front bathroom window. His truck was there. All day my body had been tingling at a fever pitch. I climbed the stairs and slowly walked on down the hall, my heart throbbing in my chest, adrenaline racing under my skin.

I stepped into the bedroom, through the closed door, and turned. I thought I'd have a minute or more to arrange myself on the bed for him. But he came at me immediately from behind, arms snaking around to grab me to him like I was about to fall—one arm at my chest, one at my midriff. I sucked in a gasp and my eyes went wide. I slumped down, excited, surrendering.

"Don't scream," he hissed. "I've been watching you. I've seen you walking home from school. I've wanted to take you for months." He grabbed the book from my hands and threw it to the floor. He tossed my glasses on the nightstand. "You don't need those." I was glad I'd kept my contacts in. The room came into focus. I wanted to see him. He dragged me back to the door and pushed me up against it, pressed my cheek onto the white panels.

I kept trying to turn my head to meet his eyes, to find Blake behind the mask. He'd shove me back, saying, "Keep your face against the door." He had such powerful, dominant energy. It was difficult to pretend to be scared; I felt safe. I was already moaning it was so attractive.

He held my arms fast behind me and tied them together at the wrists with a scarf. "I told you I've been watching you, little girl. How could you expect to be treated any other way, dressing the way you do?" He pushed my hands up behind me. "Keep them there," he demanded. "You have such fine, long legs," he said and flipped the back of my skirt up, then gasped. "And such a sweet, white ass. So cute." He fondled my butt cheeks, pressed up against me and breathed against the nape of my neck, into my ear. *Oh my god.*

I squirmed to see him and he pressed my face against the door. He let my skirt and arms drop to nibble at my neck and pushed his whole body against me. I felt how hard he was and began to massage his cock through his underwear.

"And you say you're a good girl," he admonished.

"I am a good girl," I insisted. "Who are you?"

"You don't need to know that. I live just up the street, though. I see you all the time."

I strained to see his face and he pushed my cheek back once again. "There are rules," he said. "The first one is that you may not scream."

I nodded.

"Say it after me."

I was reluctant in my reply, hesitant and soft, high-pitched with my words. "I must not scream," I said.

"Second is you must not look at me."

"But I want—"

"Say it!"

"I must not look at you." I didn't intend to uphold that one.

"You must do what I tell you." That was much easier.

"I must do as I'm told."

"What *I* tell you."

"I must do what you tell me."

"That's right."

He lifted my skirt up again and his hands found the plug in my ass. "What is this? Huh? What is this?!"

"It's—just something," I said.

"You're a naughty girl."

"I get straight As," I insisted.

"And you think that makes you a good girl?"

"I am a good girl!" He ignored me.

"Where did you get this?" He fingered the plug so that the vibrations sang through me.

"After my mom left for work I took it from her bedroom."

"And you wore it to school all day."

"Yes."

"Get over here," he said, yanking me away from the door and throwing me against the bed where I crumpled. "Stand up," he commanded. I tried, but my ankles were splaying in the unfamiliar heels and with my hands tied behind me all I could do was flop like a fish on the floor.

He helped me up quite tenderly, taking care to shield his face from my eyes. Then he slipped my shoes off, careful with the straps, one by one. In spite of all the roughness he implied, in spite of his strong, work-callused hands, he was exquisitely tender with me.

"Now get on the bed," he said, turning me and pushing me toward it. I hinged forward at the hips but I couldn't manage to get my body up because of my secured arms. "Get up there!" he said.

"I can't. I'm trying."

He lifted me and slid me on the purple satin blanket so that it bunched up below me. I heard him move away for a moment. "What's that sound," he said. "You know what that is?"

I heard a buzzing and recognized my little friend. "No," I said.

"It's called a vibrator," he said, placing it against my clit. *Mmmm.*

I shrieked and rolled away when it got too sweet and as I did he'd move it, placing it slightly deeper.

He pulled away the vibrator away all at once and I relaxed for a moment, enjoying the reprieve as much as I did the assault. "Who put these on here?" I heard the pull of Velcro and knew he was opening the leg restraints I'd painstakingly put on the bed earlier. It had taken me forever. Our mattress was extra deep; I'd had to use extensions to get them to the right length. He put one restraint snugly on each of my ankles. "Who put these on here?" he demanded.

"I don't know," I said.

"Isn't this your bedroom?"

"No, it's my parents'," I said. "And when my daddy gets home he's going to call the cops."

"You think I care? You think your daddy's really going to advertise to the world what happened to his little girl here? Slut. He won't want any part of you."

"What are you going to do to me?"

"You'll see. Don't be so impatient." I squirmed and fought as he fixed the restraint on my leg. I kept trying to see him.

Once, I did manage to find his pupils with my own. His eyes flew open and I caught a glimpse of righteous indignation in them before he surged across the bed and put his palm over my eyes.

"What did I tell you," he demanded in my ear.

I whimpered.

"What did I tell you?"

"Not to look at you."

"That's right. Do you want to be punished? Is that it? Tell me how I should punish you."

"I don't know. Please don't hurt me."

"You want a fat, hard cock in your mouth, is that it?" And suddenly I had one and he was thrusting deeply, ramming against the back of my throat. I gagged.

"No, little slut. You like that too much." He pulled out another silk scarf and balled it up, then gagged me with it. My mouth was instantly desiccated. "I'll have to punish you if you scream," he said. "Don't even try. No one will hear you anyway."

He returned to fixating on my white, round rump and pussy. He licked my clit, pulled me to him. I moaned until he started to yank at my pink skirt and I fell out of the moment, scared he would actually damage it. I'd paid a lot of money for that skirt. I made a panicked sound against the gag.

He pulled the scarf out of my mouth. "I told you it would do you no good to scream."

"Please don't ruin my skirt," I said hurriedly.

"You're worried about your fucking skirt?!" He almost broke character. I could see him turn aside from me, a smirk on his face.

"I have to wear it to school tomorrow," I pleaded.

"Fine. Fine!" He undid the latch with care, unzipped it gently, and loosened the straps from my legs so he could slip it off. He snapped the top of my black thigh-highs against my leg. "I like those. They're staying on."

He turned and tossed the skirt lightly to the floor. I took the opportunity to struggle in earnest, pulling and twisting my legs away from him as he grabbed them, turning my shoulders and body to try to get another glimpse of his gorgeous eyes, shorn head. He lunged against me and pushed my shoulders back down. "You tryin' to escape?" he laughed. "Where did you think you were going to go?"

"I don't know," I said. "I just want to see you."

"So you can identify me to the cops, after? I don't think so. What do you really want? You want this rock hard cock inside your wet lips?"

"I want you to kiss me."

"You want me to kiss you. Where?"

"My lips."

"Which ones, little girl?" he asked even as he dove in to kiss me on the mouth. His kisses were different, aggressive even. Had I had only those kisses to identify him, I wouldn't have known him.

He reattached the restraints to my ankles, and I felt one of the cords give, realized the restraint was attached to my leg but not the bed. "I'm just going to untie you for a moment so I can slip your shirt off," he said, beginning to work at the silken knots holding my arms behind me. I waited until the moment my arms were loose and scrambled to get away, groping for purchase on the slippery comforter. He pressed one hand against my back like I was a baby, flattening me against the bed, my head at the edge. "Take your shirt off," he commanded, hunger dripping from his voice. I struggled against the press of his hand. He slipped his second hand under my shirt and said again, "Take it off."

I obeyed. He undid the snaps from behind and never even saw the cute Barbie pink and black bra. "I'll have to hurt you if you move, you know," he whispered and released his hold on me. He slipped out of his clothes.

He came up alongside me, stroking his beautiful cock right at eye level. It was all I could see. "You ever seen one of these before, little girl?"

I shook my head. "No," I assured him, letting my eyes widen. It was so easy to be in character. He flipped me on my back, pulled my shoulders so they were in alignment with the edge of the bed, let my head drape over the edge, then slid his hardness in my mouth. "I know you like that, little girl." I moaned. He fucked my mouth then, hard. I wouldn't have been able to take him so deeply on my own. He kept jamming against the back of my throat. Sometimes I couldn't breathe.

"You like that, little girl?" he asked again. I nodded. I did. My eyes were tearing up and he must have seen. He pulled out.

"What do you want?"

I couldn't stand it. "I want you to fuck me," I whispered.

"What? I can't hear you."

"I want you to fuck me."

"What?"

"I want you to fuck me!" I half shouted. I didn't want the neighbors to hear.

"And you want me to believe you're a good girl." He smiled.

I didn't say anything, just looked up at him hopefully.

"No," he shook his head. "I'm going to make you beg for it."

"I am begging."

He couldn't take it anymore. The foreplay had gone on long enough and he was so ready. He rolled me back onto my belly, leaped onto the bed and straddled me, and took me in a single, hard thrust to his hilt. He leaned in close to my ear, still deep, throbbing in me. "You're not a virgin anymore."

I shuddered.

"Does it hurt?"

"A little," I admitted. "I kind of like it."

He rammed into me, faster, harder. I grabbed at the bed covers as the silky blanket slipped all over and bunched up more underneath me. I squealed, moaned, screamed. Oh my god. We were so good together. I was tight and wet for him, he filled me up completely. I said none of this, just reveled in the sheer joy.

"What if I get pregnant?"

He leaned in close, fucking me even harder. I felt his breath at my ear. "Then that's your problem, isn't it," he said. "Isn't it?"

I nodded.

"Say it."

"That's my problem," I stuttered and hoped that we were making a little boy. I went back to moaning. My cunt was on fire.

"If I'd known you'd like it this much I would have visited you much sooner," he told me. "Little girl like you all hot and heavy for my cock. You bet I'd have come sooner." No pun intended, I think. "Slut," he said, slapping my rump.

"The nuns never—said it would—feel this good," I managed to gasp out in spurts as he rode me.

He slapped my ass again. "They couldn't handle a whole school full of sluts like you now, could they?"

His rhythm intensified and he got quiet. I squeezed him with my cunt, made the tunnel even tighter for him and was gratified to hear his shuddering moans and guttural, through-his-teeth screams.

"Oh," he said, suddenly vulnerable, "I'm gonna come." His clenched scream intensified and he collapsed against me with the groan of final release.

We lay like that together for a while, his sweat covering me. I squirmed underneath him and he finally let me see his face. I stared at him, smiling, enchanting, seducing. I pulled him to me and he kissed me softly, the way I'd been hungering for. We made out for a while; I sank into those blissful Blake kisses.

I ran my hands over his chest muscles. "Were you in the army?"

"No," he said. "But something like that. Forced labor, certainly."

I think of his time in prison, how he was still paying for that stupid mistake. I was entranced by how large his eyes were, how softly green, like spring moss in fog. His gaze mesmerized me. He started to pull away.

"No," I said, holding onto his arms.

"You want more of me?"

"Yes," I said, wrapping my legs around his waist as he crawled above me. I lifted my hips off the bed and rocked against him.

"That's right. Wrap those long, sexy legs around me.

He was instantly hard again and this time he took me in standard gear, slow, steady, loving, sensual. I was blown away by the force of his love.

He rolled over, eyes closed, breathing hard. I leaned over him, all smiles, and licked the sweat from his forehead. I blew lightly on his chest. "God damn," he said. "That was the strongest orgasm. Takes so much out of me."

He breathed for a while; we cuddled. He got up to relieve himself and when he returned from the bathroom, he was himself. I slipped back into the part of myself I called Aleah.

"Hi," I said, standing up, glowing, ignoring the shackle and cord dangling from my leg, and it was like I was seeing Blake for the first time that day and all of the ache I'd felt missing him at Black Butte swept over me. I was so happy to see him.

"Hi." He stepped in to kiss me. He fell back to the bed and we lay together a little while.

He touched me and I ached for him, feeling the succubus within me pulsing against its cage of skin. I was going to have to leave him, I kept reminding myself as if it would somehow dull the pain when my actual time of departure hit.

Blake started kissing me, softly at first. I shook, moaned, fought back tears.

"Are you going to be okay?"

"No," I said. "No."

"Shh," he breathed into my hair, holding me softly. I lifted my chin up and found his lips, kissed him again. He kissed me harder, pulled me in tight, and we grew furious in our hunger for each other, teeth clashing, sucking hard at each other's lips, devouring.

"How was Black Butte?'

"I already told you."

"I want to hear more."

I thought for a minute. "Here's how it was," I said. "Everywhere I looked I wanted to show you the magic of it. I would stay up at night to watch the moonlight on the rocks and think of how much you'd love it. I wanted you to be in the cabin with me, playing house in the woods. And I was there with

Glen, who was angry and still in love and wanting me. Everywhere I looked, you were missing. All I want is you, Blake." I looked at the clock. "When do you have to leave me?"

"Not now."

"Yes, but what time do you have to go?"

"What time is it?" he countered.

"Blake."

"I have to go at 5:30."

"It's after that now."

"No," he said with yearning, his face contorted. We never had enough time together. That much I knew was true. "Fuck me," he urged, pulling me on top of him. "Fuck me."

I obliged him, of course.

If it was possible, his orgasm was even stronger than before. We surrendered to peaceful bliss after.

"You are beautiful," I said.

"Thank you," he said softly, kissing my eyelids, the tips of my ears. I lay my head down on his chest.

"So, do you still love me?" I said, half teasing from when he'd asked me that, half wanting to hear it.

He nodded. "I love being with you. I love what you let me do to you."

"Is it so hard to say?"

He nodded, pulling me close.

"Why?"

"You know."

"Tell me anyway."

"It complicates things."

"It makes me feel like less of a whore," I countered.

He looks me in the eyes. "Love doesn't change, Aleah."

"Okay." I could accept that. And yet part of me continued to demand that he open to me. I slid over to look at the time. "I said deeper or not at all," I reminded him of the talk we'd had when we'd first admitted to love.

"If you want me, you have to keep falling down the rabbit hole with me."

"I want you, but I can't follow you."

I knew it was true. It still made me feel sick to my stomach.

I ran my hand over his shoulder.

"We're too alike," he said. "This would never work."

"It would be great and you know it," I countered.

"Yeah."

I shifted so that he was cradling my head on his shoulder. I kissed his chest. Twirled the wiry, curly hairs on a carefully manicured finger. It felt like home when I was with him. I raised my eyes to him. "Thank you," I breathed. "Thank you so much for waking me up. I needed it so badly."

"Yeah," he said. "You're welcome." I mock punched him. "It's been fun watching you come alive. Besides, I needed it too." His voice trailed off.

"You okay?"

"Just exhausted. Cami was a maniac this weekend. I had to fuck her Friday night, Saturday morning. Saturday night she went to the bar and brought her boy Carter home so we had to fuck again. Sunday morning and night too with Carter and she wants to go to the bar and fuck him tonight again. I'm pissed. I said, 'Aren't you getting enough?' and she tells me it's sex that she actually looks forward to—as opposed to the sex she has with me."

I lay my hand flat on his chest. First of all, I couldn't begin to imagine feeling that way about him. Damn, she was so amazingly wrong for him.

"Then she said I needed to find a friend to bring home so I told her I wanted it to be someone like Carter, a friend that we can hang with as well as fuck. She whirled on me, 'So you want to fuck Aleah.'"

I was riveted. "What did you say?"

"I said I'd thought about it. She said, 'You know as soon as you stick your dick in her she's going to fall in love with you.'"

"Nice. What did you say?"

"I told her I could handle you, that if we explained all the rules up front it would be okay." He grinned. "I've got her mostly talked into it. Won't it be great?"

I felt sick. "No," I said. "It really wouldn't. I want no part of Cami in my sex life. What part of you thought that was a good idea?"

"I was kidding, Aleah." He groaned and pulled himself out of bed, to his feet. "I have to go. We'll have more time Thursday. I'm alone on the jobsite and I can get off early," he promised. He started to get dressed. "God, I'm so high off you." Quickly, he cleaned up. In the mirror I saw how pink my lips were, how perfectly and wildly my hair framed my face. I tried to tell him how utterly amazing the afternoon was. He pulled me in close and shushed me, kissed me. "I love you," he said quietly, my face cradled in his hands.

I reveled in the sound of his words a moment before responding. "I love you," I said. The energy, the mental connection, the pure joy I felt in his presence… Yes, this was love. My body echoed with the reverberation of his touch, with the hunger he invoked. Distance wouldn't change it.

"Shh." He put his finger to his lips and then slipped out the door.

My phone rang a few minutes later.

"Oh my god, do you know how fine you are? You are so fine. You are so hot," Blake gushed without preamble. "I was watching you walk out of the garage and you literally took my breath away. That pink skirt, your glasses, those braids. That skirt was just perfect."

"You hadn't seen that before, huh?" I said, realizing then that of course he hadn't. He'd never had reason to see my professional attire. I rarely wore it anymore as it was.

"I can't believe how you surrender to me." With his words my body remembered the feeling, blending in to the character I was playing, flowing easily with his lead. It felt like melting inside. The sensations lived just under my skin, the heaviness of relaxation, the airiness allowed by my trust for him.

"I love how you are so—not aggressive, not controlling—" I was actually searching for the word. "I love how dominant you are," I said.

"You have no idea, Aleah. I've wanted to do this for years." I'm glad for a moment, that I got to be the actress in a role he wanted filled, a little surprised he'd never managed to do it before. "I've been wondering where I could hide, how I'd make sure Glen wasn't around."

I blinked in disbelief. "You've wanted to do this for years *with me*?"

"Yes." He said it like it was the most obvious thing.

Book Three

Chapter Twelve

I re-lived Blake's feral and dominant lovemaking every time I walked through the bedroom door. If I looked closely, I could see the leftover lipstick staining one of the door panels, where he'd pressed my face against it. I chose not to clean it. Glen wasn't sleeping in there anymore anyway, he'd have no reason to see it.

I couldn't stop the flashes of memory from invading all the time. I found myself smiling at random moments. I was so happy in his love, so happy I glowed. There were light bruises under my tan at my wrists and knees. I'd press into them now and again, enjoying the memory evoked by the pain of the tenderized flesh. I loved that he had finally marked me; there were so few ways he could stake any sort of lasting claim on me.

I felt the days we had left slipping away. I was going to leave. Thursday Blake called and said he could only stop by for ten minutes. A quickie. I was disappointed.

"Can't you come early?" I begged. "I had plans for you today."

He sighed. "I'll see what I can do."

"Are you wearing a belt?"

"I am. I'll call you."

"Blake," I caressed his name with my tongue. "Before you go. I just wanted you to know that my pussy is freshly waxed and she is swollen and wet for you." *Who was that talking*? I surprised myself.

"God damn." He stopped talking to cough. "All right. I'll find a way to see you later."

Somehow the hours passed in a sprint. I walked out of the bathroom and jumped when I saw him lounging on the bed, waiting for me.

He laughed. "Now what plans do you have for me and my belt, little lady?"

"No patience at all," I admonished, shaking my head. "Do you want to ruin the surprise?"

"Pretty much."

I laughed and dropped the robe I was wearing and wrapped his belt around my waist, fastening it long and low across my hips. I was about to tell him he had a handle.

"You giving me a handle?" he said. I half snorted, nodded. *Mind reader.* I walked to the bathroom.

"Where are you going?"

"Come and see." He followed me. I hinged at the hips in front of the mirror and arched my sweet cheeks up to him as I lay my chest on the counter.

"No, come here." He patted the edge of the bathtub. "You waxed for me, let me see her."

I caught his gaze and held it as I hoisted my ass onto the counter. I put one foot up on it so that my knee was at my shoulder and my swollen nether lips were exposed to him. I kept his eyes trapped as he knelt in front of me. "You can see her here," I said. He groaned buried himself in my pussy and I felt my body reward him with warm juices. He took his time, playing with me, his tongue lapping, sucking... Of course I got self-conscious after a while.

"What is it?" he said. Unlike Glen, he always noticed.

"I don't know. I just get stuck in my head up here all alone."

"Yeah, I can feel your energy shift."

I loved him for that. I slid off the counter and turned back to my original position in front of the mirror. He put his hands on my shoulders and pulled me up, trying to turn me so he could take me from the front.

"You have a handle for a reason," I said, turning away. "I want you to take me from behind."

"Okay." He took me, beautifully. I loved how wet I was, how deep in I could take him in that position. My toes swiveled inward and I arched my back for him. In the mirror I could see the svelte line of my belly, my thigh. I looked so hot. My hair was a halo of blonde. My brown eyes were tinged orange amber with desire.

"I don't need a handle," he said. "You have so many already." He put a hand on my hip, and one on my breast, then slipped the first down to find my clit. I gasped as he played with me, pounding his cock into me, little shivers.

He was so handsome in the mirror. Our gazes locked. His teeth were clenched and he groaned. And then he took it up a notch or eight. I mean, he took it way up.

He unbuckled the belt and snaked it around my throat. Gently, he lifted the hair from the nape of my neck and took out the slack in the brown leather. I don't have the words to tell you how sexy it was. My clit began to twitch; my leg trembled, shaking with a palsied frenzy. I gasped against the restraint. I could only take air in shallowly—I had trouble breathing, but still I leaned forward against the belt so that it stayed taut. His cock slid hard into me over and over; I arched my back to take him deeper as darkness seeped into the sides of my vision. He shouted and we succumbed to bliss, his cum filling me up while my body shook in delirious orgasm.

He stood up and braced his hands on the either side of the counter around me. I pushed myself up off the counter and melted back into him, letting his strength hold me up. I stared at us in the mirror. He loosed the belt's grasp on my throat and took in fresh lungful of air; the world seemed electric. My hair was floating, my lips so red, my eyes serene.

"We do look good together," Blake said.

"You know what's funny?"

"Mmmm?"

"Glen kept telling me—when we were at Black Butte—how beautiful we were together. You and me. He always used that word, beautiful. Like he was watching art come alive in front of him."

"Well he was," Blake said. *No ego there,* I reminded myself.

He stumbled to the bed. "I haven't come that hard since— since the last time."

I felt delicious. We had a little time left to spend together in afterglow. We lay there, happy.

"It's never like this with her, you know."

"Like what?" There was so much goodness to choose from.

"Peaceful. I'm never at peace except when I'm with you. I like you best, Aleah Porter. You would make a fucking fabulous wife."

Shutup. Shutup, shutup, shutup. I closed my eyes and blocked it out. *Blake Porter did not just call me that. He doesn't mean it. I can't go there. Fuck it all, I can't.* I told myself I didn't even want to. That path was so rife with conflict.

I swallowed hard and managed to say, "Shut up." I buried my head in closer to his heart. I felt like a pendulum swinging from hungry to joyful and heartbroken in a single motion.

"Listen, I need to lie low," he said without preamble when he called the next day. He paused and I could hear the intake of breath, envisioned the cigarette smoke as he exhaled.

"I get that. But Blake..." I couldn't help myself. "It's not like we have a lot of time before I leave for good."

He took another drag. "I can see where you're coming from. All I know is it's starting to bleed over into my real life."

His *real* life. That hurt. "I knew this would happen. It's why I keep trying to stop."

"I know. Last night I started to spank Cami I was so frustrated with everything. And the more I thought about the situation the angrier I got and the harder I hit her. I scared her. She isn't you. She can't take what you take. She doesn't like what you like."

I knew I should be concerned when I heard this, and part of me was. But most of me was freaking throbbing with desire. I was so turned on. I want him to bruise me. My clit started pulsing and swelling. "Is she okay?" I said, but my voice was husky.

"She's fine. I didn't hurt her. I just can't ever be happy with her while I have you."

"It would be easier for me to leave you if I knew you were happy."

"Well then. I'll come over, one more time, we'll have some fun, we'll break up, and you'll move on."

"Sure," I said, not really acknowledging it. "Come on over." I hung up the phone to cry and get over myself. I knew he was teasing. I knew we were dancing on lies.

I wore my red and white checked dress from Amsterdam, white thigh-high stockings, my Franco Sarto pumps, a cream colored bra edged with scalloped black lace, a black vinyl thong. I lay on my stomach on the bed and kicked my feet up, ankles crossed, facing away from the door.

Blake told me later he crept into the room and just stood there for a while, watching me. I'd left him a beer on ice downstairs and two more up in the master sink on ice. He said he'd been planning to come in with a cup of ice and it was like I'd read his mind. When I'd called him that morning he just started laughing. He'd just picked up the phone and was debating whether or not to call me. I'd woken that morning when *his* alarm went off at 5:45. I am not a morning person. We had the strongest, strangest connection. I was collecting all the evidence I could find.

After he'd gotten his fill of looking at me, he jumped on top of me and straddled my back, grabbed my arms. I hadn't heard a thing because I had my iPod on and Sadie hadn't barked. I screamed. We had three crazy wonderful hours together. In character. Out of character. The thong didn't make it through the afternoon. The rest is all a delirious blur in my memory.

The next day was Saturday and Glen went over to Blake and Cami's to work on one of Blake's home improvement projects—payback for Blake having helped us with the fence. But he didn't leave before we'd had an emotional discussion about what went wrong in our marriage.

"What was it exactly?" he'd said. "I just don't understand what caused everything to fall apart."

"Really?" I said. "I told you everything last October, when we had that first come-to-Jesus talk about how unhappy I was. I've been telling you for years. You know, the broken promises. How disconnected I felt, how I needed someone to talk to. How important it was to me to try and have a baby."

"And?"

"And? And your response was to take up Zen meditation for several hours a day."

"What needs to change?"

Was he actually still fighting for me? Glen had the strangest sense of timing.

"I need to move away from here. You know how much I hate Seattle and the lack of sun and how I'm always, always cold." I didn't feel it necessary to say how hard it was for me to see him so firmly attached to his mother's apron strings because his family was only fifteen minutes away. How he always picked his family over me, never made me or us a priority.

"I would do anything, Aleah, right now, anything to save our marriage."

"Are you serious? What the fuck, Glen? I am leaving in a week." I shook my head and stared at him. Did he really mean it? I'd loved him once, very much loved him. Enough to commit to him for life, enough to marry him. Could we really begin again? What if we were away from all of this, from the dark gray days, from my infidelity?

"Serious as death," he said.

"Move to Austin with me," I said before I'd thought it through any more.

"No." It was his immediate response. He hadn't even given it a moment's consideration, just a reflexive, "No."

"Okay. So much for doing anything to save our marriage."

"Fuck you," he said.

I looked at him. I opened my eyes and just looked at him, this man I'd married. Did his promises, his earnest words ever mean anything? What could I trust about him? Did I even know him at all? I turned and walked away.

"You'll hate Austin," he said a while later, after I'd maintained my silence.

Before he left for Blake's he sent me links to YouTube videos of giant Austin-area centipedes eating mice and articles about police brutality. And, of course, he reminded me of the misogynistic culture rampant in the Texas legislature. I was glad he'd rejected it out of hand, actually. I didn't know why I'd even extended an olive branch in the first place.

"Listen," Glen said when we got home as he embraced me gently. "I'm sorry. That wasn't fair, this morning. You're right, it was out of the blue and we've already made our decisions. I want us to be friends. You'll always mean a lot to me. C'mon. Let me take you out for a burger at the pub."

"Okay," I said. I liked this Glen.

The waitress set down our first pints and my phone rang. It was Blake. I stepped outside to answer it.

"Hey baby. You want to come over tonight?"

"Why, what's up?"

"I'm getting ready to send Cami over to her boy Carter's for the night."

"I'll let you know. I'm at a restaurant. I'll call you back."

"Who was that?" Glen asked as I slid back into the booth.

"Blake," I admitted.

"What did he want?"

"For me to come over tonight."

Glen snorted. "I thought things were over with you two."

"They pretty much are," I said. "I think I could leave Blake alone if he would leave me alone. But it's like pot. If it's in the house, I smoke it."

"Seems like it's pretty one-sided to me, Aleah. According to Blake, you're the one having a hard time letting go."

I blinked at him. "What do you mean?"

"Oh, he made it pretty clear today that it is always you calling him. You sound like you're like a cute little high school girl with a crush." He was almost sneering. I knew he was going through a lot, that it was difficult to fight for this friendship, but I didn't appreciate him attacking me.

"Right, because it was me that just called Blake, right Glen?" A look of confusion clouded his face as he realized the truth of what I was saying.

"You know he calls me all the time," I said. "He called me—" I looked at the call history on my phone, "four times today starting at 6:30 in the morning."

"I didn't know that."

"He calls me two or three times a day, every day, Glen."

"He made it sound like it was just fun for him, like you were crushin' on him but there wasn't anything he was doing to spur it on."

"He doesn't want you to think less of him for fucking your wife."

"Oh."

"We do talk about ending things."

"I see your point. I mean, it's clearly not what he painted it to be. Actually, I'm pissed at him for lying about you. He made me think less of you, Aleah. Thank you for telling me."

I felt a sense of disappointment about Blake that I hadn't been prepared for and I was touched to find an unexpected ally. Glen did love me in his own backward way. He didn't like to see my honor impugned or maligned.

I nodded and picked up the phone. "I'm going to let Blake know I'm not coming over. And then I'll go home with you."

The phone rang in my hand as I was walking outside to call him. It was Blake. "I don't think tonight's such a hot idea after all."

"Funny, I was just calling to tell you the same thing."

"How are you?" he asked and I was quiet for a while, trying to find the words. "Okay," he said. "You don't want to talk. I'll just get off the phone."

"No, Blake. My heart is breaking. I'm fine and I'm going to be fine, but my heart is breaking. I'm leaving next weekend for good and I don't want it to end ugly."

"C'mon it's all been so much fun."

"Stop it. Stop compartmentalizing me. Stop shutting down on me. Stop belittling what we have. If you love me at all you should let me go. Don't turn me into a meaningless fuck buddy. Don't talk about me that way to Glen."

"Look," he said. "I was with my wife all weekend long and it was you I couldn't stop thinking about, you that I wanted to be with. It was you I wanted to see today, you I want to see every day. When I'm on my way home I have to fight the urge to turn up the Parkway to come see you. Every fucking day."

"Oh," I said. "Thank you." Through the window I saw Glen pulling his credit card off the tray and pocketing it. "I have to go. Can I call you later?"

"Yes. Please do."

It was such a bitter, bittersweet heaven.

I called him from the garage when I got home from the pub. I explained again why I didn't want it cheap and tawdry. "This isn't 'just fun' for me, Blake Porter. Let me go if you can't take it, let me go. Don't trash my name."

"Hush, hush," he said softly, when I let him get a word in edgewise. "It's me I'm protecting. I have to build some kind of armor around me or everything I feel for you will break me. It's not that I think you're going to fuck things up for me with Cami, it's that it's too hard for me not to let it bleed over. She's on me like a hawk now. I have to push you away or she'll know without a word."

"I'm all or nothing, Blake. Just let me go."

"You don't understand," he said. "I can't. Our connection is so strong, it's like I can't bear to be away from you. You know, the first time you left me, when you said 'Goodbye Blake Porter' and walked away, my heart shattered. Every shred of emotion I'd ever felt for you crashed over me. I ran halfway down the road, following you. I was so sad, heartbroken. And then you came back," he said and it was like dawn breaking in his voice.

"I know." I sighed. "It's like we have an elastic cord between us and it stretching between us, always drawing us back together no matter how far we're apart. I can feel you everywhere, I know when you're thinking of me because out of the blue I'll flood with your desire and know it's you. Then you'll call."

"I feel it too."

"I want you to be happy, you know. I don't think I can handle both of us being miserable."

"You know what it's like. Cami's a wonderful woman. Competent, caring, a great mother. She works hard. That woman has more energy… But after ten years, she still doesn't know me. It's like Glen. Glen is a great guy. But he doesn't get you and he never will. I get you. You get me. It's always been that way. It always will be."

Tears rolled down my face.

"When I'm with you," he kept on, "it's like you are just and extension of me. You touch me exactly where and how I want to be touched."

"It's so natural with you."

"Plus, you're so fucking hot." I could hear his grin.

"You're mighty fine yourself, sir."

"And your kisses. Your kisses are the best." I knew what he was comparing me to; I'd give him that one. "You know, it doesn't matter how long we go without seeing each other... My attraction for you is always just as strong as the first time I saw you. God you were pretty. Those tight little leggings and that huge sweatshirt. You were my Uma. You were always going to be mine. And then Glen says, 'There's Aleah; there's the girl I like' and he's pointing at you and I have to follow the man code. You were supposed to break up with him. You were supposed to end up with me."

For a moment my mind chased that alternate future and I saw a translucent path to the side of the one I'd taken, bathed in sunlight and laughter. I ached to go back and take that path.

"I knew you weren't happy, even then."

"Why do you say that?"

"Because, back in that apartment when we were all practically living together, he'd fuck you and I'd hear every fucking moan, Aleah, every one, through those paper thin walls and all I could do was fuck that chick I was seeing harder so that I wouldn't have to think about him fucking you."

"I had no idea," I said. "But why did you think I wasn't happy?"

"Because he'd fuck you in the morning and I'd hear how quick it always was, and how one-sided and you'd stumble out of your bedroom completely hungry, just dripping with lust. You'd sit next to me and watch cartoons with me and that girl. I'd be kissing her and running my hands on your thighs, sticking my finger in your tight, tight pussy. I knew I could have had you right then," he said. "I knew it."

I had completely forgotten all of that—those amazing early morning erotic interludes—until he said those words and then Cami's words from the first ballistic episode came back in a flood and I knew he'd told her about this at some point. That's what she'd meant when she'd said she knew all about the apartment.

"I completely blocked that out," I said. "I swore you hated me. You were always bitching at me, always angry with me for something petty. You wanted to put masking tape down the middle of the living room—"

"So I would be forced not to touch you. So I'd obey the man code."

"You treated me like the girl you hated in fifth grade."

"What? The girl I loved in fifth grade, maybe. The way I always teased you? The way you hugged me, every hug our full bodies came together, Aleah. Every hug you gave me, I'd feel your body against mine. Every inch."

It was true. It had always been so easy to fall against him, fall into him, our bodies fit so well together. "I know."

"I can see myself when I'm sixty three, my face buried in your pussy, eating you up. It will still be like no time has passed, like we were watching TV together yesterday."

I took some time with that. "I need a minute," I said. "I'll call you later." I put the phone down and lit a cigarette. I lost myself a little, in the dream of his words, in what it would have been like if I'd done like he'd said, if I'd said no when Glen asked me to marry him. I felt the ache of that missing happiness. He had me again, the bastard. He had me.

Six days. All we had left was six days. Everything was ending just as it was getting great.

Blake came over early on Tuesday. He'd called and given me twenty minutes notice. I left him a care package of toys including scarves, restraints, feathers, rope, and scissors on the staircase and raced to get ice in the upstairs sink and then shower, shave, slather on lotion, and get dressed. I'd already decided on a completely rip-off-able outfit and ended up with cutoffs, a pink T-shirt, dark blue silk lingerie that wasn't my favorite—including the G-string from our first time together that was completely uncomfortable. I came out of our walk-in closet, took one last approving glance at the casual sexy of my outfit and hair in the bathroom mirror and scrambled to get into position before he—suddenly his arms snaked around my neck and he yanked me to the ground. I was so startled I screamed. He clamped a hand over my mouth and I felt like a trapped animal, breath heavy, eyes wild, suffocating and relaxing at the same time. I fought him in bursts but he was too strong to get away from.

"I've heard all about you," he said. "My friend couldn't help bragging about what a good little slut you are, what a fucking whore."

"No!" I protested. *Oh, it was on.* I was so wet. I fought half the time to get away and half the time I fought the urge to move closer. "I'm not a whore, I'm not."

"The way you dress? The boys you tease? I see you, your sexy clothes, the looks you give them. My friend says you like it all. You're going to find I like it rough, little girl."

I whimpered and tried unsuccessfully to escape his grasp.

"Little girl, I'm your new daddy," he said and, lifting me under my ankles and neck, threw me on the bed.

I tried to escape at every opportunity. He'd corral me, and I'd spin away on the silky sheets, roll onto the floor. Once I made it to the bathroom. "Where're you gonna go?" he drawled. I looked at the window and he lunged at me. I struggled against him, I bit him.

"Now you need to be punished," he said and slapped my ass as he shoved me to the carpeted ground. I fought and he grabbed my throat, pushed me down, cut off my air. I was so turned on.

He ripped my shorts open and played with my pussy, said, "You think I wouldn't notice you biting me, those pretty little teeth in my flesh. I'll bite you, girl." Then he clamped something over my nether lips. "You know how it feels, now."

Whatever it was, it pinched like hell. At first I thought maybe he'd gotten some clit jewelry but looked down to see it was one of my hair clips. You know, the ones on a spring with about ten giant teeth. Goddamn that hurt. But I never said the safety word we'd agreed on. I squirmed. I tried to get it off. He repositioned it. Fucking ouch. Even so, I was so, so, so wet for him.

He growled and slid me along the carpet, still holding my throat. "Get up," he said, pulling at my shoulders. "Get up!" He got me back on the bed, threw me face down and put the dog collar on, turned it so the D-ring was in the back. He tied my arms behind me with scarves and tethered my legs so that I was on my knees, my ankles tied together and then attached to the D-ring on my dog collar.

He positioned me on my side, at the edge of the bed. "I heard you like cock, little girl," he said, plunging in hard from where he stood beside me, ramming hard against the back of my throat. He was so rough I had trouble breathing.

I scraped him with my teeth and he grabbed my hair, and said "No teeth!" He fucked my mouth hard and came so fast. Everything was happening so quickly. He tasted divine.

"You're such a bad girl," he said, walloping me hard on the ass. He hit me several times in succession, each time bringing me closer to release. Throughout the afternoon he spanked and clawed me. I was so excited by the possibility of scars and bruises. My whole body throbbed.

He played with the ties again. As he worked on tightening the straps, he said, "Let's see how bendy you are."

"Please daddy," I almost croaked. I caught his eye for a flash and then looked demurely down. "Please can I have some water?" I looked up at him through my thickly mascara-ed lashes. "I'm so thirsty."

"I'll give you something to drink," he said, stroking his cock several times before disappearing from view and returning with ice water. He gave me a few sips and then took the cup away. He changed my ties so that my legs weren't bound at the knees anymore. My pussy was more accessible.

He slid me forward so my bent knees hung over the edge of the bed. It was a deep plunge for him and he rammed his cock hard against my cervix. He pummeled me that afternoon, hitting me while he was fucking me. It was the strangest sensation of pleasure wrapped in pain. He screamed as he came, growled and bit me, then collapsed against the pillow after plowing throw two orgasms in quick succession.

He picked me up tenderly and placed my still-tied body alongside his, stroked my hair, cooed while he cradled my head against his chest. Tears of release flowed down my face. I let them. Such sweet afterglow. Heaven.

Home. “Shh,” he murmured until I’d quieted.

“God you’re so tight,” he said. “I’ve never had a woman so tight. How do you stay that way? Feels amazing, the way I fit inside you.”

We fell back into character. “So, you’re my little fuck toy?” he asked, yanking on one of my nipples. “My little slave?” I started rubbing against him. “Oh no. This isn’t about you. I wonder how much I can sell you for?” he said, pushing my head down so I could suck on him. “Couple hundred dollars an hour?”

I looked up at him with scorn. “I’m worth far more than that,” I spat.

“So you are a whore. My little slut,” he said affectionately.

The next hour was a blur of fucking. He took me in the ass, in the pussy again, again. He came easily five or six more times. I don’t know how often I came, it was wave after rolling wave. Plenty. So good. So amazing. I know I’m a broken record. I don’t care. The crack of his hand on my ass. He used a belt to whip me, too, leaving delicious swathes of red welts across my buttocks. So exciting.

“I don’t know where you end and I begin,” he said after, as we lay in each other’s arms.

“I had this dream last night,” I said as I noticed how his skin melted into mine. “I was at your place and you weren’t there but everyone else was, so I left and then you called me to come back and only you and Cami were there. She was wearing those slutty leopard skin pants that she has to use safety pins to keep together and she was not happy to see me. We started arguing and I was defending myself against her suspicion when the power went out from the storm outside and you dragged me off to the bedroom, your hand clasped over my mouth. I went limp in your arms and you whispered that it would be a while before she could find us. You started to fuck me and we were both getting into it when Cami walked in on us. I kept saying, ‘Blake’, but you just ignored it. After a few minutes she started yelling at us and we sat up on the bed. You told her you were done with her, that you realized you wanted to be free of her. You took my hand in yours. She faded out like a ghost. I looked up at you and asked, ‘What are you saying? You want to be with me?' and you laughed and cupped my chin in your hand and kissed my tears away. 'Yes, I want to be with you,' you said. I couldn't believe it. I was so happy."

To his credit, he sat in the glow of that. He actually shed a few tears. To his credit, he said nothing.

"I've been thinking more about what you said the other day; I said I love everything about you and you said I didn't know everything about you."

Blake stroked my hair back from the temple. "Where's this heading, woman? You want to know all the skeletons in my closet?"

"I don't care what skeletons are in your closet," I said. "I want you to understand how much I love you."

"I don't think I want to understand that," he said, rolling over on top of me, kissing me hungrily, yanking my top up to kiss my belly.

"Blake, can you just hold me?"

"Oh, baby needs to snuggle?" he teased.

"Uh huh"

"You're such a girl."

"Yes, I am."

He rolled on his back and pulled me to him, tucked his arm around me. Everything was ending. If I had things to say, I needed to say them now. I breathed with him for a while and then I said, "I have a gift for you but I don't think you'll be able to accept it."

"What is it?"

"More happiness than you know what to do with. More understanding than you can comprehend."

He sort of cried into his hands, a half sob and looked at me, his eyes a somber gray. "How did I know you were going to say that?" He sat up, caressed my belly with his hand. "It can't go down like this."

"I know. You can't leave her for me." Goddamn it. "I just want you to know, Blake Porter, my gift to the world is my ability to see possibilities in people and to make dreams real. I am this way because my parents loved each other so deeply." I didn't have to say that he wasn't giving his children the same gift.

"You don't have to tell me any of this."

"I do, because I'm leaving you."

"But I know it all already. I know you."

"I have to know I've said it all." Fuck. I really was pulling out all the stops.

"It makes it harder for me."

"That's why I do it." Did he not know it was my job to hold his feet to the fire? I squinted at him. His words seemed incredibly selfish until I saw his clenched hand at his side and remembered that it cost him to lose me, too. There was no winning for Blake Porter, no matter his choice.

"Thanks, thanks a lot."

We kissed and I told him I loved him and he said he loved me. Tears welled in his eyes.

I heard the clatter of dog feet below and the squeak of the garage door through the open window. I jumped up to see what was going on and caught Glen coming out through the back of the garage. "Fuck," I said. Blake was already halfway dressed. I looked at my watch. 4:00 p.m. Glen never got home before 6:30. Not without having planned it. Not without telling me first.

I dashed for the closet, threw my clothes on, and was barely able to run a brush through my hair before Glen burst into the room. "What are you doing here," he demanded.

"Glen," I said calmly, walking out as I wrap my hair in a ponytail. "Blake's just here to finish the house inspection. We were just getting started." I wonder how red my cheeks were, if I'd been beaten somewhere visible to Glen.

His eyes narrowed. "Where's you clipboard?"

"In the car," he said.

"We were just getting stoned first," I said. "Do you want some?"

"This whole room smells like sex and you think I'm going to believe that shit?" His temple pulsed with anger. "I don't think so. I don't think you can keep fucking *my wife*, Blake Porter," he shouted. "You're going to have to face some fucking consequences."

"Glen, what are you doing? What are you talking about?" I said.

"I'm talking about this sick, fucked up affair you're having with *my wife*," he said, still staring at Blake. He skewered me with his gaze next. "And you think you can just leave and let him get away with it."

"What?"

Glen actually took a swing at Blake and then a light dawned across his face and he reached for his phone, but Blake had Cami on speed dial. Blake got to her first, and skated past Glen as Glen was still finding her number. Blake was down the stairs before I would have even been able to act, I was so shocked at what was happening.

I made a grab for Glen's phone and managed to hang up mid-ring before he yanked it back out of my grasp.

"What are you doing?" I said again.

"I told you," he said, slapping my hands away from him, shoving me back away as he redialed. "You both have to face the consequences of the sick, fucked up thing you've been doing right under my nose. There has to be natural justice in the world. Blake doesn't get to get out of this Scot free."

"We had an understanding!" I yelled at him. "You fucking encouraged it."

"And you took it way further than I would have thought possible," he said. "Consequences, cunt."

I couldn't get over that he was letting a woman do his dirty work, that he couldn't punish me himself. Even when he was standing up for himself he was a wimp. I heard her voicemail recording and Glen left a message saying, "Cami, I know Blake is keeping you on the phone and he'll do it until you get home because he doesn't want you to hear what I have to tell you. So, expect company because I'm coming over. I have some extremely interesting news for you about how your husband has been fucking my wife." His voice faded as he walked purposefully down the stairs.

Oh shit, it was on. I had half an hour before he was there. Half an hour of them talking. Make it fifteen minutes. I couldn't overestimate things. Some amount of time for her to lash out at Blake but I couldn't count on that. Half an hour for her to drive her ass up here to face me down. An hour and fifteen minutes. I grabbed my packing list, glad I'd gotten everything but the essentials down. I prayed that the bug was full of gas and packed it to the gills, leaving just enough room for Sadie to have a little cave on the back seat. I was taking my dog. It was time to go.

I'll give her this. The woman scared the shit out of me. I knew she was a crazy motherfucking bitch. I just didn't know how crazy.

Book Four

Chapter One

Adrenaline galloped through my system. I gulped for air, needing more and more oxygen for the flight I was about to take. I knew I had to run. Cami would be after me in no time at all. Even so, I couldn't leave town just then. My muscles felt jittery under my skin. A thousand grubs, larvae, writhed in my abdomen—or so it felt. I could barely see the road in front of me. My vision faded in and out. I knew I could black out at any moment. I couldn't drive. Not far. Instead, I called Jennifer.

I told her I was in trouble with Glen and I needed a place to stay. "Come over," she said. I managed to drive the short distance to her house, blinking against oblivion the whole way, the windows cranked for air. She had tea ready when I got there. I put Sadie in the back yard and tried to keep breathing. I sank into her comfortable kitchen chair, gratefully noting the curtains drawn around the nook. Jennifer sat quietly while I told her what was going on as simply and directly as I could. "I've been having an affair with Blake Porter. For almost six months." My heart beat overtime. I felt flushed as I spoke. I figured my whole face was red. Everything hurt.

She looked up, like she was picturing something in her head. "That actually explains a lot," she said. "Why didn't you tell me?" I could hear the unspoken words, *I'm your best friend.*

"I'm sorry I hid it from you. I'm really sorry, Jennifer. I know I could have trusted you. It just wasn't something I talked about with anyone at all, for the longest time... Except, Glen found out, well, encouraged it, actually." I told her a little about his enthusiasm, about our threesome. "But then he came home early today and walked in on us. He went ballistic and left about half an hour ago to tell Cami what he knows."

"Oh, fuck," she said appropriately. I loved that she never judged me, just took it in.

My phone rang, skittering across the kitchen table top as it vibrated. Looking down, I saw the name on the readout and started shaking. *Cami.*

"Don't answer that," Jennifer said.

"I'm not going to."

"Good." Jennifer reached out and gently placed her hand on mine, softly squeezed me in reassurance that all would be okay, that she at least still loved me, then pulled her hand away. "So, what are you going to do?"

I shook my head. I was really doing this. This was really happening. "Leave town a few days earlier than planned. Maybe tomorrow."

"Sleep here tonight," she said without hesitation. "You don't need to see any of them ever again. I'll move my car in the street. Come, put yours in the garage."

My phone beeped to let me know I had a voicemail. I ignored it, vowing to delete it, and moved my car. It was the sanest thing I'd done in a while. I was grateful for her refuge.

Then I listened to it.

"Really interesting. Found out that you seduced my husband to have a threesome with you." Cami's voice took on a tone I'd heard at work before with her next words, one aimed at making her target break into tears. I felt my heart clench. "You are going to talk to me and you are going to really take responsibility for a whole bunch of bullshit that's been going on. And I understand you tried to seduce him on Tuesday night before I kind of 'gave permission' quote unquote." I noticed a weird pain radiating from my thighs. "Now your husband thinks that you've been fucking him for weeks. SO HELP ME GOD," her voice crescendoed and collapsed into a focused rage, her final words issued through a nearly clenched jaw, "if it's true, I will kill you. I will fucking beat the living shit out of you. You will talk to me. And you will tell me the truth."

She didn't exactly give me a lot of incentive to call her back. And, given her history of punishing honesty, I decided then and there that I would never talk to Cami Porter again. Never.

I struggled to breathe as the reality of the situation seized my body. I could see Jennifer's lips moving, but nothing registered through the ringing in my ears. My cheeks flushed and drained. I felt alternately freezing and roasting. My breathing shallow, my lungs pumped furiously to get enough oxygen. Jennifer reached out, her calming hand on mine.

"Give me that," she said, taking my phone from me. She replayed the message for herself. She touched the screen a few times and I assumed she deleted it. Probably for the best. Part of me thought evidence of a death threat might not be a bad thing to have.

"Ignore her. Cut the cord, Aleah. It's all you can do now," she said and handed me back the phone. "Whatever she sends, just delete it right away."

I could feel everything crashing around me. I'd never see Blake again. His life was exploding around him. It was what we never wanted. It was why I was leaving the state in the first place. Glen couldn't have waited four fucking days and let everyone find their own peace? Those kids. Oh god, what was going to happen to those kids?

I told Jennifer as much as she wanted to know. Probably more. It was a few hours before my phone rang. We both started a little at the sound. "It's Blake," I said.

"Don't answer it."

"I have to."

"You don't."

I picked it up. "Hey there," I said.

His voice was aggressive and full of emotion. "Aleah, it's Blake," he said, as if I wouldn't have known unless he told me. "Why does my wife think that you and I have been having an affair?"

"Why does your wife think?" my voice trailed off. "I don't know, why would she think that?"

"Yes, and why in the world does Glen think that we had a threesome? What the fuck is going on with you guys?" Blake sounded like a bad actor reading his script for the first time.

I struggled to keep up with what he needed me to say. I was never good at thinking fast on my feet.

"I don't know what you're talking about," I said. "Why would you ask me that?"

"She's listening!" Jennifer hissed at me, making a knifing motion across her throat. "Get off the phone."

"You sound funny," I said. "Is she listening to this?"

"You bet I'm fucking listening to this, you two bit whore. You have been lying to me all this time and Glen just served up your head on a silver platter. You are going to pay for what you've done to me and what you've done to my family."

I took Jennifer's advice and hung up.

"She was listening." She stated the obvious.

"Yeah."

"Girlfriend, I have been in your shoes and it is not pretty."

"Oh my god." I collapsed on the bed next to her. "She has so much venom and she's so focused on *me*."

"What did you think was going to happen?!"

"I thought she'd be angry with Blake for cheating on her."

"No, *Glen* is angry with Blake." She was shaking her head. "Haven't you seen any movie, ever? Women always blame the other woman. Otherwise they have to face the idea that they're not sexy enough or attractive enough or interesting enough to keep their own man. Not many women are going to choose that route."

"Well, when you put it that way." I was SOL. Though I'd heard Jennifer's husband David talk about how affairs are, at their core, symptoms of "fucked up relationships," I'd failed to take into account denial and the other woman syndrome. I felt stupid. Glen had grown almost protective of me up until the end, had been angry at Blake for lying about me. He thought that by informing Cami of our affair he'd be punishing Blake. Now I knew better. He was putting the bitch on me. Well, fuck, what did I know? Maybe he hated me for what we'd become. Maybe that was the clarity he'd reached at the Buddhist retreat I'd sent him on. Maybe he knew exactly what he was doing.

I shuddered a little at the thought. I couldn't believe that of Glen. He'd promised to love and cherish me. I had to believe these were unintended consequences.

"What are you going to do?"

"I don't know." I knew Jennifer had had had a few affairs back in the days before David. "What did you do, when you were in my shoes?"

"Oh, I ran." She placed her hand on mine, warmth radiating from it, and gently squeezed. "You love him, don't you?"

A tear fell. "I do." I nodded. "Goddamn it."

I got texts from Glen's sister. *'lying cunt how dare you hurt my brother like this?'* and *'your a fucking whore fucking his Best Friend behind his back.'*

And one by one all of our mutual friends sent me texts:

'how could you, fucking cunt. Succubus'

and

'wow, I never really liked you but I never knew what a whore you were,'

and

'lying whore cunt bitch sicko'

Every text rattled me. Every chime set me on edge. I felt hunted by the immediacy of the punishment.

"Power your phone off," Jennifer urged.

I shook my head. "I can't." I couldn't say it out loud, but I knew this was the modern day equivalent of the village pillory. I felt the sting of every lash. I should have shut it off. But this was the punishment that they were meting out and I, who had broken the rules, had to stand for the consequences as Glen had dictated. I owed him that much, at least.

My afternoon was peppered with joy. I'll spare you most of it. I knew Cami and Glen were spreading the story. Glen's family. All of our friends. I was glad I'd never given him my girlfriends' information. Neither Glen nor Cami could cut me off from everyone and everything. And thank god for the constant balm of Jennifer's presence.

'you sick bitch! fucking homewrecker! Fucked up sick perv'

I couldn't understand why Glen and Cami would want everyone they knew to know everything. I mean, if my husband cheated on me, I wouldn't want to scream it to the world. Apparently, that was just me. Cami declared I was a fucking slut on my wall and I deactivated my Facebook page.

From Glen's mother: *'your dead to us.'* At least that one felt a little more like relief than shame. I'd never have to cringe at her grammar again. Or eat her bland food. Or watch her floss her teeth with her hair at the dinner table. It wasn't exactly relief, but it was a lot less painful than seeing friend after friend that I cared about, people I'd known for a decade, step away from me and my life as if I were nothing and never had been. Slowly, I was becoming a ghost. If I were dead to them, perhaps they'd leave me with no reason to live. Or, I imagined that was their hope.

I surrendered to exhaustion and slept fitfully for about two hours. I awoke, not knowing where I was at first and then everything hit me anew. I stared at the ceiling for hours, my stomach in knots, and I cried. The voicemail Cami left reverberated in my head like Princess Leia's message to Obi-Wan. Except more sinister. "*So help me God, I will kill you. I will fucking beat the living shit out of you. So help me God, I will kill you.*"

Glen called me in the morning. I'd barely rolled out of bed, but had managed to get on some jeans and a T-shirt, and was working on my first cup of coffee.

I picked up. "Look," he said. "Something had to happen. I'm not saying I'm sorry for what I did. But Cami is going batshit crazy over you. Ballistic. She wants to kill you. I mean, she literally wants to kill you." He sounded like he was on the verge of hyperventilating. "She wants me to set up a goodbye lunch date with you so that she can go instead of me and beat the living shit out of you. I wanted you to face the piper, Aleah. I didn't want it to get violent." Once again his Zen Buddhism worked in my favor.

"I guess it's too late for that now," I said, my voice cracking. "You should have considered those kids. You should have considered that woman before you let all hell break loose."

Glen's tone took on a fierce quality. "Don't you even begin to put this on me."

"I was already gone, Glen. I was four days away from being gone for good. For all the pain to be over. Did you think I was just going to hang around forever for the joy of being Blake's mistress? I was leaving and now I'm gone. I'll arrange to get the rest of my stuff sometime. Put the house on the market. Goodbye." I hung up. I didn't care how I sounded. I knew why he'd done it. I understood. In his shoes I might have even made the same choice. I just didn't think he thought it through. In fact, I know he hadn't. Cami would have relaxed as soon as I left town if he hadn't told her. He could have let it die. But no, he had to unleash the beast.

I slugged down a few cups of coffee before grabbing up my keys. I didn't like goodbyes. Who did, really? Jennifer thrust a warm knit cardigan at me and put a necklace over my head before she hugged me. "It gets cold in Arizona, too," she said. She always had something perfect for me. I never knew what to get her. I felt completely inadequate as a friend. What a fuckup I was. What a complete fuckup.

"I'll miss you a ton," I said, tears streaming down my face. "I'll call."

"Do," she said. "Keep me posted about the Cami-monster. Stay strong, girl. I'm proud of you." Her hazel eyes glistened with tears. I didn't bother holding mine back. Everything was ending and I'd brought it all on myself. I didn't deserve any of her kindness.

I fled Seattle. Took the five south to Portland. That was typically as far as my stamina would take me in a single jaunt. I'd done that three-and-a-half-hour stint more often than I cared to recount, so often after my father died, while my mom was alone, before she moved to be with the snowbirds in Tucson.

Cami started a series of vitriolic assaults through a string of voicemails, each starting with "And also," as if we were having some sort of brainstorming session and she was just adding ideas to the white board.

"And also, you are a lying piece of shit and you are going to have to live with that."

A few hours later: "And also, really nice you've been fucking my husband all these months. Very, very nice. And nice try on the phone there, too. Wasn't that fun? I listened to every fucking word your filthy dirty mouth said. Basically, you're the biggest piece of shit I've ever met and I hope you fucking rot in hell. Have a nice fucking life you fucking cunt."

Fueled by adrenaline, I pushed through Portland, down to my alma mater in Eugene. I stopped at Fred Meyer's and bought myself a Duck keychain and a University of Oregon T-shirt. Who knew when I would be back in Eugene? I stopped at Track Town Pizza for a taste of college and my youth. I could just stay here, I thought. I'd always loved Eugene. It was the only city I'd ever been to where, driving into it for the first time, it already felt like coming home.

Who was I kidding? It wasn't far enough. Blake was a car ride away. So was Cami. It wasn't nearly far enough.

Another voicemail: "And also I'm setting up a lunch with your boss so that she knows what a selfish, manipulative home-wrecking cunt whore you are. Cannot wait to do that, that's going to be delightful." Her voice grew thick as she held back tears. "You have no idea how you hurt my family and my babies." I could almost see her body wracked with pain; I could certainly hear it. "You have no idea what you did to those two innocent, sweet little darlings, let alone me and Blake and our whole fucking family, extended and all. Everyone fucking hates you. HATES YOU. FUCKING HATES YOU."

That one, I had to give to her. That one got to me. She hit me upside the head first with job security; I hadn't seen that one coming. And then the hardcore punch to the stomach, the kids. Followed by the heated flush of shame as I felt the radiant hatred of a community channeled through Cami's bitter words. Touché, Cami Porter. Touché.

They kept coming and coming over the hours and days. I deleted most of them. I should have just powered off my phone. I don't know why I didn't. Except a sick hope that she'd kick him out and it would be over and we could be together. We'd paid the price, surely. We'd abandoned marriages, lives, children.

This is where I understand if you hate me. I didn't feel guilt. I didn't feel guilt for celebrating a loving relationship and fabulous sex with a man that

I had known for over a decade and loved as long. I didn't feel guilt for wrecking a home—they'd done that work on their own in my opinion. I felt shame. I felt the shame of the naked person in the spotlight who is told it is shameful to be naked. I felt defiant. I felt righteous. And I felt cut off, with no hope real hope of return. And sad and lonely and hopeless, those things too.

I pushed on south, past Roseburg, past Ashland, through the winding hills. There were a few crazy stretches on the highway there through the mountain pass. I was grateful for the challenge of the road to take my attention from the pain, even if briefly. I stopped in Yreka and got a room. I splurged and got one where I didn't think I'd spend the night wondering when the roaches were going to start crawling over me, or if I'd step on them on the way to the bathroom. I snuck Sadie in and let her up next to me on the bed. At least she just loved me. There's something to be said for the unwavering love of a dog. Damn, I was grateful for it.

I got up in the morning and forced myself to eat bacon, eggs, hash browns and a healthy dose of coffee. I bought a few muffins for the road and made myself pee extra hard before I left. I didn't want to have to stop too soon.

I started crying again when I got on the road and I cried for hours and hours until I couldn't cry any more. I drove and I cried. And I sang. I sang because all of the songs still made sense. And I knew Blake was doing what he had to do to save his marriage and his kids and I was giving him the space he needed to do that. It's boring to read about crying and tears, I'm sure. I would have been bored myself if it weren't so painful. So just take my word for it. Buckets of tears. Wailing. Aching. All that.

I know I sound like a stupid schoolgirl. I know I don't deserve your compassion. All I can say was that when I was with Blake Porter, I was his. He was my heroin. When I was without him, all I did was yearn. There was no controlling the raw need I felt to be with him. And so I cried.

My phone rang and I glanced down at the screen to see Blake's name. My heart seized with panic and joy simultaneously. It could be Cami, though. It was probably Cami. I didn't pick up and after a minute, I saw that a voicemail registered on the phone.

I pulled over at the next rest stop to listen to it. “Ahh.” The message started with Blake’s voice releasing a deep sigh. I could hear the stuffiness in his voice, the result of days spent crying making him sound like he had a bad cold. His voice was ragged on the phone; it sounded hollow, like it was propped up by smoke and bones. I knew he had cried as much as I had. “I had to let you know I’ve...” He sniffed. Another deep release of breath. “I’ve lost everything.” He paused, a deep breath. “I’ve lost everything. My wife, my marriage, my kids.” His gusty breath echoed through the recording, punctuating each word. He didn’t mention me. I didn’t count. Not anymore. I knew this. “Cami cut me off. I’ve lost everything.” His voice found its normal cadence as he began to tell his story. “She talks to Glen. He talks to her. Hourly. They’ve been sharing, fillin’ in, puttin’ pieces together. Everyone knows. Everyone. Glen and Cami have turned everyone against me. And I am. Yeah.” His voice dropped to a whisper. “I lost it all. I lost everything.” Another big breath, a quaking, “*Oh my god*.” The message ended.

I sat in my car. What did I do with that? Why hadn’t I picked up the phone? Sadie whimpered and I leashed her up to take her to the dog zone. A pinprick of hope sparked in my chest. He was talking to me. He had reached out to me for a reason. He hadn’t lost everything. *He could still have me.*

It had only been a few minutes. I called him back. “Blake,” I started, sniffling.

He sobbed. “Don’t call me!” he shouted and hung up. He sounded irate.

I’d been wrong. I let that sink in.

I ached on through the miles, down I-5. I was numb. I drove on, the remnants of adrenaline coursing through my body still. I drove on the fumes of fear and pain.

I made it to L.A. and looked up an old college pal, Julie, who was a raging lesbian and a perfect friend for the moment. Someone who knew me enough to care and who was removed enough from my main circle of friends that I could be completely honest and tell her everything, over several bottles of wine, about the empty years with Glen, the many times we'd talked and he'd promised change that never came to fruition. I told her about Blake's flirtation with me during our house inspection, when I realized what he was doing.

I told her about Valentine's Day. "Oh honey, I would have left his ass right then," she said of Glen. "I wondered about you, getting married right after your father died. I wondered if you weren't looking for something that wasn't there, jumping on to the first available ship."

My phone rang. I picked it up and saw Blake's name on the readout. "Don't," Julie said. She was right. I put the phone down. We sipped our wine for a few minutes until the voicemail notification beeped. I swallowed. "I have to listen. It might be..." I didn't dare voice my hope aloud.

"Put it on speaker," Julie urged, sitting forward in her chair. Part of me wanted privacy. Part of me wanted support. I hit speaker and play.

Cami's voice came on, confident and direct. "Blake and I would both like to leave you a message that you're a fucking cunt bitch whore." She spaced the last four words out evenly. I heard a muffled, "Here you go."

Blake breathed into the phone. "And thanks, for all this. Really."

"Fucking cunt," I heard Cami say in the background. Blake breathed heavily into the phone. "She ruined your fucking life. Tell her." Cami again.

"You ruined my fucking life. You ruined my fucking life. I have nothing. You fucking cunt." Blake fed venom into his words. My heart fluttered erratically, my chest clenched with pain, like fingers of electricity spasming out from my heart. His breath sounded raggedly over the line. And then, "Ahh, fuck." It was almost a whisper.

"Tell her to fuck herself," Cami coached.

"Fuck," Blake said, and the message ended abruptly.

"Fuck," Julie echoed. I picked up the phone and listened to the message again. I knew exactly what he was doing and why he was doing it—there was no other way to keep Cami and his kids without attempting to destroy me—and still it hurt. I listened to it until I could get past my own selfish pain and hear what was going on. I pieced together what I could. He was trying to save his marriage. He was doing anything and everything she wanted in an attempt to appease her. He had to give her total control, let her act out her little revenge play. And yet, from how he couldn't bring himself to repeat what she was saying, I knew he loved me. Had he hung up so abruptly on purpose? Without letting Cami know? So that he could go on a pretend rant and say anything she wanted, things he knew I'd never actually hear but that would appease Cami? Was he even now trying to protect me, too?

Julie ordered in some divine chicken concoction with risotto and grilled asparagus spears. "You're good for my soul," I told her.

"You know it." She caressed my cheek and stroked the errant strands of hair framing my face until they fell in behind my ear.

"Kiss, kiss," I said, suddenly uncomfortable. "I have to get back on the road."

"You're kidding. You're staying here tonight."

"I can't. Too restless. Besides, I like night driving."

"No, hon. We've had three bottles of wine. You're not driving."

"I think I am." I stood up, and suddenly the world buckled around me. I sat right back down. "Or not," I said. "But first thing in the morning I have to go."

I woke with a raging headache, drank some orange juice and downed more Tylenol, left snoring Julie a love note of thanks for her hospitality, and got on the road. I drove obsessively to get to Tucson and my mother's that night. I drove through the desert, past the wildfires in Palm Springs, their black smog choking the sky. I couldn't get over the line of trucks on the road to Las Vegas through the Mojave. Like a wall of moving steel. Crazy. It was a warm night with a strong breeze. I drove with the windows down and let the hot air dry my tears. I drove with a single goal in mind: don't hit a truck.

Sadie helped me fend off real and imagined lecherous men at the rest station I stopped at. I was the only woman in a sea of rough truck drivers. The rest stop was crowded like a street in Vegas. More than a few of the men looked at me, then to Sadie, and then away. I ruffled the fur of my trusted companion, grateful I'd chosen a German Shepherd and not a poodle for my four-legged friend.

I made it to my mom's at 3:30 in the morning and, not wanting to wake her, fell asleep in the reclined driver's seat.

Chapter Two

Rapping on the window woke me up and I squinted against the harsh bright sun.

"Aleah, you made it, come inside," my mother said, pulling me out of the car and into a hug. She ushered me and Sadie into her little adobe home and hugged me again and gave me so much love. She got me some water and put me into bed as she got ready for work. It had been a while since I'd seen my mom. We weren't always close. I was grateful for the warm reception.

Over the next week I got my room set up; a small bookshelf, an ironing board for a desk, computer plugged in, a full bed with a foot of clearance and I was as home as I was going to get in my sixty-four square foot adobe prison. Everything in my mother's house had to be in its perfect place at all times. Every surface bleached clean. Every dog hair removed from the premises as soon as it was shed. My mother liked to go to bed at 8 p.m. She was a light sleeper. I'd stay up for a while, working or writing down these words to try and let go of all the pain. She complained that the writing I did at night was too loud: the clacking keys echoed off the tile and ricocheted down the hallway to where her bedroom was, three doors down. I felt restricted, like I'd come to a convent.

I took to going to coffee shops with my laptop so that she could sleep. I'd work until their 2 a.m. close and zoom home on the empty Interstate under crystalline stars.

She complained that the door opening and closing and my feet walking down the halls in the middle of the night also woke her up. I knew well from my mother that children should be seen and not heard. I kept going to the coffee shop.

I also started gambling. The nearest casino was just ten minutes up the freeway. Slots are pretty and distracting. Loud and blinky and hours slide by with your dollars. It was good to focus on anything other than Cami and Blake. I played nickel slots. I never let myself lose more than $20 a night.

I didn't like myself. I had no appreciable savings and nowhere else to turn. I was thirty-two years old and I had just moved back in with my mother. This was not exactly a high point in my life. In short order I lost twenty pounds and gained bags under my eyes from all the crying and not sleeping.

To her credit, my mother left me alone a lot to mourn whatever it was she thought that I was mourning. She didn't pester me for details, she didn't try to console the inconsolable. It wasn't in her nature anyway. I let her think whatever she wanted, that I was ashamed that I'd lost my marriage, whatever. That I was crying over Glen. Whatever.

We went out to eat a few times, my mother and I. Linner was her favorite meal. She liked to get the senior special at the local Mexican joint. The food was awful but cheap. The service was slow (and sloppy and frenzied) because the place was always jam-packed with seniors. During the lulls in our conversation I'd tune in to each of the tables around us like they were radio stations, listening for something interesting. Easily eighty percent of them had something to do with disease or dying. Some story of insurance or cancer or diabetes or estranged relatives or horrible health care costs (usually accompanied by a dig at Obamacare) colored their lives and this is what they shared with one another. The whole city felt sickly. I couldn't stand it. Moment by moment I was beginning to hate my life.

Everything about the desert struck me as alien. All the dry creek beds. The multitudinous cacti. The landscape barren of trees. The flat land made me feel like prey under a hawk's eye, and worse, it gave no boundaries to the city. I could see the network of ticky-tacky little houses and concrete would continue its slow takeover of the desert lands. Humanity was a cancer here.

The heat waves slithered off the pavement like dancing cobras. Even for me, a sun lover, it was too much. I couldn't wait to leave from the moment I got there.

As the days wore on, Cami started to leave me alone. Her text messages came less and less frequently, until I had an entire day from morning until bed with not a single text. And then another. And another. Had she figured out that I wasn't the one who had betrayed her? I began to relax. Maybe I could move on after all.

Then, sitting at the café one evening her name popped up in a Gmail chat window.

**hahaha* whore, I just luv hearing about what a sick fuck u r. I know about you throwing up in my kitchen after deep throating him.*

Adrenaline. My hands shook. I immediately made myself unavailable to chat and then worked through the settings until I figured out how to block her permanently. I was jittery from the intrusion, but also puzzled. What she described had never happened. My phone rang a heartbeat later. Of course, it was Cami. She left a voicemail. I listened to it, still feeling sick in my stomach at the sound of her voice, at receiving her animosity.

It wasn't that I felt guilty. I felt persecuted. Unjustly, even. Yes, hate me. I don't care. I have to be honest with you. I had no respect for this woman. She didn't deserve Blake. She never had. She didn't treat people like human beings and she didn't deserve to be treated like one. Hate me if you must. Go ahead. The rules of the heart don't always follow the rules of law.

Curiouser and curiouser, Cami spoke at great length with some glee about how Blake had told her all about my sick rape fantasies. The thing was, I didn't have any weird ass rape fantasies. I'd never heard of what she was describing. The thoughts flew through me like lightening. *He's lying to her. He's actually protecting the sanctity of what we had together.* It was still just ours. *Ohmyfuckinggod.* She didn't know about any of it, really. He might have been fighting to keep her, but part of him was protecting me, too. I was kind of amazed at his brilliance, the fine line he walked, how he trusted that I'd understand him.

Cami kept up the cyber assault. In spite of her barrage, in which she constantly told me how much Blake hated me, I kept thinking about how right it all had felt, how wonderful every moment had been, how it belonged to us and us alone. I tortured myself by listening to our songs, the ones on those first playlists we'd made for each other. I had to let him go. I didn't want to.

Another week of her harassment continued to send worms under my skin. I felt riddled with wounds. How was she still fixated on me? It had been six weeks since I'd left. She sent more emails insisting on an apology.

U really take it. Such a coward. Do you think you can lie to me and repeatedly seduce My Husband for months and not answer to me? You are a disgusting excuse for a human being ....everything you ever did for my family was only to be close to him.
Everything about you is sad. You will answer to me. You will apologize or I'll keep reminding you what a sick, selfish sack of shit you are until the day you die. I will never stop. You were a total sex addict and now you will pay the price. I'm at least getting the help I need. You on the other hand, are a lying, cheating home-wrecking whore.

Another came the next day.

You can talk to me on the phone or in person. Up to you, but you WILL give me closure on the hell you created. Choose, quickly.

I genuinely wondered why she put so much power in my hands. She wouldn't fix her marriage until I cowed to her power play? I didn't think so. She was fucking batshit crazy. I shared her love notes with Jennifer, to get her opinion on how to handle this particular barrage. It felt bigger, somehow. Laser focused. Jennifer's response helped.

What a bitch. Ignore her. She's delusional if she thinks she can control you this way. She thinks she has power over you? Hilarious. Delete. Delete. Delete. Did someone say restraining order?

Restraining order? I laughed, but didn't seriously consider it. She hadn't done anything to me physically. Was I being oversensitive to all of this? Did I need to just suck it up?

The assault continued the next day.

You'd better call me, bitch. You owe me an apology,
slut. I know where you are, whore. You can't hide from me
forever, fucktard. I can tear your world apart the same way
you have mine. One conversation, one apology and you
can't even face me for that. You would deny me closure
and the ability to move on. Slut. Whore. Bottomfuckingfeeder.

The stress of her assault was taking its toll on my nerves and my body. I was losing weight steadily. More than was healthy. I wasn't sleeping well. I felt on edge all the time. Cami's terrorism was doing its job. Still, I had no intention of capitulating. I took Jennifer's advice seriously and started researching what it would take to get a restraining order. I had recorded Cami's death threats. I felt legitimately scared of what she was capable of. It wouldn't be a bad thing to protect myself.

My mother's home phone jangled me awake the next morning. It switched over to voicemail before I could get to it. The readout showed a 206 number. A Seattle area code. Curious. I poured myself a cup of coffee. The red voicemail notification light on my mom's phone started blinking. Mom was at work. I couldn't help myself. I listened to it.

"Hello. You don't know me, but my name is Cami Porter. I know your daughter, and I have some really interesting news to share with you about her. I would welcome your return phone call so that I can let you know what kind of help she needs." She left her phone number.

Fuck. I felt like I'd been punched in the gut with a medicine ball. My body started shaking. How had she gotten this number? It was unlisted. Did she have my mom's address, too? I erased the message, called the phone company, and had her number permanently blocked. I felt like I was slowly being herded into a corner. Meanwhile, the emails kept coming.

You owe me an apology, I need closure. Call me or I will come and find you face to face. You know you don't want that. I'm not fucking around. All you have to do is call me, answer my questions without lying every third sentence, provide a heartfelt apology, and we'll be done.

I didn't believe her. I knew her too well. I knew she would get a taste of power over me and, because she was so hurt, control over the one hurting her would be beyond addictive. If I felt harassed now, all I had to do to feel truly subjugated and to lose all shred of anything I had left was to give in to her demands. I stayed strong and silent. Still. She scared the fuck out of me. The next message grew even more ominous.

You have made your choice by not calling me. It's been weeks and weeks of sheer hell and more than enough time for you to call me and explain yourself. It's on now.

Another email came later that afternoon. It was just one line, an ultimatum.

You have through this weekend, that's it. Then all hell breaks lose on you, bitch.

I'd lost most of my friends. I had a few staunch girlfriends who were still willing to endure listening to my tears. I had my mother. I had myself. My world, small before, had shrunk to the size of a cave. I was burrowing deeper and deeper, hoping never to be found. And yet, the further I went, the harder it seemed she tried to find and trap me. I was scared, yes. But not broken. I was not going to let this woman break me. I took it as a sign of personal resilience that even under her relentless assault, I could find it in me to be irritated by her poor spelling. I knew I wasn't perfect. But neither was she.

The hounding took its toll on my body. My hair was brittle and ragged. Hollow eyes greeted me from the mirror. I felt thin, like I was slipping away, like I could blow away on the wind and it wouldn't matter. This, coupled with the ache in my soul for Blake, my longing for Blake. I still had so much love for him. It burdened me every day, the yearning for him. I still held onto the beauty of what we'd had. I'd flash on moments, like the one in the garage towards the end of the affair. We were talking about how Glen and I had gone through and split our belongings. "Whatcha gonna do with the flagstone?" Blake asked.

"I dunno."

"I'll take it. What about the box fan?"

"You can have it."

"And the bicycles…. And the..." I looked up to find him staring intently at me, like a fox hypnotizing his prey, completely feral. My hair stood on end, electrified.

"You can have it," I whispered. He was on me in an instant.

With him I was sensual, creative, generous, aware, alive, and happy. God, I missed that sense of everything being right, the bliss.

Blake called the next day. I couldn't bring myself to pick up, not knowing who would actually greet me if I did. The voicemail indicator on my phone dinged and I listened to it. It was Blake.

"Please, Aleah. Please. I had to face Glen. You have to give her that satisfaction. For me? Please?"

Oh despair, that's what you feel like.

Glen called that evening. We hadn't spoken at all since I'd arrived in Arizona. I looked at the number for a while before deciding to pick up. I wondered if he yet regretted his decision to tell Cami about the affair. I wondered if he still felt self-righteous in his tattling and that Cami and her kids were better off having the affair exposed. I wondered if he were calling to apologize.

"Hello?"

"Aleah, thank God," Glen said. It was actually him. I breathed out a gust of relief. I hadn't realized until that moment how much I'd feared Cami had gotten a hold of his phone. "I have to talk to you."

"Let me get somewhere more private." My mother had just returned home from work. I'd gotten in the habit of going for drives while I talked on the phone, so as not to be overheard. I waved hello-goodbye to her as I walked out the front door to the car.

Safely ensconced in the driver's seat, I said, "Okay. How are you?" I turned the key to start the engine and cranked up the AC.

"I'm fine; I'm fine. I have to talk to you, though. It's about Cami."

Of course it was. Was he calling to coerce me into apologizing to her? Did he think he still had any influence on me?

"What is it?" I said, already irritated.

"Erik wanted me to call you." Donna's husband, Blake's brother-in-law. "He said it wasn't fair what was happening and you needed to at least know what was coming." He stopped talking and the silence between us grew.

"So, what's coming?" I said at last.

"I don't know how to say this. Cami hired a private investigator. She knows where you are. She's getting a gun. She has plane tickets for Tucson for next week. She's planning to show up on your doorstep."

My heart froze and then started beating rapid fire. I gulped for air. "To do what?"

"I don't know, exactly, but it doesn't look good. She's gone off the deep end, Aleah. She's on all kinds of pills, hard drugs. I wouldn't put anything past her right now. I would. I." He halted. "I'm afraid for your life, Aleah," he said and his voice held the trace of a caress, a memory of the love he'd once had for me.

"Oh." It was too much. "Okay." I hung up the phone.

I pulled out of the neighborhood and took the old quarry road into the desert. It was like that, where we were. Civilization and then nothing. It was obvious that humanity was a barely-tolerated blight on this bitter landscape. Everything was hostile. Thorns and burrs, poison and fangs, wild javelinas, no water anywhere. I passed over a dry creek bed and pulled to a stop where the road dead-ended into nothingness. The sunset had faded as I drove, the inky night was speckled with stars. The world was the same, but I was not.

I cut the engine and got out of the car. I skirted past the barrier into the brush. It was a stupid thing to do and I knew it. Any number of evils lay in wait to hurt me. Snakes or scorpions or pigs or even the fucking plants, but I didn't care. I sat down on the gritty dirt and scraped my clammy hands on the ground, needing to feel the earth. Jittery, nervous, and hollow—these had been my primary feelings for weeks. Except for the occasional bug noises and the distant roar of the freeway it was quiet there. I suffocated in the quiet. I had a hard time drawing enough air in my lungs. It felt so thin, like I couldn't breathe deeply enough. I started to hyperventilate and sob at the same time. I gave into it, let the heaving of my lungs take over, the overwhelming sense of despair. The depth of the cry took over my being. I don't know how long I sat there like that. Probably not long by the clock. But long enough for my world to change. I wasn't just harassed anymore. I was prey. I wanted to die.

But I couldn't. Cami had brought my mother into this. I needed to protect my mother. Overloaded, I shifted into hardcore rational mode. I couldn't afford the luxury of fear anymore. I couldn't have Cami showing up on my mother's front door with a gun. Fuck. I had to come clean with my mother. Fuck.

I didn't know what would happen. At the very least I owed my mother an explanation. I wasn't looking forward to it. But, if she was going to hear the news about me one way or another, I wanted it to come from me. This whole thing was exhausting. I never imagined it would get so messy and ugly. I'd never been in trouble like this.

I got up off the ground and dusted the sandy dirt off my body, gathered my resolve like a cloak, got back in the car and drove to my mother's home.

She was in the living room, watching DVR'd Ellen on TV. She'd changed into her slippers, but otherwise remained perfectly groomed, her hair molded by infinite hold hairspray into solid-state precision, her clothes lintless and creaseless. This woman strived for perfection in her life. I'd always failed her. At least this would be nothing new. "Aleah, hello again," she said and then looked at me. I'm sure I looked a sight, puffy eyes, bloated red nose. She paused the recording. "Is everything all right?" She rose from the couch, extended a hand toward me.

I felt my gut clench and, before I lost my courage, blurted out, "Mom, I made a big mistake and I fell in love and had an affair."

"Oh," she sat down. "I've been wondering what was going on. That explains a lot. What." She pursed her lips and held out her hand again. "Well, tell me what happened."

I told her the bones of my story with Blake, how wonderful it had been, how weird it had gotten with Glen (sparing the sordid; this was my mother) and how the affair had been discovered, why I'd left early, why I'd been so sad.

"I'm glad you trusted me with the truth, Aleah."

"The thing is, Mom... That's not all of it. Cami's apparently gone insane. She hired a private detective and found out where I am. She's got a plane ticket for Tucson and she is bringing a gun. She scares me. She's been harassing me for weeks. I am going to go downtown to get a restraining order tomorrow, but it won't go into effect until she's served and I don't know when that will be, or if it'll even happen before she gets on the plane."

"God, Aleah. What did you get yourself into?"

"I know." I looked her straight in the eye. "I'm sorry. I am so sorry to bring this to your doorstep. I'm so sorry to include you in my mess. It's the last thing I wanted. You don't deserve this." I meant it. When was all the pain going to end? It just kept rippling outward, trapping more people in its web.

Book Four

The woman I'd lovingly referred to as an ice queen anytime a stranger asked me about her pulled me tightly against her cashmere sweater and kissed my hair, my cheek. "It's okay, Aleah," she whispered. "We'll get through this." The lingering scent of the Chanel No. 5 she applied to her wrists every morning hit my nostril just then, the same as it had when I was four years old. She held me close as sobs wracked the length of my body; she stroked my hair as she held me, held me, held me until the sobs wore me out and I remembered that she was also my mother, and that she loved me.

Chapter Three

I went to court first thing in the morning and filed for an anti-harassment order. The judge, after dealing with case after case of domestic abuse—with actual bruised and battered women who had poverty and shitty educations to contend with as well—looked at me like I was troubling her with a catfight. "And your concern with this person in Washington State is what exactly?"

"Death threats," I said. "I have them recorded. She's reportedly purchased a gun and plane tickets. I don't want her near me or my family."

The judge sighed and looked down her nose at the papers, then at me. She shook her head a little, but signed the order. I got the papers and overnighted them to the King County Sheriff's Office in Seattle. I called and spoke to the sheriff, asked how the whole process worked.

"Well, when we receive the papers, there's a day or two for processing, then we'll try to serve them. The no contact order won't go into effect until the papers are served."

"If there's any way you can speed it up, I'd appreciate it. I have it from a mutual friend that she's bought a gun and intends to visit me. I'd rather not have things end up that way."

"I can understand that." The officer's voice softened a bit. "Tell me this woman's name again?" I did and could hear his pencil scratching over the line. "And how can I find her?"

I did what I could to fill in the blanks as to where he could find Cami during the day, though it had been some time since we'd worked together. I didn't know if she still consulted to the same client or if she'd been reassigned since I'd moved on. I explained as much and gave him the name of the parent company; he could call and find out. He promised to be on the lookout for my documents and to do what he could. I thanked the officer for his help and hung up.

Then the waiting began. I forced myself to work, to read, to write. The waiting was excruciating. All I could think about was Cami and that gun. Everything I did, I did distractedly. I knew I'd have to go through my work again after the current crisis had passed. Or not. I mean, there was a chance this was going to end with a bullet in my heart. Or head. Ugly. I shook my head. Was there any other way out?

I thought hard about Blake's appeal. The truth of the matter was that there were any number of ways Cami could have approached me where I would have been receptive to a dialog and certainly willing to offer a sincere apology. She happened to pick bullying and threats, which pretty much guaranteed a closed door with me. Now that I'd chosen to enact it, I wasn't going to nullify the restraining order once it was in effect. But I owed it to Blake to tell him as much. Or so I told myself. I'd have taken any reason to call him, any at all.

I dialed the phone and he answered, "This is Blake." His voice. Oh, that clench in my heart.

"Blake, it's Aleah."

"Yeah." Just like always. "How are you?"

"Don't ask," I said, clenching back tears. "Lonely."

"I know, baby," he whispered.

I got to the point. It was killing me to be on the line with him. "Listen, I've gotten all those emails from Cami. All those threats. And I can't call her."

"Why not?"

I didn't want to tell him about the restraining order. I figured surprise was my friend in that endeavor. I wanted no chance of her evading papers being served. "Because it will only fuel her need to punish me. Because she's cruel. Because... Oh, Blake. I didn't want any of this. I was *leaving* already.

I'm so sorry." The pain of the past few months crashed over me.

"I know," he said. "I know you didn't. I have to try to make it right with her, you understand?"

I did.

"She's hurting the kids. Always picking fights with me in front of them, screaming, crying. They're always crying and screaming, too. They don't know what the fuck is going on. Meanwhile, she's obsessing over every detail, making me go over the calendar with her. Asking about this date, that time. I've been honest with her when I could. Except I didn't tell her everything about the week we spent together. And our first kiss. I told her it was mutual."

I was in part grateful that I'd been right and something special had been shielded from her. At the same time, his unwillingness to claim the first kiss was further evidence that he was missing his *cajones*, unwilling to claim his own feelings for me, unable to be real. I shook my head at myself. Stupid. What had I expected?

All of this pulled me right back to my broken heart.

"Please apologize to her," he begged. I hated him a little for it.

"I won't do it. Don't ask me again."

"Glen got to punch me. Let her take a swing."

"She bought a gun, Blake. She is threatening to kill me. Go fuck yourself." I thought about Cami's barrage of hate mail, her shaming voicemails. "And beyond that, trust me; I've been punched." It felt good to be a little angry.

"Yeah. I haven't really been privy to what she tells you."

"Blake, the message you left for me was 'You fucking cunt whore, thank you for ruining my life.'"

"Yeah. I'm sorry about that. I was limited in what I could say."

"I'm sure." I felt suddenly sad for reasons I couldn't yet name.

"Look," he said. "I'm seeing two different counselors. My life is gone. I am doing whatever it takes to hold my family together. I want to run screaming, every day, all the time. But I won't leave, not until I've exhausted every option to stay with my kids." I could hear the drag on this cigarette and wished I had a pack of my own. I felt thin and shaky all at once and I wasn't mad at him anymore.

"Cami set me up with my own email account. It was her idea, that we get separate accounts." When they'd gotten married, Cami'd insisted on a joint email account. I'd always thought that was weird. He told me his new email address. "She wants to rebuild trust."

I snorted. Like I believed that. "Did you set up your own password? Have you checked for keyloggers?"

"Yes. Yes. She means it. It's my personal account."

"You checked the filters? The rules?"

"Yes. You could email me something and it would just go to me."

"I could email you something like what?"

"I don't know. You could write an apology and if I thought it would help, I could give it to her and she could read it. That way you wouldn't have to talk to her and everything would be solved."

I didn't have to consider that for long. "I don't think it's a good idea."

"Aleah, please. You have no idea what it's like here. Listen, she's crazy obsessed over you, about your disappearance. She won't talk about anything else and she won't move on, she swears, until she knows you feel remorse. I promise if you write an email she won't see it unless I think it will help."

A shout in the background and then Blake said, "Listen, I have to go. Call me if you want to talk. I'm lonely, too." I felt a clench of panic in my belly. Our call was ending and I missed him desperately already. I knew what I had to say.

"I'm not going to call you, Blake. I think we should leave each other alone."

He cleared his throat. "Of course we should." He sounded like his voicemail recording, cheery but empty. I hung up the phone. I couldn't bring myself to say goodbye.

I knew Cami. I knew she was more tech savvy than Blake ever would be. I knew whatever he had set up, she would have set up a way to bypass it, to see his email. Hours passed. I played Candy Crush. Blake's words ate at me:

She swears she won't move on until she knows you feel remorse. I knew the next day the restraining order would arrive in Seattle and the day after that it would be served. Supposedly the day after that was the day Cami had plane tickets for. I could slide an apology in under the wire and still obey the letter of the law. Then the restraining order would go into effect and we would leave each other alone and it would all be hunky dorey, as my mother would say.

Somehow I found myself at my keyboard with a browser open. Maybe it really would diffuse the bomb that was Cami. Maybe one little email would bring peace. I didn't believe it, but I also didn't want to look back on my life and think of myself as a coward. Was I in the wrong in this?

I started to type. It wasn't something I'd actually send, of course. I wondered what I'd write, how I'd write something that would sound like it was written for him, but really the ultimate message would be for her. Of course, she would see it regardless. It became a game. What did I need to say to make things right, the way they should be? I started to type.

Blake,

I am so sorry for all of the pain. I know it lines your face every moment of every day. I spend every day mired in sadness. I find it difficult to eat. I don't sleep well. But I know I'm not alone. I know everyone else is hurting worse than I am. I'm so sorry. I am especially sorry that Davis and Desiree have to deal with the aftermath.

I didn't think the aftermath was my fault; I thought it was Cami's idiocy, fighting with Blake in front of the children. It was as close as I could come to any kind of apology to Cami.

You and I both know we weren't going to be able to leave each other alone until we were out of one another's reach. I chose to move away so that you could get back to your family and Glen and I could move on our separate ways. Since leaving Washington I have talked myself out of calling you a thousand times or more. You have to know I could have lashed back at Cami's attacks, that I have plenty to hurt her with, that this could have become so much uglier. I have been doing everything I can to give you both a new beginning without reference to me.

That much was true. I had plenty to hurt her with, just no reason to engage.

Regardless, she will only be hurt more if she talks to me. Especially since she thinks I lie about everything. Chances are damn good she will walk away from any conversation with me even more enraged than before. Think about it, Blake. You have to know there is no satisfaction that can come of this. Giving in to her obsession will only make it grow.

You keep acting like I'm the lucky one with a fresh start. I've left _everything_ behind, too. I have been dealing with a broken heart, a destroyed marriage, vanished friendships, financial difficulties, and not least, the constant threat of Cami's retribution. Please understand that I'm giving you all that I can in regards to saving your marriage & keeping your family together. It is hell to be cut off from you. Nothing has changed for me. Take the clean break, Blake. Please let me go.

With love,

Aleah

There. That was all I could say. I hit send before I could stop myself. Then I stood up and backed away from the keyboard, banging against my chair in the process. I turned and left the room. Oh fuck, what had I just done? I went into the bathroom and cranked on the shower. I stripped and stood there, waiting for steam before I stepped into the too-hot water. I wanted to wash the whole world away. I stood there and I cried. I'd thought I'd cried out all my tears, but they just kept coming.

I found my way to bed and dropped into the cool sheets, exhausted. It was hours before I woke, a sliver of intense moonlight crawling across my face the culprit of my sleep. Compulsively, I went to my desk and jostled the mouse to wake up my desktop computer. I refreshed the browser with my email.

To: Aleah

From: Blake

When I told her I'd talked to you and you'd admitted you were hurting and that you'd been crying and said you were sorry, she changed. She started to get over it. She was warm and nice—for the first time in weeks she didn't bring you and us up every hour on the hour and fly into a rage.

Then I got your email and I struggled with whether or not to tell her that you emailed me but that is what she said she needed. So I let her read your email. It backfired. It all came crashing down again.

Would you, could you please just apologize plain and simple but with some feeling? She wants an apology for the lying you did, for how you made her doubt her sanity. Please help me. I am running out of options.

Blake

Fucking asshole! Seriously. I'd known Cami wouldn't be happy with what she got. I felt vindicated and full of rage at the same time. I had had just about enough of this shit. No, I wasn't about to contact her directly. I would reply though. I took my time. I crafted the perfect email. I spent hours on it. I knew she would read it, too. I knew she would read every word a thousand times. I chose them carefully. I knew she would think I actually intended it for Blake's eyes only. I could play her like a fucking violin.

From: Aleah

To: Blake

Blake,

Goddamn it. Of course sending her that email backfired, dumbass. When are you going to figure out that Cami & Aleah don't mix? It doesn't matter what I say; any communication between me and her will only make it worse. Furthermore, you are still lying to her, so there's a good chance that (if I were to talk to her, which I'm not) when she starts asking me questions, my answers aren't going to corroborate yours. Do you really want to face that? At best, I'm a lying shit (in her eyes) and she gets caught trying to figure out what's real and what's not—and stays trapped in that mental hell for a long time. At worst, she actually believes the truth of my words and then you're really fucked. Either way, we all lose. You say you're running out of options. My not contacting her IS your best option when it comes to this.

What I don't understand is why you think it's a good idea for me to talk to her. The web of deception we created was part of what we signed on for when you said you couldn't see it ending between us. I knew if we were discovered I'd write off Cami's friendship and my marriage would be dead over. You said if she found out, you'd be able to talk her down; it would be ugly for a while and then she'd come around and everything would be fine.

That was it. Right there. My silver bullet in the middle of this email. It was true, he'd said that a few times. But by me saying it in this fashion, as something she would overhear me saying back to him, I was in essence throwing down a gauntlet she wouldn't be able to refuse.

There were several times over the course of our time together when I asked you why you were risking so much, and over and over again, you said it was your risk and you'd decide when it was too hot in the kitchen. I trusted you to be answerable to her if it did come to that. It was my naiveté to think her focus would only be on you if we were found out. The truth is, Blake, you and I both walked away from our families in February.

I'm living with my consequences. Complete and utter fucking heartache aside, lost friends aside, my mother finding a way to call me a failure at life aside, I've lost my marriage, too, and a man who loved me, and maybe I didn't give it enough of a chance because I let you into my life.

Cami has a set idea of what will supposedly bring her to closure, *and that includes me behaving in a prescribed way. But even if she handed me a script, I'm sure I'd read the words with the wrong inflection. This isn't about her needing closure, it's about her need to control and she doesn't and won't control me. Furthermore, she doesn't trust me. I already gave her a heartfelt apology, just like you asked, and she's not satisfied. Any exchange between Cami & me will only make things worse. Just like it already has.*

Yes I lied to her throughout this year. Yes, I felt like a shit doing it, but I chose to do it because I loved you more than I loved her. So, I'm evil and she should feel free to hate me. But that's where this ends. I didn't break my marriage vows to her. Her need for closure with me is a story she is telling herself. She is choosing to be stuck.

I'm sorry, Blake, but I won't contact her. Please don't ask me to again.

Yours,

Aleah

I got a flurry in my stomach before I hit send. But I clicked the button anyway. And then I sat there, stunned.

I still hoped she would leave him. She wouldn't though, if she hadn't yet. I knew this. And so I started hoping that she would die young. Really young. I hated her. I hoped the seeds of doubt sowed by my email would linger with her and eat at her from within. I hoped that cancer filled her bones and organs. I hoped she drank herself into a car wreck.

I didn't feel sorry for her. I didn't want to apologize. I had no love left for her. I'm sure the same was true of her for me.

I looked at the desktop clock. 4:48 a.m. I clambered back into bed and fell to sleep, feeling more relieved than I had in weeks. It was after 11 a.m. when I awoke. Morbidly curious, I found myself back at the computer, toggling the mouse so the computer would wake up, too. I had another email from Blake.

To: Aleah

From: Blake

she got to this email before I did and it is over... I have to move out and she is selling the house and taking the kids...

FUCK

There was really only one way to respond.

To: Blake

From: Aleah

Oh my god, Blake. I am so sorry. You said this was your private account... I had no idea she could get to it. Fuck. I am so sorry.

I think that was the first time I lied to him. I was certain I'd never, ever hear from him again.

Chapter Four

My mother made me eggs in a basket for breakfast the next day. She was an amazing cook. Gordon Ramsey, watch out. I mean, she made them gourmet. Fried to perfection in grass fed butter, attended by just the right amount of handmade hollandaise. Tasting that concoction reminded me again of childhood, how sweet it had been, how gentle. I was licking my fork when my phone rang—a ringtone I reserved for numbers not in my contact list. It was a 206 number. Seattle. I pursed my lips. Did I dare?

"Aleah, answer your phone already!" my mother snapped and I did as she commanded, reflexively, not at all surprised at her power over me.

It was Sheriff Donnelly. "I'm calling to inform you that the papers have now been served directly to Ms. Porter—"

"How did she take it? I mean, was it you that served them? How did she seem? Do you get a sense of these things?" I knew I should shut up and let him talk, but I couldn't seem to. "She bought a gun," I blurted out. "Plane tickets."

"You do get a sense, sometime. But I don't always know if it bears out." He was deliberate in his speech, his words spaced as if he considered each one individually. "I will say this." He paused. I could hear him stand up, his breath grew heavy in the phone. I heard his keys jangle, imagined him hefting his pants over his paunch as he cradled an ancient, corded phone, shoulder to ear. Had he forgotten his belt? "I will say. I—"

"Donnelly." A second voice.

"Ms. Clayton, all I can say is the papers have been served." He was done deliberating. His voice picked up speed. "I've got to go. Stay safe, now." The line went dead. He'd been about to say something else, but what? I rubbed my hands over my face, massaging the stress in my jaw.

"What is it? Who was it?" My mother. I felt like I was seventeen again. I couldn't wait to get out and away from all of this.

"The sheriff. The papers have been served."

"Oh, good. Well, that's that." She looked at me calmly. I wished I could share her relief. What had the sheriff been about to say? He'd tell me if she seemed malicious, wouldn't he? If she'd gotten them and was going to break them, wouldn't she have done so already? Already started harassing me again? Had it worked? I had to trust that it had.

Still, I moved through my days wearing a shroud of brittle anxiety. She could decide to break the order at any time. I lived on coffee. I smoked the last of my tiny stash of pot in the bathroom after my mother left for work. I kept the window open and the vent on and took a shower right after. I hoped her nosy, goody two-shoes neighbors wouldn't report me.

My mother and I went to Scottsdale for the weekend. Just in case the restraining order hadn't been enough of a deterrent for Cami. Just in case she still boarded a plane for Tucson. There was really no need for us to be there. My mother and I managed to survive each other's company, in spite of my continued tears. I cried myself to sleep every night. I would never see nor hear from Blake again. I had destroyed his family. I'd shut him out.

Glen finally sent the separation papers. When they arrived, I called and asked him to talk me through them. I'd expected him to be cold, calculating even, but we spent nearly two hours on the phone and it was a gentle conversation, even tender at times. I told him I was so sorry for all the pain I'd caused him. I was glad to have that chance. He seemed, at least, to finally be over me. Our "goodbye" had a sad finality to it.

"I guess we'll never hang pictures of *us* on the walls again," I said.

"Probably not. You know, the people I talk to think that the lull we faced happens in every marriage. They say you should have weathered the storm."

Bullshit! I blinked, surprised at the clarity I felt, but I managed to keep my mouth shut. And then I didn't. "Weather the storm?! I weathered the storm for probably seven years, Glen, waiting for someone to join me in the cockpit and be my co-pilot. In case you have forgotten, I was still *weathering the storm* when you asked ME for a divorce. I weathered the fucking storm, and it isn't derelict to end a relationship that will never work. It isn't normal to stick with mediocrity when you know what better feels like."

There was silence on the other end, and then a gentle click. I sighed, hoping he could find his way to peace with me. I found myself surprisingly at peace with him.

The weeks droned on. I still wanted Blake. I still missed him.

"Available," Jennifer quipped during one of our phone calls. "Next time pick one of those."

"Right." As if there would be a next time.

The weeks droned on and I ached for Blake. I couldn't bring myself to resent what my friends and mother labeled as his cowardice, his selfishness. I understood him. His words hurt, everything that had transpired since I'd left Seattle hurt, but the thing was, I still wanted to see him again. It was all that I wanted.

I spent my days at coffee shops. I'd pull all-nighters and come home to crawl in bed after my mother had left for work. I met the barest of my commitments at work and somehow managed to hang onto my job. Days bled into one another; I couldn't tell one from the next. I'd fall to bed exhausted, emotionally drained from the wanting, the pain of separation.

One night in December, I woke up to starlight; I looked at the clock and saw I'd only been asleep for forty-five minutes. It was early yet, not quite eight o'clock. I shook my head, fell back to the pillow, and closed my eyes. I wanted to turn my computer on, though. The moonlight shone strongly through the slatted blinds. It seemed like I had to turn on my computer. *It's such a beast, though. It takes forever to power up*, I argued with myself. *Just do it.* Okay. I flung the covers over and crawled to the edge of my bed closest to my laptop and grabbed for the machine.

A moment after I opened Gmail, my IM chat popped open.

BP: Hey, it's me. Its Blake.

Of course I was instantly suspicious.

BP: for real. I'm at the library. I got my own thing going now.

There were long pauses between words as he typed. I knew he wasn't good with a keyboard; he never had to use one for work. If Cami were acting like him, I doubt she'd think to slow down her typing speed. I was shaking so badly as I read I could barely control my mouse. Did I trust that it was him? Did I respond?

This is what I'd dreamed of. It was happening.

AC: hey

It was all I could manage.

BP: sigh

I could feel it, the flood of connection like he was right next to me.

BP: Aleah, I have to tell you, words can't express how sorry I am for all of us. I knew you were doing everything you could for me by staying away. And then l I asked for your help and everything got fucked up. I HATE THIS. I hate this whole damn thing. I hate me for hurting so many people out of my selfishness

AC: Oh darlin'. I knew what I was signing on for.

BP: I know

BP: This hurts so deep. I can't forget what we had. But I have to. She's going to let me try. I have to do all I can for the kids. I moved out for a while. Now I will move back. But I couldn't go without contacting you, just once.

AC: I understand. I was doing okay letting you go until you contacted me. Then it all came crashing back and it's so hard.

BP: Fuck I know. I want to run to you now but if I did it would all be over for this family. I have to try. You won't hear from me for a while because of that.

AC: Understood.

He was saying goodbye again. It was my last chance to say it all.

AC: I will always love you. You will always nothing but understanding from me. I know you. I want you to be happy. I want your kids to have their dad, who is SO GOOD with them.

BP: Thank you. and hey. all the shit that you have heard from Cami is just that. shit. lies and deception... I wish things were different.

I want to run to you now. I reveled in that. I was a fool. I closed my laptop. I tried to fall back asleep, buy my thoughts were spinning. An hour passed.

I opened my computer. Everything in my head revolved around him. I knew it wasn't healthy. I knew everyone around me was sick of it. I sent him another message.

AC: I miss you.
BP: sob
AC: ?
BP: i am crying on my keyboard
AC: seriously? Don't do that. Easy to ruin a keyboard that way.
BP: ya
this HURTS
for what it's worth
I LOVE you. I am so thankful I have you.
you are and have always been my fantasy

I lost myself in his words.

AC: oh... I love the way you love me. I never dreamed ...
BP: You KNOW that goes for me as well
just a kiss. A good one at that. and look where we are
AC: I dream of being next to you
BP: I want so much to stroke your hair. kiss your cheek. hold you close
But I gotta go. Library is closing. Nighty night princess
AC: nn

And then it was over. He was gone again. I don't know how I did it, but I fell quickly to sleep and slept blissfully for the first time in ages. I dreamed of him.

I went on missing him. Since he'd contacted me it felt like somehow there was a future there that I couldn't just walk away from. Goddamn it. I was waiting for him to move out, let me know where he was. Damn it.

After we'd broken apart the first time, he'd said it took me leaving him to figure out how much he loved me. It felt like every day I was newly realizing what I'd lost. How very much he meant to me, how we belonged with one another. How could I still have so many tears for him? He was doing all he could to stay there. He was not going to come for me. I tried to make myself believe it.

The holidays came and went.

I found myself in a strange limbo. Part of me—a big part—wanted to see what would happen with the Porters before I made any decision as to what to do with my life. Donna was one of the only friends who saw things my way. Her words had a way of making things more or less bearable. I called her for solace. "Cami just needs to go away. Stay in Arizona for now, Aleah. Be with your mom for a while. But the kind of love Blake has for you, that doesn't go away. He won't forget you. Their marriage will fall apart and he'll come and find you. We'll see you back here."

I couldn't stay much longer in Tucson, though. I knew I was wearing my mother thin. I was wearing myself thin. It was a holding place, not a landing spot. Austin was everything I wanted. I'd been there five years before. Not too big. Friendly. Eclectic. Great food. Sunshine. River. Happy people. University town. Blue town.

I enlisted the aid of a few different apartment hunters to help me find a place in South Austin. One that would take my German Shepherd and my measly $800 a month in rent. They found one. I'd move in March first. Just in time for SXSW.

I made plans to go back to Seattle in the middle of February. Just three days, a long weekend. I knew I wouldn't be able to see Blake. But I had to pack up the rest of my stuff from the house—my furniture and books and things—and get all of it on a moving truck to Austin. It was time.

It was still mid-January, though, and bitter cold. It was hard to think I'd be in sunshine. It was hard to truly get excited for a fresh start. *Fake it till you make it, Aleah. You've done this before, I told myself. You can do it again.* I holed up in my room that evening, working on the laptop until my mother rapped on the wall to let me know the clacking was keeping her from sleeping. I curled up in bed with a book for a distraction and fell into a restless sleep. Something woke me a little after 1:00 and, just as before, something told me to go to the computer. I checked my email. Instantly, I received an IM from someone named Cole Hawkins.

CH: Its me.

AC: Who r u?

CH: Blake. She set me up. She's seen everything in the other account. Chats, email.

AC: How do I know this is you and not her?

I got a series of IMs in rapid succession: his nickname, his favorite NASCAR driver, the places he wanted to take me that he didn't want to take Cami, my favorite songs.

AC: Hi, B. Is there a line I can call you on?

CH: Haven't moved out yet. Call my cell.

Damn. How had he not moved out yet? I got dressed—warmly because it got freaking cold in the desert at night—and crept out to the swing on the back porch. I hoped the hiss of the sliding glass door wouldn't wake my mother. My fingers shook as I dialed his line. I was actually going to hear his voice. It had been months and months. If I were Jules Verne I could have gone around the world since I'd last heard his voice. I was shaking. My bones hurt from tightening against the cold. The stars were bright crystals, sparkling in a black sky. The air burned my lungs with cold as I took it in and turned instantly white as I blew it out in the night.

He picked up the line. "Hey, there."

Suddenly, I couldn't feel the cold at all. "Hey, there. I take it she's not home?"

"She passed out cold. Came home from the bar stone drunk and abusive. I have to be careful not to bruise her when I'm trying to keep her from punching me. She'll use it in a heartbeat as evidence of domestic abuse. And she's the one trying to hit me."

He sounded like he had a lot to unload, but when he didn't say anything for a while, I said, "I'm so sorry, Blake. Where are you?"

"In my truck. In case she's pretending. I mean, she's snoring like a fucking hippopotamus, but you never know with that bitch." I actually giggled at the hippopotamus part. "It's fucking cold. Freak snowstorm this weekend."

"It's cold here, too," I said, curling up tighter on the swing. "I wish I'd grabbed a blanket." My hair was still damp from a late shower. It was already crunchy. Everything seemed crystalline in the cold.

"I wish I was there to hold you, baby," he said and just like that my body was on fire. "I'm so sick of it. Everyone looking at me like I'm the filthiest thing they've ever seen. My own dad wanted to punch me in the gut but he turned out to be the only one I could talk to. He knows everything now. You have people you can talk to, don't you?"

What was going on? Something had definitely changed. "Yeah," I said. "I got people. It's crazy to hear from you. I was half asleep and I got this strong urge to turn on my computer."

"That's because I'd been reaching out to you with everything I had, willing you to get on." I stared at the stars as I took that in. They glistened in the black sky. I could almost see the cold. Blake was always so tough on the outside, such a man's man. I'd forget about his spiritual side. I'd forget who his mother was, a true pagan witch, drawing down the moon sky clad and all. She didn't visit often, but I'd met her once or twice.

"I wanted to call. Then the first thing you do is ask if you can call me."

"Connection."

"I know. And Aleah, just like that I'm at peace again. I don't know where I'm at, but I do know that I'm sick of people telling me that I'm sick. I do know that what Cami's putting me through is way more retribution than is called for and maybe you were right all along and a divided house is better than one filled with such ugly fighting all the time. She won't stop in front of the kids. It's like she's deliberately hurting them. It's because I'm there. She wouldn't do it in front of them if I weren't there to skewer. They're hurting. Me being here is hurting them."

"Oh, Blake." I didn't really know what else to say. I let him talk.

"I miss you every day. I think about you every goddamned day. You know, Peter at work said something. He said I needed to make a choice. Be what everyone thinks I should be and kill myself in the process or relax and embrace my inner freak. And that was just about the sanest thing I've heard in a while. I mean, I've groveled and I've given and I've walked the line. No one cares a damn that she slept around, too. She's got everyone believing I'm a sex addict.

"I keep falling for her technology shit. I'll set up a new email and somehow she'll know about it and know how to access it."

"She probably installed a key logger," I said.

"Sure." I knew Blake was out of his element. He pressed on. "Tonight we were going to burn all the shit you'd ever given us as a gesture of moving on. Cami was excited. She was in a good mood, actually. I made the mistake of logging into that email account earlier and I left her alone in the office for half an hour. I came and found her and said 'Let's do this.' That's when she told me it was over, she wanted a divorce. Told me she was taking the kids to New York. She told me to move out. It was because I said I loved you. Then she went to the bar. On the way out she told me if I ended up with you she'd make sure I never see my kids again."

"She can't do that, Blake."

"She's going to do her damndest to try. She actually said she was afraid I was going to molest our children. To my face. That's pretty much what made me snap. Right there. She's not even trying to make things work. She's still on a witch hunt. It's been months, Aleah. She won't even try to get over it."

"Why are you still living with her?"

"I have to try to make things work. She keeps letting me try." He told me Cami had gone from depressed to violent. She was drinking heavily, popping handfuls of pills she purchased on the internet. She was a frazzled wreck and looked like a zombie.

"She keeps saying she can't handle the betrayal. She tells me at least once a day that her counselors think I must hate her to have treated her the way I did, that I am a sociopath."

"Oh my god," I said. "Have they met her?"

"I did this to her, to them," he said, meaning the kids.

"We did this," I said. Maybe for the first time, I understood my role in all of this. I felt a shame I hadn't before. "I'm sorry." I knew it wasn't enough.

"Thank you." He paused a moment and I heard his lighter spark. "I mean, they're not monsters," he said. "They're good people, loveable people. Why can't we love them?"

"I tried," I said. "I really tried." I actually started crying. I didn't realize how judged I'd been feeling, how much pressure had built up around the idea of the broken marriage being my fault, because I hadn't tried hard enough. "But it was so hard. It almost killed me." I mean, I had been starting to think about who to give stuff to." I stopped a moment, realizing that while it felt suddenly like there was no time or distance between us at all, a lot had changed.

"How are things?"

Blake blew out his breath. "They're hard. They were crazy for a while, insane crazy. I've been having anxiety issues. Panic attacks. I have to pull over sometimes, when I'm driving. Cami was obsessed with you. The restraining order was a smart move. Took all the wind out of her sails. She barely mentions you now."

"I didn't know what else to do."

"I know. And I know all kinds of shit happened since the last time we saw each other. And I know you wrote me off. All I know is that all my life I've never felt anything like the bliss and the deep, deep love that I feel when I'm with you."

My stomach fluttered. Fuck. I loved the way he loved me. I said, "If you're drunk and fucking with me..."

"I'm not. I told you. I had to talk to you.

"Why?"

"I'm getting there," he said. "Patience, woman." He paused a moment. He always did like to tease me. "You know, after all these years of my mom telling me how wonderful Cami is, today she finally says, 'I've always known she'd never be right for you, though.' I told her 'fuck you.' Why couldn't she have said that eight or ten years ago?"

"I wonder the same thing about my mom and Glen. She never liked him. I think they were trying to let us make our own mistakes."

"Well, they picked a hell of a time. The thing is, Aleah, I think you're all the woman I need. I don't think I can quit you." His voice grew husky. "I have to see you. I can't decide without seeing you again. Come back for a while, will you? I need to know for sure that I can walk away from them." He stopped talking and when I remained silent, said, "I know this is a major head fuck."

It was. But in those tiniest of moments I'd already decided to extend my trip. I'd rent a house for a week instead of staying in a hotel. "I don't know what to say."

"She actually is taking the kids back home to Jersey."

"For how long?"

"A week."

"When?"

"Middle of February."

The same time my trip was already planned for. "I'll think about it," I said. I couldn't wait to see him.

Chapter Five

I floated through my days. Arizona sunshine began to sing of spring; I actually spent days by the pool. Not in a swimsuit, but in the sun. I felt like those first albino tulips as they pushed through dirt, cold and naked, in my mother's garden. I felt like I could reawaken to the beauty of life. I'd rotted enough in the darkness, hadn't I? For every month I'd sinned I'd spent a month in this hell. I judged the price fair.

I know. I know! I'm a monster. You're thinking it, or you should be. How could I feel as though I'd paid for my sins? All I can say is it wasn't just any woman whose husband I chose to dally with, but Cami, a woman who'd always scared me and, because of that, who'd never earned my trust or respect. Of course I hadn't anticipated the extent of her backlash. My gut clenched when I thought of the mother she'd become to those children. I feel sick over that, still.

Oh, and Glen. Poor Glen. I feel pity for him now, most of the time, when I think of him. I hope he's happier. The truth was, I'd fallen out of love with him so long before things fell apart and neither of us really noticed. We were comfortable. Comfort can be its own devastation. Now, when I think of how our relationship was, I liken it to daydreaming at the poker table and finding everyone staring at me, waiting for me to act on a hand I'd folded a thousand years ago in my head.

The three weeks passed as they would, slowly. Blake called three days before my departure. I could tell immediately from his voice something had changed. "Listen," he said. "Cami filed divorce papers yesterday."

He paused. I could scarcely breathe. Was he going to ask me to be with him?

"I'll have almost nothing to live on after she gets her share of my paycheck. Seriously, I don't know how I'm going to live. She's getting custody and said if I ever see you again she's going to the judge. She says she'll tell him I molested the kids, and take them out of state."

She was back up to her antics. Fuck her. I'd play poker with her anytime. "She can't say that, Blake. It's not true. She can't prove it because there's nothing to prove. It's just a threat. She's bluffing."

"I can't see you when you're here, it's too risky." He kept talking as if I hadn't said anything. I heard him breathe. I couldn't so much as blink; I froze in the wake of his words.

"And I can't not see you either," he said at last. "I'll call you in a few weeks."

"I'll be there in three days, asshole." Seriously, what the fuck was I supposed to do with that?

"I know. It's— I have nothing left."

"I guess that leaves me with nothing, too." I hung up, destroyed. I kept expecting he would call me back. For three days I expected it.

No one thought it was a good idea for Blake and me to be together, except me. Jennifer thought he was destructive and generally bad for me. My mother made no bones about telling me she thought I'd be coming home from Seattle in a body bag. But I loved him and I was in love with him and I loved who I was when I was with him. I was that stupid, hopelessly devoted lost cause who would never get her man. I was that pathetic girl. I just couldn't see it in myself. I didn't let myself believe it. I would find a different ending. I got on the plane.

He called an hour after I arrived at the house I'd rented. It was a sweet little thing in Queen Anne. "Can I see you tonight?"

I nodded.

He must have heard it. "What's the address?"

I gave it to him.

"Six o'clock," he announced.

My body zinged with that constant inner fire of desire, a Pavlovian response to his voice that relayed from toes to crown to fingers. I felt utterly radiant.

I made a lunch date with Jennifer for Café Flora. The food was divine. It'd been almost a year since that fateful Valentine's night with Glen, the one that catapulted me into Blake's waiting arms. I told her about that night, how Blake had been pursuing me, Glen's lack of attention to any of it. I even told her how I'd been touching myself in the bathroom stall, thinking of Blake.

"Girl, if I had known it was that bad I would have booted your ass out of that marriage so fast." I loved Jennifer's white ass California bitch speak, like she had soul or something.

"I did the best I knew how to do."

"I know." She took a sip of her Perrier. "Well, you seem like you're in a good place now."

"Really? I hope so." Time would tell. Six o'clock or thereabouts. As the waiter poured tea, I suddenly flashed on the idea that maybe my mother was right. Maybe I would be coming home in a body bag. Fuck. Was I foolish to believe him? Would it be Cami showing up at my door that night, with that gun loaded and ready? I hated myself for doubting. But I doubted, a little. All the traffic was too slow and all the music too loud as I drove home. I'd grown used to Arizona's wide open freeways. Breathing in Seattle always felt like I was wearing a corset, crowded. There were too many eyes everywhere. And it was fucking cold and gray. Of course it was. Fucking Seattle. I hadn't missed it at all.

It hit me hard as I crossed the 520 bridge. Blake and I were in the same city. Just knowing that reawakened the raw woman inside of me. I was aware of how plump and warm my lips felt as I sucked on the straw of my ice water. I imagined the business men in their suits and BMWs around me, desiring me. Blake and I were in the same city. I was a real woman again, slick and wet for want of him.

I went to my home away from home and made myself ready to see him. I took a shower and re-shaved my legs. I went over my pussy with a fresh razor. I put on simple creamy silk lingerie, a long-sleeved, scoop-necked maroon dress, and combed my fingers through my wet hair. No makeup. I didn't need it smeared all over my face. I'd keep it simple, go Seattle natural.

Six o'clock came and went. I huddled on the couch, flipped channels on the TV, and tried not to feed my fears. It was another hour before my phone rang. Blake. Part of me knew he was calling to cancel.

"What's up?" I said, expecting the worst, sure he'd changed his mind. *He isn't coming to see me after all.* Or the very worst, he was calling only to offer a distraction for Cami, who was on the doorstep, gun-wielding, and ready to fight. I felt I was going to be sick.

But all he said in a very husky voice was, "I'm running late."

"Okay," I said. He didn't say how late, just hung up again. It was as if every connection took supreme daring for both of us. We were tentative in this dance, both of us wondering if we were really doing this.

I tried not to look at my watch, but then he was another twenty minutes late.

Thirty minutes late.

Forty minutes late. I thought he was going to call again, tell me he wasn't coming over after all. At 7:49, I heard the creak of the screen door and the doorbell sounded. I caught my breath in my chest. I felt like a mouse ready to bolt for the nearest hole. I forced myself to rise, to go to the door.

If it were Cami with a gun behind the door, I wouldn't have the slightest idea what to do other than call the cops, so I brought my phone with me, poised to dial 9-1-1 if necessary. The door had frosted glass windows on either side. I could see a human-shaped shadow through them; that was all.

But then I noticed the peephole. I'd seen a movie once where the guy in my position had put his eye up to the keyhole, blocking the light to the keyhole and letting the killer know his victim was behind the door. The killer put a bullet through the victim's eye. I hoped that if it was Cami on the other side of the door, she hadn't seen all of the movies I had. Who was I kidding? Of course she'd seen that movie. All this I thought in a flash as I moved toward the peephole and looked through to see Blake on the other side. I almost started crying, the relief ran off me so palpably in my shaking body as I opened the door.

He slipped in—a motion so delicate he could have been dancing—and glanced around the room like a hunted creature.

My face flushed as he entered. I could feel the heat emanating from my cheeks. Fiery sparks danced over my skin. I wouldn't have been surprised if my hair had stood on end, I felt so head-to-toe electric. Blake and I were in the same room. I fought to draw breath against the shallow container of my rib cage. My gaze lit on his face, trapped by what I saw there. "Oh, Blake," I said.

This was not the man I had known. This man had been damaged. I saw it in a heartbeat. I saw it in his shadowed eyes, his furtive stride. I saw it in his countenance, and the stubble on his jaw. Who the fuck was she to treat him in such a way as to render him to this? Oh my god. I wanted to fucking kill her. Some people should die. That's just... Go ahead. Think whatever you want of me. I promised myself honesty here, for you. I want you to know me. That's all I want. I'm hoping that's enough to forge this bond. But it starts and ends with honesty. I won't have anything else with you.

"You're here," I finally managed to say to him. They weren't quite the words of welcome I'd envisioned, but neither was this the homecoming I'd expected. Feeling daring, I leaned in close—the smell of his aftershave intoxicating as my lips neared his throat, almost touching until he pulled away.

"I'm here," he whispered. "But... I don't know yet. I don't know."

I understood, or so I thought. I wanted all of him, all at once. And it felt like I was going to implode if I got it all. "It's like I just saw you yesterday."

"I know," he said. A slip of a smile played at the corners of his mouth. "Show me around."

I did. It didn't take long. I reached for his hand, but he wouldn't accept mine. I shrugged. He needed a moment for this to become his reality again. I would give it to him. The cottage was a sweet one bedroom with a kitchen, dining room, and a personal theater. In eras past it had probably been a sitting room, but a television that big couldn't be housed in anything but a theater. And that was the extent of it. A tiny side porch. A picket fence. Old-fashioned porcelain crockery in the kitchen.

We existed in this half-believing state, luminous. Without kissing, only almost touching. I walked him back to the couch. I stood in front of him, took a step in closer. I let my cheek rest against his. He didn't resist. I turned my head softly to his lips and dusted a few kisses on them. They were dry and cracked against mine. I felt him tense and then he couldn't hold back. He opened his lips to me, we tasted each other again, so soft and so sweet.

One kiss and that was all. He pulled away and sat on the couch.

"I don't think I can stay," he said. "I'm paranoid, scared that Cami has a PI trailing me."

I looked at him hard. "The blinds are drawn in the front. We're in a windowless room with the door closed. I traveled two thousand miles to see you. She is three thousand miles away. I mean, she is, right?" He nodded. I got a little mad. "I can't take you anymore," I said and walked out of the room. I paced to the bathroom and realized I had nowhere to go. This was ridiculous, anyway. We of all people had no reason to avoid each other, no reason to fight. I walked back to where he sat and kneeled on the cushion next to him so that I was facing the back of the couch. I leaned in and pulled his face to mine, demanding that he kiss me. "No," he whispered, kissing me all the same.

I let my hands drift down as I sucked at his lips, his tongue. I unbuttoned and unzipped his pants.

"No, I'm not ready." He made no move to stop my hands.

"You want me to stop?" I kissed him deeply. "You want me to stop?" I stood up and pulled him to his feet, slid his pants over his hips. His cock thrust proudly against the rough cotton of his briefs.

He said nothing, only groaned. I took his pants off, getting on my knees to do so. "Tell me to stop and I will," I said, rubbing my face against his briefs, breathing deeply, the musky smell of his cock intoxicating. I slipped my hands under the elastic and took off his briefs. He didn't stop me. I pushed him back onto the couch, slipped my panties out from under my dress, and straddled him. My cunt yearned for him, I came at him in a rush, lowering myself onto him—aah!—I rode him hard, dripping wet. We didn't last long. How could we? We were overwrought. He came quickly and grabbed me to him as he shuddered my name. When I came after I felt like the goddess had showered me with rainbow flowers. I sighed and sank down against him. I closed my eyes. I'd longed for this and it was here. I'd never let myself forget this moment.

Paranoia forgotten, he fucked me four more times that night. The way he touched me, the way he looked at me, the way he understood me... I couldn't get enough. Neither of us could. We went to bed and snuggled and fucked, and fucked, and fucked. I woke him up at five to ride him again and told him I'd dreamed of him bringing me a ring. "We had the same dream," he said and took me up the ass. I can't believe how good everything felt. I resolved to ride that happiness as long as I could.

The days passed by in a blur. I wished I'd brought my calendar so I could fill it in with little blue boxes. We fucked in every place possible in that sweet little cottage. We'd relax on the lover's couch from time to time, him sitting upright, me curled up next to him with my head in his lap. "I can't tell where I end and you begin," he said. Probing for a boundary I realized it was the same way for me; I really couldn't tell. "It's so nice to just be. To not be ruled by suspicion. She plays these fucked up games with me, Aleah."

Cami. Our conversations always went back to Cami. "After she read those chats where I told you I love you, she went ballistic in front of Desiree. She started screaming, 'You love her, you love her, you can go!' Shrieking. 'Go play your fucking twisted games together. It's over. I want a divorce.' Then my little girl says, 'Mommy, who does daddy love?' and Cami screams, 'He loves Aleah and she's going to be your new step-mom!'"

"Oh my god," I said. I mean, what a thing to put on your kid. I don't care how much you're hurting, you don't do that. "Blake, she really is psychotic. You are writing everything down, right? The nights she comes home late from the bar, passes out. You're keeping tabs, right?"

"That's just it," he says. "We're tight on money. I asked Cam how we were paying for all her beer and she said she had a new boyfriend, one who always picked up the tab in exchange for fucking him as much as she wanted."

"That's insane." I know. Who was I to talk? "So, you're writing it down, right?"

He pressed on, ignoring my question, which gave me all the answer I needed. "I think she's staying drunk because in her more lucid moments she's forced to confront the truth she doesn't want to see."

"Which is?"

"Well, what really torques her is knowing what a great mother you would be to our children." *Our children.* His and mine. I went doe-still. I listened for all I was worth.

He pulled back and regarded me as if seeing me with new eyes. "You'd be such a fabulous mother, Aleah."

"Thank you." I flashed on an afternoon when I'd come over to babysit. Blake had gotten home to find Desiree sitting in my lap on the kitchen floor. I'd been rocking her back and forth in my lap singing a Lyle Lovett song about riding a pony out on a boat on the ocean.

Desiree had burst out laughing, "That's silly!"

I'd looked at Blake and kept singing. He'd looked away, but not before I'd seen him wipe a small tear from his cheek.

It was our last night in the cottage. I ordered in Chinese and we sat on the couch, struggling with chopsticks, sitting as close to one another as physics would allow. "How fucked up would it be if you got pregnant?" Blake said out of the blue.

"It would be pretty crazy," I said, hating how he played with my emotions.

"I love kids. I want eight or nine of them." He was in a light mood, almost the Blake I used to know. Even the shadows had retreated from under his eyes. I wished I could share his mood. My plane was leaving in two days.

"It doesn't matter, I'm not fertile. If I were, all these years without birth control would have resulted in something." I sighed and pulled away from him, a little. I didn't want to talk about the one thing I wanted most and would never have. "You better figure things out, Blake Porter."

"I think I am, Aleah Porter," he said. Aleah *Porter*. I wanted to fucking punch him. I felt like I'd taken a medicine ball to the gut.

All of a sudden the energy changed in the room. Blake scooted away slightly, but turned to me and leaned in. His voice took on the husky intensity I'd come to associate with his raw honesty.

"All this time you've been telling me how it's better for me to be whole even if I can't be there every moment for my kids. That if I am healthy, then I can be so much more with them. This time with you is the happiest I can remember being in years. Since before Cami. My panic attacks are gone. My anxiety is gone. You are my angel. You help me find my confidence, help me be stable. I can be a better dad like this a few days a week than I can if I'm there in her hell seven days a week. I finally get it."

"Do you?" I said. "Then take me out of the shadows. Make this real. I'll stay by your side. I know what I'm getting into."

Anger flashed in his eyes. He was irritated with me. "Why is it so important that I announce this to everyone? So you can clear your name?"

"Like I care about that anymore," I said. "I just want to be able to look your sister in the eye."

"Oh, Donna knows. She knows what I have with you is way bigger than anything I ever had with Cami."

I just shook my head.

"I'll prove it to you," he said.

"How are you going to do that?"

In response he got out his phone. He called Donna and said he needed to see her, and gave her the address. He didn't tell her about me.

I was a bit nervous when she arrived. She kept shaking her head and saying, "You two." But then, it was Donna, one of my closest and dearest friends and it didn't matter all the shit that had gone down, or at least it didn't matter as much as it had. We all sat down in the theater.

"You're not pregnant, are you?" she asked.

"No," I said. Blake snuggled up next to me on the couch and draped his arm over my shoulders. Like we were teenagers at the movie theatre. I wanted to cry I was so happy. It melted away so much pain, his willingness to claim me in front of his sister.

"I don't know what I'm doing," he said. "All I know is I'm happy when I'm with this one."

Blake went out, ostensibly for a smoke, but I knew it was to give us time to talk. "You know, I wondered what was up when Blake called. I knew something was different. He sounded peaceful. Happy even. But mostly peaceful. Before tonight I haven't heard so much peace in my brother's voice since before he met Cami."

I sat with that for a minute. I knew how much Donna prized peace. It was high praise.

"I've missed you girl," I said.

"I know it. Me too, darlin'," she said. "Good luck with that one." She jerked her head toward the door Blake had exited through. "I don't envy you a bit. He's been to hell and ain't comin' out soon."

I laughed. It was all I could do. "Love hurts."

"So it does. Because of those kids."

"I know. But he's better for them when he's happy. They're happier with him. He's happy with me. I don't understand why he's letting Cami's abuse be passed on to them."

"He can't see it like you can, Aleah. It's because of our mom, how she used to treat him. She'd in one breath pull him close and shower him with sweet words and love, tell him how he was her little man, her angel, her knight in shining armor, then in the very next breath she'd remember how our dad had treated her, and push him away. Sometimes she'd actually spit at my brother. She'd tell him how evil he was, how much she hated him, how he needed to get away and leave her alone. I'm telling you, Aleah. It was fucked up."

Suddenly, everything about why Blake had stayed with Cami clicked into place. I understood why he couldn't leave her. I wasn't asking him to leave a controlling bitch, I was asking him to leave the embodiment of his mother and I was asking him to take a leap of faith that a happy life could actually exist where he was just loved and not hated. It was something he couldn't believe in because he'd never seen it in real life. I was a fairy tale. I might have well have been asking him to go to Oz.

Chapter Six

For our final night together I booked a room at the Salish Lodge, overlooking Snoqualmie Falls. I got there at four and checked in. He got there after work, around five.

"I remember this place as being very expensive," he said.

"I remember it being worth it," I said, lounging back on the most comfortable bed in the world.

"They wouldn't let me in at first. You didn't give them the right name."

"What name was I supposed to give them?"

"Aleah Porter."

I jumped up and hit him hard, on the bicep. He immediately grabbed me and dragged me out to the balcony. Before I knew what he was doing he had taken his belt off and lashed my wrists to the wrought iron railings. He was a shadow behind me in my peripheral vision. I heard the button pop out of his jeans and the zip of his fly, I heard him grunt as he jerked down his briefs. He drew up close behind me. I felt his back against mine, his breath rushing hotly through my hair. "You're not going to be a virgin after tonight," he whispered as I felt the length of his hardness press against my ass crack. Mmmm. He hiked up my skirt, thumbed the thong out of the way, and plunged deep into my wet, hot, waiting cunt, right there on the balcony in the twilight, the massive river rushing to fall below us, in plain sight of anyone who wanted to watch from their balcony. He slapped my ass raw with his open palm as he pummeled me with his huge cock and screamed when he came. Miraculously, no one seemed to notice. Or maybe they were just enjoying the show. I know I loved every moment of it.

He pulled his pants up. "Thank you, I needed that," he said as he unbuckled my arms and unwound his belt from the railing. He kissed me tenderly and led my shaking body inside, to warm up, to get dressed for dinner.

I wore a blood red cocktail dress with a plunging neckline and shoulder straps. My necklace covered my throat in a cascade of low-grade but extremely large rubies I'd gotten for a song at the Tucson Rock & Gem show. I wore red sandals fastened with a red ribbon that criss-crossed up my legs before tying at the calf.

"You're the sexiest creature I have ever seen," Blake said in my ear as he sidled up to me. "I have something for you." He slipped his hand under my dress, then pulled my thong down a few inches and probed for my hole with his thumb. "A present," he said, slipping the tip of a rather large and, thankfully, lubed plug into me. He pushed it home slowly and I gasped. You could probably say it put a spring in my step. I'd forgotten how sexy it was to wear a plug for him.

The hotel's restaurant was still decked out for Valentine's Day, which had flown by us, somewhat unnoticed. I had brought presents for Blake, gone forgotten the day before, but brought them to dinner and was glad for the décor. Though they looked slightly tired, there were red roses and sprigs of baby's breath at every table. We were seated near the fireplace at the back of the room.

"You look so lovely," the hostess said to me as she walked us to the table.

"Doesn't she," Blake beamed. "Those are rubies in her necklace, real ones." He'd asked me about them in the elevator.

"Low grade," I amended, smiling. He pulled my chair out and scooted it for me as I sat. He sat down and took my hand across the table. Anyone looking at us could have seen it. He looked dashing. I was entranced.

"Every man in this room is jealous of me tonight," he said, gazing at me intensely. "You are insanely beautiful, Aleah. You are radiant."

"The girls are all jealous of me," I said. "For how well you treat me."

"It's not that hard," he said. "You taught me that."

He ordered venison sausage chili and I opted for the duck risotto. Our appetizer arrived shortly after—mussels swimming in a white wine, butter, and garlic broth. Everything was divine.

I passed the presents I'd carefully prepared for him across the table.

"You didn't."

"I did. Happy Valentine's Day."

He opened the littlest box. "An iPod," he kept saying in his best southern. It seemed retro to get him an iPod, but I knew his construction grade phone wasn't app-savvy and he'd always said he wished he could listen to music while he worked. "I always wanted one of those. Didn't think I'd get one, though." His eyes were shiny. "Thank you." He looked at the window across the room and swallowed; I could see his jaw tighten. "You know," he said, turning back to me, "I can't think of a single thing Cami ever got for me because I actually liked it. She always got me things she wanted me to have, trying to make me into the person she wanted me to be. Fancy suits. Spa visits. Cologne." He tapped the iPod on the table. "I love this. I know I've never even mentioned it to you and still you knew."

He glanced at the Quick Start guide and turned the silver player on. That's when he found the menu and saw that I'd already loaded around 800 songs for him. "Holy shit," he said.

"Enjoy," I said. "You deserve it."

He unwrapped the candle next and closed his eyes as he brought it to his nose and inhaled. "It's you," he said. "Oh my god, I'll be able to smell you forever."

"For when I'm away," I said.

"I love it, Aleah. All of it. Thank you for everything."

We held hands at the dinner table. "It's so easy to be with you," he said in obvious amazement. He started talking about the house he was working on, his day job. He stopped mid-sentence and gave me a curious look. "I know you can't—or don't—but I like that you act like you care about all this."

"I do care." I did.

There was no baggage, just two people out for a nice meal. In those hours I knew ecstasy.

"You're so strong and sexy," he said. "So much more than when you were with Glen. I woke something up in you. Confidence. You've changed the way you dress, the way you walk. You've even changed the way you drive."

"*Head Over Feet*" came on the sound system. "We'll play this song at our wedding," he said. I blinked. I couldn't even let myself acknowledge he'd said it. All of my dreams were coming true.

He picked up my left hand, and examined my empty ring finger. "You never had a diamond."

"I don't like diamonds."

"I know. I always figured I'd get you opals when it was my turn."

His turn.

"Opals, really?"

"Yeah."

"They're my favorite."

He gave me a look that I'd come to identify as an acceptance of disbelief. "That's funny," he said huskily, "Because an opal is what you are to me. Multi-faceted color, sparkling from deep inside, with flashes of fire."

I melted.

We talked and told stories for hours.

"See," I said in a teasing voice as we finished our cheesecake.

"What?"

"We can do more than just have sex. We can talk for hours."

"Oh, I know, Aleah. I know."

"I think you're waiting for it to wear off sometimes."

"Expecting it to, maybe. But it never does."

We sat on the balcony together, after we'd made it back to the room. I brought his iPod and, as we sat there under the stars, huddled together each with an earbud in one ear, I told him some of the meanings behind the songs and why I'd put them on. He turned to me, a pained look in his eyes.

"I think I love you," he said. All I saw was torture and vulnerability shining out of him, like those words were the worst possible outcome he could envision. “You have to write about this. Some people are never this happy, ever. The need to know this kind of happiness exists.” He didn’t sound very happy. This wasn’t how I wanted to spend my last night in town.

“Come on,” I said, taking the earbud from my ear and rising. “Let’s go inside. I have something else for you.”

“You don’t.” Blake groaned. “I didn’t get anything for you. I wanted to.”

“You’re here,” I said. “That’s enough.” The whole night was magical. I brought out my second gift bag full of presents I hadn’t wanted him opening in public: a Japanese rope kit, a soy candle that, when burned, created a pool of warm wax you could pour onto your lover, wrist cuffs made out of thick leather with a two foot long chain between them, a small leather cat o’nine tails.

“Oh my god,” he kept saying as he drew each item out of its magenta tissue paper. “This is the best Valentine’s Day. Ever.” He sat down with right away with the rope book that came in the kit and intently examined each of the designs before settling in on the most intricate pattern. “This one,” he said. “I want to see you like this.”

“Okay,” I said. “But light a fire first.”

The fireplace was already set up, ready to light with newspaper and wood to burn. I loved this hotel. Blake started the fire with a match. I turned the lights down low. He put music on and lit the soy candle. “Are you ready?” he asked. I nodded. He proceeded, over the next hour, to very carefully tie a series of intricate knots all over my body using a single length of soft black rope. He started with a loop around my neck, and tied several knots in a row, each about six inches apart down my belly, so that the rope hung from my throat like a comically long bolero, past my knees. He arranged it so that a knot hit just above my clit, and pulled the two strands of rope through my legs. I stood stock still as he patiently looped the ropes around my thighs, through the partitions he’d created earlier and back around. He tied a series of butterfly patterns across my belly and sides. My arms ended up secured behind my head, elbows bent, hands clasped at my nape. The rope played along my clit in the most tantalizing tease that left me tingling and throbbing simultaneously. He left my ribboned shoes on, but otherwise I was dressed only in rope.

I stood next to the fire when he was done, letting him survey his work. He'd come in close for a moment and adjust a strap, then step back to take in his handiwork. He sighed and came close in again, kissed me softly in the hollow of my throat. He ran his hands over my erect nipples, down to my navel. He sank to his knees, his hands cupping my womb. "I've got to give you a baby, don't I?" he said so matter-of-factly, like it was done except for the doing of it. He blew on my skin and I trembled like the brittlest leaf on the wind.

What was he doing to me? He was breaking all the rules. I needed more assurances before I could dream like that. "Well. I hate to break it to you, but if it hasn't happened yet…" I didn't mean to be flippant, but I was tired of hoping for something that clearly wasn't in my cards.

He knelt at my feet and untied my shoes. He re-wound the ribbon in figure eights around my ankles so that they were bound together, too. I kept breathing, praying I wouldn't lose my balance and tumble to the floor. Blake kept a light hand on my body to steady me, then swooped me up into his arms. He carried me to the full-length mirror in the bathroom so I could see myself. I stared at how pretty everything was, how artfully each aspect of my sexuality was positioned. Even my clit was butterflied, exposed. My tits were arranged just so, perked up by the restrictive knots, a perfect display. I was beautiful. Blake carried me to the bed and draped me, stomach down, over two pillows so that my ass was poised in the air. He pulled my legs wide, knees bent, ankles tied. I leaned forward on my elbows over the pillows, helpless. He adjusted the ties so that I could relax against the rope. Freedom through constriction. I let go completely. I stopped trying to do anything for myself. I let the rope hold me. I felt his hands rushing over me like a soft breeze, and then felt the absence of him as he stepped away. I heard him rustling in the bag of goodies I'd brought.

He was beside me before I sensed him, whispering in my ear. "You've been an exceptionally naughty girl," he whispered.

"I'm sorry," I said. "I won't be bad again."

"I think you will. I think you like it."

"What will you do to me?" Everything inside of me poised like a horse ready to fly out of the gate. Excitement, desire. I needed to feel the lash. I needed the pain.

I yelped and blinked in surprise at the sudden heat on my ass, then the subtle pressure of hardening wax.

"I'll do whatever I want, little girl." He whipped me then, loving me with every stroke. The lash licked and bit my ass, a nibble here, a tease there. It was more of annoyance than any kind of punishment. I giggled.

"I know, this is kind of absurd," Blake said, breaking character. I heard the small whip land on the floor. His hands splayed against my rump, covering it. He caressed me, rubbing my flesh to warm it. In spite of the fire, there was a slight chill in the room. I began to shake. His hands roamed, rubbing my back, my legs, my shoulders. "Are you warm enough?"

"I will be."

"I can't get over how sexy you are. No one—no real girl—is this sexy. God." His hand pulled back and flew against my ass with a smack. I cried out involuntarily and his hand fell again. "I want to cover your ass in bruises," he said. It was poetry to my ears. He hit me, again and again until my whole world was pain. The best kind of pain. I was sure my butt was pink and tinged with rose-shaped spots of purply red that would blacken as the bruises bloomed. I couldn't wait to see them. It was so sexy. It would be a while before I would be comfortable sitting down. The plane ride home the next day would not be pleasant. Tomorrow. I didn't want to think about it, so I put it out of my mind.

At long last, Blake removed the plug he'd placed in me before dinner, and fucked my reddened ass. I adored how tight my asshole was, but also how much more of him I could take since I'd been wearing the plug. It was a noticeable improvement. He came in my ass, then stepped away for a bit. He came back smelling faintly of soap and I felt the scratchy softness of a warm, wet washcloth as he wiped me clean, too. He worked his way over my body with kisses, from my toes to the back of my knees, the inside of my thighs, my breasts. Then fucked me again and came in my pussy. And on my breasts. I trembled in the ropes when he was done.

"God, I love you," he said over and over. And then, "I didn't just say that aloud, did I?"

"Over and over," I said.

"Oh. Shit." He smiled and raised my chin with his finger, planted a soft kiss on my lips. "I love you. Let me get you out of this."

He went to draw a bath and then came back to me. He untied every knot, one by one. Centimeter by centimeter he released me from bondage. I didn't even try to move. I was jelly. An amoeba. As each appendage was freed it flopped to the bed. I couldn't feel my arms or legs. They didn't belong to me. I was floating, happy. Everything was bliss.

After he'd undone the knots along my spine, Blake rolled me onto my back and released the last series of knots, ending with the one at the base of my neck. I lay there, limp. He could have done anything with me. He scooped me into his arms and carried me to the giant bathtub. He stepped into the water and sank down, never dropping me, never coming close to hitting any part of my body on the walls or ceramic. He cuddled me from behind as the heat soaked into my muscles. I cried a bit. More than a bit. My body wracked with sobs. Aftershocks, I suppose. I'd never been beaten like that in my life. Not even close. He wrapped his arms around me and just held me while I cried it out.

"You're all I need," he whispered. "It's okay." He stroked my hair until I'd calmed.

It didn't take long. "I'm okay. It's okay," I said after a few minutes.

"Good," he said. "Then you won't mind if I fuck you again."

"No," I whispered. "I will not." He slipped around from behind me and fucked me missionary style, hammering my back against the wall of the tub. I wrapped my legs around his hips and reveled in him pumping into me like a fucking bull. He was amazing and huge and gorgeous and in that moment, he was mine.

We finally went to sleep at a quarter to five. We woke up two hours later and ordered room service for breakfast. Eggs Benedict, thick slabs of bacon, blueberry pancakes, coffee, juice, a fruit bowl, a bread basket. I was starving.

All good things have to come to an end. Why had I thought the week would last forever? "I have to catch my plane. We have to get out of here," I said.

His breath caught in his chest. "This is it, then."

"It is," I said. "So, did you figure it out? Are we together, now? Is this for real? I need an answer, Blake. You can't keep dragging my heart around."

"You need it now?"

"Yes. I came to Seattle like you asked. You've had a chance to see if you could be happy with me."

A look of genuine pain crossed his face. He sank to the bed and put his face in his hands, staring at the floor. Finally, he looked up. "I can't envision how we can ever be together," he said. "She'd find a way to keep me from my kids. They need me, Aleah. I need them. I don't know what I want. They keep pulling me back to her. I can't walk away."

"She's divorcing you, Blake."

"I know, but it's just something she has to do. She wants a clean start."

I was way too easy for him to walk away from. Rage seeped through my muscles, pooling under my skin. "Fine," I said. "Go back to her. Let her destroy you. I'm done with you. I'm done! God damn it. You don't get to treat me like this, not ever again." No one did. I actually slapped him.

"I deserved that," he said.

"You deserve much more than that," I said. "Get out. Get out of here!" I was screaming then.

He picked up his packed bags and he walked out the door. He walked out of the fucking door. I couldn't even cry. Worse, I was so sore and bruised I could barely move. It was going to be one hell of a plane ride back to Tucson.

Chapter Seven

My mother wasn't home when I arrived. Probably at work. I didn't even bother to unpack my bags from Seattle; instead I started packing up the belongings I had in Tucson. I was moving to Austin. That wasn't changing. It hurt to move my body. Everything hurt. I relished the pain. I couldn't even cry. I felt dulled. As I packed, I realized I hadn't done the one thing in Seattle I'd set out to do: all of the rest of my things were still at what I'd come to think of as Glen's house, waiting for me to arrange their transport. Fuck. I'd have to go back. But not now. Maybe not even soon. The house seemed to be languishing on the market. Who knew when it would sell?

Sadie, at least, was happy to see me. Her back legs, I noticed, were getting worse, splaying more on the tile as she tried to walk on it. The vet had told me she'd be particularly prone to hip dysplasia and I could tell the degeneration was starting. I hated to see her like that. She'd been my constant companion since she was two months old. She was only six now. I vowed to do some research, maybe change her diet. Up the glucosamine intake.

A week passed. I never made it out of that dull fog. My mother and I existed in the same house together, avoiding each other. I knew she wasn't proud of what I'd done in Seattle. It didn't take a rocket scientist to look at me and see that my dreams had once again been dashed. I was sure she couldn't wait for me to get out from under her roof, to take my drama elsewhere. I couldn't wait, either.

Finally, moving day arrived. I packed my bug to the gills and boxed up whatever wouldn't fit. My mother said she'd UPS the packages to me.

It was ten a.m. before I was ready to go. Already the sun beating on the hood of my beetle made the car uncomfortably hot to the touch. "I guess this is it," my mother said. She stood on the lip of the drive, arms folded against the wind. Her hair moved as one object, buffeting her face. "Good luck, Aleah."

"Thanks, Mom." I wrapped my arms around her in a brief hug. She unfolded her arms and encircled me. I could feel how skinny she'd gotten. I could feel her ribs and her hips and the bones in her arms. She seemed fragile to me, suddenly. Made of iron, for sure. But fragile. Her skin seemed a little brittle, like that brown wax paper you sometimes get at the butcher. "Thank you for being here when I needed you," I said. "I appreciate it more than you know."

It took a few days to get to Austin in my little yellow bug. That sort of boggled my mind. I was moving to a state in which I would cross the border and drive for an additional two days before I reached my city of choice. What's more, my city of choice was smack dab in the middle of the state. If I wanted to reach whatever backwater state was on the other side of Texas (Arkansas? Mississippi? Louisiana? Alabama? Fuck if I knew, but I'd put money on it being one of those four. So much for public education.), I would have to drive an additional day or so to get to the other side. I'd heard once that the landscape of the west was so grand that a man either rose up to meet it or was crushed by it. Something like that. Anyway, the west had nothing on Texas.

Sadie and I overnighted at a skanky roach motel in Fort Stockton. I was tempted to buy a bumper sticker that said, "I wasn't born in Texas, but I got here as quick as I could." I couldn't quite bring myself to buy it though. I'd buy it now, in a heartbeat. I'm somewhat enamored of that poor grammar, whereas before I'd have been a twinge ashamed of it. Sadie and I were on the road by six the next morning, coffee-fueled. After hours and hours of driving through near-empty country, roadside farmer's stalls began to pop up, hawking strawberries. Hill country towns flowered here and there and then began to appear in earnest along the freeway, intermingled with broad pasturelands full of oak trees and goats or sheep or cows or horses… even bison. There were fences everywhere. Fences tamed the west, I remembered dimly from somewhere. *And barbed wire.* Giant black birds roosted in the tops of some of the scruffier, dead snags. I wondered if they were a kind of hawk. It was only when I came upon the remains of a deer on the road and a bevy of vultures scattered to the sky that I realized what they were. They were so much bigger than the vultures in Arizona.

Soon the towns grew more frequent. Then they lost their edges and one bled into the next, civilization crowding in. Fredericksburg, Johnson City, Dripping Springs. Lanes multiplied. Before I knew it, I was coursing into Austin's south side. From the top of one of the freeway's impossibly high flyovers the city skyline rolled out before me, gorgeous and shining in the light. High rises the color of brick, creamy stone towers, and green glass played along my sight, but also the trees and the river. I'd made it. My heart sang. I'd never seen so much sun. I was flooded with happiness, starting my new life. I put Muse's "Feeling Good" on and blared it through my open windows as I flew over the asphalt into town.

I followed Siri's instructions and turned off on Congress. As I drove up the avenue, the presidential dome of the capitol of Texas stood before me in stately grandeur, glistening in the distance. Sweet and funky little shops lined the promenade. Ice cream shops and candy stores, antique shops and bookstores, costumers, milliners, and restaurants. Not a McDonald's or a Wal*Mart among them. Nothing I recognized, everything completely individual. I loved the town already. When I looked at someone, they looked at me and smiled or waved hello. I was so startled, I waved back. What the fuck? Friendly people too?! I actually had a tear roll down my cheek, I was so much in love.

I turned on Academy, by Doc's whose billboard sign proclaimed, "The madness is coming. Drink/eat while u wait." I snaked my little car back up into the hills above Congress.

I made it to the apartment manager's office, picked up the keys and moved my few possessions into the living room. It was a dumpy little shoe box, that apartment. Living room/bedroom, kitchen, tiny bathroom, and a patio off the back. One small squarish box. But it was my cheap little shoebox in the middle of town.

I noticed that all of the screens on the windows and patio door had been shredded by the previous owner's cat. I rang the front desk and told Management about it. They said they'd get right on it. I felt immensely satisfied, like I'd come to a place I could make a home. I could find friends here. I could do this. It would be a while before the divorce went through, but I already felt free of the trappings of my marriage. I felt so much distance from Glen I could barely remember him at times. I didn't let myself think of anyone or anything else.

I emptied the bug's contents, making a pyramid of boxes in the middle of my empty living room. Furniture would have to come later. I took Sadie for a stroll around the neighborhood. After a few minutes it was obvious she was in pain from the way she carried herself, so we turned around and walked back to our new home. I felt strange, hollow around the edges. I needed something. I put Sadie's leash in a drawer in the kitchen and I realized I was hungry. I wasn't just hungry, I was starving. I needed food. I smiled. It felt good to be hungry. I had an appetite for life again. I was moving on.

I took myself out to dinner. I had a steak. I was in Texas, after all. I was a Texan now. Fuck the years I had spent with Glen as a vegetarian. I promised myself I would eat a lot of steak.

Back at the apartment, the mountain of things I'd piled in the middle of the living room looked like Mt. Kilimanjaro. No fucking way was I dealing with that right then. I'd left my blow-up mattress on the edge where I could get to it easily. I dragged it to the bedroom and turned on the auto-inflate feature. Sadie cowered and barked at it as I soothed her. *Oh, Sadie.* I rummaged about for blankets, but all I could locate was my pillow. Exhausted, I called it good enough and collapsed on the flocked blue vinyl. Slumber claimed me. I slept deeply and woke up to the sun streaming in through the windows. It felt good to be alive.

I walked down to Congress Avenue and strolled over to Jo's Coffee. "I love you so much," was spray-painted in red cursive letters on the side of the key-lime-pie colored building. A few minutes later, armed with a large coffee and the barista-recommended breakfast tacos—whatever those were—I sat down on the porch to watch the inhabitants of my new world walk by. I scarfed the tacos down. Filled with eggs, potatoes, and cheese, they were unbelievably satisfying. I saw that everyone else put salsa on theirs. Breakfast tacos. Who knew? More importantly, why hadn't the rest of the country clued in yet?

The air had grown heavy with humidity, and oppressively hot as I'd sat under Jo's metal roof. The trudge back up the hills to my apartment was pretty taxing. I dropped back to my air mattress and took a nap. I welcomed sleep's cradling arms. I cocooned myself in it. Untold hours later I rose and made myself busy settling into my new home. I hung up my clothes, unpacked my boxes and my computer. I set up a temporary work station so I could at least make some money. Not for the first time, I was grateful for the job that travelled with me, that let me work from home, wherever home happened to be.

My refrigerator was empty. That needed to be rectified. Plus, hunger gnawed at my belly. I smiled, realizing I was in the birthplace of Whole Foods. I took the afternoon for a jaunt to their flagship store. Everything was fine, I told myself. I was going to be fine. I loaded up the car with six of those reusable shopping bags worth of groceries. Fresh fruit. Coconut juice. Avocados and pineapple. Grass-fed rib-eye steak. I felt like I was on vacation. I knew I needed to settle in. I found a routine that worked for me. It went like this: eat, work, eat, nap, eat, walk, eat, sleep. After a few days of this, I realized I was hungry and tired all the time, in a way I never had been before. My body felt strange, like parts of it were waking up that hadn't been awake in ages. I liked being in Austin, I told myself. It suited me.

I let myself believe this for a few more weeks. I told myself it was because I was healthier than I'd been in a while. Then the nausea started. I didn't actually throw up. I'd eat something quickly and quell the urge, but after combating the urge to vomit a few times, another thought occurred to me.

Book Four

Though I had no need of it—force of habit being compelling enough for me to always know the last day of my previous period—I walked to the kitchen and looked at the calendar. I was about a week late, but that was nothing new. Still. I walked to my bathroom's medicine cabinet and rummaged around until I found a Clear Blue Easy stick. I'd been buying them at Costco when I lived in Seattle, in bulk. Damn things were so expensive I couldn't bring myself to leave them behind.

I peed on the stick. In a matter of moments it produced a gigantic blue plus sign. I mean, it seemed like biggest plus sign I have ever seen. I'd seen so many negative results before. It took several moments for the realization to hit me. I shook my head. It was lying to me. I couldn't get pregnant. I threw the damn thing away and grabbed my sole remaining stick. I peed on that, too. Gigantic plus sign, again. The biggest.

I decided the kit had to be defective and someone was playing a sick joke on women in America. Clear Blue was the leading brand, after all. I went to the closest drugstore. I don't remember getting there, or which one it was Siri took me to. I bought a different brand and Siri directed me home. I peed on a different kind of stick.

I was pregnant.

With Blake's baby.

The storm that had been threatening all afternoon arrived at that moment with a roaring wind. The crepe myrtles in the courtyard slammed against the glass of my patio door. A huge flash of brilliance seared my vision, immediately followed by a deafening crack that morphed into a roar as sheets of rain flooded my porch. Everything was bigger in Texas. There was a plus sign on the stick.

I swallowed against my disbelief and wandered around my apartment in a stupor, listening to the heavy rain until I finally collapsed on the pseudo bed. I had spent my entire marriage trying to get pregnant and *now* it happened? Now, really? Now that I had finally moved on? I did not mean to lead this interesting a life. I swear I did not. I might have cursed some deity or eight in that moment.

And praised. I was pregnant. I was actually pregnant. I was pregnant with the baby of a man I loved. *Oh my god.*

What does one do in a moment like that? I did what any little girl would do. I called my mother. "I have some news," I said.

She breathed out heavily. "I see you made it into Austin all right." I could tell she was irritated. It was true, I had been there for a while now. I could have called. Then again, she could have fucking called me if she was worried about it. I gritted my teeth.

"I did. Thanks. All settled in now." I didn't need the guilt trip. I'd just have to be a shitty daughter in her eyes.

"Well, that's good—"

"And I'm pregnant."

Our words collided over the line.

"What?"

"I'm pregnant. You're going to be a grandmother." I smiled. It was starting to feel good. I was pregnant. I was actually excited to tell someone. I was pregnant. I was going to have a baby. I was going to be a mother. I was going to raise a child. I couldn't help but be happy. I didn't care about how hard it would be. My smile filled my entire body.

"Oh, Aleah." My mother colored my name with disdain. It took her no time at all to come to a conclusion. "You can't keep it. No way. It will be the worst decision of your life. You will come to hate and resent that child for what he's done to you. You should terminate it. The sooner the better."

I blinked. That was all the time it took me to respond. "I don't even know what to say to you, Mom." I wondered if that was how she'd felt about me. Had she come to hate me for what I'd done to her? Did she wish she'd never had me? My cheeks grew hot. I recognized I was angry. "This child is my miracle. I am not going to kill it." Even as they came out, I wondered at the forcefulness of my next words. "You should think about whether or not you want to be a part of your grandchild's life—or mine—and if the answer is *yes* then you'd best get supportive of me and fast. I won't tolerate your negativity, Mom. Not now. I don't need it. I love you and I want you in this baby's life, but you're going to have to want to be a part of it, too. I won't hear another word against it."

"Oh. Okay. I see."

"All right. Well, let me know." I didn't have anything else to say. I hung up the phone. I forced my shoulders to drop, and pushed the stagnant air from my lungs. I'd had enough. I tried to shake the tension out of my head.

Days passed and I grew more and more used to the notion that I was going to be a mother. I hadn't told Blake. I didn't know what to think about telling him, about what might happen. I was bearing his child. I mean, I knew I had to tell him sooner or later. That was the only ethical thing to do. I knew what I feared. What if my being pregnant wasn't enough to bring us together? I know that sounds like I was trying to trap him. What I was actually doing was considering if opening my heart to him again was a risk worth taking. Did I go for the moon? Or did I just move on, take the free pass to Start-overs-ville and leave everyone and everything in the past?

Then I thought about my father. My beloved father. Where would I be without him? He had understood me like no one else ever had. I didn't think any of the things I loved about myself would have been there without my father. It had been one of the best relationships of my life. Of course I wanted my baby's father in his or her life. Of course I did.

I wanted to tell Blake to his face, to see his eyes. I wanted this to be our miracle, not just mine. But my credit card was beginning to feel the burden of all of the extravagances I'd been splurging on since leaving Seattle in the first place: Thousands of miles of gasoline, airplane tickets, food, and moving into the apartment. I didn't know how I could keep it up. I told myself I still needed to arrange to have my furniture brought to Austin, and camping out in my own place with a blow-up mattress and card table as my only pieces of furniture was beginning to grow stale. I mean, I was working, but my income was nothing like what I'd been used to, living with Glen. I'd have to pay attention to things. My credit limit was only so high.

I came to the honest realization that I simply couldn't afford another trip to Seattle. I had to save for the baby, for the insurance deductible, for the future. I told myself when push came to shove I didn't have to be there for the movers. Glen could see to at least that much.

I texted Blake. *Need to talk. Call me.* My phone dinged back almost instantly.

I got my own place. Finally moved out. I miss you. Will call tonight.

He'd been waiting for me to reach out to him. For once, he'd let it be my choice. I guess things hadn't gone as smoothly with Cami as he'd hoped. Maybe he couldn't make himself love her after all. *Oh, fucking hope. I want to murder you*, I thought. The afternoon hours took forever to pass.

I felt the jangly cloud of nerves take over when Blake called that night. I picked up the phone and let it ring in my hand a moment, my stomach heaving to keep enough air in my body. I felt like throwing up. I answered it up just before it would have clicked to voice mail. "Hello?" I managed.

"I just wanted to hear your voice," he said.

"Here it is," I said.

"Cami's lost it completely. She launches into me every day about you, again. Still. She won't let me back in. She won't trust me. She's calling me a sick fuck because I like to watch porn. 'I suppose *she* would watch it with you,' she says, talking about you. Then she'll tell me I'm a sick fuck for liking it, and I can't control myself and that's why we're getting a divorce. Last night I told her, 'No it's not. We're getting a divorce because you don't understand me and you don't get me and you never have and you never will. You don't give a damn about me.' She started screaming again, 'That's because you're a sick fuck, blah blah blah.'" He sighed and I could hear him drag on his smoke. "I'm done."

"You seem like you're in a different place." I let it all wash over me. He seemed a little more confident.

"I'm safe now. She talked to a lawyer and found out that she can't just up and leave with the kids. She tried to manipulate me into signing a document that would release them, at which point I knew she couldn't take them without my permission. She kept telling me she wanted them to be surrounded by love and not by sex addicts like me. I told her I wouldn't let her take those children away from me and I won't. So I moved out."

It was late and I didn't want to hear about Cami anymore.

"So, I wanted you to call because I have something to tell you."

"Say it already." He chuckled.

I took a deep, heaving breath, and another. "You know how you kept saying you needed to put a baby inside of me?" I couldn't go on. My words tried to form a bridge of understanding between us. I needed him to make the leap. I was so afraid of saying it aloud.

"What are you saying, woman?"

I was going to have to say it. "I'm pregnant."

"Oh, fuck," he said.

"Yeah. That's exactly what I wanted to hear."

"I'm sorry, baby. It's just—it changes things. You're pregnant. Wow." He sat with it for a minute and when next he spoke, the tone of his voice was bemused. "Are you sure it's mine?"

I actually laughed. We both laughed. Maybe things were going to be okay after all. I imagined the way his smile lit up his eyes from within, remembered again how intoxicating he was.

"How far along are you?"

I told him and we talked about the pregnancy for a while. "I bet you're radiant," he said. "I bet you're a fucking Madonna. Oh, I wish I could be there."

"There's room here for you. Come on over."

"I wish I could. But you know where I need to be. We need to get you and that baby back up here." I heard him let out a heavy breath. "Ah, shit. You know I'm going to have to tell Cami. We're going to have to work all this out."

I didn't want to know that, but I supposed he was right. If I was in this, I had to be in it all the way. He could tell her. I could leave her well enough alone. "You could wait a little while, before you tell her, couldn't you?"

"Yeah," he said. "Yeah. I could do that."

"A few months."

"A few months," he agreed.

I remember them as a deliriously happy idyll. He'd call me in the morning, in the afternoon, on the way home from work, after dinner, before bed... It felt like we were spending our days together. And yet I spent those months alone and lonely. I stayed in Austin because it was just too messy up north. Divorces needed to be finalized. Tempers needed to retreat. Sometimes I'd go to meet-ups for expectant mothers and attempt to make friends. But not really. Not the way I should have.

I missed Blake.

I made baby plans, read baby books, saw baby doctors, and scoured garage sales for baby things. I hit twenty weeks and found out our little bean was a girl. I texted Blake an indecipherable photo that the technician somehow knew how to interpret and the words: *It's a girl!* I had to find the right name.

The following day the UPS man dropped off three huge boxes of baby supplies. There were tons of diapers stacked neatly in one box. The others contained clothing, a portable high chair, toys, a baby bath, washcloths, socks. There was no card, but I took note of the zip code. I guess when my mother got on board, she really got on board. I mean, it seemed like everything but the crib. I called her that day and said my many thank yous. I told her I'd missed her. I had.

I'd already found a crib on Craigslist for a hundred dollars. Same story for an organic mattress for the baby. I ate hamburgers all the time. And guacamole. And pizza. And breakfast tacos. Lots of breakfast tacos.

Blake texted me back: *You should name her Chaos.* I knew he was only partly joking. It hit me with a twinge of melancholy, but a little smile, too. I missed him.

He called me that night. "So, I was dropping off the kids at Cami's when your text of the ultrasound came through. She saw it. She figured out that you're pregnant." I could hear from his tone there was a lot more he wanted to say.

"How'd she take it?"

"How'd she take it?" His tone intimated I should know better than to ask. "She flew off the fucking handle. It's opened up all sorts of questions. 'When is she due? When did you fucking knock her up? Where were you?

Where did you do it?' She called me a fucking liar among other choice words. All I've been is pleasant to her. It's not like I've been courting her. I'm just trying to get along. Needless to say, she's not happy."

"I gathered that much. What did you tell her?"

"No more than I had to. She stormed out of the house anyway. I haven't seen her since. I'm still at her place with the kids. She's probably passed out at her fuck buddy's house."

The next morning I got a new barrage of ugly text messages from my old circle of friends. Why hadn't I changed my number? I knew the answer. I hadn't changed it because I wanted Blake to be able to get through to me. Stupid ex-friends. As if I cared about any single one of them anymore. Cami was still trying to hurt me, just doing it within the confines of the restraining order. She was probably just taking people's phones and using them to fuck with me. So that's how it was going to be. I started blocking numbers.

Donna called, at least, and asked me directly what was going on. I confirmed I was having her brother's baby and that she was going to be an aunt again. I didn't really have much else to say. Neither did she. "You're family, Aleah," she said before hanging up. "Always know that."

Blake called me a few hours later. I didn't know what to expect. His voice was jubilant. "She caved," he said. "On everything. I can see you, I can still be the father my children need me to be. She's letting me go. She's going to let us be together."

I closed my eyes, trying to let that sink in. "What?" I needed to hear it again.

He repeated himself. "She finally came home looking tired and defeated and I told her I wanted my children, I wanted her to find a man to be happy with, and I wanted you. She is letting me walk away. She knows she's not going to win. She's conceding. She only has three conditions."

Of course she did. "What are they?"

"First: that we have to get married before you return to Washington."

Did she think that was a deterrent?

"Second: that you never see Desiree and Davis. Third, she wants you to call and apologize." There it was again, the apology.

"I've told you," I started.

"No, listen. It's everything we've wanted. We can make it ugly forever or you can do this one thing and she'll walk away. Everything will be easier. You know it will. Call her tonight, after the kids are asleep. Let her rant at you and answer her questions. Please. Do it for me. For us. For our baby."

"I'll think about it."

"Please," he said. "This one little thing is all that stands between us, Aleah."

"I'll think about it."

That afternoon, I found out that Glen landed a buyer for the house at a sale price of just over a hundred thousand more than we'd paid for it, less than two years prior. Hallelujah! That solved my money problems in a fell swoop, even after taxes and broker fees. It opened up possibilities. I thought about what Blake had said. I *could* try. My baby deserved that much. I could apologize and we could get married and my baby could have a family. A few words could change my life. I could be brave enough for that.

I charged my phone and spent the afternoon crafting an appropriate apology, one I could deliver without feeling like I was betraying myself or lying, one that could actually be heartfelt. I ended up keeping it as short as I dared. I didn't want to accidentally pull a trigger and set her off.

Eleven my time took forever to roll around. I didn't want to call before their kids were all the way asleep. They were two hours behind me now. At 10:55 I went out onto the back patio and sat on the cement. It was warm outside, humid. The wind was stronger than I expected. I looked over my scrawled apology, the one I was going to read to Cami. I picked up my phone and I called her. She picked up, she didn't say anything.

"Cami. It's Aleah."

"Well." The phone crackled with her pent up energy. "You've had plenty of time to think about what you are going to say to me." Her words came out in a charged cadence.

In truth, I'd though very little about saying anything at all to her, ever again, until that afternoon. I'd always been so adamantly against playing her reindeer games. Still, if this would end it, I would do it. I told her, "I am sorry, Cami, for all the pain. I'm sorry for everything you and your children have gone through and I'm sorry for the lies." In spite of myself, I choked up as I spoke. My voice was laden with shame. "You didn't deserve any of it, Cami. I was horrible to you. I apologize."

She was quiet a moment, drinking it in. "Thank you for that. It wasn't so fucking hard, after all, was it?" Strangely, she was right. I knew this woman. I had considered her to be a good friend, once. It wasn't as hard as I thought it would be. I survived, and I felt better somehow, too.

Mollified on that count, she launched into a new line of attack. "So you've won. He's yours. I mean, you can have him," she said. "I certainly don't want him. What I don't understand is how you can think he's not lying to you with every breath. I mean, ask me anything. You and I have been like sisters. I'll tell you the truth."

What a complete snake. Was she so desperate to tarnish my image of him?

"I mean, if I were you, I'd head for the hills. How can you trust him?"

I sighed. "I just do, Cami." He didn't have any reason to lie to me. I didn't have any reason to keep talking to her.

"Whatever. Speaking of sisterhood, how could you have ever, *as another human being on this planet*, have treated me the way that you treated me?" I could see the incline of her eyebrow, the thrust of her index finger in my mind's eye.

"I have no excuses." It wasn't any of her business, who I was, what I'd been going through, or why I'd made the choices I'd made. She could have known, if she'd just opened her eyes. I left it at that. I wasn't here to defend myself.

"You're trapping him with this pregnancy. You engineered this whole thing to trap him." This was the Cami I knew and loved. I could sense her eyes narrowing with the accusation. "You should get rid of that baby. He'll leave you, too. Just like he left me. There will be someone else."

"This isn't about trapping Blake," I said. "Cami, you don't wait for a child for ten years and then abort the one that's given to you, planned or not, optimal conditions or not." My voice cracked. "I'm not giving up this child. I can't. I have wanted this for too long."

"You must have deliberately come up here when you knew you would be ovulating."

Obviously, I did ovulate during the time I was there. But… engineer the trip around that? It was laughable.

"I'm waiting."

Finally, I said. "Look. None of this was premeditated. I didn't try to set it up and I don't have any excuses and I don't have a time machine—"

She pounced on that. "What would you do if you did?"

I thought, but only for a moment. "I'd go back twelve years and act on my first attraction for Blake, before he met you. Before I married Glen."

She was stunned into a moment's silence. "That's honest," she said. I realized from the sound of her voice she'd thought I would say I'd go back to before the affair and restore *her* happiness.

"I don't have reason to be anything else."

"Would have saved us all a lot of pain and trouble." She was deflated. "Well, let's get this over with. I want to be sure you understand my conditions." She launched into her rules.

I interrupted her tirade "—all of which would change if Blake and I were married."

It threw her off the edge. She started screaming. "That is *so far* in the future it doesn't even matter," she sobbed. "You are so unbelievably foul. I don't even know how you can be called a human being. I never want to see your face again. Never!" She hung up. It was over. I sat there and shook for a minute. I wished I had a cigarette, but I'd given those up months ago. Then I realized, that was the worst of it. The much dreaded and long avoided phone call was over.

Blake was mine.

The next day I got this email from Cami:

I'm not saying the following to hurt your feelings, but I asked Blake what would happen to you if I took him back and gave him his old life back. He said you would be history...WHY do you think you can love someone who puts you second, bullshits you with every breath he takes and deep down KNOWS you trapped him with this pregnancy?

You now know you can get pregnant...why not wait until you meet someone who will put you first, love you only and is not a sociopathic, pathological liar and will not kick you to the curb at the drop of a hat? You should care about yourself and any children you may have in the future more than that.

Sincerely,

Cami Porter

I forwarded the message to Blake, but changed the header to "I thought it was one conversation and we were done..." I texted him: *Check your email.* He called to soothe me.

"Ignore her, baby," he said. "She's just hurting. She lost and she knows it."

We hadn't spoken since I'd gotten off the phone with Cami. I told him how it had gone, how she'd tried to push me away from him, how poisonous she was. He wasn't happy to hear it.

"All she's been doing to me all day is urging me to go to Texas, go stay with you, and raise my new family."

She was an idiot for not knowing him better. As if he would leave his children.

I was an idiot for trusting her to keep her word.

I got a text from Blake the next morning: *It's hard to say, but I need space and time from you. I hope you can understand. I will understand if you can't*

wait for me to get my life together. I don't expect you to. Go be happy. So sorry to do this by text. I can't do this when I hear your voice.

Was he fucking kidding me? The bastard was actually attempting to break it off with me via text message. I called him before I knew what I was doing. "I'm having your fucking baby and you promised you would never, ever abandon me and now that is exactly what you are doing. Coward! Coward!" I cried.

"I know. I know. I want you, Aleah. I want us and our baby. I just can't manage it all right now."

"You can't manage it?" I was dumbfounded.

"It's just too hard right now, with Cami…"

"You understand that you keep choosing to stay in hell, right? You understand that we could actually be happy together, that we could get married. I'll move back to Washington and you can be with all of your family."

Silence, and then I heard a slow exhalation. "I need some time to consider things. I need some time to think."

"I thought we were happy, Blake. Weren't we?"

I heard him snuffle. He was crying.

"I love you," he said.

I understood in a flash. I was a fool. My heart broke again. How did I keep letting this happen to me? My hands fluttered to my growing belly. In that moment I found it in me to be strong for my little girl where I never had been for myself.

"But not enough," I said. "You don't love me enough."

There was silence for a while. I waited. I realized I didn't need his confirmation. If he'd loved me enough, things would have been different. Even so, I waited for his words.

"I guess not," he said.

I nodded, finding resilience that had been hiding. I shut the window in my heart, the one I'd kept opening to let him in, and I barred it. It might have been my twentieth time quitting Blake, and I knew it was the one that would stick. If I were to go back and choose a moment when things were truly over between us, it would be that moment right there.

"Okay," I said. "Okay." I felt myself nodding, sucking in huge breaths to fight off the threatening hyperventilation. I told myself I was giving my girl a good future. I was not going to model this roller coaster, co-dependent relationship for her. "I'm done," I told him. "I'll never let you do this to me again."

I really was done. Except for the tears. Except for the endless tears. He didn't call the next day or the day after that. I didn't call him either. I stopped counting after thirty-eight days.

Chapter Eight

I enrolled in a Lamaze class at the local hospital. Included was more information about the process of giving birth and having a baby than I ever realized I'd need to know. Every week I'd show up alone and everyone would show up with their spouse or their sister or their mom or their doula... I received a few strange looks at first, then just pity as they realized I really was alone. I shouldered through it. I was learning. I could support myself.

My baby girl is a kicker! She'll be a night owl like her momma, I wrote in my pregnancy journal. I dreamed of what it would be like to share this journey with a partner by my side. I still thought of Blake. I wondered what was going on with him, but not enough to find out. All I knew was that as long as Cami pulled his puppet strings I wanted nothing to do with him. He called every once in a while. I didn't answer. He didn't leave messages. It was better that way.

I had one of those little heart monitoring machines. You put a microphone on your belly and connect it to headphones. At first there's a lot of white noise. You tune it and sometimes find your own heartbeat, but then keep searching until you find the rapid, rapid beat of your thriving baby's heart. My baby was so serene, inside of me, growing. It calmed all my anxiety, listening to that. Sometimes it was the only thing I had to smile about. I often fell asleep listening to her heartbeat.

Sadie's legs grew worse. My constant companion and friend struggled to walk. It broke my heart, seeing her difficulty, knowing how much she loved to run. Over a matter of weeks, her back hips degenerated to the point that when she moved, she simply dragged her back legs along behind her. It was hard for her to go outside to pee, let alone poop. The time came when I knew I had to find a mobile vet. I was so tired of watching things I loved die. I woke up early that morning. I watched her sleeping at my side. She whimpered with excitement, and all of her legs were twitching. She was in a full out run in her dreams, chasing a ball or a squirrel I guessed. The vet arrived and we went outside to the communal yard. Sadie rolled in the grass and lay down, her head in my lap. I stroked her head while the vet snuffed out her heart. Sadie would never feel pain again. Me, I cried for days. I'd wonder if the tears were bad for the baby and then I'd cry some more. I cried for everything.

Over time, my tears dried up as the baby grew inside me. That's not to say there wasn't still pain, but I knew I needed to change my life and I couldn't do that moping around in my little shoebox apartment. I started going for daily walks around Lady Bird Lake. I started doing my work in coffee shops instead of at home. I started to say hello to people.

Glen sent an email on our tenth wedding anniversary. We were actually still married. It read: "I still ache almost every time I think of you. I wonder if that will ever stop." I hoped for his sake it would. The divorce went through shortly after that. Not with a bang, but a whimper.

My time grew near. My daughter grew heavier by the day. Every movement I made was governed by her, how I slept, how I walked, what I ate, how long I sat, when I peed. At seven months I'd lost the ability to sleep through the night. My breasts had started leaking. My hormones were training me for night feeding. Honestly, I would have rather had the sleep than the conditioning.

I went into a light labor the Friday morning of my 41st week. The contractions were strong, but infrequent. Sometimes they came very close together; sometimes they were as much as twenty minutes apart and I wondered if I were in labor at all. I watched my favorite TV shows, *Downton Abbey* and *Firefly*. I skipped the season with Lady Sybil's death, though. I figured that was for the best. I knew the contractions needed to be regular before I could go to the hospital. I didn't sleep much that night; the contractions were too strong to let me do more than doze.

I woke in serious pain, contractions were still erratic. I drew a warm bath, with Epsom salts. I told myself I was floating, floating, floating away in my head, away from the pain. I remembered when pain was a release, when there was nothing I could do about the next time the whip or the hand was going to flog my raw ass again, how relaxing into the rhythm of it had its own reward. I did that with my birth. In my head, I gave in to it.

In that way I made it through the first day and night of labor.

The next morning, I sat on the toilet. It was where I spent most of my time when I wasn't in the shower or tub. You know how often pregnant ladies have to pee, except this time, I just kept peeing and peeing. Like three times as long as Tom Hanks in *A League of Their Own*. Finally, my bladder emptied. I got up and took a few steps. Warm water gushed down my legs. That wasn't pee. That was my water breaking. Shit just got real.

"I should go to the hospital," I said out loud. I dug out my phone and called a cab.

It was the most painful car ride of my life. Thankfully, the hospital was only fifteen minutes away. I felt every bump in the road keenly. I wanted to cry, and let myself.

"This woman is in labor," the cab driver barked to an attendant as we got to the hospital's main drive in front of reception.

"Is she registered here?"

"Can we get her a wheelchair?" the driver countered, like a badger. It occurred to me I hadn't paid him. I wanted to tip him well.

"Oh, of course," the orderly said

"Yes, I'm registered here."

The cabbie helped me into the chair once the orderly had wheeled it over.

"Thank you." I looked at the cabbie. "And I need to pay you. How much do I owe you?"

"Not today, ma'am." He actually tipped his hat at me. "Good luck."

I couldn't help it. I burst into tears. I always found such kindness in unexpected places. "Thank you," I said.

They took me to the maternity ward. It was Saturday. My doctor didn't normally work on Saturdays. He'd taken a special liking to me and had given me his cell phone number, in just such a case as this.

"I'm sorry sweetie. It's my wife's birthday. I'm hosting a party for her. Even if I wanted to, I couldn't be there. You understand."

I didn't. This was the doctor I'd built up all my trust with. This was the doctor I knew. He'd abandoned me. I had nothing to say.

I'd only once gone to one of his colleagues, Dr. Englund, when my doctor had been on vacation. She had asked when I'd scheduled my C-section for and actually snorted when I said I was planning a natural delivery. "You'll feel those contractions once and be begging for the epidural," she'd said. "Where is your husband?"

"I'm single," I said, feeling every bit of it.

"Not even a baby daddy?"

I wanted to hit her. Instead, I said, "No, not even that," but I'm pretty sure it sounded like "Wow. Is your bedside manner always this good, you evil whore?"

Of course, Dr. Englund was on call when I was admitted. After thirty minutes, she lost patience with my still irregular contractions and forced me on Pitocin, a contraction-inducing drug. Every time the nurse would visit, she suggested pain medication, which I steadfastly refused—having been educated about the risks they presented to the baby, I wasn't about to take those—and then she'd crank up the Pitocin another notch. Twelve hours went by. The Pitocin drip was up to maximum. Each contraction was a new demon clawing its way through my abdomen, shredding muscles with its dull and dirty talons. I'd squat through them and let go, collapsing to the hospital bed, then rise to squat through the next contraction. I did this for hours and hours, grateful for the stamina my yoga practice gave me. I felt as though my body was literally going to split in two to have this baby.

The cabbage-like little nurse came in. "Doctor says if you don't relax she's going to have to put you on the table. We think the baby's cord is wrapped around her head. She wants to cut you open." She tapped her watch and leaned in conspiratorially. "It's past dinner time, you know."

"But if I get the epidural, she'll let me try to avoid the surgery?"

"She'll try. Not for long, but she'll try," the nurse confirmed. I allowed them to bring an anesthesiologist in to give me an epidural. I was whimpering from the pain when the anesthesiologist arrived. He looked like Mr. Rogers. "It's okay," he said. "You're so brave. I don't know if I've ever seen anyone so brave." Another contraction wracked me as he set up and he helped me get into position for the needle. We let another contraction ride through me.

"They're getting closer," he said. "You'll need to be super still for me, even if one hits you, okay? You can't move. It's important." I knew why. I could be paralyzed if I moved the wrong way at the wrong time.

One more contraction took hold and the nurse took both of my hands in hers.

"Aleah, look at me," the doctor said. Of course he was behind me, so I couldn't see him when I looked up, but the nurse met and held my gaze as I gritted my teeth against the pain. I wondered if she was someone's grandma. "It's good," I said as the contraction started to ease. "Go."

I will admit the relief of the epidural was immediate. It was like a cool gel settling over a burn. It put out all the pain. I fell almost instantly to sleep. The Pitocin-induced contractions kept working my body, muscling the baby through my vaginal canal. The nurse woke me up when my cervix was dilated to ten centimeters. Everything in the room erupted in a flurry of motion.

Dr. Englund started screaming at me to "Push, push, push!" No joke. It's not just in the movies. I did my damndest, thinking about bearing down, straining. I could feel nothing at all. "Push!" the doctor screamed.

"She's turning red; she's pushing," the nurse said. I couldn't feel a goddamned thing. I didn't know what I was doing. I thought I was pushing. I focused my brain waves on my abdomen and sent the message. I was trying to push. I felt like I was trying to move some object outside of myself with my brain, like a child practicing telekinesis on a bowl of cereal, and as effective.

But then my baby slipped out and the doctor caught her. "The baby is peeing on me!" the doctor screeched. I wanted to laugh. My baby girl was already on my side.

"Aww, this is what we wait for, isn't it doc," the nurse said peering over the little thing, attempting to swaddle her. "This is the magic moment."

"I want to hold my baby," I said, "My little girl, I want her."

"She's not clean, the cord isn't cut," the nurse said, taking her from the doctor.

She was crying; she was cold. "Give her here. I don't care." To her credit, the nurse handed her over. My baby nuzzled up to me and almost cooing, latched on to a nipple like it was something she'd done a thousand times before. I drew her swaddling blanket up over her. I cradled her, my baby, to me and drew her near, as close as I could. And as I breathed deeply of her intoxicating newborn scent, I knew we would always be that close. I wouldn't let it be otherwise.

I feel this intense yearning still. Every time I sit in the rocking chair and nurse, I remember Blake between my thighs, one way or another, the sheer number and intensity of the orgasms we gave each other. I feel my breasts respond your suckling, a painful tingling begging for release. I've never felt like more of a woman.

You are his last and best gift to me, Lorelei. I see him every time I look at you. And I see myself, too. I see us, together. You are our love made manifest. Blake wanted me to write this book so people could know how good it could be. I knew I had to write it for you.

These are my secrets, little girl. These I give to you in perfect trust, because the love contained within them is what created you. Know now, as

I do, that you are my miracle. I wrote all of this for you because—someday, when you're much older and you're ready—I want you to know me as a woman. I want you to know yourself and celebrate yourself as a woman. There will come a time in your life when you'll have big choices to make and you'll make them however you do. I want you to know you can always come to me, and I'll listen, and I'll love you no matter what.

I miss your father still, but I don't ache for something that's not going to be, not anymore. I'm building a new life here. I'm finally joining the momma and baby groups. We have friends here, Lorelei. There are good people still on this earth, in this city. My old life is over, in ashes. I didn't realize when I stood there in the aftermath, ash in my hair, ash on my face… I didn't realize how wonderful my life would become again. I am grateful to you for that. I will always be grateful to Blake for you, for all the beautiful lies that resulted in the truth of you.

In my heart I was able to forgive myself even, because of love. Love is the truth that trumps all wrongdoing. There was a purity in what Blake and I had that transcended immorality. Our love was enough; its power was so strong all I could do was surrender to it. There was never any other choice.

I'm finishing this story while you still suckle at my breast, before we've had any fights or times of misunderstanding, and before we've had the chance to be overcome by the wear and tear of the day-to-day. In these moments I see you so clearly as a human being; your soul shines through your eyes. We understand each other perfectly, right now. We won't always have this, I know. It's part of the human condition. We'll go through rough spots. Mothers and daughters do. But you will always be the same person I'm with now. And I will always be here for you. It's you and me together now, Lorelei. I can't wait to show you the world.

I only have one wish for you. May men find you and dash their unworthy hearts upon your gorgeous shores. Taste them all, my dear. Let one pass, but choose wisely.

Know that any of them are yours for the taking.

The End

Author's Note

This book wouldn't be what it is without the amazing help I got along the way from my first readers. Special thanks go to my critique partners, Julia Hornsby and H. Claire Taylor, to A. Penn and M. Bach for unbounded friendship, and to my husband for his insight, never ending support, and for the countless hours he watched our children so that I could write.

If you enjoyed this story, it would help immensely and I would be ever so grateful if you would leave a review for it. It's easy to do and only takes a few minutes. New authors are dependent on word of mouth and reviews to get noticed and generate enough sales to keep writing. We writers need all the support we can get. I would very much appreciate yours.

Lastly, I'd love for you to visit me at www.sarahatlas.com. You can email me there and let me know what you thought of the book. Join my mailing list to keep up on the latest releases, get free stories and be privy to other giveaways. I can't wait to meet you!

Yours,

Sarah

About Sarah

Sarah Atlas doesn't remember a time when she didn't know how to read. She filled her childhood with books and started spinning stories at an early age, writing her first novel with a friend in seventh grade. Her earliest forays into erotica started in college. *All the Beautiful Lies,* a mainstream erotica, is her first published novel. Sarah lives with her family in Austin, Texas. Please join her story club (free!) at www.sarahatlas.com to keep up with the latest.

Want more Aleah & Blake?

You can find them in this erotic short story on Amazon.com for only $0.99.

http://www.amazon.com/Precious-Cargo-erotic-fantasy-romance-ebook/dp/B00PCRP67I

www.ingramcontent.com/pod-product-compliance
Lightning Source LLC
Chambersburg PA
CBHW031449260626
47154CB00016B/215

* 9 7 8 0 6 9 2 3 9 2 9 1 1 *